P9-CDD-594

THE
Unlikely
ESCAPE of
URIAH HEEP

THE
Unlikely
ESCAPE of
URIAH HEEP

H. G. PARRY

REDHOOK

Redhook Books/Orbit
Hachette Book Group
1290 Avenue of the Americas
New York, NY 10104
hachettebookgroup.com

First Edition: July 2019

Redhook is an imprint of Orbit, a division of Hachette Book Group.
The Redhook name and logo are trademarks of Hachette Book Group, Inc.

The publisher is not responsible for websites (or their content) that are not owned by the publisher.

The Hachette Speakers Bureau provides a wide range of authors for speaking events. To find out more, go to www.hachettespeakersbureau.com or call (866) 376-6591.

Library of Congress Cataloging-in-Publication Data
Names: Parry, H. G., author.
Title: The unlikely escape of Uriah Heep / H. G. Parry.
Description: First edition. | New York, NY : Redhook, July 2019.
Identifiers: LCCN 2019000762 | ISBN 9780316452717 (hardcover) |
ISBN 9780316452724 (ebook)
Subjects: LCSH: Characters in literature—Fiction. | Ability—Fiction. |
Family secrets—Fiction. | GSAFD: Fantasy fiction.
Classification: LCC PR9639.4.P376 U55 2019 | DDC 823/.92—dc23
LC record available at https://lccn.loc.gov/2019000762

ISBNs: 978-0-316-45271-7 (hardcover), 978-0-316-45272-4 (ebook)

Printed in the United States of America

LSC-C

10 9 8 7 6 5 4 3 2 1

*This is for my sister: teacher, writer, Time Lord, Jedi Knight.
Thanks for being wise, funny, and brave.*

Dr. Charles Sutherland, age twenty-six

Notes for article "The Autobiographical Form in Great Expectations *and* David Copperfield"

- Think about the nature of memory, guilt, irony, self-reflective narrative voices.
- Child David as victim, drawn directly from Dickens's memories. But child Pip as criminal, also based partly on autobiographical material.
- Cf. Hodgins, esp. 267–89.
- I don't know. Sometimes I think my brain opened as far as it could go when I was about seventeen, and its doors have been just stuck there ever since. And now they're ossifying and collecting cobwebs, and things are spilling in, swirling around for a bit, and then flying out again. And someday they'll start to swing slowly shut, and I'll be left in the dark with nothing but a few rustling fragments of thoughts that get thinner and weaker every time I use them. Like tea leaves.
- And sometimes I think I can do anything.
- Brilliant, Charley. That is probably called the human condition. And you should probably just get back to work.
- What about Uriah Heep? How does he fit in?

I

At four in the morning, I was woken by a phone call from my younger brother. He sounded breathless, panicked, with the particular catch in his voice I knew all too well.

"Uriah Heep's loose on the ninth floor," he said. "And I can't catch him."

My brain was fogged with sleep; it took a moment for his words to filter through. "Seriously, Charley?" I said when they did. "Again?"

"I've never read out Uriah Heep before."

"True, but—you know what I mean." I rubbed my eyes, trying to focus. The bedroom was pitch black and cold, the glow of the digital clock the only fuzzy source of light. Next to me, I heard Lydia stir and turn over in a rustle of sheets. I had a sense then of being suspended between two worlds: the sane one in which I had fallen asleep, and Charley's, reaching to pull me awake through the speaker of my phone. It was a familiar feeling. "That's Dickens, isn't it? You know you and Dickens don't mix—or...mix too well, or whatever it is the two of you do. I thought you were sticking to poetry lately. Those postmodern things that read like a dictionary mated with a Buddhist mantra and couldn't possibly make any sense to anyone."

"There is not a poem on earth that doesn't make any sense to anyone."

Even half-asleep, I could recognize an evasion when I heard it. "You promised. You promised it wouldn't happen again."

"I know, and I meant it, and I'm sorry." He was whispering, presumably trying not to alert the security guards roaming the university campus—or perhaps not to alert Uriah Heep. "But please, *please*, Rob, I know it's late and you have work tomorrow, but if they find him here in the morning—"

"All right, all right, calm down." I forced exasperation out of my voice. There were times when he needed to hear it, and times when it would only tip him over the edge, and right now he sounded dangerously close to the edge. "You're in your office? I'm on my way. Just try to keep an eye on him, and be down to let me in the building in ten minutes."

He sighed. "Thank you. Oh God, I really am sorry, it was only for a second..."

"Ten minutes," I told him, and hung up. I sighed myself, heard it go out into the darkness, and ran my hand through my hair. Oh well. It wasn't as though I was *surprised*.

"It's my brother," I said to Lydia, whom I could sense watching me with sleepy concern from the other side of the bed. "He's having a crisis."

"Is he all right?"

"He'll be fine." Lydia didn't know the form my brother's crises took, but it wasn't the first time he'd phoned me with one. It wasn't even the first time in the middle of the night. I had no idea who used to help him while he was living in England, but since he'd come to Wellington, I seemed to be on speed dial. "He just needs some help with a problem. You know how he is."

"You've got a trial this morning," she reminded me.

"I know," I said. "I'll make it. Go back to sleep."

"You can't fix all his problems for him. He's twenty-six."

"I know." She was right; he did need to learn to deal with these things himself.

Uriah Heep, though. I'd never read Dickens myself, but I'd learned to have an instinct for the names, and that one didn't sound promising.

My brother works as a lecturer at Prince Albert University of Wellington, which I can, as I promised, drive to from my house in about ten minutes, provided I stop only to pull on a pair of shoes and shrug on a coat over my pajamas. It's a tricky road in the dark, skirting the central city and winding up into the foothills of Kelburn. I missed a turn, and found myself on the wrong side of the botanic gardens. Wellington's like that. The city itself is nestled between the harbor and the hills: too far one way, and you hit the ocean; too far the other, and you're facing a wall of impenetrable forest sloping up into the clouds. It's not a good place for my brother, whose relationship with "too far" has never been a healthy one.

The campus is perched halfway up the Kelburn hills, a tumbling assortment of buildings on either side of the road connected by an overpass. They're old buildings, by New Zealand standards, but they probably don't seem that way to Charley. Until three years ago, he'd been at Oxford, where referring to a building as old meant someone was studying in it a thousand years ago. I'd been there on a family visit once, and had felt the dust-stifled weight that comes from centuries of scholarship and ancient stone. I wasn't certain I liked it. It felt too much as though it had come from the pages of a book. The Prince Albert campus, just over a hundred years old, still feels as if it was built by people. Most of its office blocks started life as a settler's house, and even its grandest buildings are infused with the labor of Victorian colonials re-creating England in basic scaffolding. When I think of Oxford, I think of the still peace of the summer air; here, the air is never still, and rarely peaceful. That particular night, it was raining lightly, and the streetlights caught the drops in a mist of silver. When I got out of the car, the haze clung to my face and stung like ice.

I think Charley had the door to the English department open before I could even knock. In the light spilling from the corridor behind him, I could see his eyes huge and appealing, his unruly mess of dark curls and baggy sweatshirt making him look smaller and younger than he was. He's very good at that. It didn't mean I wasn't going to kill him this time—I was—but maybe not when he was completely beside himself with worry.

"He got away from me," Charley said immediately. As usual in a crisis, he was talking almost too fast to be understood. "I tried to stay with him, but I had to call you, and... and my cell phone was in my office, so I had to go there, and then once I called you I tried to find him again, and he..."

"Hey, slow down." My left shoe had a hole in it I hadn't noticed until I ran through the puddles. I could feel my wet sock squelching inside it now. "Take a breath. He has to still be in the building, right? He hasn't got a card to swipe out, and the building locks down after dark?"

"That's right," Charley confirmed. He took a deep breath, obediently, and released it. It didn't help. "Unless he breaks a window, or someone left one open—"

"Any sign of that?"

"No. And I've looked in every room. But I can't find him."

"We'll find him," I assured him. "Don't worry. It's only some nasty Victorian with no eyelashes." I'd Googled the character on the way here, which might have contributed to the wrong turn I'd taken. Apparently he was an ugly redheaded clerk who tries to ruin the lives of the main characters in *David Copperfield*. Also, there was a rock band named after him, which sounded cool. "Not like that time you brought Dracula out of *his* book, when you were eight."

"Vampires have weaknesses," Charley said darkly. "Stoker wrote them in. People are far less predictable."

I couldn't argue with that. "Come on. Let's start in your office."

I'd never been in Charley's office before, but it was exactly how I'd pictured it: complete chaos. Mugs littered the desk and peered out from bookshelves, books spilled from every nook and cranny, and the computer was buried beneath pages of scribbled notes. The battered armchair by the window was the only thing clear of clutter, because it was obviously where he sat in order to clutter everything else. It was a Charley-shaped hole in the mess, like an outline at a police crime scene.

There was no sign of a wayward Dickensian villain, but I could smell the faint tang of smoke and fog that I'd learned to associate with Dickensian England, amid the more usual smells of books and stale coffee.

"What were you doing here at four in the morning, anyway?" I asked. I was out of breath: we'd climbed the stairs to the ninth floor so as not to alert Uriah Heep of our coming. The elevators were notorious for breaking down in this building anyway. I remembered that from my undergraduate days, although my classes had usually been at the law campus in the central city.

I'd never been in the English department, and right now it was eerie in the dark. Reception was locked off, and the corridors were a labyrinthine world of shadows.

"I was finishing an article," Charley answered. "Well, I was starting it, actually. Someone wants it by next week, for an anthology. And I just—I don't know, I'd actually proposed something about the autobiographical form in *David Copperfield* and *Great Expectations*, but I became very interested in how Uriah Heep was functioning as a scapegoat for middle-class anxieties in *David Copperfield*, and the means by which he's constructed as a threat to the social order, and I was reading and thinking about him quite closely—"

"And he sprang off the page," I finished grimly. I'd heard it before. "You couldn't just put him back?"

"He was too fast. He knew what I was going to do, and he wasn't going to let me."

I shook my head. "You shouldn't be here in the middle of the night."

"I got caught up." He sounded apologetic. "Anyway, it's better to work when no one's around, in case something like this happens."

"I suppose, but you know it's more likely to happen when you're tired. And *definitely* when you're caught up."

"I didn't mean it."

"Never mind." I picked up a paper from the top strata covering the desk, filled with the least legible version of Charley's handwriting. *LOOK AT pg. 467*, it began. *Model clerk—model prisoner—Heep is his own parody—becomes what people expect him to be—commentary on 19thC hypocrisy—fear of* squiggle squiggle—*shape*-squiggle—squiggle *David's own* squiggle—*like Orlick and Pip from GE—Fitzwilliam writes on this in* squiggle—"You say you were thinking about him as a threat to the social order?"

He nodded unhappily.

The figures Charley summons from books are always colored by his interpretations. Charley calls it postmodernism at work. The last thing we needed was for this latest one to be colored by danger, however theoretical.

"All right." I tried to think. It was hard, when I had been sound asleep twenty minutes ago. Unlike Charley's, my brain doesn't work well in the hours before dawn. "You know this character. Where would he go?"

"I don't know. He doesn't go near an English department in the book. I suppose we just have to look for him."

"Charley—!" I bit back a surge of temper just in time. It was more than temper, really. I hated this. I'd always hated this, but I hated it more now, here, in my city.

I looked out the office window. Beyond the campus, the ground dropped away dramatically, and Wellington spread out like a blanket. Down in the distance, I could see the glittering lights of the central city, and past them the long curve of the harbor and the dark of the ocean. Outside the mess my brother worked in, it all looked impossibly clean and young and bright.

"Do you think we should check the library?" Charley asked.

I forced myself to focus. "Would he *want* to get to the library? Is that where you think he'd go?"

"Possibly. I have no idea where he'd go."

I pinched the bridge of my nose. "Charley, I have a big trial coming up in a few hours. I'm expected at the courthouse at nine. It's my job. There are people depending on me. I can't just keep looking all night!"

"I said I was sorry! I knew I shouldn't have called you."

"You shouldn't have had to!" So much for keeping exasperation out of my voice. I had never been very good at that. "How many times does it take? Just keep your thoughts under control when you read a book! It shouldn't be so hard!"

"Maybe you should go. I can deal with this myself. It's not your problem."

"It *is* my problem, though, isn't it? It's always my problem. You make it my problem when you bring these things into my city and into my life."

"I didn't mean to."

"It doesn't matter what you mean! It's what you do. It's what you always do."

"I said I would deal with it myself," Charley said. His face had hardened. "I shouldn't have asked you to come here. Just go home, Rob. I mean it. I don't need your help."

I might have gone. I don't think I would have—I hope I wouldn't have. But I was furious, and I could already feel fury pushing me to say and do the things I tried to avoid. It just might have propelled me out the door.

Except, just for a moment, I looked at Charley again. There was something there, in the tilt of his head and the lines of his face, that I'd never seen before. Something hard, and cunning. There was a glint in his eyes that could almost have been malice.

All at once, Charley's notes flashed up before my eyes, and I felt cold.

Shape-squiggle. If my brother's handwriting hadn't been so terrible, I might have worked it out sooner.

As I said, my brother's creations are always colored by his perception of them. Sometimes this is slight, and manageable: a shift in personality, or a blurring of appearance. But some colorings are deeper and stranger, and the deeper he gets into literary theory, the stranger they become. Traits that are metaphorical in the text become absurdly, dangerously literal. A shy character may come out invisible. A badly written character might come out flat. The Phantom of the Opera walked in a little cloud of darkness, and all Charley could say about it was that it was a half-baked theory about pathetic fallacy and his concentration slipped.

Dickens, as far as I know, has no shape-shifters in his books. But somehow, Charley's Uriah Heep had come out as one. And he had been standing in front of me from the moment I entered the building.

"Where's my brother?" I said slowly.

The thing that wasn't Charley looked confused. He did it well—he got the nose wrinkle just right—but it didn't matter. I knew now. "What are you talking about?"

"You weren't down at the door because you were waiting for me." I could feel the pieces start to fit, the way they did on a good day in court when a hostile witness said just the wrong thing at the right time. "You were down there trying to get away before I arrived. Sometime after Charley called, you took him out of action somehow and stole his key card. But I arrived too soon, didn't I? You had to let me in, and bluff it out. That's why you told me to leave; that's why you're trying to provoke an argument. You need me to storm out and leave you here alone, so you can get away."

He shook his head. "Rob, you can't possibly..."

"You should have known me better than that," I said. "Or Charley should—I suppose you know me from his memories. I wouldn't leave him in danger just because he was getting on my nerves."

"You've done it before," Charley said. My stomach twisted, because I knew what he meant.

"Yes, I have," I admitted. "And that's why I'd never do it again. Where is he?"

I didn't wait for the impostor to lie this time. I pushed my way past him, out into the corridor. "Charley!"

The corridors were lit only by the light spilling from Charley's office. It might have been my imagination, but I thought I heard a faint sound in response.

"Very well." The voice from behind me wasn't quite my brother's anymore. I turned around quickly, and the face wasn't my brother's either.

For the record, Uriah Heep is a very ugly character. He had a face like a skull—cadaverous, I think the Internet had said—and a skeletal body to match: tall, pale, thin, with red hair shaved far shorter than I'd thought the Victorians went in for, and reddish eyes without eyebrows or eyelashes. His jeans and sweatshirt had changed with him to a black tailcoat, funereal garb. His limbs twitched and writhed, apparently without his input; I thought, inexplicably, of the branches of the tree at the back of our childhood house. I was more interested in the knife in his hand. It was a modern box cutter, and he held it like a dagger in my direction.

"I should have known better, Master Robert," he said, "than to think my umble self could fool a gentleman of your station and fine schooling. Do forgive me, won't you, Master Robert? It was on account of my being so very umble and unworthy."

"Don't give me all that." I mastered my shock, and hardened my tone. "I don't even like Dickens. Where's my brother?"

"Oh, you mustn't think I've hurt Master Charles," Uriah said, with a laugh like someone grating iron. His voice was honey and rusty nails. "No, no, someone in my umble position—"

"God, literary critics must have a field day with you," I groaned.

I saw it then: a flash of hatred, right across his face. And then, all at once, the knife was at my throat, and I was against the wall of the corridor opposite, a bony hand on my shoulder holding me there. It was so quick, I didn't even have a chance to flinch. The blade touched my neck; it stung, but didn't cut. My heart was beating so loud and fast it filled my entire body.

"I never asked for this," Uriah hissed. "I never asked to be poor, and ugly, and the villain of the piece. I never wanted to be obsequious, and insincere, and deadly. I never wanted to fall in love with a woman that was always destined for the hero of the novel."

"I'm sure you didn't," I managed. It was my best attempt at conciliation. It might have been better to keep quiet. "But that's not our fault."

"Master Charley brought me out." His face, inches from mine, melted from the shadows. "And now he wants to put me back in. In my place. Just as everybody's done, all my life. Well, I won't go, do you hear me? I won't. This world out here—it hasn't been written yet. For all I know, I can write it for myself. I don't have to do what the story says. I can do whatever I want."

I couldn't help but laugh at that. "You've got a lot to learn about the world out here, don't you?"

The blade dug deeper. A thin drop of blood was suddenly warm on my throat, like a shaving cut. Whatever Charley had managed to do to Uriah Heep, he was no longer merely a nasty Victorian with no eyelashes.

"Look, fine." I tried to speak very carefully, without my voice trembling. "Go, if you want. Just tell me where my brother is."

"Why should you care? I've seen you, you know, in his memories. You don't like him. You wish he'd never come here."

"That's not true," I said.

"Yes, it is." Uriah shook his ugly head. "You'll be better off without him anyway, with what's coming. He's going to be right at the heart of it. Stay out of it, keep your head down, and don't look too closely at what's going on, that's my umble suggestion, Master Robert."

Curiosity momentarily overcame my fear. I frowned. "What do you mean?"

"Just what I said, Master Robert. You stay out of it. It don't concern you. And you won't want it to."

"What doesn't concern me?"

"The new world," he said. "There won't be a place for you in the new world."

Down the corridor, one of the doors burst open. I turned toward the sound on instinct before I had registered what it was. My brother came out.

It was definitely my brother this time. He was wearing the same clothes as the Uriah Heep version of him had been—maybe those were all the clothes of our world that thing had known well enough to copy. His hair was the same mess of curls in need of a haircut. But I had been right. He did look different. His face was softer, and less sure of itself, and his eyes lacked that touch of cunning I'd seen in the copy. I suppose in a Dickens novel evil is real, and it shines out.

He stopped short at the sight of us. The knife was still at my throat, even though Uriah Heep turned to look at him at the same time I had. Then he raised his head.

"Let him go." His voice had that touch of an English accent I'd noticed at odd times since he returned from overseas. "I'm here now. It's over."

"With all due respect, Master Charley," Uriah said, "you were here at the start. I tied you up and put you in a cupboard."

"Well," he said rather weakly. "I'm back again."

I took a chance then. Uriah was looking the other way; even had he not been, my heart was now beating so fast I couldn't have held still a moment longer. I grabbed Uriah's wrist and wrenched the knife away from my throat.

Uriah lunged forward with a hiss. But I was prepared for his wiry strength this time, and adrenaline was flooding me with strength of my own. I kept a tight grip on his wrist, twisting it farther away from me; at the same time, I grabbed his other arm and clung on for grim life. It really was like holding a writhing skeleton. His bones stood out through his clothes, and his unearthly wail was that of a specter. The knife clattered to the floor.

"Now!" I snapped. "Put him back!"

"No!" Uriah cried. There was hatred there—seething hatred—but also real despair. It made me feel sick, despite myself. "You have no idea what it's like in that book. They always win. *They all hate me and I hate them and they always win!*"

"I know," Charley said. He sounded unhappy too. "I'm truly sorry." He reached out and touched Uriah on the shoulder, and deep concentration swept over his face. And suddenly my hands were closed around nothing at all. There was a flare of light, and between one heartbeat and the next Uriah Heep had vanished. His screams lingered even after the sound of them had faded, like the smell of Victorian smoke and fog still clinging to the air.

Lydia was right. I really did need to start letting Charley sort these things out for himself.

II

I was four and a half years old when my brother was born. He nearly died before he drew his first breath. Everybody thought he *was* dead, for a long time—complications during delivery, the doctor said. They had abandoned all efforts to resuscitate him, and wrapped him in a blanket, ready to be taken away and cremated or whatever they do to infants. My mother was holding him when he started to cry. Everyone thought it was some kind of miracle, and most of them were sure he'd suffer some kind of long-term brain damage. That's very funny, in retrospect.

I wasn't one of those there to see the miracle. I was meant to be. He was born at home, in our rambling old house out in the country; the plan was for me to be there, too, to pace the living room with my father while my mother fought to bring him into the world. For some reason, they thought this would be good for me. But he came early, by quite a bit—setting the pattern for the rest of his development, though certainly not his punctuality—and I had been sent to stay for the weekend with Grandmother Sutherland. I remember being brought to see him the next day, bundled up in his crib in the room I had helped paint for him. Apparently all I could talk about before he came was the fact I was going to have a little brother; apparently I was very excited about it. And yet, I must not have really understood what it meant, because I remember being silenced by surprise and awe at the sight of him: how real and solid he was and yet how small and fragile, the way his huge, dark eyes reached into mine and tugged at my heart. I'd expected the baby to have blue eyes, like me. I remember that Mum and Dad left the room for some reason, perhaps to go get my things out of the car, and he began to whimper fearfully at being on his own. And I remember knowing, at that moment, that I would do anything—I would kill the whole world—to keep him from being scared or hurt.

"Don't worry," I said. "I'm here. I'll look after you."

I can't remember if he quieted at the sound of my voice; probably not. He never really gave me moments like that. But I remember I was going to be the best elder brother ever. I wasn't one of those children who was jealous of a new baby in the house. I was going to teach him everything I knew.

At eight months old, he began talking. Really talking. If he ever needed the usual infant sound play and noises, he worked them out himself, in his head, without any help from us. When he spoke his first words, they were in proper sentences, and grew more proper by the day: he'd be so frustrated with himself if he didn't know the word for something, or if the syntax was wrong. About that time, I taught him the names of all the colors in his room, which was mostly yellow. I think that was the last time I ever taught him anything.

By two years old, he was reading my books. By three, he had read most of our parents'. People started to call him a prodigy; others, more cautiously, used the term "highly gifted."

And at four, he began to bring people and things out of books. It started small. There would be scents lingering in the air after he'd been reading: a cake baking, fresh country grass, ocean spray. Our mother found him with a funny-looking paperweight one day; when she asked where it came from, he said, "*Nineteen Eighty-Four.*" And then, one day, she walked in to tell him dinner was ready and found him playing with the Cat in the Hat.

Most people, I think, would be justified in losing their head when their four-year-old conjures a Dr. Seuss character from thin air. Mum, impressively, kept hers. She told him firmly to put the cat back right now; I doubt Charley had any idea he could do so, but he obeyed, and found he could. Then she took him by the shoulders and told him that he was never to bring anything out again. Ever. To be fair to him, I think he really tried, and still does. But, apparently, there are some things even he can't do.

I wasn't there for the arrival of the Cat in the Hat either. I seem to miss all the family stories. This time, I was at a friend's house, in town. Mum told me about it when I got back, and she told me that it needed to be a secret. Charley would be taken away from us if I told anyone, she said. We all had to keep him safe.

There were plenty of times when I thought I wouldn't have minded Charley being taken away, as long as it wasn't anywhere too horrible. I didn't understand, growing up, why everything was so easy for him, even things that weren't physically possible. I was confused, and then I was resentful, and then I was bitter. Gradually, the protective hold he'd taken of my heart loosened, or I learned to ignore it. I wanted to show him things, and instead he kept trying to show me. He wasn't what I'd been expecting in a little brother.

When he was thirteen, he left to study at Oxford, on the other side of the world. I left that same year to study law in Wellington, an hour's drive away. I fell, with increasing delight, into a world of courtrooms and cafés and city streets; he was enveloped in books and language and ancient halls. Outside of Christmas holidays and birthdays, we had almost no communication with each other. When he phoned me late at night from England three years ago, I almost didn't recognize his voice.

"Hi, Rob," he said. "It's me. Um. I don't know if Mum and Dad have told you, but I've just been offered a position in Wellington. I'd be flying over to take it up next month. Is that all right with you?"

"Why wouldn't it be all right with me?" I said, and knew my whole life as I had built it was over. Charley couldn't help it; I understood, even at my most bitter, that this was true. It was nothing he did, or at least nothing he did on purpose. It was simply what he was. He had come into the world trailing dreams and stories and improbabilities, and I knew he would come into my city doing the same.

III

He caught me just after I phoned you," Charley explained as we drove along the predawn road. Wellington was barely stirring below us; a few lights were beginning to flicker on in windows, and the sky had an orange-gray sheen that promised a rainy morning. "He had a knife—I suppose he'd found it in the storage closet. He tied me to the radiator with those plastic ties that only pull one way. I've always hated those things. They're just a smug reminder that sometimes life doesn't allow a do-over."

I shook my head. "Is that in character? Tying people up with plastic ties?"

"Actually, I think that's my fault too," Charley confessed unsurprisingly. It had to be, didn't it? "I was formulating an idea about how Uriah Heep and Orlick from *Great Expectations* are both shadow versions of the main characters—I think some of Orlick got mixed up with Uriah. It's the sort of thing Orlick does to people."

I had no idea who Orlick was, and didn't care. My heart was still pounding. "Just…stay away from the Victorian melodrama late at night. If you absolutely *have* to work with narrative, go for the Jane Austen. The worst that can happen there is a broken heart or two."

"That's an oversimplification of Austen," he said distractedly. He was rubbing his wrists where the plastic ties had bit them.

"Then leave the oversimplifications alone! Honestly. You made Uriah Heep a shape-shifter?"

"I just meant that he shaped himself to conform to society's expectations, but did so in a way that was a parody of those expectations and a means of rising above them. It was metaphorical."

"Then stay away from the metaphors too," I said. "At least outside business hours. I mean it. That one wasn't just irritating, it was *dangerous.*"

"I'm sorry." He paused. "Are you sure he didn't hurt you?"

"Of course I am, idiot." He'd already asked me this five or six times, in between apologies. Charley takes contrition to excess. It makes it hard to be angry with him, but very easy to be irritated. "He barely touched me. You're the one who looks like he can't see straight."

"I'm much better now." He's always light-headed after he puts something back, and a bit tired. It doesn't seem to bother him as much as it does those around him. "You didn't need to drive me home, honestly. I could have ridden."

"You do realize the wind got up to a hundred kilometers an hour last week, don't you? And you're talking about riding uphill roads into the bush?"

Charley shrugged. "I could manage. It's a moped, not a bicycle."

"It's a death trap. That thing should have been scrap metal years ago. Either the brakes don't work, or you've yet to reliably master them. Besides, by your own admission, you've been awake for two nights running. Letting you get on that thing would constitute criminal negligence."

"I got you out of bed at four in the morning to chase a Dickensian villain through Kelburn campus. I think you could actually murder me at this point, and not a jury in the country would convict."

I snorted at that, despite myself. "Please don't think I'm not tempted. You're very lucky I got it out of my system with the Uriah Heep version of you, and now I can't be bothered going through it all again. How'd you get out of the closet?"

"Oh," he said with a yawn. Now that the excitement had died, he was fading fast. "There were copies of *Le Morte Darthur* in there. It took me a while to reach them with my hands tied; in the end, I had to kick the shelf over. But once I did, I could read out Excalibur, and then it was easy to cut myself free."

I stared at him. "You pulled out Excalibur?"

"There's a turn coming up," he reminded me, and I quickly put my eyes back on the road. We were winding up into the bush that bordered the city. Parliament was at the bottom of the hill, as was the district court where I was due in just a few short hours.

"It wasn't hard," Charley added. "It's a significant object—it's easy to have a reading strong enough to bring to life. It was a lot harder to use it to free myself. I think I nearly cut my wrists. But I heard you call my name. I knew that meant you'd worked out whom you were really with, and that meant you were in danger. It was my fault. I had to do *something*."

I wasn't quite sure what to say. I half wanted to thank him, but felt it would make my anger with him somewhat less convincing. In the end, I contented myself with, "Does that make you rightful king of all Britain or something?"

"Wrong sword. Excalibur was from the Lady of the Lake. I think it just makes me the person who needs to tidy up the mess in the closet tomorrow. Today." He yawned again. "So what's your case?"

That took me by surprise. "What?"

"You told Uriah you had an early trial. What is it?"

Now I had to wonder what else he had heard me tell Uriah before I realized who he was. Nothing I wouldn't have said quite literally to his face, I suppose, but I had been angry. "You don't want to hear about my trials."

"Why not? Maybe I could help."

"They're about the real world. Facts and figures. You've never lived more than half in the real world your entire life. Besides—" I broke off.

"What?"

"Nothing. I mean—you're practically asleep. If I start to tell you about my work, you'll be out in five minutes."

That was true, but I had been about to say that I didn't need his help. It was what I might have said as a teenager, saturated with resentment, and what I knew I still said, deep down, whenever he told me something I hadn't known or his mind jumped lightning fast to a conclusion before mine could get there. It was what I had come too close to saying in Charley's office. I didn't want him. He'd ruin everything.

"No, I won't," Charley said. I think he missed the words I'd left unsaid, but I could never quite tell with him. "Try me."

"Forget it." I hesitated. "Charley?"

"Hm?"

I almost didn't speak, but it had been nagging at me too much.

"Uriah Heep—just before you arrived on the scene, he said that something was coming. A new world, I think were the words. He said you would be at the heart of it. What did he mean?"

"I have no idea," Charley replied. His brow furrowed. "I must have missed that part, trying to get out of the closet. Are you sure he said that?"

"Pretty sure. He had a knife to my throat at the time, so I was paying attention. He doesn't know anything you don't, though, right? He can't."

Some of the smart ones do seem to have more of Charley's memories than others. When we had Sherlock Holmes in our spare room for a few days, back when Charley was seven, he knew enough about the modern world to pass for a friend of the family and beat all our high scores at Pac-Man. But still, they're from Charley's head. They can't tell him anything he doesn't already know.

"There *has* been something strange building lately," Charley said hesitantly. "Have you noticed? Perhaps in the last year, but more so in the last few weeks. I keep seeing things out of the corner of my eye that don't seem right."

"At the university?"

"No—well, yes, once or twice. I was in the stacks of the library a while back, and something ran past me very fast, about knee height."

"It was probably a small child. They do exist, you know."

"Why would there be a small child at the university library? Looking for volume three of *The Decline and Fall of the Roman Empire*? Besides, when I went to follow, the door slammed shut in my face. That door is heavy. A small child couldn't unhook it and slam it shut on me like that. And it hasn't only been the university. I was at Cuba Street the other week, and...this will sound strange, but I swear I saw the Artful Dodger buying muffins."

"That does indeed sound strange. It also sounds impossible. I suppose it explains where Uriah Heep got the idea from after all."

"Not the new world part. I've never heard that before in my life. And—"

"What?" I asked, after the pause had lengthened beyond the usual limit.

"Nothing. You haven't noticed anything?"

"I notice a lot of things. The only truly strange things I've ever noticed in this city are what you bring to it."

"You were the one who said Uriah Heep told you—"

"I know, and I'm sorry I mentioned it. It was just a phrase. I'm sure it's nothing."

"Nothing is nothing." He paused. "That didn't come out right. What I mean is, phrases are important. That's what I'm trying to teach my poetry students at the moment. Words are chosen very carefully. Stories are built from words."

"This is reality, not story. Reality is built from facts."

"'There is nothing more deceptive than an obvious fact,'" Charley said, which sounded like a quote from something. He shook his head before I could reply too sharply. "Sorry. You're right, I'm practically asleep. Perhaps he was just playing with you. He's Uriah Heep. He does that."

"Exactly," I said. Since this was what I wanted to hear, I didn't push any further. But I knew it hadn't sounded like that at all.

Lydia was getting dressed by the time I had dropped Charley off and come home. She works as a hotel manager at City Limits on Courtenay Place, and her days either start very early or go very late— sometimes both. I had started this one a little earlier for us both.

"Is your brother all right?" she asked as I shaved and she put on earrings in front of the tiny bathroom mirror. (We still needed to renovate the bathroom.)

"He'll be bouncing off the walls again in an hour or so." Which meant I should probably at least phone him at some point during the morning and remind him not to be an idiot. Charley after accidentally reading a character forth has a bad history of being so fascinated with the result that, as soon as dizziness and exhaustion have worn off, he'll accidentally-on-purpose do it again.

"And are you going to tell me anything more about what the problem was in the first place?"

"Does it matter?"

"Of course it bloody well matters!" She finished putting in her earring, and turned to face me. I immediately began to prepare my defense. "I want to know what's going on. I care about your brother, too, you know. I like him. And for the life of me, I can't imagine what he could be involved in that requires you to be pulled away at all hours of the day or night to go to his aid. He just isn't the type."

It wasn't the first time she had asked this, and I knew it wouldn't be the last. I couldn't answer. It wasn't just that I had never betrayed Charley's secret to anyone, or that I wanted to protect Lydia from having to keep the secret herself—though both of those reasons were constantly on my mind, sometimes nestled so closely I couldn't tell where one ended and the other began. I just knew that once I did tell her, the shape of our lives would be irrevocably altered. I wasn't ready for that. I had fought too hard for our life.

"You know him," I said as carelessly as I could. "He's hopeless."

"No," she countered, "he's not. He may not know what day of the week it is half the time, but he didn't earn a PhD by the age of nineteen on the other side of the world by being completely hopeless. Something was very wrong last night. If it wasn't, you would be able to tell me what it was."

"It was wrong last night," I conceded. "It's right again now."

"As simple as that? Whatever the problem was just vanished into thin air?"

"That," I said, "is exactly what happened."

"And you vanished it?"

"No, actually. He did. But I helped."

"I'm sure you did." She actually meant that; her look softened. Human nature being what it is, I wondered if I'd sounded a bit pathetic. "I don't mind you wanting to look out for him, you know. I get it; he's your brother. I have four of my own. I know what it's like. I just don't see why it has to be such a secret. And, I have to admit, I wonder if it would be better for both of you if you let him fix his own problems sometimes."

I realized that she had been lying awake thinking this out while I was gone, for her benefit as much as mine. Lydia's like that. We've been together four years now, and I'm constantly amazed by how long she can think over her own feelings, working at them patiently until she's straightened out the knots and tangles and can lay them out in words. I, according to her, am more likely to use words to deliberately confuse myself and others. And I am in the practice of law, so she's probably right.

"You're probably right," I said to her. "But I can't exactly ignore him when he phones in the middle of the night in a panic."

"No," she conceded. "I didn't mean that. You should have let me come too, you know. You came and helped move my parents into their new house last month."

"That was carrying boxes. And eating your father's cooking, which was amazing. This... could best be described as a family thing."

Lydia's big on family things. One side of her own family is Māori and the other is Greek, and there are a lot of enthusiastic relatives in her life at any given time. She will usually accept that definition, at a push. This time, she gave me hard look, but mercifully didn't push any further.

"Well," she said instead, "if we're stopping to get breakfast in town, we'd better get a move on. And if we're not, one of us needs to learn to cook in the next three minutes, because Thursdays require more than last-minute toast and possibly expired yogurt. You know this is true."

I kissed her—partly because I wanted to, partly to thank her for trying to be understanding about what was not really understandable at all.

When I first came to Wellington to study law, I came because it was the cultural and creative capital of the country. It was where laws were made, and where art was made. It was where governments rose and fell in the House of Parliament named the Beehive, where lively discussions sparked over coffee in quirky cafés, where students drank to flashing strobe lights in the small hours of the morning. I had been there only once or twice, on school visits. I knew its inhabitants always complained about the weather and the hills: it was famous for winds that tore through the city at up to 250 kilometers an hour, rain that lashed its coast to ribbons, and steep slopes, dark with ancient bush, on which wooden colonial houses perched like roosting wood pigeons. I didn't have feelings about that. I was eighteen and ambitious, and I wanted to build a life in the city. I didn't need, or expect, to fall in love with it.

I did fall in love, of course—for all the things I had no feelings about, plus a few more. Now I know that almost everyone who lives in Wellington is in love with it, many of them fiercely, passionately, jealously. It's just customary to express it by complaining about weather and hills.

On that day, I was glad of the wind tugging at my coat; I was glad, too, of my sleek office building, thrumming with people and ideas. It helped drag me the rest of the way out of Charley's world. In the rush of an ordinary day, Uriah Heep's threat or warning seemed ludicrous. If it weren't for the tiny blade cut rubbing at my shirt collar, the whole thing would have felt like a dream. I collected my files for the day, clarified a few last-minute details with the paralegals, and crossed the road to the district court. I finally argued the case I'd been preparing for months, the lingering tiredness from my early start burned away by the peculiar cocktail of adrenaline and conviction that always kicks in about five minutes into a trial. I don't have the feel for language my brother does, or the intellect. I'm articulate enough when I need to be, and I'm bright enough to get by with a good deal of hard work. But I love the feel of a case coming together. It becomes real, at that moment. I had the exhilarating sense, as I often do of being in touch with the heartbeat of the city.

When I came out of the courthouse at lunchtime, still riding a crest of exhilaration, I saw a child by the side of the road. A boy, quite small and frail, maybe eleven years old. I would have thought he was waiting for someone, but in all the crowds going past, nobody seemed to spare him a second glance. Perhaps I wouldn't have, either, except that I was almost certain he was looking at me. He was wearing an old baseball cap and oversized sunglasses, so I couldn't see his eyes. But I could feel them.

I moved toward him, on impulse. I couldn't just leave him there. It was the middle of a school day, in the middle of the city. It didn't feel right. *He* didn't feel right. This was Lambton Quay, the heart of central Wellington. Parliament was across the road; the railway station, in all its redbrick glory, was opposite. It was a clean, solid area. He was a ghost in the middle of it.

"Are you all right there?" I asked. "Who are you looking for?"

The boy was gone before I had taken three steps. He didn't run, just ducked his head quickly and walked away, as though he'd been caught staring at something he shouldn't. A shiver went down my spine that I couldn't name. There had been something very familiar about him.

I entered our office building cautiously. This had nothing to do with the boy; I'd shaken off the incident over the walk back across the road, reassured as usual by the bustle of the wind and the crowds. I was avoiding Eva Rusch, the firm's lead partner. I knew there were new interns in the building, and that it was my turn to take one of them on for the week to prepare them for the summer. And I know they needed someone to look after them, and I should have been happy to oblige. Lydia had told me as much the other night, and she was right. I usually would have been—younger interns, however brilliant or hopeless, were refreshingly easy to look after compared to my younger brother. But it had been a long, difficult morning, and I was not in an obliging mood.

I was almost safe, actually opening my office door, when I heard the telltale rap of heels on the corridor floor.

"Oh, Rob," Eva said, catching my arm with a smile that said she knew what I was doing, and that threatened me with disembowelment if I didn't stop. "There you are. Come meet the new summer interns. People, this is Rob Sutherland, one of our best solicitors; Rob, this is Carmen, Frances, and Eric."

I sighed inwardly, turned to say hello, and found myself face-to-face with two pleasant-looking young women and Uriah Heep.

Dr. Charles Sutherland, age nineteen

Extract from notebook (leather bound, green)

I know it's a secret. But one day it might not be. One day people might want to know what it is and how it works, and the knowledge might not be there. I would tell them, but the day might come only after I'm dead. So just in case, I want to write down what I know—or at least what I think—about how it works.

This is how it works. I think.

I'll be reading. Of course I will. Well, if I know something thoroughly enough—a poem, or a very specific piece of text, something small—I can sometimes just be thinking. But usually, I need the sight of words on paper. It has to be paper. That's me, I think, not the magic or the ability or whatever term applies. Words aren't the same to me on a screen. I can see them, but I can't connect with them. They're too hard and bright; I float on top of them, like a leaf on the surface of a pond. Words on paper are quiet, and porous; in the right mood, I sink down between the gaps in the letters and they close over my head.

Words and paper. That's the easy part.

So I'll be drifting in words, absorbing, and the words I absorb will be racing through my bloodstream. Every nerve, every neuron will be sparking and catching fire, and my heart will be quickening to carry it through faster, and my eyes will be tearing ahead to take in more and more.

This isn't magic yet, or whatever the word is. (It's always annoyed me that I can't find the word.) This is just reading a book.

And while I'm reading, the new words I'm taking in will connect to others already taken in. That reference to blue is the third this chapter, and it always goes with wealth. That phrase is from the poem earlier. Deeper. That's a reference to the myth of Orpheus. That's a pairing of two words that don't usually go together. Wider. That's a symbol Dickens employs often. That typifies Said's writings on Orientalism. Points of light. They make a map, or a pattern, or a constellation. Formless, intricate, infinitely complex, and lovely.

And then, at once, they'll connect. They'll meet, and explode. Of course. *That's the entire point.* That's how the story works, the way each sentence and metaphor and reference feeds into the other to illuminate something important. That explosion of discovery, of understanding, is the most intoxicating moment there is. Emotional, intellectual, aesthetic. Just for a moment, a perfect moment, a small piece of the world makes perfect sense. And it's beautiful. It's a moment of pure joy, the kind that brings pleasure like pain.

This isn't magic yet either. (Or whatever the word may be.) Still just reading. Or literary analysis? Are they different things? This is just reading deeper.

Sometimes—often—at that point of explosion, someone or something will arrive. It's as though I see them properly, and I see them so clearly that they manifest. I can remember doing it for the first time when I was four, before the time with *The Cat in the Hat* that drew my parents' attention. I was reading *Nineteen Eighty-Four.* I still didn't understand everything about *Nineteen Eighty-Four*—if I had, Child Protection would have probably needed a call—but I understood the paperweight. The main character, Winston, buys a paperweight—glass, with a piece of coral enclosed inside—at an antiques store. He and his lover, Julia, have it in the attic where they go to escape the attention of their evil government. ("The paperweight was the room he was in," Orwell says, "and the coral was Julia's life and his own, fixed in a sort of eternity at the heart of the crystal.") When they are discovered, the paperweight smashes. I understood, right then, how a piece of coral in writing could be the hearts of two people, and a glass paperweight could be the world they create: safe, protected, yet infinitely fragile. In life, a paperweight was a paperweight. In a book, when it broke, it could leave you exposed on the floor. I remember catching my breath in awe at this, and then the smooth, cool feel of the paperweight in my hand. Instead of the coral, there was a tiny attic inside it, and a tiny Winston and Julia safe in each other's arms.

That part is the magic, in that it's a step further than most people's reading or analysis goes. It all feels one and the same to me, but that's where the line crosses from the accepted to the extraordinary. (I like the word "extraordinary." *Extraordinarius.* Out of the common order. More than ordinary. Ordinary plus extra. It looks like "extraordinary," but is in fact just the opposite. If I could make that a noun, the way "magic" can be made a verb, then that would be a good word for what I'm talking about.)

Rob thinks I can't stop it from happening. That's true, often. If something strikes me unexpectedly, and I don't catch myself in time, then whatever it is has come into the world, and it's too late. But I learned when I was very little that I could also do it deliberately. If I just concentrate very hard on the character or object, their role in the book, their purpose or meaning or textual composition, they can come out. And honestly, I do that more than I should. I've told you how it feels. It's a shadow of that, when done deliberately, but still. Even if I can technically stop it, how can I help it? And why should I? It doesn't hurt anybody.

Putting them back hurts, sometimes. Not always. If they go back willingly, they just slip away, back into textuality. I'll feel a wash of dizziness, but only for a moment, like a tide pulling out and crashing back in again. But sometimes, especially if they're accidents, they resist. Then, putting them back is like willingly taking a hammer blow to the skull. It's difficult, too, because it feels counterintuitive. To pull them out, you think of them, or some facet of them, as close and as deep as you can. To put them back, you think of their place in the wider story—it's a little like adjusting a camera lens from deep focus to wide focus. It requires you to know the whole book, not just the tiny fragment you've brought to life. It also requires you, right at the moment you know the character best and have taken possession of them, to unknow them, to let them fade out of your sight and concentration, to lose them in a wider story. And it's hard, when your brain has an idea, to force it to let it go. I'm used to it, so it doesn't bother me in any practical sense. It bothers me, though, because I don't know why some of them resist, or what they believe themselves to be resisting. It feels, momentarily, like dying. I wonder what it feels like for them.

So that's how I think it works. It's about interpreting, understanding, visualizing, connecting. Basically, still reading a book.

I never sent that paperweight back, the one from my four-year-old *Nineteen Eighty-Four*. I still have it, on a high shelf where nobody can stumble on it. Sometimes I get it down, and watch them in their safe, fragile, perfect world that is smashed in the narrative, but not as an idea.

("How small, thought Winston, how small it always was!")

IV

There were two cars parked outside my brother's house when I arrived. When Charley opened the door, I could hear the low murmur of voices inside.

"Oh, hi, Rob," Charley said. "I didn't know you were coming."

"Well, no," I said, probably irritably. I don't think I realized how worried I'd been about not being able to get hold of him, until I saw him there completely oblivious. "No, you'd have to be psychic to know, because you weren't answering your phone. As usual."

"Did you call?"

I didn't quite trust myself to answer this. I had, of course, been calling all afternoon. I'd tried his office phone and, when he didn't answer, assumed he wasn't in his office. I'd tried his cell phone and, when he didn't answer, assumed everything from his untimely death to the theft of his phone by magpies. I tried the English department reception, where I learned he had finished classes at three and gone to work from home for the rest of the day. I tried e-mail, knowing I might as well try a message in a bottle. When five thirty came, and he still hadn't replied, I'd finally given in, rang to tell Lydia I'd be home late, and came to knock on his door.

"Yes," I said. "Yes, I did call. Are there people here?"

"Well, yes. Sort of. I mean—it's the rest of the History of the Novel course. We always meet on Thursday afternoons to talk about next week, and sometimes we come back here rather than use one of the offices."

"And...that was a 'sort of' because you're uncertain they're here, or that they're people?"

"Because they're technically here, but they were just on their way out. Why? What's wrong?"

"I need to ask you something." I hesitated, then lowered my voice. "Uriah Heep—has he come out again since this morning?"

Charley frowned, and glanced over his shoulder. He stepped outside and closed the door behind him. "No," he said, matching my near whisper. "No, of course not. I haven't had any time to work with Dickens today at all."

"What about before? Was that the first time you'd read him out?"

"Yes."

"Are you sure?"

"Definitely. Why?"

"Because he's just started work as an intern at the firm."

He was silent for a long moment, then shook his head. "But—how can—? Are you sure?"

"Definitely," I echoed him, without thinking. "I know him now, trust me. He's calling himself Eric, and he's wearing modern clothes—but it's definitely Uriah Heep. I hate to say this, but that feeling you had? I'm starting to think you were right after all."

Charley was silent a moment longer. "You know, I think I probably need coffee at this point in the conversation," he said finally. "The others really were just leaving. Do you want to come in?"

The truth is, I sort of love my brother's flat. It's hopeless, but it's hopeless with style.

It's a tiny one-bedroom town house further up the hill from the university, right on the outskirts of Highbury, so while the university and the city are nestled within walking distance, there's nothing around it to walk through but a lot of bush and a few other houses winding up a long, steep road. And that's fine—that goes for a lot of houses around these parts—but this one manages to combine isolation and limited square footage with total lack of understanding of the laws of home design. Its one bedroom is an attic up a rickety staircase; the kitchen, dining room, and living room are all one wood-paneled space; the bathroom, tucked behind the stairs, is both freezing and ungainly. And, of course, Charley has filled every spare inch of it with books. Books cascade over the surface of the desk in the corner by the window, climb in staggering towers up the walls, pack the bookshelves, crouch on the stairs. They hide in the kitchen amid the pots and pans, frame the old fireplace that hasn't burned in years, bury the coffee table in front of the couch. I found one in the fridge once, though he swears that was a mistake.

This time, the books on the coffee table were doubling as coasters for a ring of half-empty wineglasses, and three people were gathering their belongings: a bearded man in a checked shirt, a younger, lankier man with glasses, and a gray-haired woman in a pink cardigan.

"This is my brother, Rob," Charley introduced me. "Rob, this is Brian, Troy, and Beth. Troy's tutoring on the course, and Brian and Beth are lecturing."

"Oh!" The older woman, presumably Beth, looked at me with interest. "A pleasure to meet you. Charles has often spoken of you."

I shook her proffered hand. "Really? What does he say?"

"That you're a lawyer in the city, and that you're intimidatingly organized."

"He also says he suspects he drives you insane," the bearded man, Brian, added.

"Well, he's right." I tried to speak normally, when really all I wanted was for everyone to leave. "I think he says something similar about you. At least the last part."

"I think I say things like that about everybody I know," Charley said. "Beth, you wanted those books back from me, right? I'll see if I can dig them out."

"Don't let me chase you all away," I said, praying very much they would let me chase them away. I was in no state to make polite conversation with academics—at the best of times, possibly, but certainly not now. I wasn't convinced that Eric wasn't going to come knocking at the door.

"No, no. I need to get back to the kids, anyway," Brian said. "I'll run you to the train station, Troy, if you like. Good to meet you, Rob. I'll see the rest of you next week."

"Second to last week of term," the younger postgraduate sighed. "Thank God."

I waited, with increasing impatience, as Charley rummaged through the shelves while Beth studied me curiously with blue-gray eyes.

"Here's one of them, anyway," Charley said at last. He emerged from the shelf, a red hardcover in his hand. "It was on the mantel-piece. God knows why. Beth, I kept meaning to ask you—have you seen a box of notebooks, about twelve of them, all different sizes? I know they were there by the potted plant when you and Troy were here last month, because Troy asked about them, and I know they were here after you both left, because I put them somewhere else. But I have no idea where that was, and I haven't seen them since."

"I remember the box you mean," she said, with a wry glance in my direction, "but I have no idea where it could be. Frankly, Charles, in all the times I've been here, I've never once been able to work out where you put anything."

"No," he conceded. "Neither have I, and I live here. I'll dig out the other two books and give them to you next week, I promise."

"There's no hurry: it was this one I wanted over the weekend. I'll leave you two to talk." She hesitated, as if she might be about to say something more, but all she said was, "It was nice meeting you, Robert."

"You too," I said.

I waited until I heard the sound of the car pull away down the long, winding road before I turned to Charley. The house suddenly seemed very quiet.

"I'm sorry I missed your call," Charley said, before I could speak. "I don't know how that happened. I only had an hour's sleep before the morning faculty meeting, so I'm a bit all over the place this after-noon. Would you like coffee? Or there's tea, I think, somewhere."

I didn't want to test Charley's definition of "somewhere," so I accepted coffee. The last of the afternoon sun was fading from the room; outside, the trees were beginning to press about the house. The bush surrounding the city always does that at night.

"Tell me about Uriah Heep," Charley said.

"I didn't really talk to him." I sat down carefully amid the wobbling paperbacks on the couch. "We only saw each other for a moment. He's one of the three new interns we have at work—they're shadowing us for a week before they come back for the summer at the end of November. Eva introduced us. We shook hands; we parted ways. That was it. Is there any way you could have brought out Uriah Heep without know-ing it? You've done that in the past, with other characters."

"Not since I was about six." He stopped rummaging in the kitchen to look at me. "I know the feeling too well now. I don't have a Uriah Heep out there, Rob, I promise."

"I believe you," I assured him. "This is going to sound strange, but I knew right away it wasn't you. I've met your Uriah Heep. This one felt different—it was cruder, somehow, and less well formed. I know those things can shift if your reading of them does, but they never grow *lesser*, do they?"

"No," he said. "They don't." He was silent. "So what exactly are you suggesting? Someone else read out their own version of Uriah Heep?"

"Exactly. And…call me paranoid, but it's a little odd that he ended up, of all the places in the world, in my office."

"After what my Uriah Heep said this morning," Charley said slowly, "I'd have to agree."

He came over with a mug in each hand, and handed me one.

"Here," he said. "It'll have to be black, sorry. Milk goes off really quickly, doesn't it? But at least I found the phone. It was right next to the milk bottle."

"In the *fridge*?"

"I don't know how that happened." He settled himself cross-legged in the armchair opposite me. "Could you tell me exactly what he said to you?"

"There isn't much more to tell. Like I said, it was a quick meeting."

"Still." His eyes were thoughtful. "If you could talk me through it…"

I took him through the meeting, prompted occasionally by his questions. Uriah Heep had appeared suddenly. I'd seen his over-red hair, his corpse-like pallor, his long limbs. I'd felt the clamminess of his hand when I'd been forced to offer mine. I'd heard a London accent when he'd said he was pleased to meet me, oiled over by the obsequiousness that seemed to go with the territory. When I mentioned his surprising youth—he could have passed for eighteen—Charley nodded.

"Alfred Grossman," he said immediately. "He did an article on Uriah Heep as a perversion of Victorian childhood innocence."

"You think it was him?" I asked, surprised.

"Oh God no," Charley laughed. "I've met him; there's no way he summons figures out of books. He's the most boring man imaginable. Besides, he lives in Michigan. I just meant that whoever it was, they might have modeled this portrayal from his article. That would explain his name too. *Eric; or, Little by Little*—it's a school story that was published eight years or so after *David Copperfield*. Grossman uses it as a template."

"I've never heard of it."

"You're lucky. It's like slow torture—unless you really like Victorian morality tales where everyone dies at the end, then it's hilarious. Eric also means 'ruler,' of course. I wonder if that's relevant."

None of that sounded particularly promising. "Does that help us? Is that article hard to find?"

"Nothing's hard to find these days," Charley said. "As long as you can navigate search engines. It's something to look into." He hesitated. "Do you think you're in danger?"

That startled me into laughter. "Actually, Charley, I was more concerned about you."

"Me?"

"Well...yes." I set my cooling mug down on a nearby hardcover. It was still full. I don't drink black coffee. "I mean, I'm a good lawyer, I'm decent at pub quizzes, and I can cook excellent pasta, but none of that's likely to garner interest from literary characters come to life. I have a feeling that if they're beginning to show up at my work, it's probably because my brother is a linguistic genius who can bring them to life."

"But they don't need to be brought to life," Charley pointed out. "They're already alive. They need to be put away again, if anything."

"Maybe that's what bothers them."

He nodded slowly. I could see him turning my words over in his head, as one might handle a potentially lethal reptile that must be studied for the good of science.

"Do you think—?" he started to say, then stopped short.

So did I. Over the faint rustle of the wind in the trees outside, the evening had been split by an unearthly howl. The hairs rose on the back of my neck. I suddenly realized how dark it had become, just in the twenty minutes or so we were talking. Too dark for half past six on a spring evening in October.

"What is that?" I asked him.

"I think," Charley said slowly, "that's the cry of a gigantic hound."

V

Between the darkness and the reflection in the glass from the lights inside, it was difficult to see out the window. I would have grabbed a flashlight, gone out, and checked around the house myself, but Charley gave me a look as though I had lost all reason when I suggested it.

"One howl doesn't necessarily herald the Hound of the Baskervilles," I said. "You're right by the bush out here. There's a wildlife sanctuary around the corner. It could be anything."

"Like what?" Charley asked—reasonably, under the circumstances. It was getting colder. Fog was beginning to curl from the grass outside. Perfectly natural animals howled all the time; they didn't affect the weather.

I didn't get a chance to answer, because then we both saw it. A green luminescence in the darkness, coming from the gully. A second later, I realized that the light had been flames, and that the flames wreathed the head of an animal. I saw a glimpse of red eyes, flashing teeth, bunched muscles beneath black hair. The head was at the height of the lemon tree in the garden. Dog shaped, roughly, but like no dog I had ever seen.

"What *is* it?"

"I told you," Charley said. "It's the Hound of the Baskervilles."

I couldn't really argue anymore. It was.

"Why is there fog outside?" For some reason, my mind was snatching at irrelevant details. "It was warm a moment ago."

"There's always fog," Charley said distractedly. I had a feeling he didn't mean in Highbury.

We'd been rural kids, Charley and I. We grew up on a large section surrounded by dairy farms. We knew how to deal with vicious dogs; I'd even dealt with a few vicious cows. But this looked bigger than any dog I had ever seen. And it was breathing fire.

On cue, the howl came again. This time, it was much closer; a harsh, rhythmic rasp, which I had barely registered before, became a little louder in its wake. It was the sound of a dog panting.

"Did the front door just shake?" Charley asked very quietly.

"I don't know." I found myself whispering as well. "Look—I'm sure it will go away. But if it *doesn't* go away, can you put it back?"

"It's not mine," Charley said. "I don't know how."

"Well, how do you usually do it?"

"I think of how it fits into the wider story, and I concentrate on that—but this isn't my reading. I don't *know* where it fits. I don't know what kind of reading it is."

I took his word for it. I know nothing about literary criticism, or bringing things out of books. If a mechanic tells me he can't fix my car because the thingumajig will no longer connect with the whatsit, I don't bother to argue.

"Well, it seems large and scary," I said instead. "I haven't read the book, but I thought the Hound of the Baskervilles turns out to be a normal dog?"

"Nobody pictures that," Charley said. "Not in the early parts. You're not supposed to."

The cry came again, louder this time, and this time there was a decided bump against the door. Charley flinched, and took a step backward.

"Are you okay?" I asked, though I understood why he might not be. My own heart was pounding.

Charley took a while to respond. "Oh...yes," he said. "Just...this is sort of my worst fear come to life right now."

"Isn't *Hound of the Baskervilles* one of your many favorite books?"

"That doesn't mean it doesn't scare me to death. The opposite, actually. When I was five I couldn't even open it unless I was hiding under the bed with a flashlight."

"I remember."

"I know it's not really a ghost dog from the depths of hell. I know

Holmes proves it's a hoax. But that isn't the experience for the early parts of the book. Oh God."

This last came involuntarily as the door shook and rattled; on the wood outside, I heard hard nails scrape.

"Do you have anything to fend it off with?" I asked. "You know: a poker, or a baseball bat or something."

He shook his head vigorously. "I don't have a working fireplace and I don't play baseball. Anyway—it's the *Hound* of the *Baskervilles*. It's not going to be deterred by a flailing stick."

"Steady," I said, as if my blood hadn't turned to ice. "What about a kitchen knife?"

"In the top drawer." He took a deep breath, trying to calm himself. "But honestly, those knives can't even cut tomatoes anymore. I keep meaning to get them sharpened. Hold on—there's Excalibur, if I can find *Le Morte Darthur* again."

"I'm not going to attack a spectral dog with a medieval sword, Charley! They shoot it in the original story, don't they? If you must bring something out from the pages of a book, don't you have books with guns?"

"It's not that simple," he said. "It has to be—I don't know, it would have to be an important gun, one with meaning and context. I can't just reach in and pull out a hot dog because the protagonist eats one on page twenty-six."

"I thought you said everything in a book has meaning."

"It does! That doesn't mean it means what you want it to mean!"

"Well, find one that does! You've got a whole bloody library here!"

"I don't—there's Chekhov's gun, obviously. But I don't know if I have that anywhere—maybe in Abrams's *Literary Terms*—"

The door shuddered; the blow shook the house and set the lights above us swinging. A book fell to the ground, with a soft thud like an echo. I could hear growling, and that terrible, rhythmic panting. The door's hinges groaned.

"It's going to be through in a moment," I said. "We need to move."

There was no response, and I turned quickly. I realized then, rather belatedly, how scared he was. Charley talks very fast when he's nervous, or ill at ease; when he's truly, deeply terrified, he goes quiet.

Right then, he was not only quiet, but frozen. I felt a familiar protective tug in my chest, and as usual I pushed it away.

"Charley!" I snapped.

He still didn't move; it was only when I grabbed him roughly by the shoulder that his eyes flickered toward me.

"Upstairs," I told him. There was literally nowhere else to go: Charley's flat has no back door, and if it did there would be nowhere to run that way but a bush-covered gully. "Move!"

With a supreme effort of will, Charley shook himself out of whatever had him in its grip, nodded quickly, and started to run as I pushed him away. He stumbled, picked himself up, and made it to the stairs, me close behind him.

He had reached the top and I was on about the third stair when the door flew from its hinges. The hound was in the room.

I've seen some strange things emerge from books over the years—you should have seen the house when Charley was reading Kafka—but I've never seen anything like that creature. I suppose it was a dog, but it more closely resembled a cart horse crossed with a gargoyle: enormous, so black it made the dark around it look gray, with luminous green fire roaring from its open mouth and coiling about its neck and flanks like a lion's mane. It growled, like a freight train rumbling through, and its eyes gleamed red. I only caught a glimpse of it as I froze in horror, and then I was tearing up the stairs and through the door that Charley was holding open.

I collapsed onto the ground at the foot of Charley's bed, and he slammed the door shut. There's not a lot of furniture in that room—honestly, it's a bed in a cocoon of books—but there's a small writing desk by the window, and I got up to help Charley drag it in front of the door. We were both breathing hard, and he was shaking visibly. I probably was too.

"Did you see it?" he asked me.

"No," I lied—I knew he hadn't, and he was frightened enough without hearing the details of that thing. "Look, that's not going to hold it for long—the front door's much sturdier, and it tore through that like paper."

"No." He pushed his hair out of his eyes. "No, I know. Give me a second, I'm thinking."

"Well, hurry up." I could hear the sound of padding footsteps on the staircase.

"I know," he repeated. Then his face lit. "Of course, obviously…"

He dived for one of the piles of books that circled the walls. I ran my eyes around the room quickly, looking for anything to use in case of the worst. There was a paperweight on the desk, but that would be like throwing a pebble at an elephant. I went instead for the desk lamp, which had a fairly solid metal base, and ripped the plug out of the wall so I could hold it like a club. The scratches were at the door again; I heard growling and whining, and then the door quivered on its hinges.

"Charley!" I urged, then groaned as I saw which book he had pulled out from the bottom of the pile. "Oh, not him again…"

There was a flare of light, and then a familiar figure was standing beside us.

I hate it when Sherlock Holmes comes. I didn't use to mind so much when I was little, although the way he and Charley talked always made me feel left out and—I suppose—superfluous. But since that day when I was eighteen, I've always felt his cool gaze on me had something of real disdain. Most of Charley's creations presumably know about that day, depending on the memories they carry from him; Uriah Heep was only the first to mention it. But Holmes was there. He knows firsthand what I did—or didn't do. And I'm sure he's probably deduced more about me from it than Charley would have the heart to.

"Dr. Sutherland," the great detective greeted my brother. As usual, he showed no surprise at suddenly finding himself in a twenty-first-century house. "Always a uniquely unexpected pleasure."

My brother's images of Sherlock Holmes have shifted over the years, but he can never be mistaken for anyone else: tall and lean, with dark hair, a hawklike nose, and piercing eyes (not literally piercing, fortunately—that can happen). This version looked a little older and more human than the ones I'd seen in my brother's teenage years, but still absolutely formidable.

"We're in the middle of a crisis here," I told him.

"So I gathered," Holmes said, a little coolly, I thought, though I might have been oversensitive. "When two people are hiding in a bedroom whilst the door is being battered from the outside, it's not difficult to deduce a crisis is in progress."

"I'm so sorry to bother you," Charley said. He had shut *The Sherlock Holmes Novel Omnibus* and scrambled back to his feet. "But the Baskerville hound is outside, and you dispatch it so well in the book…"

"How kind of you," Holmes said, with a smile in his direction. He looked at the closed door, which was trembling under repeated blows, and tilted his head to one side as he considered. "But I'm afraid that won't work in this case. That is no mere hound you have outside the door. You have the nightmare version, the version of legend, and I'm afraid it will be very much impervious to bullets. It was believed to be, after all, before I shot it."

"But you *can* do something?" The panic was rising in Charley's voice again. "Please, you have to. It's your book."

"I can't do anything," Holmes said. "I'm afraid you'll have to handle this yourself."

"How's he supposed to do that?" I demanded. "There's a—I don't even know *what* that thing is outside the door!"

"*You* know what it is, Doctor," Holmes said to my brother. He was perfectly grave now, and ignoring me completely. "A cross between a bloodhound and a mastiff, aided by a cunning preparation of phosphorus. And mortal—not supernatural. You simply need to read it back the way it should be."

"But it's not mine this time!" Charley protested. "I can't put it back."

"Perhaps not. But you can argue with its interpretation. You do it all the time—on paper, at conferences. Think of it as an academic dispute. And in this case, you may consider yourself justified by the text itself. You would correct a colleague or a student who tried to read the hound as a pure Gothic monster, would you not?"

"Of course. It's an ordinary dog. You unmask it through deductive reasoning. The entire book is about the power of science and intellect to disprove fear and superstition. But…"

"Exactly," Holmes said. "This…creature out there, whatever it is, is a misreading and an affront to the most basic Sherlock Holmes scholarship. Correct it. That, after all, is how I truly defeat the monstrous hound, is it not? Not merely by shooting it. By disproving its very existence."

"I don't know how."

"Yes, you do." He took my brother by the shoulders, and looked into his face. I was focused on the door, but still there was something hypnotic about his voice. My ears were drawn to it, even under the sounds of our death trying to tear its way to us. "You know why the reading is wrong. You know the clues my author placed in the text to hint at the hound's proper origins. You know how the text resolves itself. You know the thematic reasons why there cannot be a ghost in the universe of Sherlock Holmes. Your only difficulty is that, at this moment, you are in a state of terror. Your heart rate has increased, your breathing has quickened, your pupils have contracted, your muscles have tensed, and you are *no longer thinking clearly*. That is precisely the effect the hound is designed to have. It scares people to death. Sir Charles Baskerville died of heart disease and terror at the sight of it; the convict on the moors broke his neck trying to escape it. You need to overcome your fear, and quickly, because when it breaks through that door—as it assuredly will—it will almost certainly be too late."

Charley shook his head. "I can't—"

"You can," he said firmly. "Sutherland, I am not in the habit of flattering people with false estimates of their abilities. You can."

The door was creaking under the strain now—fortunately, the landing was too small to give it a run-up, or it would have battered it down already.

"Rob," Charley said. "What did it look like?"

"I said I didn't—"

"I know, but you must have—you wouldn't have been so far behind me if you hadn't stopped to look. Please, I need to know this."

"It was huge," I said. "And black. And breathing fire. It was—I don't know—"

"'Never in the delirious dream of a disordered brain could any-thing more savage, more appalling, more hellish be conceived than that dark form and savage face which broke upon us out of the wall of fog'?"

"Yes." There was fog creeping in from under the door now. It was deathly cold; I saw the hair rise on the back of my hands as they gripped the lamp. "That."

"Good," Charley said. "Thanks."

He opened the book to a different page, and began reading.

"Very good," Mr. Holmes said softly.

I turned back to the door, disturbed as always by the intense concentration on my brother's face. I knew that look very well: it was there when he brought something out, or when he put something back, but sometimes just when he was reading or writing or staring out the window, oblivious to the rest of the world. I don't think I ever go that deeply into my own head. I always have the irrational fear that he might not come out.

"All right," I heard him say to himself. "We're told that the dog was bought in London from Ross and Mangles, the dealers in Fulham Road. There's a characteristic attention to prosaic detail, precise locations…and the word used is 'dog,' no longer the more Gothic 'hound'…"

"Be careful," Holmes instructed. "Keep your focus on the hound outside the door. You want to change it, not create another."

That was a thought.

The hound was still growling and scratching. The fog was still thick. The door jolted, and the desk scraped against the floor.

"Charley…"

"'But that cry of pain from the hound had blown all our fears to the winds. If he was vulnerable he was mortal, and if we could wound him we could kill him…'" He was keeping his eyes resolutely on the paper, so tense it was as though he were trying to shy away from the air around him. "That's classical logic. It's conditional implication— the 'if–then' structure is echoed. And it's from Watson, which is notable—deductive reasoning is now worked into the fabric of the narration, and not just personified in Sherlock Holmes…"

"It's getting through," I said.

Holmes raised a finger to his lips, and I shut up.

Charley drew a breath quickly, as if something had hit him. I heard a startled yelp from outside the door.

"Got it." He was very pale, and there were beads of sweat on his forehead. "God, I hate misreadings of Conan Doyle."

"It's still out there," I said, although I had definitely felt a change in the air. The fog had lifted, and with it the terrible sense of oppression;

the fear from downstairs loosened its grip on my stomach. That yelp had not sounded supernatural. It sounded like a dog in pain.

("But that cry of pain from the hound had blown all our fears to the winds...")

"Let it in, Mr. Sutherland," Holmes said to me. "And be prepared to use that lamp you've been waving so enthusiastically."

I glanced at Charley, who nodded. I pulled the desk away from the door.

The handle must have already been jiggled, because without that desk, the door swung open on its own. Behind it, teeth bared and hackles rising, was a dog.

It was still a terrifying dog. It was the size of a small lioness, with a jaw that could have cracked a person's skull in one bite. Something was smeared around its mouth that gave off a chemical glow. It was clearly bewildered and furious. But it was just a dog.

I had time to register this before it sprang at us; on instinct, I jumped in front of it and gave it a sharp rap on the nose with the lamp. It yelped and pulled back, snarling.

"Go on!" I yelled at it, waving the lamp in its direction. "Go on, get out of here!"

It hesitated for a moment. Then, as I lunged for it again, it turned tail and ran. I heard it clatter down the stairs, its great lolloping strides practically overlapping each other, and then there was silence.

"Poor brute," Mr. Holmes said. "It must have been very confused."

"I know," Charley agreed. "I always feel sorry for the Hound of the Baskervilles."

I took a flashlight and went out to have a quick look around the garden for the hound or anybody who could have conjured it, but there was nothing and nobody to be seen. When I came back to report this, Charley was saying goodbye to Mr. Holmes.

"Are you sure you don't want to stay?" he asked, a little wistfully. "This could be described as a real mystery now."

"And I will be here if you require my assistance," Holmes said. "I always am. But you won't. Any expertise I have in the manner of your abilities, Dr. Sutherland, comes entirely from your head. It's time you began to trust it."

"Uriah Heep knew something about what's going on," Charley said. "Do you?"

Holmes shook his head. "No. No, I don't. If Heep has any specialized knowledge from being a literary character, I regrettably do not share it. But I do have one piece of advice for you, in that regard."

"What's that?"

"There is a street." Holmes sounded uncharacteristically hesitant. "In the heart of the city. Turn off Cuba, go down the Left Bank past the old bookshop, and you should find it. It didn't exist until two years ago, but now every time you call me through I can feel the knowledge of it tugging at my brain."

"I've been down that way countless times," I said. "There's no street there. Just a lot of shops."

"I know," Holmes said. "It is utterly impossible, and yet it exists. Which, of course, must mean that it is not impossible at all, merely unlikely."

"And you think we'll find answers there," Charley said.

"I don't say so. But it may be a place to start." He shook Charley's hand, a clear signal that the interview was over. "Good luck, Dr. Sutherland. It really is always a pleasure. Mr. Sutherland," he added, with a nod in my direction. It seemed a little warmer than usual.

"Thanks for your help," Charley said, and closed his eyes. The room was briefly suffused with light, and then the great detective was gone.

Charley sank unsteadily onto the sofa behind him, and rested his head in his hands.

I was shaken myself. It was one thing chasing figments of Charley's imagination around the house. We all, our parents included, saw that as part of the furniture of family life by the time he was six, as we might a dog that ate the couch or an aunt that insisted on buying socks for Christmas. Irritating, but unavoidable. It went, somehow, with the special teachers and the university degrees by fifteen and the heavy tomes on literary theory lying about the place. It went with Charley being in the family at all. This was suddenly much bigger than our family.

"I'm sorry I was so useless there," Charley said, pulling me back to the present. "It was just that I'd read that book so many times—"

"Don't worry about it." I didn't tell him that I'd been terrified too;

if he had somehow missed it, I would rather he didn't know. "Are you all right?"

He rubbed his eyes, looked up, and nodded. "Mm. I've never done anything like that with the hound before. It's fascinating. I've only ever had my own readings—now I know there must be some that are stronger than others. I suppose it's exactly like Mr. Holmes said: it's an academic dispute with some else's interpretation. I'll have to try it myself—I mean, when my head's not spinning so much. Not with somebody else's reading, but if I could read out an interpretation, then try to refine it in some way—"

"You're not supposed to be reading out anything! For God's sake, Charley, can you not just let things alone? You're not a child anymore. You should be able to refrain from reading things into my home city by accident. You should *definitely* refrain from doing it on purpose."

"I didn't have anything to do with this one. It wasn't me. I told you that this morning, you know. That something was happening."

"I know." I sat down next to him, and leaned my head against the back of the couch. I was starting to feel as if I'd run a half marathon in the last quarter hour. "And I'll say I'm sorry for not believing you, if that's what you want. But don't start reading things out, all right? We have enough trouble when you do it by accident."

"We might need it. If we're up against someone who can do what I can do, I might need to be able to do it better."

"We're not up against anyone," I said firmly. "Whatever's happening, we need to distance ourselves from it, quickly."

"It's a bit late for that," Charley pointed out. "My front door's missing."

"Exactly. Let's take that as a warning, and back off. If that thing had come ten minutes earlier, you would have had people here, do you realize that?"

"Maybe," Charley said. "Or maybe whoever it was was waiting until they left. There's only one road out of here. It would be easy to see the cars leave."

"But my car hadn't left. I was still here. Are you saying that was a mistake on their part?"

"I don't know. But either way, I'm already in this. I'm a part of it. It *is* my business. You don't have to be involved—I understand if you'd rather not. But I am."

"Why? Why does the word of a Dickensian sociopath and a visit from a phantom hound involve you in anything?"

"Because of the impossible street. The one Mr. Holmes spoke about, the street where there is no street, the knowledge that makes no sense."

I pinched the bridge of my nose. "Firstly, I fail to see how knowledge of any kind of street constitutes an obligation to fight the Hound of the Baskervilles. Secondly—I know the area Holmes mentioned. There is no impossible street. There's not even an improbable street. Holmes is wrong."

"*Sherlock Holmes* is wrong?"

"Why not? He might be infallible in his book; this is the real world. However well he knows Victorian London, he doesn't know this city."

"Neither do I," Charley said. "Not as well as I should, definitely not as well as you do. But he isn't wrong. I've felt it, too, exactly the way he described. I've never quite put it into words, but I know there's something there."

I felt a shiver down the back of my neck—although, that could also have been because it was a cool night, and Charley's house now had no door.

"You never said anything."

"I couldn't. I couldn't even think it. I almost said something to you this morning, but—I knew that whatever it was, it was tied up with everything I wasn't supposed to do or think about. I know you believe I don't try hard enough to be normal—"

"Oh, don't give me that. Nobody asks you to be normal. You make it sound like we hold you back—you had everything. You went to Oxford at thirteen, for God's sake."

"I didn't mean that!" Charley caught himself. Honestly, he doesn't have a temper to rein in. It's almost funny to see him try: like watching someone work very hard not to drown in a puddle. "All right then. I know you believe I don't try hard enough to be...I don't know, an ordinary, plausible sort of abnormal. Does that work? I promise, I do try. I just don't think this is something I can make go away by trying very hard not to think about. I'm sorry, I really am. But this is my problem."

And then, of course, there was no way I could back out. There never was. I had left him alone to deal with his own problems once before; I knew I couldn't face doing it again.

"God, you're a pain." I drew a deep breath, exhaled, and felt my world tremble around me. "All right. We'll have a look at this street—assuming there is a street. If this starts getting too dangerous, though..."

Charley nodded, too quickly. "Absolutely. I understand. Thank you."

"And I think we should tell Mum and Dad. They need to know about this." I tried not to sound as though I desperately wanted our parents to tell us what to do. Perhaps I really wanted them to tell Charley what to do. They'd always been better at getting him to stop than I was.

This was probably exactly what Charley was thinking. "Please don't—not yet. Perhaps after we find the street—if we find the street. They'll only tell us to stop."

"They'd be right."

"They'd be wrong. This is important."

"Important to who? To you?" I shook my head. It was an acquiescence, but an unwilling one. "Your friend Brian was right, you know. You do drive people insane."

"I know," he agreed.

The unnatural dark the Hound had brought with it had lifted from the sky outside. The real night would come soon. It had been a very long day.

Millie

The Street was quiet in the early evening. The wind from the world outside had chased her home, but here the air was still and crisp with the promise of frost. The sky above was steel blue; the gas flames burning in the lampposts barely showed against the lingering light. Millie Radcliffe-Dix drank it in with pleasure, and with satisfaction. So often, when she returned from her day job, crises rushed to greet her—she rather braced herself to meet them, if truth be told. Sometimes she even enjoyed them. This time, the line of crooked houses seemed already asleep.

One, however, would be only just waking up. She knocked on the door to the house nearest the wall: one of a row of near-identical doors that lined the quarter mile of cobbled road. When there was no answer, she opened the door, and stuck in her head.

"Dorian?" she called. It was always best to give warning, in his case.

"Up here," the languid voice called back. "Just in time. I was on my way out for the night."

"I bet you were," she said, possibly too low for him to hear, but then it wasn't really meant for him.

The room at the top of the stairs was more of an attic than a second-story bedroom: dark, dusty, low of ceiling, and creaky of floorboard. In the middle of it was a laptop on a desk, lit by flickering candles. The man at the laptop was beautiful enough to stop a heart at fifty paces. To all appearances, he was young, perhaps seventeen years of age. Seventeen, though, has an unfinished quality, and this man was a work of art. His hair was a wave of softest gold. His skin was polished ivory. His cheekbones were sharp enough to pose a flight risk. His eyes defied all metaphor. People who looked into them without fair warning tended only to report, incoherently, that they were blue.

Millie was aware of this effect, of course. She tried to contain it by encouraging him to stay away from the general public as much as possible, or at least to wear sunglasses. Fortunately, she had a daily reminder of what lay beneath it. It enabled them to stay on friendly terms, or at least for her to remember to watch her back.

"Dorian," she greeted him.

"Millie." Dorian leaned back in his chair, stretching his perfect limbs. "How very industrious you look this evening."

"Thank you very much."

"It wasn't a compliment."

"I know." She leaned against the desk next to him. "Anything to report? Before you disappear into the world?"

"You say that so disapprovingly," he said. "As though there were any better place to go during the night, and any worse place to go during the day. In fact, there was one of those very dull disturbances reported in the Prince Albert University English department last night. You know, campus security going up with little flashlights, finding things slightly rumpled and nobody in sight. You always like me to tell you those."

"I do," she said cheerfully. "And you have, and I like it. Nobody in sight at all? How about nothing?"

"Well," he conceded, "there did seem to be a medieval sword lying in an unlocked closet."

"Jolly good. Anything else?"

"Just this." He turned the laptop toward her. The light from the candle opposite, burnt almost to a stub, cast a reflection on the screen. "It came up in the police reports. Possible Fagin sighting?"

Millie tilted the screen away from the glare, and read the lines there briefly. She nodded in satisfaction. "Good show, Dorian."

"It's what I live for," he said. "Oh wait, it's not. But it's what *you* live for, and you have my soul in a wardrobe, so…"

"It warrants a couple of hours out of your misspent nights." She scrolled down the page a little, taking in the details. The police had apprehended a man attempting to pick a pocket down on Vivian Street in the small hours of the morning. The victim had chosen not to press charges, given that nothing was taken and the man appeared drunk. Innocent enough, but Dorian had noted a few Dickensian traits, such as the man's predilection for calling the arresting officer "my dear." Dorian had a good eye for such details. "Interesting. I'll have a look before I go to bed."

"Excellent. One should always have something sensational to read in bed. Does this business with campus security have anything to do with the rumors?"

Millie was startled out of her thoughts. "What rumors?"

"You know what rumors." She did too. "The change in the air. The ticking of the clock. The coming of the new world. All that."

"No," she said. "This has nothing whatsoever to do with all that. But I would very much like to know what does. I have no idea where all that nonsense is coming from, and nobody seems to be able to tell me."

"You don't believe there's truth to it then?"

"There's truth to everything," she said. "What I would appreciate are some facts. Why? What do you believe?"

Dorian shrugged. "I believe anything, provided it is quite incredible. One of the things I happen to believe is that truth is always independent of the facts."

"That's the spirit," she said. It was the only thing to say when Dorian started in that vein. She pushed the laptop toward him, careful not to knock over the inkwell. "E-mail this to me, will you? Before you pop off to your Tinder date or nightclub or other regularly scheduled corruption."

"The Street shifted again last night," he said. "Only a few inches. Most of you were asleep; I don't think anybody else noticed this time. Perhaps Heathcliff, if he was brooding at the window. But I felt it."

She had felt it too. Unusually for her, she had not been sleeping soundly the last few nights. "Well," she said, "I would very much appreciate some facts about that too."

VI

The next day, I showed Eric around. Frances and Carmen, too, but it was Eric who consumed my attention.

As I'd told Charley, he looked younger than the other Uriah Heep, and he had the crisp suit and haircut that any burgeoning lawyer might be expected to have. If I hadn't met Charley's version of the same character, I would never have seen anything odd about him. Since I had, I could see that his face was thin and waxy, and his thick-rimmed glasses did not entirely conceal lashless eyes the color of blood. Under his suit, I could see how thin and elongated his limbs were. And I could see the same crawling, wheedling manner that in the other Uriah had alternated with flashes of murderous fury. The other interns recoiled from him instinctively when he came close.

I approached Eva about him when I was supposed to be going to my lunch, and caught her on the way to her own. It was when she was least inclined to chat about random interns, but also least inclined to question my interest.

"He just seems a little odd, that's all. Where does he come from?"

"He comes from the School of Law, like the others," she said around the manila folder between her teeth. She was using both hands to fight her way into her coat. I helped yank it over her shoulders.

"I meant before that. Who are his family?"

"You sound like an Eton schoolmaster. 'Is he the right sort?'" She tucked the folder into her massive leather handbag, and turned to face me. "I have no idea, off the top of my head. I'll e-mail you his CV. Actually, I was going to do that anyway. He's asked if he could shadow you for the rest of the week—subject to your approval, of course. But it makes sense. His interests fit."

Of course they did. That would have been the entire point. If I hadn't recognized him, I would have had no reason to say no. The question was, should I say no now? It would sensible, and safer. I didn't know what he wanted, but it couldn't be good.

I thought of Uriah's glowing red eyes, and the cold press of the blade on my throat.

"Sure," I said. "No worries. I'll keep an eye on him."

At least I had the advantage of knowing who he was, when he didn't know I knew. If there really was something going on, I might not be so fortunate next time.

He was a good worker, I had to admit. If I hadn't known who he was, he would still make my skin crawl, but I probably would have formed a favorable opinion of his prospects. He stuck to my side like glue throughout three meetings that afternoon, listening intently all the while. Given a data collation task to do, he set to it with a vengeance, his head bent so his nose was almost touching the laptop in front of him. The tap of his keystrokes filled my quiet office. When I suggested he take a ten-minute break for coffee, he took it as might be expected.

"Oh, thank you, Mr. Sutherland. So kind of you. But really, that's not necessary. No, I'm fine as I am, thank you. I want to finish all this before I go home this evening."

"Where do you live, Eric?" I asked, just to hear what he'd say.

"Oh, here and there, Mr. Sutherland," he said whimsically. "I share a flat at the moment, with some like-minded people. Very like-minded. Almost like family. I hear you have a younger brother, Mr. Sutherland?"

A shudder went down my back. If I'd been hoping to throw him off guard with my inquiry about his homelife, he had beaten me at that game.

"Where did you hear that?" I asked as casually as I could.

"Oh, someone must have told me." His eyes glinted behind their spectacles. There was no way he could realize I knew who he was. I was sure I hadn't given myself away, and he certainly hadn't. And yet... "He works at the university, doesn't he? Up there on the hill?"

"He does."

"It must be nice," he said, "to have family so close. You must see a great deal of each other."

"Not if I can help it." I'm not sure quite how much I meant it. Sometimes I did mean things like that. This time, I just wanted to tell him, whether he understood or not, that he wasn't getting to Charley through me.

"Really, Mr. Sutherland?" was all he said. "I would, if I were you."

I stayed late, making sure Eric had left, and because Lydia had the car I had to walk down the road to Cuba Street. Still, I waited half an hour before I heard the distinctive buzz of Charley's yellow moped. A 49 cc engine probably can't be expected to sound very good, but it should be able to compete for audibility with a broken hair dryer.

"Sorry," Charley called as he wedged the death trap into a small parking space. I sometimes think he apologizes reflexively whenever he sees me. "I had a couple of students stay late to talk to me after the tutorial, and then Natasha needed to see me about the conference we're organizing for November."

"They have you organizing conferences? Have they seen the state of your fridge?"

"Luckily, the conference won't be held in my fridge," Charley replied. "And the committee doesn't need me to remember to buy milk—at least, if it does, I've forgotten."

I think he was joking about the last part.

Cuba Street is the bohemian end of Wellington, a cascade of cafés and comic book stores and secondhand record shops that smell of dust and incense. On a Friday after work, it was bustling with students and young professionals, and had the atmosphere of an evening street market. The bucket fountain, its gaudy primary colors bright in the fading sunlight, splashed water over the pavement, and the chatter of diners eating outside was interwoven with heavy metal blasting from a nearby pub and the sound of a busker's guitar. The sky was pale blue, and went on forever. Some of the eeriness of being alone in my office with Eric drained away. This just wasn't the kind of place where Dickensian villains crawled out of the woodwork. It looked too young to have bred them.

"We should go for lunch here some weekend," I heard myself say. God knows, I didn't consciously intend to take advice from Eric.

"You and I and Lydia, I mean. She keeps saying she wants to see more of you when you're fully conscious."

"Oh," Charley said. He looked surprised, but pleased. "Yes, of course. Whenever you want."

"Not this weekend, though," I added. "Because Lydia's visiting her sister tomorrow, and I'll probably have work to do."

"No," he said quickly. "No, of course not. I'll probably be working too. But sometime."

I wondered, not for the first time, why I always felt the need to punish my brother for being too willing to come when I called.

The Left Bank Arcade is just a collection of redbrick and wooden shops off Cuba Street: an overflowing bookstore, a wool shop, a jeweler, a couple of arty designer clothes shops, and one or two restaurants. Lydia thinks it's ramshackle and charming. I don't think about it very much at all. At this time of evening, the shops had just closed, and it was more or less deserted.

"What are you expecting to find?" I said as Charley stepped forward and looked around. "The Artful Dodger having dinner at the Mexican place?"

"I still think I saw some version of the Artful Dodger buying muffins around the corner," Charley reminded me. For someone who deals with metaphors for a living, he can be very literal. "And we did spend yesterday evening with the Hound of the Baskervilles. But no. Mr. Holmes said it was an impossible street."

"There are no streets here," I said. "It's just a square."

"He said past the bookshop."

"The bookshop's closed. It's all closed."

"Well, we're not trying to buy a book, Rob," Charley said patiently.

I hate it when my younger brother speaks to me as if I have the IQ of a cabbage. Even now, it freezes my brain completely. He knows this, of course. It's the closest he ever comes to picking a fight with me.

Charley wasn't capable of letting me feel condescended to for more than a minute. "I don't know what I'm looking for," he said, by way of apology. "Except that it must be here, somewhere."

"I thought you felt you were being pulled here."

"It's only a tug, not a map reference. And I've been resisting it for so long. It's hard to suddenly start to listen. What's that?"

I looked at where he was nodding. "That? What do you mean, what is it? It's the alley. Have you really never seen it before?"

"I've tried to avoid this place, remember? Even the bookshop. It felt dangerous. What is it?"

I had actually never thought about what the alley was. I had no idea if that was the name for it. It wasn't strictly an alley, but I'd never called it anything. It's just a short tunnel through two buildings. The question threw me, because I was so clearly expected to know more.

"It's just leftover space," I hazarded. "It connects the Left Bank Arcade with Victoria Street. People cut through it to get to Cuba Street, if they're coming from that direction. Sometimes homeless people sleep there."

This was a description, not a definition, but Charley didn't seem to notice. "Can we look at it?"

I laughed. "I can't imagine anyone would stop us."

Entering the alley is a plunge from shabby, sunny courtyard to urban grime. The roar and swish of cars from the road and the low thrum of a generator fill the space. Pipes snake overhead, and the walls on either side are awash with graffiti. It's not a very literary location. My only memories of it involve being very drunk in first year, so my brain couldn't help but supply vivid images of what exactly the sharp, sickly smell in the air might be.

From the interest on his face, Charley was seeing something different. "It's a liminal space," he said.

"What do you mean?"

"A threshold. A gap between two places or states of being. Like the time between night and day, or a secret passage between the walls of a house."

"I know what liminal means," I said, although I hadn't heard that application of it. "Why does that matter?"

"It probably doesn't. I just like liminal spaces. They're important in literature—in all branches of culture, really. But in story and folklore, they're where the impossible happen. The spaces between."

"Pasifika culture has a concept called the *va*," I said, despite myself. It was something we'd learned about in law school. "The space between two people, or cultures. Sort of an imaginary landscape, made up of the social, personal, and spiritual bonds that comprise the relationship."

"Really? I've never heard that before."

"That's because you're embarrassingly English. I wouldn't believe you grew up here sometimes, except I was there."

"Well, it's fascinating. So could you see conversation as navigating a liminal space?"

I shrugged, already wishing I hadn't spoken. "I suppose so. I think the only thing that happens in liminal spaces in modern cities is they collect rubbish."

The place was strewn with it, tied up in plastic supermarket bags. People seemed to be using the alley as their own personal dumping ground.

"And homeless people, you said," Charley reminded me. "Anthropologically speaking, 'rubbish' is just a word for material unwanted or out of place. Forgotten things that slip between the cracks. That's what we're looking for."

I had stopped listening. Something had caught my eye, between the gaps in the rubbish. I nudged one of the bags with my shoe.

"What are you looking at?" Charley asked.

"Nothing." He waited, and I shrugged. "There's an extension cord going through the wall here. There's something odd about it. I don't know what. I suppose there's no reason it shouldn't be here, except that I can't tell where it's going..."

Charley crouched down beside it. I had wanted to do that myself, but had been too embarrassed. People did pass through here, sometimes.

"Oh," he said after a moment. His breath caught. "Oh, I see it."

"What do you see?"

"There *is* something odd about this cable," he said. "It's going through the wall."

"Cables go through walls all the time."

"No, they don't. Cables go through holes in walls."

I felt a chill. Because he was right, by a pedantic twist of grammar. There was no hole in this wall. There wasn't even a kink in the plastic where the cable entered the wall. That was what looked so odd. The cable slipped through brick as though it wasn't there.

"It *is* there, though," I said as if someone had argued otherwise. I touched the wall above it, leaning over the rubbish bags, and felt it rough beneath my palm. I hit the surface hard, just to be sure, and my hand made a satisfying smack against the brick. "That's a wall."

Charley stood slowly. "I know." He reached out, and laid his hand against the wall.

His hand went through it.

He jerked it back immediately, at the same time as I made a convulsive movement forward. We stared at each other, and then at the wall. I tried to think of something to say.

"That was strange," Charley said, before I could.

"It was." I felt cold. "Is it—is that wall not real? Is it an illusion?"

"No," he said. "No, you were right before, it's a real wall. I felt it, while my hand was passing through. The layer of paint over top, and the brick underneath. It's just—it's also a real door."

"That doesn't make any sense."

"I know." He shook his hand, as you do to shake off pins and needles. "I think we've found it."

It wasn't a street, at least not yet. It didn't seem to have anything to do with literary characters, or books, or the Hound of the Baskervilles. But I didn't argue. It was certainly impossible.

Charley broke the silence. "I'm going through, if I can."

"You can't. I mean—physically, you probably can, for all I know. But it would be stupid."

"I know." He really did. His jaw was set the way it always used to when he was trying to be brave. "But I've tried to avoid being stupid for two years. I think it's better to do it now and get it over with. Do you want to try to come through as well?"

"How? You saw—it doesn't want me. It's just you."

Story of my life, I thought. I didn't mean it, but the metaphor was too neat not to think it.

"Well, my clothes are going through," Charley said. "Thank goodness. So it's not just me, it's things that are in contact with me. I think I could probably bring you through as well. If you hold on to me, and don't let go. You would really have to not let go, though."

"Oh, don't worry," I said. "I won't."

Which meant that I had already made the decision, didn't it? It would have been nice if my brain kept me informed.

"Give me your hand," I said. "Before I change my mind."

That made him smile, just a little. "Thank you."

"Don't thank me. I should be trying to talk you out of it."

"You'd succeed. But I'd come back later. I know I would."

He held out his hand, and I took it. A breeze blew through the passage, stinging grit against my face. In the distance, a busker was playing a guitar; someone was laughing. The world had never been more real. I remembered, for no reason at all, that I was supposed to pick up bread on the way home.

We went through the wall.

VII

I felt nothing. My vision went dark for a moment, as though I'd passed through a shadow; perhaps there was a tiny jolt, more emotional than physical. It seemed to take no time at all, and yet when my eyes cleared, it seemed as if a great deal of time had passed. The light was different: lower, quieter, more golden, more shadowed. The air was colder, and still. It even tasted different, pungent with smoke and fog.

We stood in a long, narrow, crooked street; a Victorian street, or older, paved with cobblestones and flanked by teetering buildings. The lower stories of the buildings were old storefronts—a sweet shop, a saddlery, an umbrella shop—but the upper floors looked residential, with windows open and wash hanging out. Lampposts lined the side of the road, their glow hard to make out against the twilight. The air was hazy with fog.

"Oh," Charley said.

I had to swallow a few times before I could speak. Fog and bewilderment caught in my throat. "This is completely..."

"It's *beautiful*." His face, when I looked at it, was soft with wonder. "Don't you think it's the most beautiful thing you've ever seen?"

"It's a very nice thing," I said. "What *is* it? Is... are we in England?"

I knew the answer before I spoke. England hadn't looked like this in at least a hundred years. I'm not certain England had ever, quite, looked like this. It was a little *too* much like an illustration of Victorian London, complete with a sepia tone and a misty, unfinished look to the buildings stretching into the distance.

"It's not England," Charley said, without taking his eyes from it. "I don't know where it is. I think I've seen it before, someplace, or something very like it. Perhaps in a book."

"But this isn't a book." I resisted the urge to grab him. He was right there. I only felt that he was drifting away. "This is real. We came through the *wall*. And there's a street back here. What looks like a street from a hundred and fifty years ago. This...you know this is not remotely normal, don't you?"

"No," he said, but distractedly. "No, I think—"

He stopped, and so did I. Doors were opening, and shutters on the windows above our heads.

"Charley..."

"I see them," he replied.

I saw them too. Figures were coming toward us out of the mist: a little old woman in a shawl, a little girl in a blue dress, a man in a red velvet cape with a sword at his side. A woman in a white leather jacket stalked toward us, at least seven feet tall, her stark white face and black hair both beautiful and terrible. Three men in breeches and cravats emerged from the same house as if in one movement, their classically handsome faces oddly identical. From the sidewalk, grinning and leering, was a young urchin that I knew, having seen the musical *Oliver!*, must be the Artful Dodger. And those were the ones who were remotely human. One man passed the nearby lamppost, and I recoiled as the light fell on a face that was no face, only a blank, featureless white globe, curved like an eggshell or thin porcelain.

Of these, one stepped forward.

From the first glance, I knew he wasn't real. He was a figment, the kind Charley pulled from books, larger than life and more vivid. His rugged, swarthy features had the air of something elemental, half-animal and exotic. Still, he might have passed for an unusually well-built man, if it hadn't been for his eyes. Under the bristling black brows, they burned—literally burned—with flickering black flame. Something like that is hard to ignore.

Charley frowned, then his face cleared. "Heathcliff," he said, with something like awe.

I recognized the name, though I'd never read *Wuthering Heights* and knew nothing about its antihero save that he was a bit of a lunatic. Through my unease, I felt a thrill. It was only the third time I knew we were certainly standing in the presence of someone else's reading.

"What can you mean by this?" the figment demanded. His extraordinary eyes flared. "Why have you come here?"

As usual when Charley is confronted, his assurance faltered. Some of the exultation died from his face. "I—we came through the wall."

"Of course you came through the wall! And for what purpose did you come through the wall? You have the look of no fictional characters I have ever read. Explain yourselves!"

I can't explain myself, I'm afraid, sir, because I'm not myself, you see. God knows where that quote came from, or why I had it in my head.

"We're not," Charley answered. He was growing nervous, which never boded well for his ability to explain anything. "Fictional. I mean—we just—"

The man took a step closer to him. "How dare you enter this place? Speak!"

"Hey!" Somehow, I found myself moving between them. Anger of my own had flared in my chest. "Back off."

The man's hand flashed into his coat pocket, and suddenly I was looking down the barrel of a pistol. Not just a pistol. On either side of the barrel were two long, spring-loaded blades. My heart jumped.

"Heathcliff!" one of the strangely identical men called from the door. His voice was deep and resonant, and could have come from the BBC; so, for all its anger, could Heathcliff's. "Have some decorum, man, for pity's sake."

"Pity!" the man snorted. "I have no pity! The more the worms writhe, the more I yearn to crush out their entrails! It is a moral teething; and I grind with greater energy, in proportion to the increase of pain."

This, by the way, was the book Charley read cover to cover three times one summer holiday at the beach, when he was eight. Sometimes, I'm amazed he turned out as well as he did.

I took advantage of Heathcliff's distraction, and grabbed at the barrel of the gun. I don't know what I was thinking. Perhaps I meant to wrench it from his hand, but if so I only knocked it sideways. The explosion of the gunshot was so loud it shook every nerve in my body. The spring of the knife blades rebounded; Heathcliff let out a snarl of pain as a line of blood streaked across the back of his hand. The pistol scuttered through the air and across the cobbles.

He looked at me then with real rage on his face. His teeth bared.

"Charley," I said without looking behind me. "Get out of here. Now."

"Not without you."

"Of course not. I'm coming with you. Just—"

And then Heathcliff reached for the lamppost next to him, tore it from the earth, and brought it down toward my head.

I should have been used to things like this. There are no rules to what a fictional character may or may not be able to do, given the right reading. But this was so unexpected, so completely insane, that I almost didn't duck out of the way. When I did, it was a split second too slow. I felt the edge of the iron catch my temple—glance it, really, but a glancing blow from an entire lamppost wielded by an enraged Victorian antihero is pretty significant. Pain exploded in my head; I stumbled, and hit the ground hard. My vision flickered, and red dots danced in my eyes.

"Stop!"

It was a female voice: clipped, English accented, and ringing with authority. "Heathcliff, you put that lamppost down this instant! You know how difficult those are to come by."

The man glowered, his eyes burning. Then, to my astonishment, he lowered the lamppost. I stayed tensed.

"These two came through the wall," he said. "They could offer no explanation. Their souls have no calling to this street of—"

"Oh, do shut up, there's a good chap." The owner of the voice stepped forward out of the fog.

From the sound, I'd expected someone old-fashioned, out of an Edwardian novel: her voice had same the precise, period-drama ring of the others. She was a perfectly ordinary woman, about my age, the sort of young professional you'd see on Lambton Quay any day of the week. She wore a well-cut gray suit with a long coat and scarf, her dark hair was twisted neatly at the back of her head, and her makeup was perfectly applied. (Trust me, you don't live with Lydia for four years and not know more about makeup than you want to.) The only odd thing about her was the way she strode across the cobbles to the giant named Heathcliff and folded her arms.

"You know I keep telling you not to attack anything that moves," she said. "This is why we don't let you out of the Street. It's like when you started throwing knives in the supermarket."

"It's not like the supermarket!" he protested. "They've intruded! They came through the wall and couldn't explain why they were here."

"Heathcliff does have a point"—one of the identical men spoke up—"alongside his collection of misanthropic Byronic neuroses. The newcomers might be dangerous."

"They're not," she said. "I know these fellows. They're quite harmless. Where's your knife-gun, Heathcliff?"

"It fell in the gutter," Heathcliff muttered.

"What a shame. Don't worry, I'm sure you'll find it again." She turned to us, and looked us up and down. The confidence on her face slipped when her eyes fell on Charley, only briefly, then she pulled it back about her like a coat on a cold day. Her lips curved very slightly. "You can get up now, Rob. Nobody's going to kill you."

"Yet," Heathcliff said, with dark menace.

I got to my feet awkwardly. My head was still spinning. "I don't understand. How do you know us?"

"He knows me too." She looked at Charley. "Don't you?"

"Yes…" Charley said. He was staring at the woman in growing wonder. "Yes, I do. But you can't—"

"You're Charles Sutherland," she said. "And I'm Millie Radcliffe-Dix."

VIII

I was there when Millie Radcliffe-Dix came out of her book, though until that moment I'd forgotten about it. It wasn't anything unusual, by Charley's standards.

We shared a room in those days: Charley hated being alone in the dark. Well, maybe alone wouldn't have been so bad, but we could never be quite sure that he was. When he was four, he came into my room three nights in a row because there was a monster in his wardrobe. Dad found it hiding on the fourth day. It was from *Frankenstein*, which he'd been strictly forbidden from reading before bed. I'm not sure why he couldn't just put it back: I asked him about it a couple of years ago, and he could only vaguely remember the whole thing.

"I think I didn't have a strong enough conceptualization of what it was," he said. "You have to understand where something fits before you can put it back. That, or I was just scared."

Our parents moved him into my room after that. I didn't mind, not then. I kicked up a fuss when I turned thirteen, by which time he was eight and old enough not to conjure his worst nightmares—or at least to put them away himself without too much bother.

At this point, I was ten and he had just turned six. We were doing our homework in our room in the evening, me at the desk, Charley stretched out on the floor. There was a brief flare of light, and I heard Charley say, "Oh!" rather quietly.

I turned and saw a little girl, maybe my age or a little older, wearing a short green dress with green-and-black-striped stockings and a sturdy pair of boots. Her brown hair hung in curls about her face, which was mischievous and freckled. There was a tawny-haired monkey sitting on her shoulder. She wasn't from around these parts.

"Charley!" I complained. "What the heck?"

"I'm sorry," Charley said, but he didn't sound entirely sorry. "I didn't mean it."

"I should jolly well hope you *did* mean it," the little girl said. She sounded older than her age, and very English. "I was about to be captured by a horde of smugglers."

"I know," Charley said. "That's where I was up to. And I think I did mean to pull you out. I sort of called out to you to look out in my head, and there you were."

"You were supposed to be doing your math assignment," I said to him, rather self-righteously, considering I had been drawing pictures of dinosaurs on my own homework sheet. (Charley, thank God, never went through the dinosaur phase I did. I mean, can you imagine?)

"I was going to," he said. "I just wanted to finish the chapter."

"You could at least have been reading something good." Again, this was a bit much coming from me, who at the time only read books about dinosaurs. "Not the umpteenth Millie Radcliffe-Dix Adventure."

"They *are* good," he protested.

"No, your brother's right," said the girl who was presumably Millie Radcliffe-Dix. "They're awful trash. They're formulaic, badly plotted, and entirely without literary merit."

"I don't care," Charley said complacently. "I like them. They're like the books I used to read, when I was younger."

"You're six," I informed him.

"You can be younger than six, Rob." He winced as the monkey jumped across to his shoulder and tweaked his hair. "Ow."

Millie whistled, and the monkey leaped back into her arms.

If you haven't read them, *The Adventures of Millie Radcliffe-Dix, Girl Detective* are stories of an intrepid orphan, adopted by a wealthy family, who with her pet monkey Vernon battles pirates, smugglers, kidnappers, and thieves every summer. They were published by an obscure writer in the 1930s and '40s; I have no idea why we had the full set on our shelves, but Charley was going through a phase of devouring them with the avidity he otherwise reserved for Dickens, Austen, and literary theory. I suppose I can't blame him, given what he was being tutored in at the time. *War and Peace* has got to be a little dull for a six-year-old, whatever his IQ.

"Well, put her back," I warned. "Mum and Dad will go mad."

"Do I have to?" he pleaded.

"Yeah, you have to. Don't give me that look. It's not my rule."

"I don't want to go back," Millie interrupted. She sat back on Charley's bed, her curls bouncing around her face. "I was about to be taken by smugglers."

"It always works out by the end of the book," Charley promised her.

"I know," she said, rolling her eyes. "And then it starts all over again, summer after summer, with me never changing or getting a day older than eleven. Thanks awfully, but no. I think I'd rather stay here, and grow up and be an accountant or something."

"You've made a crazy person," I said to Charley.

He gave me a look that for him bordered on the irritated. "You can't do that," he explained to the girl. "It doesn't happen. There isn't an older version of you. I've read the last book. You just go back home and get commended by the police and have cake and ginger beer, same as always. Even if you did stay here, you wouldn't grow up."

"Watch me," she said.

Vernon the monkey broke the stalemate then. He'd been sitting on Millie's shoulder, his little beady eyes glancing around the room with interest; suddenly, without warning, he leaped through the air and onto the bookshelf. I made a grab for him, but my hand closed on empty air. All that happened was that my chair flew from under me as I got to my feet. He clambered up the shelves, then down onto the desk; fortunately, Charley had scrambled up off the floor and lunged to shut the half-open door before the monkey could get to it. Every once in a while, my brother was good in a crisis.

"Catch it, quick!" I hissed at him. "And put it back! I don't care how horrible it is!"

He made an obedient attempt to snatch Vernon from the desk, and barely caught his tail. Vernon screeched, I saw a flash of teeth, and Charley jerked his hand back with a cry.

"Ow!"

I caught the monkey around the middle then, as if it were our old tabby cat. It hissed, and writhed, but I held on tight.

"Quickly!" I ordered. Charley, after a second's hesitation as he looked at the flailing limbs and bared teeth, reached out and laid his hand gently on the monkey's back. I saw the brief, intense look of concentration flit across his face, and then I was holding nothing at all. All at once, the room seemed very quiet.

I breathed a sigh of relief, and turned around. That was when I saw that Millie was gone too.

"Hey," I said. "Where is she? Did you put her back?"

"I don't know," Charley said vaguely. As usual after he'd sent something back, he looked rather white; this time, he was shaking his hand and looking at it critically. "Vernon bit me."

"Charley…"

"She might have gone back with Vernon," he said. "I don't know. They came out together; maybe they function as a metaphorical duality. My finger's bleeding."

She wasn't there anyway, so there was nothing else I could do but give it up. I sneaked Charley into the bathroom and put antiseptic on the bite on his hand, like Mum did with cuts and scratches, though looking back I suppose Vernon couldn't have had any diseases that weren't written into the book. Then we went back and did our homework. I did wonder, when it started getting cold and I went to close the big window, but by then it was too late. I never saw Millie Radcliffe-Dix again after that, except on cover after cover of the books Charley left lying all over the house. I assumed she was back in those books, and Charley never summoned her again.

IX

It was an ordinary flat. Completely ordinary, exaggeratedly ordinary. It was neither overly large, nor the tiny shoebox that had been my first central Wellington flat. It was painted off-white, with a clock and a generic Monet print gracing the walls. It had a couch, and a dining table, and a little bench covered in photographs. It had a fireplace. For a flat overlooking a Dickensian nightmare street, it was trying far too hard.

Millie sat down next to me on the couch, holding a cloth in one hand and a tube of antiseptic cream in the other. She was one of those people who make the couch bounce when they sit.

"Here," she said, handing me the cloth. "There's no electricity here, so no ice pack. But I've got it nice and cold for you from the well in the pub courtyard. I'll just put this ointment on the cut, then you can hold that to it for a while, and you'll feel good as new. Well, that's a lie, but you might not be too unsightly tomorrow. Don't worry, I'm rather good at first aid."

I felt the coolness of her hands as she dabbed cream over my eyebrow, and then the sting.

I had read Millie Radcliffe-Dix's adventures, though not for a long time. "Millie was an adventurous little girl," the narration would begin. "She had a tall, lanky body, and her corkscrew curls tumbled about her shoulders when she played with her monkey, Vernon. If Millie liked you, she was a kind and loyal friend. But if you were cruel or cowardly, then watch out! For Millie had a fierce temper, and she could not stand to see a wrong done."

The adventurous little girl now had to be thirty or so, if my memory served me. I could see traces of her still in the determined chin, the arched eyebrows, the direct gaze of her chocolate-brown eyes. But she was no longer tall or lanky. If anything, she was tending toward short, and comfortably plump. There was no sign of a pet monkey, and any curls were pinned tightly under control. The woman I was seeing was a force of nature: a hurricane that pats you on the back sympathetically as it blows you over. She wasn't real—I'd seen her come out of a book, or Charley's head, or both. And yet somehow, impossibly, she'd grown up.

"Awfully sorry about Heathcliff," Millie said. "He's not really a very stable manifestation. We think he's a postcolonial reading—or perhaps he just misses the fictional moors. Either way, he's certainly very angry all the time. And they're all on edge at the moment, with everything that's been going on."

"That's all right," I said lamely. The rush of adrenaline from facing Heathcliff was starting to hit me. I was shaking, and hoped the other two hadn't noticed. Her words caught up to me a moment later. "What's been going on?"

"Where did this place come from?" Charley asked from the window seat. He was barely able to tear his eyes from the scene outside. I couldn't see anything from where I sat, but I could hear the sound of footsteps over the cobbles, and the murmur of voices rising from below. "Who made it? And who's that helping Heathcliff pick up the lamppost?"

"The White Witch," Millie said, and I thought of the alarmingly tall woman in white leather. "She's good with lampposts. I don't know if anyone made the Street; none of us do. I wondered if you'd made it."

"No," he said. "I wish I had. None of this comes from me—only you, I suppose, but that was a long time ago."

Millie shrugged. "Well, it's jolly useful, and it's ours now. What on earth are you two doing here?"

Charley started to answer, but I interrupted.

"Look, I'm sorry, but you can't be Millie Radcliffe-Dix. You can't be. She was a little girl—I saw her. And these things—the things my brother makes—don't grow like human beings. Do they?" I turned to Charley for confirmation, but he only shrugged helplessly.

"I—I don't think so. I never kept one out of their books for long enough to see…"

"I say, let's go easy on the term 'things,' shall we?" Millie said it mildly, but I felt the sting. "The others don't age, or none of them have so far, and we have some who are centuries old. But I do. I can't explain that either. Perhaps I just wanted to. I mean to say—who wants an endless summer of adventures trapped in perpetual preadolescence?"

"Who doesn't?" I replied, though I didn't really mean it. Eleven was hard enough the first time through.

"So you *did* run away when I was distracted with Vernon," Charley said. "I always thought something wasn't right. When I put him back, something was missing. And—I think I've been feeling you in my head, all these years. I was too young to recognize the feeling, and after a while I got used to it. It was you, wasn't it?"

"Vernon distracted you to let me get away." Something like pain crossed her face. "He knew that I wasn't going to be able to grow with him still there. So he distracted you, and I got out the window and ran."

"I'm sorry," Charley said. He did look genuinely stricken. A metaphorical duality, Charley had said of Millie and Vernon back then. I think he'd made that term up—he was six—but I knew what he meant. "I could bring him out for you again, if you want. I still have your books."

Millie hesitated. "I'll have to think about it," she said. "It's decent of you, but…I'm an accountant now. I don't think an accountant with a monkey fits."

"You're an accountant?" I said. Now that I looked at her, the smart hairstyle and suit definitely said city worker, but under the circumstances I hadn't thought the implications of that through. "Seriously?"

Her head whipped around to face me. "Yes, I'm an accountant! What's so surprising about that?"

"Well," I said unwisely, "you live in a street that shouldn't exist, and talk down men wielding lampposts."

"You also say things like 'I say' and 'jolly good' quite a lot, for an accountant," Charley added. "Sorry, but you do."

"So what if I do?" Millie said. "I must say, you're jolly lucky I do talk down men wielding lampposts, considering."

"I know," I said. "I just meant—it's not exactly normal accounting behavior."

"I *am* normal! I have a very good job downtown. I make a good living. I buy groceries and go on dates with nice men at the office and get my hair done. I am normal. I'm boring!"

"Okay!" I raised my hands in surrender, and realized belatedly that the cloth she'd given me had soaked through the knee of my trousers. "I'm sorry. You're clearly normal."

"But you *do* live here?" Charley asked. He seemed unfazed by Millie's irritation. Perhaps she bites off people's heads in the books all the time. (Metaphorically. I *really* hoped that had stayed metaphorical.) "I mean—full-time?"

"I didn't for a very long time." Her flare of temper had cooled already. "It didn't exist. The night I left your house, I started walking to the nearest city, and didn't look back. I knew I couldn't risk you all finding me in your tiny hometown, and besides, I'd never seen a real city. Can you imagine? All those adventures in farms and seasides and sweet little English country hamlets. Never cities. Doesn't Jacqueline Blaine think that adventures happen in cities as well?"

"I loved those stories," Charley said, a little sadly.

"A lot of people do," Millie conceded. "I met a girl at one of my foster homes who just read the same one over and over again. It was like a talisman. That's something to be rather proud of, I suppose. We can't all be *Finnegan's Wake*."

"Oh, don't give him ideas," I said, before I could stop myself. I have no clue what that thing was that came out of Charley's reading of James Joyce, but I knew I didn't want to meet it again.

Charley wasn't thinking about Joyce this time. "Foster homes?"

"Well, it turns out that's what happens to real children who wander about the country on their own having adventures," Millie said. "And I was jolly lucky it was nothing worse. It wasn't at all like in my books, when Vernon and I would just go off on our own and camp out for days on end over the summer holidays. The police picked me up on the streets after a concerned citizen called it in. Nobody could find who I was supposed to belong to, so I was placed in care. I grew up moved around from home to home. I went to school, I won a scholarship to university, I studied accounting. Money isn't really an issue in Blaine books. I wanted to understand it. That, and have an ordinary life with a house and a mortgage, of course. Because I am in fact ordinary."

"No offense, but I doubt you have a mortgage on this street," I pointed out. "I don't think the bank would recognize the address."

I was a little worried she'd snap at me again, but she didn't. She didn't say anything at all for a while.

"We don't know where this street came from," she said, at last. "Two years ago, we just suddenly felt it. Those of us pulled from books, all over the world—and I thought myself the only one of those at the time. I was working for an accounting firm in the South Island. I tried to ignore it, but I could feel it pulling me. I booked a flight over a weekend. It was one of those Wellington days when the rain and the wind pelt you so hard it's difficult to tell which is which."

"Oh," I said reflexively. "You mean March to September."

"I turned the corner, and here I was. A few of us were already here—one of the Darcys, and the Artful, and Miss Matty from *Cranford*. Poor thing, she'd been in the real world over a hundred years, most of them homeless since tea shops started needing paperwork and business acumen and things. More came later. I resigned my job, and found another here. I've been here ever since."

"Are you in charge?"

"Why would you say that?" Her voice had a slight warning tone.

"Well, they all stopped trying to kill us when you arrived," I said. "I'd put you in charge. You talk down men with lampposts. And knife-guns."

"Look, will you dry up about that? Honestly. I'm not in charge here. I was just coming home from work when I saw you two idiots about to get beaten to a pulp by a Brontë hero. I knew you at once, of course," she added, glancing at Charley. "You haven't changed that much."

"Are there more summoners then?" Charley asked. "Is that what you call them? There must be more; all these people have to come from somewhere…"

"Not in the way you think," Millie said. "Actually, apart from me, all these people are one-offs. From what we've been able to gather, every once in a while, completely ordinary people seem to just read us into existence. They always have, it seems, since stories began—we have a Lancelot out there from the fifteenth century, though he's a rarity. Perhaps everyone has mild versions of your abilities, perhaps it's just what happens when the stars align and somebody has a pure, perfect moment of connection with a story. It's a once-in-a-lifetime thing, if that. The reader never realizes they've done it; the character never appears right in the room, as I did with you. They take longer to struggle through into the world. But you—you can bring people out whenever you want—sometimes even when you don't want. That's right, isn't it? It's from your head when you were six."

He nodded. "That's right."

"That must be why you could come through the wall, of course. It's usually only fictional characters who can get through. Everyone else just hits brick."

"That's what happened with Rob, until I pulled him through."

I interrupted then. Things were getting out of hand. "So this is where it's all coming from then? The new world the first Uriah Heep warned us about? The Artful Dodger, or whoever it was, on Cuba Street? And the fire-breathing Hound of the Baskervilles last night, that was meant to kill us? It's all part of this street you're not running too?"

Millie looked at me with a frown. "What *are* you talking about? The Artful, yes. He lives two doors down, above the Old Curiosity Shop. He goes out for food quite often—I expect you did see him on Cuba Street. But we certainly don't have a Hound of the Baskervilles, fire breathing or otherwise. Are you saying someone sent one after you?"

"Well, it showed up on my doorstep last night," Charley said. "I suppose someone must have sent it."

"It didn't come from here," Millie said positively. "And I don't know anything about Uriah Heep. Did you say more than one of them?"

"I summoned one," Charley said. "He warned us that a new world was coming. And then another Uriah Heep showed up at Rob's work."

"He didn't come from here either." She stood. The couch bounced again. "But I think we may both be looking for the same person. And I think we need to talk to Dorian Gray."

I had no chance to ask. Because at that moment, the Street moved.

X

Wellington is on a fault line. I've been here through two or three major earthquakes, and I'm used to the idea that the ground is a living thing that will arch and flex on a whim. I had never felt anything like this. The ground did indeed flex, but so did the walls, the ceiling, the sky outside. Reality rippled about us. I clutched the arm of the couch on instinct, and it warped between my fingers like modeling clay.

As quickly as it had started, the world settled back, grumbling and creaking as it did so. I sat there, shocked.

"It's all right." Millie jumped to her feet. "It often happens about this time."

"What does?" I demanded. "What was that?"

"That shouldn't be able to happen at any time." Charley sounded as bewildered as I felt. "It was as though someone..."

"Don't say that too loudly, whatever you do," Millie interrupted. She was already pulling on a lace-up boot from beside the door, one hand on the wall for balance. "Blast. Hurry up. It will be bedlam out there."

"Where are we going?" I asked. I found myself standing without waiting for an answer. Millie had that effect.

"Where I said we were going," she said. "That hasn't changed. But I need to reassure the others first. They'll be all out of sorts."

"Reassure them of what?"

"Oh, you know," she said. "Everything's perfectly all right, that sort of thing."

"And is it?" Charley asked.

"Of course not," she snorted. "If it were, they wouldn't need me to tell them."

* * *

It was a motley gathering, as you'd expect. I recognized Heathcliff; his knife-gun was back in his belt. The Artful Dodger was hanging on the fringes, grinning that irritating grin. All of them were clustered at the far end of the Street, a short distance from where the end of their reality was marked by another solid redbrick wall.

"All right, everyone?" Millie called as we approached. "What was the damage that time?"

"There's a new house," the Artful said. "Right there, by the far wall. Nice digs, actually, from what I can see. Not that you'll catch me going in."

"It's happening more often now, isn't it?" a man said. I could have sworn it was the Duke of Wellington. "That's three times in the last week."

"Nobody was hurt, though?" Millie checked. "We only grew; nothing disappeared?"

An elderly woman in a gray dress and bonnet spoke up hesitantly. "The wallpaper changed in my parlor."

"What a frightful nuisance, Miss Matty," Millie said sympathetically, though I saw a flash of real worry across her face. "When you've just bought new cushions. Still, not the end of the world. Anyone else?"

A new voice, male this time. "Miss Radcliffe-Dix!"

Edging their way to the front of the group were three gentlemen who seemed to move as one, clothed in an assortment of breeches and cravats. They were the ones I'd seen looking from the door; one of them had called out when Heathcliff pulled the pistol. Their faces were more different than I'd thought, but all looked proud, disdainful, and distractingly handsome.

"These are the Mr. Darcys," Millie said to us. "Or three of them. Darcys, Charley and Rob Sutherland. Charley, Rob, these are Darcys One, Two, and Four. Five is probably at the pool, and Three is probably at the library. They share Number 6, two doors down."

"Why are there five of them?" I asked.

"Oh, trust me," Millie said drily. "They turn up on a fairly regular basis. If there was ever a character designed for a reader to have a moment of perfect connection, it's Mr. Darcy. Darcy One comes from the turn of the eighteenth century, but most of them are just from the last few decades. There was a spate of them in the late nineties, apparently... Everything's quite under control, One," she added. "I'm taking them to visit Dorian. I say, everyone, be good sports and go back to your lives, will you? The crisis is over. These chaps are perfectly harmless."

Millie's language, I'd noticed, grew even more archaic when she was talking to fictional characters.

"But how came they to be here?" Darcy One asked. "So close to this new shift? I must insist upon being told. I have not the talent which some people possess of surrendering a situation to the management of others."

"They have nothing to do with the shift," Millie said firmly. "From the sounds of things, they saw the Artful shopping. If you want to be bad-tempered at someone, be bad-tempered at him."

The Darcys found this suggestion perfectly acceptable. They all turned away from us and toward the Artful Dodger.

"Oh, give over," the Artful sighed, apparently unconcerned. "You don't like it, you pick up your own morning paper tomorrow, all right? I'll be more careful next time."

"Next time means nothing to me," Darcy One said warningly. "My good opinion once lost is lost forever."

Millie tactfully maneuvered us past the crowd, back the way Charley and I had come, toward the wall that had brought us here. It was unnerving to see it from this side, solid and impenetrable as it had looked from the alley in the Left Bank Arcade. There was no trace of anything resembling my own city, or even my own country. The sky above my head was dark blue, and the stars coming out were unfamiliar.

"They'll calm down now," she said to us, with a nod back at the crowd. "Sorry about that. The Darcys are excellent sorts, really. They just like to explain their own character rather a lot."

"Oh God, is that ever true," Charley sighed, with feeling.

"Sorry about the lie too—or the sort-of-lie, since you did see the Artful, after all. I just don't want them to know too much about what you are."

"I don't understand," I said. "What just happened? Where are we going?"

I hoped we were going back home. I strongly suspected we weren't.

"I told you," Millie said. "I'm taking you to Dorian Gray."

"Dorian—as in *The Picture of Dorian Gray*? The one whose portrait ages instead of him?"

"It doesn't just age," Charley said, without much attention. He was too busy looking about him. "It's his soul. As he grows morally corrupt, the marks of it show on the painting, but not on his face. He looks eternally young and innocent, while his portrait becomes more and more hideous. It's ostensibly a morality tale."

"It's jolly useful," Millie said. "The condition for his being here is that I get to look at his portrait. If he's doing anything wrong behind my back, I can spot his guilt on the painting in an instant. I know we get all sorts in this neighborhood, but we try to make our villains and antiheroes behave. Or I do, at least."

I didn't dare point out that that sounded a lot like being in charge, to me.

"And what just happened?" I asked instead. "The Street growing, or changing? What was that about?"

"In a minute. Wait for Dorian."

We had stopped at the crooked house nearest the wall, and Millie was in the act of knocking, when she stopped suddenly. She turned to us, and lowered her voice. "Listen—what I told you just now goes twice for Dorian Gray. Do *not* let him know what you are, Charley, or what you can do. It could be very dangerous."

"What could he do?" I asked.

She snorted. "He's Dorian Gray. Whatever he wants. But, most dangerously, he could be afraid."

Charley nodded, as if that made perfect sense to him. "Don't worry. I'm used to hiding things."

"I thought you might be," she said.

If the Darcys were all handsome, Dorian Gray was beautiful enough to be downright creepy. His perfect features looked carved of marble; his hair was spun gold; his eyes, when they fell on us, were so wide and blue that I felt something in me falling into them. I looked away quickly, inexplicably shaken.

"Oh, yes," Charley said to me quietly, as an afterthought. "Watch he doesn't absorb your whole nature and your whole soul and your very art itself."

"What on earth does that mean?" I muttered.

"I don't really know," Charley said, almost cheerfully. "But it might have meant something to whoever dreamed him up. Maybe just don't look him in the eyes?"

"Now you tell me," I said.

The room we'd entered was dark and cobwebbed, at the top of a twisted staircase as Victorian as an illustration in an old book. Given that, I should have been most surprised by the presence of a laptop, its screen surrounded by flickering candles. But I had seen laptops before. I trusted laptops. I didn't trust living, breathing personifications of Victorian morality tales.

When I risked a second look, Dorian Gray was stretching in his computer chair. He let the stretch carry him to his feet, with the grace of a young lion. I didn't like him.

"Another shift," he observed to Millie, by way of greeting. I don't need to explain how perfectly musical his voice was, do I? "Quite a big one."

"Still no real damage," Millie said. "If anything, the opposite: we've grown. And nobody really liked Miss Matty's wallpaper. Dorian, this is Charley, and this is Rob."

"The two that caused such a commotion outside," he said. "I know. I was watching from the window."

"They're rather interested in your operation here."

"Are they?" Dorian yawned behind his hand. "Personally, I find it extremely tedious. Anything useful always is."

"And what makes your operation so useful?" I asked. I was determined not to be intimidated. I *was* intimidated, of course, by this whole situation, but that was what determination was for. "What are you doing? And why is there a computer?"

It was an old Mac laptop, the glow of its screen completely incongruous in the dark-wallpapered study. The only other light came from the fire in the grate, and the candles burning on the table.

"To his reader, Dorian Gray was an Internet predator," Millie said. "A spider in a web, master of deception and blackmail, presenting a young, attractive front to the world yet really a gross, decrepit old sinner. I think it's a bit of a stretch, personally, but it was the early 2000s. Paranoia about the World Wide Web was high. And it comes in useful for us, because it's given him unparalleled computer skills. I should mention that this is the one working Internet connection in the Street. For obvious reasons, we don't get Wi-Fi here. Or cell phone coverage."

"Or electricity," Dorian said. "Those cables passing through the wall originate at the nearby knitwear shop. Please try not to disturb them. If I need to reset them from the shop, I usually need to purchase some kind of hideous jumper to justify my presence there, and that is something for which you do not wish to be responsible."

"You don't have to wear it," Millie pointed out.

"The owners will picture me wearing it," Dorian said with a shiver. "Even to be clothed so in their imaginations is a kind of taint."

"We saw that cable," Charley said. "It was part of what led us here."

"Dorian's job, first and foremost, is to keep us safe," Millie said. "It's a difficult world to hide in these days. He keeps us away from government databases, or keeps our records ordinary in government databases, depending on the case. He tucks us away from prying eyes. He also monitors the Internet for any signs of other characters making their way toward us. When people pop into being, sometimes with odd previously metaphorical quirks, they tend to show up in police databases or on news networks. Not always, but often. We try to get in touch with them, perhaps help them get to the Street if they want to come. We've flown them in from all over the world."

"I came from the States," Dorian volunteered languidly. "But I managed my own plane ticket, of course. It's easy when you're as beautiful as me. One simply has to—"

"We're not really interested in your sordid adventures, Dorian," Millie said. "I just want you to show them the pattern."

The pattern was a spreadsheet on the computer. We clustered around it as Dorian sat down and brought up a file. I had to move twice; apparently I was crowding the great master of Microsoft Excel, and then my shadow was.

"I have a map as well," Dorian said. "But this gives you the highlights." He hit a few keys, and a series of graphs overlaid the screen. "This is the concentration of fictional characters living in Wellington in any given month—the green are confirmed, the purple suspected. As you can see, it's peaked somewhat."

It had. To me, any number of fictional characters in Wellington was a surprise, but the numbers did seem alarming.

"Most of these are the Street's inhabitants," Dorian said. "Or a few we know of who choose to live outside our borders, but are still in the area. Right now, this city has about double the known fictional population of the rest of the world combined. That's all very natural."

"There are characters living outside the Street?" I interrupted. "You mean, in central Wellington?"

"There are characters everywhere, Mr. Sutherland," Dorian said with exaggerated patience. "London. Paris. Dublin. Alaska. Copenhagen. Small towns in Italy that nobody's ever heard of. They don't all choose to live in the Street, even if they can reach it. In Wellington, I'll concede, they now tend to congregate here, but there are still many who are capable of blending into the outside world and desire a little more independence."

"Dr. Frankenstein works in the mortuary at Wellington Hospital," Millie offered. "I don't think we'd allow a lot of what he gets up to."

I didn't ask.

"The strange thing are these outliers," Dorian continued. He waved a hand at the screen. "The ones we can't track. And what's strange about them is, I've tracked most of them through police databases, and that alone. And when I say police databases, they seem to be committing real crimes. Constructs tend to be flagged for loitering or homelessness or at most petty theft. Not bank robbery—which I saw last month. You would have seen it, too, on the news. Perpetrators disappeared into thin air."

"I work in criminal defense," I said. "We would have noticed something like that. I'm fairly sure I've never defended a fictional character." But it *had* been very busy, the last year or so, hadn't it? I knew more than one police officer who'd remarked on the crime wave.

"Could Wellington be some kind of—I don't know, natural fault line for pulling things out of books?" I asked. I think I was remembering our earthquake safety talks at work. "The Street must have popped up here for some reason, after all."

"That might not have been an entirely stupid idea," Dorian said, "if it weren't for one little detail."

"They're fluctuating," Charley said. He was still looking at the screen. "The numbers are rising and falling from month to month. I'm terrible at statistics, but if Wellington were just more prone to manifestations, the numbers would be increasing steadily, wouldn't they? Unless people are moving around—"

"They aren't," Dorian said. "They're disappearing. Or some of them are. One day, I'm able to track their movements; the next, they'll seem to disappear off the face of the earth. In some cases, they never rematerialize. In others, though, they suddenly appear again, with no word or explanation, obvious and vivid as before. Now, where do they go in the intervening weeks?"

I remembered the bank robbery too. The perpetrators, as Dorian had said, disappeared into thin air.

"Somebody's taking them out of their books and putting them back in," Charley said.

"Exactly," Dorian said. He turned to look at us. Once again, I felt that peculiar wash of vertigo as his blue eyes caught mine, and looked away quickly. "Shortly after I noticed this pattern, the Street began to shift."

"As it just did then," Charley said.

"Exactly. Small tremors at first—rather like being on a fault line, in fact. Usually in the evening or the middle of the night. Small things began to change: the shape of a window, the color of a wall. Then we had a big one, at midnight, roughly two months ago. The Street heaved like a fish on the end of a line. It was most inconvenient for those with small ornaments or nervous dispositions. When the movement settled, the Street had grown."

Charley frowned. "Grown?"

"The Street ran for about a quarter mile, before," Millie said. "It stretches down that way until it hits another wall, this one impenetrable. The boundary moved farther away. We gained another hundred yards after that shift: some new houses and shops, and more road. I've been to have a look at the buildings, and they're perfectly habitable. Nobody will go near them, of course. Since then, the shifts have been getting more frequent, and each time the Street's grown or changed around us. It scares the living daylights out of everybody. Present company excepted, I'm sure."

"I don't really do living or daylight," Dorian said. "I'm a Gothic masterpiece."

"You think the Street's being shifted by this mysterious person, don't you?" Charley asked. "The same person who reads these people in and out. You think he's trying to read the Street away."

"Do you?" Millie asked.

Charley hesitated, then shook his head. "I don't know. Perhaps. This summoner, or whatever he is, must be involved somehow, or it's too great a coincidence. But the Street grows; it doesn't shrink, or give any indication it's about to disappear. I just wonder if he's trying to do something else entirely."

Millie nodded thoughtfully. "Well, whatever it is, he's dangerous. Anyone that can change the Street can change us as well—we're just as fictional. And everyone out there knows it."

"Now," Dorian said abruptly. "I've told you who we're looking for. Who are you?"

"Does it matter?" I asked, instantly on guard.

Dorian shrugged "What doesn't matter is whether or not you tell me. Millie gave me your first names, I can guess your approximate ages by looking at you, and I assume you're from around these parts. With that, I can find out who you are, and from that I can probably gauge your purpose in coming here. I do know you're not literary characters. I would have seen you online first. I'm a practiced black-mailer, sir. It's usually easier just to tell me what I wish to know."

"Easier for whom?"

"Well, for me, primarily. But it will be difficult for you either way, so it may as well be easy for somebody."

"I'm Charles Sutherland," Charley said. He doesn't believe in non-academic arguments. "And someone tried to kill me with the Hound of the Baskervilles last night."

I don't think Dorian Gray is the sort to look surprised, but one perfect eyebrow raised. "Of course," he said. "Dr. Charles Sutherland of the Prince Albert University English department. I should have recognized your photo."

Charley *is* the sort to look surprised, when the occasion calls for it, and it did. "You know me?"

"I know all the staff of the English department, and a few other relevant people. Millie has had me watching that building for two years, but never saw fit to tell me on whom my attentions were focused.

Something was going on, clearly. Disturbances at night. Figures seen at windows who disappear when the tireless security forces tromp up the stairs to investigate. That sword, a week ago—that was interesting."

"Charley!" I turned to him. "You said you'd clean that up."

"Security got there first," he said. "It was nothing—they weren't to know it was Excalibur. They just put it down to students playing pranks. I think it's still in the storage closet. Have you been *watching* me?" he added, looking at Millie.

"Afraid so, old thing," she said, wincing. "Or at least, I've had Dorian do so. Just to see if there were any disturbances. Do you mind?"

"I—no," he said uncertainly. "No, I suppose not. As long as you haven't been watching my house."

"If we had," Dorian said, "we would have seen the Hound of the Baskervilles. What did it look like?"

"Absolute evil," Charley said.

"Glorious. We should all strive to be the absolute version of something."

I looked out the crooked window at the Street below. I could see the far wall Millie had spoken of in the distance, and the buildings in front of it quiet and abandoned. I imagined them rising from the ground like a fish from the sea.

"So Uriah Heep was right," I said. I forgot, for a moment, that Dorian Gray should probably not hear about Uriah Heep. "Something is coming."

"It looks like it," Charley agreed.

"Are you referring to the new world?" Dorian asked. For the first time, he sounded genuinely curious instead of mockingly so.

"You've heard about a new world too?" Charley asked.

"There have been rumors drifting around for a year or so now," Dorian said. "They're not terribly specific, or easy to trace. They simply say that a new world is about to come. A world for us, and those like us. Some characters—Heathcliff, for one—claim to simply *know*, which is admirable in its lack of specificity but not terribly useful."

"Heathcliff isn't much on specificity," Millie said. "If he wants a boiled egg, he'll hint darkly at the metaphorical properties of chickens, and rage at the body's need for sustenance despite the ravages of the soul."

"Darcy Three heard the rumor from a character he'd never seen before, who he thought was Scrooge," Dorian reminded her. "But he, mysteriously, couldn't be found and has never been seen since. And so forth. Perhaps it's best not to meddle. A new world may be no bad thing."

"We have enough trouble to be getting on with in the old one, as far as I'm concerned," Mille said. "And I don't like the Street growing or characters fluttering in and out of reality without a good solid explanation."

"You don't like anything without a good solid explanation," Dorian said. He might almost have said it fondly.

"No, I don't. Especially not whispers of something coming that we don't understand, and as far as I can see aren't meant to."

Charley and I looked at each other. I didn't mention Uriah Heep this time, but I knew we were both thinking of him.

Millie was, too, it seemed. When we were out of the house, before we went back through the crack in the wall that would return us to reality, she touched Charley's shoulder lightly and lowered her voice. I leaned in to listen as well, even though I wasn't sure I was invited.

"Listen," she said. "Could you bring Uriah Heep back? Out of his book again?"

"Of course," Charley said, startled into being decisive for once. "Why?"

"I'd rather like to talk to him. If I come to your house, say tomorrow morning at half past eight...?"

"You want me to read him out of his book again?" Charley gave me a quick, questioning glance; I shook my head firmly.

"No," I said. "I don't think so. He was bad enough the first time."

"I'm sure he was frightful," Millie said. "But we could be prepared this time. I just think—you realize how he knew what was happening, don't you?"

"I assume it has something to do with the other Uriah Heep, at Rob's work."

"I rather think so too. The Darcys can read each other's minds. Not completely, but in glimpses—they always know where the others are, and what they're seeing or feeling. Drives them completely mad at times, as you'd imagine. I think your Uriah Heep was picking up on Rob's."

"And you think if I summon him again, he'll be able to tell us more," Charley said slowly. "But what if he doesn't want to?"

"We'll see," she said.

It felt better going back the other way. I think I could probably have done it without Charley's help: the real world felt as though it were welcoming me back. I still held on to his shoulder tightly.

We were very quiet as we walked back to Charley's parking space. I had been planning to take a bus home, but I was beginning to wonder if I really needed to walk for a while to clear my head. There was a lot to clear.

"You're not really going to summon Uriah Heep again, are you?" I asked, after a while.

"I think so," Charley said. "It makes sense. Will you come too?" he added hesitantly. "When Millie comes around tomorrow. I'd really appreciate it."

"Of course," I said, with some surprise. "Did you think I wasn't?"

"I wasn't sure," he said. The relief on his face was a little too strong for that, though.

"You've forgotten something. It's the second Saturday of the month tomorrow. We're going to Mum and Dad's for lunch."

He had indeed forgotten, even though it happened every month. "Oh, bother," he sighed. "Still... Millie's coming early, isn't she? There's probably enough time. And we can decide what to tell them later."

"They'll want to put a stop to you visiting fictional streets."

"They can't, really. I mean, I'm an adult. I don't need their approval." He didn't sound very sure of any of those things.

We reached the death trap, which had been blown over on its side. Charley hauled it upright. "So I'll see you tomorrow?"

"Make sure you buy milk." I hesitated. "Charley?"

He turned to look at me, inquiring, his helmet not yet over his head.

"Doesn't this, well... freak you out?"

Charley considered the question carefully, turning it over as though I'd asked him about the finer points of postmodernism.

"No," he said. "I understand why you're asking, but…it doesn't. School camp freaked me out. Leaving for Oxford freaked me out. This feels fine. Is that strange?"

For the life of me, I had no idea how to answer.

"I'll see you tomorrow," I said.

Charles Sutherland, age ten
Extract from diary (green and yellow stripes on cover)

Today was my first day of high school, and it was not as expected.

I thought people would want to learn in high school. Perhaps that was naive. It *was* naive. I've read enough books about high school to know better. In the future, I need to ask myself where my thoughts come from, and my feelings, too, so I'll know in advance that they might not work out.

They don't really want to learn here. Or I think they do, but they have no time to learn what's being taught. They're busy trying to learn themselves. That's probably why they didn't talk to me. They have their own complicated landscapes, and I don't fit.

Rob fits. I watched him in history, which we have together, and he knows just how to talk and laugh and be effortlessly smart but not attract attention. The trouble is, he won't talk to me either. At lunch I tried to follow him, and he waved me over to the Year Nine boys instead. I don't know if I'm considered a Year Nine, and neither did they. When I walked over to them, they stared at me, and I heard them whispering something about the genius kid. They asked me questions, and laughed when I told them the answers, and one of them became embarrassed when I corrected him, and tripped me up when I tried to walk away. It didn't hurt much, but I landed on my wrist wrong when I fell, and my new watch broke. The others became angry at the boy who tripped me then, and some of them tried to help me up. If I'd stayed, things might have gone better after that, but I couldn't stay any longer, because I would have started to cry. I went away instead, and read my book down by the bike sheds until I got deep enough that nothing could reach me, but not so deep that I brought anyone out. I'd promised Mum I wouldn't.

I learned I was embarrassing to Rob. That's why he never lets me hang out with him and his friends. I was naive not to realize that too. It's such a simple word.

I wish my hair hadn't been cut. I feel too visible. I'd never thought about being visible or invisible before, but I think I want to be invisible for a bit now. Metaphorically. Not like H. G. Wells's *The Invisible Man*. Though I suppose that could be a metaphor too. I'll have to think about it.

Yours,
Charles Sutherland

PS I just realized that *The Invisible Man* is a retelling of Plato's ring of Gyges, which is really obvious and fits perfectly and I really need to reread it. But not right now, because Griffin is hell to catch if he comes out, for obvious reasons.

PPS I don't usually say words like "hell."

XI

It turned out I was the only one of the three of us who had not read *David Copperfield*. I'd held out a faint hope that perhaps Millie hadn't, so for once I wouldn't be the only one consulting Wikipedia at the last minute. But apparently you don't live on a Dickensian street without giving yourself a thorough grounding in the classics.

"I would think you'd read all of Dickens in self-defense," she said to me. "When your brother is a Dickens scholar with a tendency to bring his reading material out of books."

I shrugged, uncomfortable. "I never had time," I said, which wasn't really true. I always meant to read Dickens. But every time I set my eyes to the pages, I felt that I was getting deeper into Charley's world, and I didn't like how vulnerable I felt there. I didn't like it now.

Besides, he could bring anything or anyone out from any book ever written. What was I supposed to do? Read them all?

We were sitting on the couch in Charley's flat, waiting for him to dig out *David Copperfield* from his room and come downstairs. When we had arrived, he came running to let us in the door—or rather, the lack of a door. A tablecloth hung over the doorway, like an inept curtain. The door itself was propped against the wall inside after the battle with the Hound.

"Charley," I had said—very calmly, under the circumstances. "What is that dog doing there?"

Charley glanced down at the enormous dog beside him. It was very large, and very black. I remembered it well, though it was less terrifying standing placidly on the doorstep than trying to break through a wall.

"Oh—this is Henry."

"I know who it is. It's the Hound of the Baskervilles."

"Well, technically," he conceded. "But the harmless version. Whoever summoned him obviously didn't bother to put him back, because when I got up this morning he was in the kitchen. I mean, he destroyed the door while in monstrous form, so it's not like I could have kept him out. I felt sorry for him, so I gave him some water and some Cornflakes, and I think he's adopted me. I named him Henry." He ruffled the dog on the head, which was at about waist height, and the dog looked up at him with his tongue hanging out gratefully. "Do you two want to come in? I'll just be a minute."

Then he had taken off upstairs, leaving the two of us waiting while he went to find the book that he probably should have had ready, considering it was why we were here. Sitting next to her, amid the usual muddle of hardcovers and paperbacks, I had no idea what to say to Millie. And now, it turned out, she knew more about Dickens than I did.

"Did things settle down in the Street after we left last night?" I asked. "Should I be worried?"

She raised her eyebrows. "For yourself? I doubt it." The giant dog padded over to us; he ignored me completely and laid his head on Millie's lap. She ruffled his ears. "But they're not used to things changing. Some of them have been around for hundreds of years; even the ones who were read into existence this decade tend to be very set in their ways. You two arriving, on top of everything else—well, I just hope they don't find out about your brother, that's all."

"Charley?" I said with a frown. I glanced up at the ceiling, as if I expected to see him through it. I could hear the occasional bump and thud. "What about him? I know what he can do is pretty unusual—"

"Unusual?" Millie said with a snort. "Rob—as far as we know, there are only two of his kind in the entire world. He has the power to shape our reality. He's not unusual. He's dangerous."

There was a clatter of footsteps on the stairs, and Charley appeared before I could say anything in reply.

"I've got it!" he called, holding up a massive tome that had to be *David Copperfield*. "Sorry, I thought I'd left it by my bed last night, but I must have put it on my desk instead, and then I think I moved more books on top of it when I was looking for it this morning."

"Did you check the fridge?" I couldn't resist asking.

Charley made a face at me, and dropped into the armchair. The book slipped easily into the crook of his arm, as though it belonged there. "Yes, actually, but I was checking it for milk. I thought you might want tea or something. Did I offer you tea or something?"

"No," Millie said. "You opened the door, said you were just looking for the book, wait right here and make ourselves at home."

"Oh," he said. "Well, did you want tea or something?"

"You don't have to do this, you know," I said. I hoped he wouldn't.

"No, I want to," he said. He said it a little too quickly. "I do. It's the most logical line of inquiry. I'm just concerned. This one didn't go so well last time."

"Will he remember that?" Millie asked. "I've never seen anyone go back into a book, much less come out again. Do we remember the last time?"

"They remember everything," I told her. "We used to end up with Sherlock Holmes around for tea on a regular basis when we were growing up. He always remembered the time before."

"That's the problem," Charley said. "Uriah will hate me even more now—which is saying something. And I've never been trying to get information out of a character before. I always just see what they have to say."

"Well," Millie said encouragingly, "let's see what this one has to say. Do we want to tie him up?"

We must have looked startled. Millie shrugged. "In my book, I used to get tied up whenever someone wanted to ask me questions."

"I never thought I'd say this," I said. "But Charley was right to pull you out of there."

Uriah Heep came into existence in a flash of light: tall, thin, cadaverous, his shock of red hair even wilder than before. We had set up a chair for him, where we could watch him from the couch. Clearly the aim was good, because he arrived as if thrown into it, legs spreadeagle and fingers wrapped around the seat. When his grip shifted, I saw the thin residue his hand left, like a snail's trail. The same thing had been on my sweatshirt after he grabbed me in the English department. I have no idea what that was about. Dickens.

Somehow, we all rose to our feet. It was instinct, as though we were in a room with a poisonous spider. Uriah Heep was not nervous. He looked momentarily surprised, and then his gaze hardened on Charley.

"Master Charley," Uriah said slowly. His eyes flickered to me and then Millie.

"Don't even think about making a run for it this time, all right?" Charley said, more sharply than I'd expected from him. "There are three of us. We're going to notice if you change into somebody else."

"I would never think of running, Master Charley," Uriah said, with simpering innocence. "Not when you caught me and umbled me in so workmanlike a fashion last time. Very good work, Master Charley, hurting such a poor, low-down creature."

Charley looked rather stricken. "I'm sorry. I didn't want to."

"Oh, I know," Uriah said. For a moment, there was a flash of hatred in his eyes. "I know."

Millie stepped forward then. "Mr. Heep," she said, with the polite-but-firm bossiness I recognized from her books. "We've a few questions to ask you, if you don't mind." Despite her jeans and hoop earrings, she was suddenly every bit the 1930s girl adventurer.

"Of me?" Uriah's mouth gaped, and two hard creases appeared in the sides of his cheeks. It took me a moment to realize this was his smile. "Now what could such fine folk have to ask of my umble self?"

"I say," Millie said to Charley. "You made a terribly accurate job of him."

"I think too accurate," Charley said ruefully. "Honestly, if you're right about this other summoner, I don't know how he manages to make the constructs do what he wants. Mine just seem to do their own thing."

"My own thing, Master Charley?" Uriah repeated. "Oh no, no. I'm quite at your disposal, I'm sure."

"You tied me up and put me in a closet!" Charley reminded him. Uriah only smiled.

"Mr. Heep, you said something was coming," Millie said. "We know what you mean now. Rob's met your counterpart, the one who belongs to the other summoner. You can see flashes from his mind, can't you? You know something about what's being planned."

"I can see things," Uriah said. "And I can tell you about them, of course I can. But I want something in return, Master Charley. Nothing at all, really, just a little promise for old Uriah."

"What do you want?" Charley asked.

"I want you to promise not to put me back." Suddenly, he was as hard as flint. "I want you to swear, on whatever you hold sacred, that I will not be going back to that book again."

Charley frowned. "Back into *David Copperfield*?"

"*David Copperfield*," Uriah spat. His limbs twitched in disgust. "It isn't even my book. It's his. Always his. I want out of it. I want to be taken to the Street, and I want to be given my freedom there."

"What does it feel like, when I put you back?" Charley asked. His guard dropped as curiosity overcame him. "Do you wake up back in your book?"

"I'll answer that, too, Master Charley," Uriah said. "To the best of my umble ability. When you promise not to put me back."

"Oh, never mind," Charley said. "I'll ask Mr. Holmes."

"Death," Uriah said. "It feels like death."

Charley fell silent. I didn't like the look on his face.

"You can't leave him out of his book," I said bluntly. "You can't even consider it. He's too dangerous."

"It's not as dangerous as it might seem," Millie said. My heart sank. I'd hoped for her support in this. "This isn't the same Uriah Heep as you have at work, remember. He has nothing to do with the summoner. Charley made him. He's a nasty piece of work, I'll grant you, but that goes for half the inhabitants of the Street. We usually manage to avoid bloodshed. I'm more concerned about the fact that the other Uriah will be able to see through him as well. We'll be wide open."

"We are anyway," Charley said. "The summoner must know where the Street is. If I can feel the pull of it, so can he—and certainly his characters can. If he means any harm to you at all, it's only a matter of time."

"That means the Street is already in danger," I pointed out. "That doesn't mean that you should *increase* the danger."

"It means that Uriah Heep is not that dangerous."

"He tried to kill us."

"He *didn't* kill us, though," Charley said. "I don't think that's in him. Not that what *is* in him is very pleasant, but I don't think we can pretend our lives are at stake."

I wasn't so certain about that. Charley wasn't the one who'd had a knife at his throat. He hadn't felt the murderous fury vibrating along the blade.

"I suppose we could keep him out of his book without letting him come to the Street," Millie said pragmatically.

Uriah shook his head. "I want to go to the Street. And not locked up in a basement somewhere. That's also a condition."

"God, he'll be asking for a Jacuzzi next," I sighed.

Uriah cocked his head to one side. "What might one of those be, Master Sutherland?"

"I thought you knew pretty much everything Charley knows?" I said sarcastically.

"I know many things, Mr. Sutherland," Uriah said. His face rippled, wavered, and then, horribly, shifted to take the shape of my brother's. Not the shape he'd taken last time, when he'd fooled me for so long. This version was a child, probably no more than eleven or twelve. In fact, exactly twelve. I remembered. The young Charley's face, grotesque on the elongated body, gave me a hard smile. "Many things."

To my surprise, Charley reacted before I could. "Stop it!" he snapped.

"Don't let him get to you," Millie said. "He's just trying to hurt you. It's what he does. We can't help how we're written."

"I know," Charley said. "But stop it. Change back, please."

Uriah looked at him a moment longer, then did so.

"Thank you." Charley was calm again now. Only the slightest catch in his voice gave him away. "Now. If we were to give you the freedom of the Street—"

"You can't," I repeated.

I think that was the first time Charley had ever ignored me. All the times he was lost in a book and oblivious to the whole world didn't count. Something has to be heard to be ignored. He heard me this time, and he ignored me.

"If we gave you the freedom of the Street, would you promise not to hurt its inhabitants?"

"Oh, I can't promise not to hurt anyone, Master Charley," Uriah said. "You heard this fine lady here. It's how I'm written. Someone so umble as me can't fight how they were written, can they?"

"I have no idea," Charley said. "Maybe. But will you promise not to betray the Street to the other summoner? The rest, I think, we could probably deal with. Can we?" he asked Millie.

"Shape-shifting, obsequiousness, and leaving slime trails over things are pretty much par for the course on the Street," Millie confirmed. She seemed to make up her mind; her own head raised with a bounce of curls. "And to be honest, if he's staying out, it's best we keep an eye on him. We can keep him watched without having him locked up—he'd have a job trying to get the better of Dorian Gray or the Artful Dodger. If you want to make the deal, we'll look after him."

"You can't possibly mean that," I said.

"Oh, thank you," Uriah said. His limbs twitched again as he looked up at Millie, and this time his gaze was both adoring and covetous. "Such a good, beautiful lady, being so kind to umble Uriah..."

"Oh, do shut up," Millie said, rolling her eyes. "There's a good chap. Just promise you won't talk to the other summoner."

"I wouldn't talk to the other summoner," Uriah said. I actually believed him. He said it too bitterly to be lying. "They're worse than Mr. Dickens, trying to make us fit their stories."

"All right," Charley said. "Then, if you tell us what we want to know, I promise not to put you back into your book when you're done."

"This is ridiculous!" I burst out. "You have no way of knowing he'll keep his word. You have no way of knowing if you can trust what he tells you."

"We could draw up a legal contract, Mr. Sutherland," Uriah suggested. "Your intern could look it over."

"Neither you or Eric are bound by contractual law," I returned. "You're not even bound by the laws of physics. You're figments of Charles Dickens's imagination. I wouldn't be so smug about it. How do you know Charley and Millie will keep *their* word?"

"Oh, their sort always do, Master Robert," Uriah said obsequiously.

"Good, honorable gentlefolk, always so kind to poor Uriah. Of course they'll keep their word. Besides, if they don't, they'll never get another word from me. They might need me later, and they know that if they've already put me back once, I won't help them. And they need my help. They don't have a choice. Do you, Master Charley?"

"No," Charley said. "We don't."

He sat down in the armchair, opposite Uriah. Charley still tends to sit cross-legged on chairs and tables—we never did manage to train him to use the furniture properly. This time, his feet were firmly on the floor, and his muscles were coiled to run at the first opportunity. But still, he sat, and looked at Uriah face-to-face.

"So," he said. "The summoner. What do you know about them?"

"Not very much," Uriah said. He leaned back and crossed his arms. "I only have glimpses, flashes. When I came through last time, I felt my other self in a room. He's there all the time he isn't working or with the summoner—he isn't put back, because they have him in the law firm now, and it's easier to keep him out than make sure he's read out the same each time. There are a few of them, there in the dark, sleeping on old mattresses. Very dark there, and cold. The rest are taken out and put back in as they're needed."

I had a sudden, unwanted image of Millie, and Dorian, and even the Artful Dodger and those weird Darcys. I imagined them lying on dirty mattresses somewhere—I thought of the basement of our childhood house, which had been a mess of cobwebs and moss and old boxes nobody ever looked through. I had always hated going in there. Once, when I was six, the door had swung shut and locked while I was down there looking for my rugby ball, and I had screamed and pounded on the door for what seemed like hours (it was about ten minutes) before Dad heard me from the hallway. I was shaking and crying when he let me out, and he had to soothe me for half an hour before I calmed down.

"That's terrible," I conceded. "It sounds like a child abuse case."

"Oh, they're not children, Master Sutherland," Uriah said bitterly. "They're criminals, all of them. The best criminals in literature, right off the page."

"What are they needed for?" Charley asked.

Uriah tilted his head a little to one side. "Ah. That's interesting. Just crime, at first, I think. Thefts, housebreakings, swindles, and so forth. I'm surprised you haven't thought of it, Master Charley. It's a perfect scheme. They can't be caught: they don't exist. By the time the police are looking for them, they're back in their books, just so many printed words on a page."

"But that's not what you were talking about," I reminded him. "You said something big was coming. Something we would be in the middle of."

"That's in his head very clearly, Master Sutherland," Uriah said. "Something coming. He clings to it in the dark, the way we cling to our revenge in our book. It's the only hope he has. He calls it the new world."

"And you don't know what that is?"

Uriah shook his head. "But it's something very big. And it involves you, Master Charley. He thinks about you all the time. You're the key to everything."

"Why is he at my law firm?" I asked.

The blood-red eyes rolled in my direction. "Why, because you're Master Charley's brother, of course. Why else?"

"I assumed that much. But I've been his brother for a while. Why now? And why watch me, rather than Charley?"

"Well, as to the second, Master Robert, the summoner probably feels that Master Charley would recognize Uriah Heep in his office. He doesn't know you would. He doesn't know I exist, and that you've seen me."

"But Eric must know," I said. "If you know he exists, he must know that you do. Wouldn't he tell the summoner?"

"Apparently not, Master Robert."

I put this aside for now. "And my first question? Why now?"

"I can't answer as to why the summoner is interested in you all of a sudden," Uriah said. "But you'll find that many things will begin to happen now. I told you. It's coming."

The new world. Millie had been right. Under the circumstances, it would probably not be a good thing at all.

"You said 'he' doesn't know you exist," Millie said after a while. "You mean the summoner? You know it's a 'he' we're looking for then?"

He gave her the Uriah Heep equivalent of a smile. "That's clear in the other Uriah's head, too, Miss Radcliffe-Dix."

"Can you tell us where the summoner is?" Charley asked.

This was what he had been waiting for, evidently. His shoulders twitched convulsively with excitement, and he sat forward.

"He's there right now," Uriah said. "It isn't so dark this time. There's a window—I've seen what's outside. I can tell you that, if you want. But first, I want to be taken to the Street. I want to be given lodgings there. And I don't want to see any copies of *David Copperfield* anywhere in the vicinity."

"I thought you trusted us," Millie said, not without irony.

"We all trust each other, I hope," Uriah said, widening his eyes. "But I don't see why we shouldn't all be careful. I'm sure you wouldn't *break* your promise to old Uriah, but he's so very umble you might *forget*, mightn't you?"

"I'm insulted," Millie said dryly. She glanced at Charley. "What do you think?"

"No," I warned. "Don't even think about it."

It was then that Millie's phone rang. She checked it, then glanced at us. "Sorry, chaps," she said. "Just a moment."

"Take all the time you need," Uriah said, generously.

I turned to Charley as Millie stepped away. "You can't do this."

"I don't see that we have a choice," Charley said. He glanced at Uriah as he said it, but didn't lower his voice. "We need his help."

Millie came back almost at once, before I could reply. "That was Dorian Gray," she said to Charley, rather than to me. "There's been another shift."

"You mean like when we were there?" he asked. "When the Street extended?"

"Rather larger than that. I need to get back. Uriah can come, too, if he must, but I need to be there."

"I'll come," Charley offered. "I might be able to help."

"You can't," I said to him. "It's past nine. Lydia's expecting us to drive out to Mum and Dad's—Mum and Dad will expect to see you too."

"You go. I'll make it up to them next month." I didn't miss the guilty glance at the floor. "You can't deny this is rather important."

"*You* can't deny that they'd kill you if they found out what you were doing."

"You can't tell them," he said at once. He caught himself. "I mean—please, Rob, don't tell them. They wouldn't understand."

"They'd understand perfectly. So do I. You've always wanted this, haven't you?"

"Reality to shift?"

"Don't give me that. It's an excuse. You've always wanted an excuse to show off what you're capable of. You couldn't just settle for being a literary prodigy, could you? You had to have this as well."

Charley sighed. "Can we please not argue in front of Uriah Heep?"

"Oh, don't stop on my account," Uriah Heep chimed in from the chair. "It's no bother at all."

I ignored this. Privately, I was annoyed at myself; I was so frustrated, I'd forgotten Uriah was even there. "So you're not coming to see Mum and Dad? And you don't want me to explain why?"

"I can't. Tell them I'm sorry for letting them down—"

"Oh, don't be. It isn't like it's the first time, is it?" And I was annoyed at myself for that too.

"Charley, you can ride with Uriah and me, then, if Rob's not coming," Millie said. If she was bothered by my withdrawal, she wasn't showing it. I don't think she cared if I was there at all. "Not to worry. I'll drop you home again when we've sorted this. We should be back in time for tea."

"Why do I feel like I'm in a Millie Radcliffe-Dix Adventure?" Charley said, with a rather weak smile.

"Well, you asked for it when you brought me out all those years ago," Millie said. She clapped him lightly on the shoulder. "Buck up, old thing. You're doing very well."

Charley came out as I was opening my car door. I had hoped he would, beneath my resentment; at least, I would have been yet more resentful had he not.

"Rob, wait," he said. He glanced quickly back at the house as he drew near, and lowered his voice beneath the hearing of anyone inside. "Don't be angry. You're right that keeping Uriah out is dangerous; I know it is. But we need him. I meant what I said in there: we don't have a choice."

"You have a choice," I corrected him. I lowered my own voice to match his, not because I cared what Uriah or Millie heard. "You can take what information he'll give you here, put him back, and get whatever else you need some other way. This is a mistake."

"Which part?"

"All of it. If you don't want to listen to me as your brother, then listen to me as a lawyer. This is not a good deal. You're letting Uriah Heep stay out in the world. You've never let a character stay in the world."

"I have," he said. "Millie Radcliffe-Dix."

"She was a mistake too. A literal one: you never meant her to exist."

"Tell that to her."

I snorted. "No thanks."

"Exactly." He ran a hand through his hair. "It doesn't matter if I meant her to exist or not. She does. I don't have any rights to her. Uriah—he's a person. Deal aside, if he really doesn't want to go back, I'm not sure he's mine to put back."

"It doesn't matter whose he is," I said, and knew I was deliberately missing the point. "He's dangerous. He knows more than he's pretending, you know. I'm certain of that."

"Probably," Charley agreed.

"He needs to be put back. It's still not too late, you know."

"It is. I promised."

"It doesn't matter what you promised! He's not even real."

Charley laughed a little. "He's pretty real, Rob."

"He occupies physical space. That's not the same thing."

"Isn't it? Besides," he added, before I could reply, "deal or no deal, I couldn't put him back now. You heard him: it's death to him. It would be as bad as what he said the other summoner was doing—worse. But I do wish it wasn't him, out of everyone I've ever brought out. He hates me."

"He's Uriah Heep," I reminded him. "He hates everyone."

"That's true. But he really, truly hates me. And they don't usually do that."

I thought of those blood-colored eyes in the skull-like face, and the way they had fixed on Charley. Both times he had changed his appearance, it was Charley's form he took. I didn't know what that meant, if indeed it meant anything.

"I won't tell Mum and Dad what you're up to," I said into the silence. "Not yet. I don't want to worry them either. But you have to promise me that you won't break into a building on the word of Uriah Heep."

"Not just on his word," Charley said. "We'll check it out first."

"I'm serious, Charley."

"Do you really think I'm not? I'm more serious than I've ever been in my life, I promise. You don't have to come with us—I won't even ask you to. I just didn't want you to feel—"

"What?" I asked, because he had, as usual, stopped without finishing.

He shook his head. "Nothing."

I knew exactly what he meant. I should have told him it was fine. I didn't. I wasn't sure it was fine; and if it was, I didn't want him to think so.

"You'd better go," I said instead. "They're waiting for you."

I half wondered, or half hoped, that he wouldn't leave. But he did, with only a fleeting glance in my direction to imply he was tempted to do anything else. Millie already had Uriah in the back of her car; Charley climbed in the front. They drove away in a trail of dust and gravel, leaving me behind.

I really needed to read *David Copperfield*.

Millie

M iss Matty's house had gone, and in its place was a new alley. The Street had also grown a further three feet, enough to warrant a new lamppost and a length of wall, but it was the alley that was causing the stir. The Street had always been one length of road. It was crooked and crenelated, like the jagged edge of a key, but it was one road. Now there was a gaping hole in the line of buildings, as though a tooth had been knocked out. In its place, the new alley spidered from the pavement. It looked to be reaching for something beyond.

There was already a crowd clustered about the entrance, but not so large a crowd as Millie had been expecting—only four, in fact. It seemed that most of the Street had decided to stay well away. That was troubling. More troubling yet was the fact that of the four that had ventured out, one of them was Dorian, who rarely bothered to venture anywhere at all.

The truth was, Millie liked Dorian Gray. She knew she shouldn't. He wasn't quite a villain, more of an antihero or a didactic exercise, but he certainly wasn't a decent sort. She had his painting, hidden in the back of her wardrobe and scrutinized regularly, to remind her of that: the bloated, pallid face, the cruel mouth, the wrinkled hand stained with blood. He didn't fool her. But he was *interesting*. More than that, he was intelligent, funny, and challenging. Many of the characters who inhabited the Street were more hindrance than help in keeping things safe. Between Heathcliff and his propensity for vengeful brooding and knife-guns, the Artful with his overdeveloped sense of mischief, and the Darcys...well, who were the Darcys... most of them were really a jolly nuisance. Dorian was helpful. He found characters lost in the world, and helped get them to the Street.

He protected them from discovery by the outside world. He could defuse irate situations with a drawling observation, usually because the situations bored him. She liked talking to him.

Sometimes, though, he could be trouble. Real trouble, not the sort that could be soothed or argued away like the trouble the others gave. When she and Charley approached with Uriah Heep, she could see it glint in his eyes immediately.

"Hello, chaps," Millie announced. Beside Dorian, Heathcliff brooded conscientiously, his diabolic face aflame. The White Witch stood beside him. They made an intimidating couple: one dark, one white as chalk, both tall, both stunningly beautiful, both able to break a person in half. Darcy Three was also present—the quiet, practical Darcy, whom Millie secretly thought of as the attractive one. (Dorian and Lady Macbeth both favored Five, but Millie thought him a little *too* reserved, and inclined to jump, un-Austen-like, in large bodies of water.)

"Hello," Dorian replied lazily. He cast a glance at Charley. "Dr. Sutherland. You've returned, have you? I wondered where our Millie was going this morning."

"I have," Charley replied evenly. He seemed to pick up on the implied threat as well as Millie; but then, of course, while he had only a passing acquaintance with this Dorian, he probably knew Oscar Wilde as well as anybody.

"What's going on here?" Millie asked. "You said on the phone that nobody was hurt."

"We lost a house," Dorian said. "Only Miss Matty's, though, which was rather an eyesore. Nobody liked the new wallpaper any better than the old."

"Miss Matty is quite well," Darcy Three said, before Millie's heart could seize. "She was at the Mad Hatter's at the time, discussing their tea shop. She is much distressed, naturally."

"I should say so," Millie said. She recovered equilibrium quickly. "What happened to the house?"

"The house disappeared to make room for *this*," the Witch said, with something approaching disdain. She waved a hand at the new alley. It looked back, shadowed and implacable, disclosing nothing.

"How?" Charley asked. "Where did it go?"

Heathcliff glowered at him. "It was swallowed up by cobblestones as a sinking ship is swallowed by the sea. Anyone within it would have gone too."

"Something must be done about it," Darcy said. "This cannot continue."

"We *are* doing something about it," Millie said. "By the way, this is Uriah Heep."

The others turned to look at him. There was a moment's silence as they took him in.

"Ugh," the Witch said flatly.

This was fitting, of course, but Millie felt obliged to give them all a stern look. "He's going to be staying with us, at least for a time. Do we have anyone that could keep an eye on him?"

"There *are* spare houses," Dorian said. "Those rooms over the saddler's, for one. Nobody wants them, because they smell of horses where there are no horses."

"Oh, I think Uriah would like to share with someone responsible, someone able to counteract any mischief he may otherwise feel tempted to cause," she said. "Wouldn't you, Uriah?"

"I am happy to be placed wherever is most convenient, dear lady," Uriah said fawningly. This time, Millie didn't censure Heathcliff's snort of disgust.

"We could keep him confined in our apartment," Darcy Three said unexpectedly. He was regarding Uriah with a look of calm, measured disapproval. As always, a single strand of hair fell in his eyes. Millie, as always, longed to flick it back, which was its precise function. All the Darcys had it; even One, who was born long before film adaptations and really should have known better. "There are five of us, all surprisingly strong and healthy given the drinking habits of an average Georgian aristocrat. Somebody is usually at home, and would be more than capable of impeding any mischief on behalf of this... person."

"I say, would you?" Millie exclaimed, with both surprise and relief. The Darcys were not known for their civic duty. "That's frightfully decent of you. Are you sure the others wouldn't mind?"

"I'm quite certain they will. But they owe me a favor. I'm still the only one of us who ever learned to cook."

"There you go, then, Uriah." Millie almost put a hand on his shoulder, but couldn't quite bring herself to touch him. "What do you say to that?"

"An honor, I'm sure," Uriah said. "To be accommodated by five such fine...gentlemen."

"That's settled then. Oh, and can you lot spread the word that we're looking for volunteers to watch an office around the clock? Uriah is about to give us the address."

"Not quite an *address*." Uriah didn't seem perturbed by his cool welcome. His eyes had brightened since coming through the wall, which, since they were red, gave them the appearance of glowing Christmas lights. "That's too much to expect of such an umble personage. I know only what he sees out the window."

"Which is?"

"Lambton Quay," Uriah said.

Millie's eyebrows shot up. "Are you quite sure?" She kept her voice mild in front of the others, who were listening with curiosity. "That's the heart of the central business district. It seems rather...unlikely."

"I don't know what's likely, Miss Radcliffe-Dix. I know only what I see through his eyes. And what I see are the old buildings that run up Lambton Quay. There are buses passing underneath; those trees down the center of the road catch the wind. And there's a McDonald's opposite. I see that distinctly."

"Rob works down the end of that street," Charley said. "It's right in the heart of the city."

"The summoner isn't afraid of being in the heart of a city," Uriah said. "Far from it. That street is the oldest in Wellington. Some of those foundations go back to the nineteenth century, to the first European settlers. The summoner likes old bones. He likes to pick over them. Don't *you*, Master Charley?"

"Very well," Millie said. She still had doubts, but she knew it was almost more important to be seen doing something. "Volunteers to watch an office block on Lambton Quay, please, Heathcliff, Darcy, Dorian. There's a McDonald's opposite, apparently. Perhaps choose someone American."

She worked on Lambton Quay as well. Her office overlooked the street. On quiet days, she could gaze out the window, and watch the oak trees rustling in the wind.

"Huckleberry Finn would probably love to go," Darcy Three said, with just a hint of condescension. "But you may be required to supply money for endless cheeseburgers. His financial situation is rarely stable."

In truth, Huck Finn was probably more financially solvent than any of the Darcys, being more open to employment, but Millie let this slide. The poor fellows could never manage to perceive themselves as anything but revoltingly wealthy.

"Jolly good," she said. "I'll give him a spare twenty or so for the work. You can spread that around, too, if you like. See if anyone else is interested."

Darcy Three nodded. His lock of hair flicked. "And the alley?"

Millie glanced at the space where Miss Matty's house had once been. It stretched out a few yards before ending in an iron gate. What lay beyond she couldn't say—perhaps nothing, save the mist that enshrouded it—but in the damp air she couldn't suppress a shiver.

"Leave it," she said. "Nobody is to go near it."

Huck Finn was very interested in the errand, as was the Artful and, for some reason, the Implied Reader. By the time they had been packed off, it was nearly midday, and the sun was burning off the worst of the morning fog.

"I should probably go speak to Miss Matty," Millie told Charley, who had been holding back trying not to be noticed. "Do you need to catch up with your parents?"

"I'd really rather not," he said. "They're not expecting me now. Besides, I don't want them to know about all this, which means I'm likely to blurt it out the second I see them."

"Will Rob keep quiet?"

"Oh, Rob *wants* to tell them, so they won't get a word out of him. It's funny how that works, isn't it?"

"People are jolly strange," she agreed. "In that case, let's get lunch."

The first time Millie had stepped through the wall and into the Street, she had found it in disorder. The buildings had been grimmer then, or seemed it. The few characters already beginning to congregate were essentially squatting, safe from the world outside for the first time in their lives, but with no food or money save what the Artful was pinching for himself. None of them had been able to carve a place in the real world as Millie had. They weren't written for work; their essential natures, unlike hers, were not fluid enough to let them hold down a job at Burger King. They had difficulty with new skills, or new ways of thinking. Darcy could have managed a grand estate, and Heathcliff could have sought complicated revenge with the best of them, but that simply wasn't helpful in central Wellington. Millie had never seen another book character before. She was shocked to see them so shabby and dirty. They clung to the Street like flotsam in rock pools; outside in reality, they risked being submerged without a trace.

She had two choices then. She could have walked away, or she could have stayed. She stayed, because that was really no choice at all. Her conscience tugged at her; and, if it hadn't, her heart had opened to the Street and swallowed it whole, and now it was lodged there, fast as a hook in the mouth of a fish pulled from the harbor, and as painful. She had walked up to Darcy One, who was trying to burn paper to keep warm in the enormous stone fireplace of what would become the Darcy flat.

"It's no good, old thing," Millie said. "This just won't do. We're going to have to sort things out."

It was her Jacqueline Blaine voice, the voice that had been out of date at the time her books were published, and that felt hollow as she used it. It was the voice of Millie Radcliffe-Dix, girl detective; she was Millicent Dix, perfectly ordinary accountant. She no longer had her animal companion, which of course in a children's book was something like her soul. She hadn't said "old thing" for almost twenty years. Her bravery had turned to bravado. But Darcy listened, and so did the others, as they trickled in. And accountants, it transpired, could at least sort things out, probably better than girl detectives.

The Street to her, dearly beloved as it was, was paved with those memories. The saddler's was where she had once broken up a fight between Heathcliff and Anna Karenina that nearly eventuated in the appropriately tragic deaths of both. (The Anna was a Victorian translation, somewhat milder than in the original Russian, or Heathcliff would not have lasted ten minutes. She left the Street for Europe three weeks later, which was a shame, as Millie had rather enjoyed her company when she wasn't working herself into beautifully written hysteria.) The Old Curiosity Shop leaked when it rained. The Darcys' doorway had once had a couch stuck in it for three months after an unsuccessful attempt to refurnish, until Heathcliff took matters into his own hands and tore it apart. She could read her own history in every line of the place. To Charley, it was new, and yet entirely known to him. She felt him light up with the beauty of the buildings and cobbles and pale blue sky.

They stopped at the battered old tea shop first, where Miss Matty bravely offered them tea and biscuits while the Hatter, her business partner, sat at the table and dunked his watch in the teapot.

"Don't you worry about your house, Miss Matty," Millie reassured her. "Anyone would be happy to put you up; you only have to say the word. Perhaps not Lady Macbeth, though. I don't think she murders guests unless there's a throne in it for her, but old habits die hard, and all."

"Thank you, dear," Miss Matty said. Her gentle face, framed by her bonnet, was regaining color. "Everyone is so kind."

"Well," Millie said cautiously. "Not *everyone*, perhaps."

Miss Matty lowered her voice, although there was nobody else in the room. "I do hate to spread rumors, but…I don't suppose you've heard the latest news about the new world, have you?"

"Not since Darcy Three met the possible Scrooge," Millie said. "We never did track him down."

"Oh, indeed. But this was only this morning—the dear Duke of Wellington encountered Mr. Maui at Mount Vic while he was taking his constitutional."

"I'll explain about both later," Millie said to Charley quickly, seeing his eyes widen. "Go on, Miss Matty, do."

"Mr. Maui said that while he was in bird form, he'd seen one of the disappearing characters—the ones that come and go. They, it seems, told him of the coming of the new world. They said, most specifically, that it was coming here."

"Here, as in the Street?"

"Here, as in Wellington, I believe. I found the phrasing peculiar. A new world, surely, means that the whole world changes, not merely a single city?"

Millie had to agree that it did. "Did he say what character?"

"I believe he was unacquainted with them. But for Mr. Maui to have imparted the information to the duke, he must, after all, have been concerned."

"Or up to something," Millie said. "He's a trickster god, after all."

Maui was one of the more mysterious figures she had encountered—and she herself had met with him only once or twice, as a slight, tattooed Māori man in a hooded sweatshirt and jeans. Most of the time, he lived as a bird in the surrounding bush, and Dorian had given up trying to track him. Nobody even knew where he had come from: a child's picture book, possibly, but sometimes Millie wondered if he had been here longer than any of them, perhaps even before printed words had come to New Zealand. For all she knew, there were several of him. If she'd asked, he would probably have lied just for fun. She didn't, though, think he was lying in this case, or up to any tricks. It tallied too well with every other source of the rumor.

"I do hope the world doesn't change," Miss Matty said. She took a sip of her tea. "I know we must move with the times, but they seem to move so fast."

The public house, a dark, low-ceilinged Elizabethan building lit by a haze of candles, was beginning to fill with diners of various shapes and sizes by the time they reached it. Lancelot and the Scarlet Pimpernel drank foaming beer by the window, Lancelot discoursing on the relative merits of broadswords in heavily accented Middle English. The Artful held court at a table in the corner, hiding a ball under a cup and shifting it rapidly as the Darcys watched. The White Witch sat alone at the bar, as cool and forbidding as a 1940s noir heroine. ("The silver Harley-Davidson on the curb is hers," Millie explained. "Cheaper than reindeer, and it does better in traffic.")

They found a place at a heavy wooden table upstairs, by the latticed windows overlooking the Street. Unusually, the afternoon sun was gleaming in. It seemed, as light and dark sometimes did on the Street, to have a quiet, numinous significance that went beyond the physical.

"How is there food here?" Charley asked, before Millie had even sat down. He seemed oblivious to the curiosity he was inspiring; his own was spilling out in all directions. "Is that fictional as well?"

"That would be jolly helpful," Millie said. "So of course not. It's more or less provided by Dorian and me. I'm an accountant, so I earn a reasonable amount, considering I have no rent to pay. Dorian does something complicated online with stocks and shares that brings in rather more. It might not be entirely legal. Frankly, I was jolly near bankrupt trying to keep this place together before Dorian came, which is why I don't question his help as long as the portrait doesn't give me cause for alarm. The Artful goes out to the shops first thing every morning—that's when you must have seen him. I don't suppose *you* do fictional food?"

"As far as I know, there's no reason I can't," Charley said. "But I can't. The one time I tried, my chocolate cake tasted like paper and glue. I suppose a Marxist reading of baked goods isn't very appetizing. Or I'm just not very food minded."

He didn't eat very much of the enormous helpings of meat pie, mashed potatoes, and mushy peas that came to their table, or the stout pale pudding, studded with raisins, that followed it. That, though, was probably because he was too busy looking out the window.

"It's a lot of work, this place, isn't it?" he said abruptly.

"Yes." She was unsurprised that it had taken him so long to think of this. To him, deep down, they were all still just illustrations come to life. "A few times I've thought it wasn't going to work at all. But it *has* to. This is the first safe place any of them have ever had. Before it came, we were all scattered across the world, alone and vulnerable—and the world isn't built for most of us to survive in. Some had a terrible time before the Street came into being."

"Like Miss Matty?"

"Like Miss Matty," Millie agreed. "Or worse. They have all the problems of illegal immigrants, to start with: no documents, no money, nobody to support them. Many of the others don't look quite human; some of them have inexplicable abilities; none of them age. If they're fortunate, they'll find other book characters to help them, but before the Street that was almost impossible. Most didn't even realize there were any others like them. They were alone in the world, and frightened."

"Frightened of what? What are they hiding from?"

"What are you hiding from?" Millie countered. "You're not a

fictional character, but you're a summoner. You hide as much as any of us. What are you afraid of?"

"Oh God. Everything." He considered the question seriously. "I'm afraid of being taken away and experimented on, obviously. But it's more than that. I'm afraid of being noticed. I'm afraid of being at the center of a new world where I'm hated and feared for what I can do."

"They'll fear you here if they find out what you are, I'm afraid," Millie said. "Summoners were only a legend to most of them. Lancelot knew of one, in the 1600s, but she was burned as a witch and all the characters she read out with her. Perhaps you and this other summoner are the first since she died hundreds of years ago. Everybody here comes from one-offs—random acts of reader connection. There are rumors of more, further back, when the written word was in its infancy. A lot of what was seen as magic in early history was probably really summoning: people reading dragons out of books, and the like."

"It would be like a self-fulfilling prophecy," Charley said. "People write about fairies; because they've been written, they're read out of books; and then they're in the world, and people write stories about them. We've read our own myths into the world."

"But as for the rest of it—they're afraid of real people for the same reasons you are. It's not hypothetical to some of them, you know, the experimentation. Heathcliff was captured and experimented on during the 1940s—he won't talk about it beyond that, not even to say which country it was, but the scars are still there. And they're all afraid of being hated. There are still so few of us, you know. Even now, with the Street, we're frightfully vulnerable."

"I felt this place arrive," he said. "Two years ago. It was an autumn night, wasn't it?"

"It was," she confirmed. "Just after midnight."

"I'd fallen asleep at my desk. It was a frosty night, and the moon was full. I woke up, for no reason, and I knew something important had happened. I just...I never knew what it was. Or I was afraid to. I tried to ignore it. I felt the pull of it, and I wouldn't listen." He shook his head. "Where did all this *come* from? It must come from somewhere."

"Where do any of us come from?" She buttered her third slice of bread, not looking at him. It wasn't a question any of them were comfortable answering. "Where do we go back to? Where did you pull me from, all those years ago?"

"I don't know," he said thoughtfully. "I never know. The simplest answer is that you're only a manifestation from my mind. If I were to send you away again, you would disappear. I could remake you again, and you'd remember me, but only because I can remember. But I don't altogether trust simple answers. Where do you think you come from?"

"My book." Her stomach tightened at the question, which she knew she had invited. "We remember our books. We remember being pulled from them. We think about returning to them. But we don't like to think about what that means too deeply. Books, after all, are just words."

"I don't know," he repeated. "We're all just words. I say that all the time. I feel it, very strongly. But I don't quite know what it means."

Millie didn't either. She felt that was true of a lot of things these days.

"That's one reason I don't want them knowing what you are," she said, with a nod at the other diners. "They don't like questioning their own reality. I hope that if I just don't explain you, they'll assume you're a reading from some obscure book and ignore you. These people are an unruly batch, for the most part. Their grasp on the world can slip at the slightest nudge. I love them all, but they can be dangerous."

"They're wondrous," Charley said. He caught himself, and flushed. "I didn't mean to word that as though you were intellectual curiosities. I know you're not. But this place is fascinating. All of it."

"I know," Millie said wryly. "You just spent half an hour downstairs talking to the Duke of Wellington about the political slant of his characterization."

He winced. "Sorry. I don't usually talk too much. Only when I'm nervous, or the other person in the conversation is fictional. And I'm only articulate in one of those two situations."

"Don't be sorry! He was thrilled. Nobody ever wants to hear him talk about his time as prime minister. They don't even want to hear about Waterloo. He's our only nonfictional occupant; I always think he might be lonely."

"I haven't read a lot about the Duke of Wellington, but I think he's from Simon Fitzpatrick's seminal biography. There's that slight Conservative bias the reviewers picked up on."

"Well, it's not surprising. History is every bit as much of a story as fiction. There's no reason a reader can't construct their own Duke of Wellington just as clearly as they might construct their own personal Uriah Heep. If you're wanting some sort of theory about what we're made of, old thing, that's the best I can do. We're half words, and half thought."

"The point where language and interpretation meet," Charley said, with what might almost have been yearning. "One of my colleagues— Beth—does a lot of work around ideas like that: semiotics, and reader response."

"She'd like to meet the Implied Reader," Millie said. "The man without a face outside, who wants to watch the office? He's a product of—what is it again?"

"Iser's phenomenological theory of reader response?" Charley said, his face kindling again. "Truly? How strange."

"I've never really understood it," Millie said. "I'm an accountant."

"It's not complicated. It's just the idea that every book has an implied reader—a sort of imaginary person the author has in mind while he's writing. I supposed in the Implied Reader's case, that wasn't visualized terribly distinctly."

"Poor chap," Millie agreed. "He's really just middle-aged, white European, and middle class."

"I wasn't really thinking of Iser, though," Charley said. "Or of critical theory at all. I was thinking of Dickens. You know, chapter forty-four of *Great Expectations*." Millie had already noticed that he liked to try for a tactful middle ground between implying people must have read the same books as him and implying they hadn't. "Estella tells Pip to put him out of her thoughts. And he says, 'Out of my thoughts! You are part of my existence, part of myself. You have been in every line I have ever read since I first came here.' He goes on, but it begins with reading. He knew, didn't he, Dickens? The way we imbue words with our own desires."

"He did," Millie agreed. This, too, veered close to dangerous territory.

Perhaps Charley read this on her face, or felt her discomfort along the thread that connected them; at least, he changed the subject.

"I don't want to sound alarmist. But if we had to defend the Street from the summoner, who would we be able to muster?"

She noted, and accepted, that he had said "we." "Let's see. Heathcliff, of course. He's not necessarily effectual so much as frightening in a psychopathic domestic-abuse sort of way, but he'll be first to attack and he has great physical strength. Matilda, though I hate to bring even Roald Dahl children into danger."

"She's from a children's book," Charley pointed out. "That makes her by definition more capable than most adults. Who else? Did Miss Matty really say we had Maui?"

"We don't *have* him. He has his own life, and it doesn't have a lot to do with a Victorian street. His ties to the land go far deeper—in general, the Street tends to attract the nineteenth-century British texts before any others. But he may join forces with us, if it comes to defending anything more than the Street. He's unpredictable. We *do* have Lancelot—the genuine medieval article. The Scarlet Pimpernel. The White Witch, if we can persuade her."

"Can she turn people to stone?"

"Fictional people—which might be enough, for what the summoner can muster. She's tried it on real people many times. She would try it on us, I imagine, except she accepted a similar agreement to Dorian Gray's in exchange for the protection of the Street. I have her wand in my cupboard. Still, I try to keep her away from Mr. Tumnus."

His eyes widened. "Mr. Tumnus is here?"

"Number 17. God knows how he survived long enough to make it here—most of the obviously magical creatures have a very difficult time of it in the real world."

"Can we please, *please*," Charley said seriously, "go to tea with Mr. Tumnus?"

"If you like. I warn you, though, he burns the toast. And the sardines are tinned."

"I don't care."

She didn't either—not just about the sardines but, suddenly, about any of it. It didn't matter who was real, or where they came from. They were here. The sun was still shining, Charley's exhilaration was spilling down the invisible link that connected them, and there was an adventure ahead of her. She just didn't feel fictional.

It was probably for that reason that when Dorian came by their table, wineglass in elegant hand, she didn't think to tighten her defenses.

"Millie," he said. "Dr. Sutherland. I thought you might care to know, Millie, that Huckleberry Finn called in moments ago. The offices in question seem abandoned, but it will be difficult to be certain until the shop on the ground floor closes. I do, however, happen to know of both a concert and a rugby game in the city tonight. Lambton Quay will be flooded with people on their way to and from the railway station. I doubt you'll have the opportunity for any practical adventuring."

"Bother," Millie sighed. "That's a bit of bad luck. Still, there's tomorrow. We should be able to break in then. Lambton Quay is reliably deserted on Sunday nights."

"Yes. I rather like to see a street without people on it. It's so entirely pointless." He looked at Charley, and shifted his voice abruptly. "This street suits you, you know."

Charley blinked. "I'm sorry?"

"It suits you. Call it an aesthetic observation; a place can suit a person aesthetically as well as a pair of trousers or a jacket. This street looks well on you. Its lights, its shades, its cobbles. We've never found someone whom it fits. It's not quite sordid enough for me, not quite I-say-old-chap enough for Millie. Not wild enough for Heathcliff, not refined enough for the Darcys. Even the Artful Dodger doesn't feel entirely suited to it, and he's our one Dickensian original. But it fits you very well."

"Thank you," Charley said uncertainly.

"Oh, it's not a compliment to fit something, unless that something is either very expensive or very cheap, and this is neither. It's interesting, though. Of all the perfectly respectable fictional people in the world, many of them Victorian, why you? A flesh-and-blood human, who can pass through our wall like fiction."

"Well, if we knew that," Millie said, "we'd know a lot more about this place than we do."

But she knew what Dorian meant. The lights and shades he had spoken of didn't just seem to fit Charley; they altered to fit him. They lightened when he smiled, and darkened when he was uneasy. It didn't surprise her: he was a summoner. But it bothered her that Dorian had noticed, still more that he had commented. To be more precise, it bothered the part of her that was still Millie Radcliffe-Dix, girl detective. It made that part of her sit and exclaim, in the Jacqueline Blaine parlance she did her best to shake, "Hello! I say, what's that?"

Since she wasn't one to wonder such things quietly, she asked as much, after Charley left to go home and feed Henry. By that time, it was deep into the evening, and the lamps were burning.

"What are you playing at, Dorian?"

Dorian turned his blue eyes on her, the picture of innocence as only a man without a conscience could be. "I don't know what you mean."

"Don't give me that." She folded her arms, and heard her bracelet jingle on her wrist. "Is it Uriah Heep that bothers you? Because I think he bothers everyone. It's sort of what he does."

"How kind of you to ask. But no, that little crawling person is no bother to me at all. Frankly, he's so uniquely hideous he becomes rather decorative. No, I'm more concerned about the person who brought him out. He *did* bring him out, didn't he, Millie? And he did it on purpose."

"Yes," she said. She wished, not for the first time, that Oscar Wilde had given his protagonist less intelligence, or that Jacqueline Blaine had been less scrupulous about allowing hers to lie. "He did. For goodness' sake, though, Dorian, keep that to yourself."

"He's a summoner," Dorian said. "Another one. You've known this for years, haven't you? That's why you've been watching him."

"He summoned me," she said. "When he was six years old. That's why he can get through the wall. But he's not the one we're searching for. He didn't summon this place."

"I never thought he did. He wouldn't have stumbled into it the way he did had he known it was here."

"Then what was all that about it fitting him?"

"I was merely making an observation. This place *does* fit him, and he fits it. And we know so little about either."

"I know about Charles Sutherland. He summoned me. I have a good deal of him in my head—the six-year-old, at least. And I've kept my eye on him a few years since. I would know if he weren't what he seemed to be."

"People change a good deal in twenty years, you know. Not me, obviously. But most people."

"He's a good sort, Dorian. And what he can do is jolly useful."

"It's jolly dangerous," Dorian countered. For the first time, something serious crept into his voice. "You say he is what he seems to be. Suppose that he is. Dull people sometimes are, just to give fair warning. What he seems to be is a person who can bring people like us out of our books and put them back. For people like us, that's the equivalent of power over life and death. You knew that, or you wouldn't have kept it from us all."

"He can't put *you* back. Only his own readings."

"As far as he knows, perhaps. He hasn't begun to experiment yet. But very well, suppose he can't. Then what did he do with the Hound of the Baskervilles? He doesn't strike me as the type to be able to kill a Gothic hound."

She thought of Henry, back at the book-infested house. "Altered it, that's all. Reread it. Made it less dangerous."

"Then he could do the same to us?"

"If he could, he wouldn't. Why should he?"

Dorian shrugged. "Why should anyone do anything?"

"You really don't like him."

"I don't like people who hold the power of life and death over me, or even the power to make me less dangerous. It's an idle fancy of mine, but idle fancies are all we have to cling to in this uncertain world."

"*I* hold the power of life and death over you, Dorian," she reminded him. "I hold your soul."

"Oh, that's different," he said airily. "We're old friends, aren't we, Millie?"

"Do stop being so Gothic," Millie sighed. "It's not half as attractive as you think."

Before she fell into bed, Millie opened her wardrobe door to make a special scrutiny of the picture of Dorian Gray. She was used to the grotesque features, even the rather horrible way she could still see traces of the Dorian she knew lurking in them. She looked at them now with purpose, making sure she could see no new traces of any planned mischief or cunning or deception in them.

She didn't see any of those, all of which she had some experience with in the past. Instead, as she examined the faded blue eyes in the sagging face, she saw something else. It was difficult to make out, except as something altogether ugly and troublesome. She had seen it before at times, but not on Dorian's face, and certainly not the face of his soul.

It was fear, she decided, after a while. That was what it was. Jealousy, and hatred, and fear.

XII

Our parents' house—our childhood home—is just over an hour's drive from Wellington along the Kāpiti Coast. As a teenager, this felt like the length of the country. I loved our house, and the farmland around it, but I wished with all my heart that it was closer to civilization. I don't wish that anymore. Now, I appreciate the way the city falls away as we drive, opening up into ocean on the one side of the road and steep fields dotted with gorse and sheep on the other. Coming up the winding gravel driveway and seeing the old oak tree waving from the back of the redbrick house always feels like slipping into a pair of comfortable slippers. Admittedly, it's easier to feel all this when I don't have to live here.

Mum and Dad were out front to welcome us: Dad tall and friendly, Mum petite and smiling. Chocolate and Tatty-Coram, the two Labradors, tried to bowl us over; my old cat, Patchwork, ignored me entirely. We took a plate of scones in the living room, its pale yellow walls and sloping ceiling unchanged since before I was born. Sitting on the couch, I had a strange hyper-real moment when all the days and years of my life rolled into one, and I didn't know if I were myself at four, at ten, at fifteen, at eighteen home for the holidays. The afternoon sun was just beginning to slant through the blinds, and the warm, sweet smell of cut grass blew through the open window.

"I love your garden," Lydia said, glancing out the window herself. "The flowers are beautiful."

"You two really need to tend to your own garden," Dad said, with his usual tact. My father is the kindest man in the world, but when I was a child trying to clean my room, he would always find the drawer

I forgot, and he hasn't changed. "The last time we saw it, the weeds were being strangled by the weeds."

"That actually seems like a system that would work pretty well," I said. "Let them take each other out."

"Excellent," Mum agreed. "The trouble is, the peas and potatoes and petunias get caught in the cross fire."

"It's Rob's fault," Lydia said. "He said he wanted a house with a garden. Then he discovered he hated gardening."

"We could have told you that," Dad said. "He made that same discovery in this very house every spring."

Lydia grinned. "What about Charley?"

"Charley—" Dad chuckled, a touch nervously, and I saw him make that quick spontaneous mental revision we all have to make sometimes when we talk about Charley outside the family. Charley's patch of childhood garden was always insanely beautiful, but that was because every year he neglected to plant anything for weeks and then read out *The Secret Garden* in a fit of remorse. "He wasn't much for gardening either. In fact, I don't think Charley saw much of the outside of the house at all, from his vantage point behind a book. He probably couldn't even describe it."

"The old tree," I said, despite myself. It felt like a betrayal of our childhood not to mention the tree. "He could tell you about the tree."

"Right, of course," Dad agreed. "You used to climb that thing all the time when you were little. I don't think you played in it much after Charley started school, though."

"Well," I said. "Charley and I didn't play together much at all after he started school."

"It's a shame he's not here now," Lydia said, too casually. "Why isn't he, Rob? Did it have anything to do with what happened the other night?"

I gave her a warning look, which she returned innocently. "No. Of course not. He had somewhere he needed to be, that's all. I don't know details. He's organizing a conference, apparently."

It was all, strictly speaking, true.

"Do you hate gardening as well, Lydia?" Mum cut in. Clearly, without knowing details, she had detected dangerous ground. "Or does your poor wasteland hold some hope of salvation?"

Lydia seemed distracted by the question, but I knew her too well to relax. "I don't know, really. I don't know anything about them— my mum wouldn't let any of us near the garden at home in case we killed the tomatoes. I thought I'd give it a try now that the evenings are getting longer, but I don't know where to start."

"I can show you what I've done, if you'd like," Dad offered. "See if we can work out what's salvageable."

"I'm sure Lydia can work it out for herself, Joe," Mum said.

"No, I'd love to see it," Lydia said. I shot her a look; it was probably true that she would, given that our garden was exactly as described, but she sounded once again a little too innocent.

I stood as Lydia and Dad left, and wandered over to the bookshelf. When I was little, it had stood in my parents' room; at some point they moved it out, I think so that Charley wouldn't go into their bedroom looking for the Dickens, and now it spanned the wall by the hearth. There were more books upstairs, of course, but these were the favorites. *David Copperfield* sat next to *Great Expectations* on the middle shelf; on the bottom shelf, with some of our other children's books, were two of the Millie Radcliffe-Dix Adventures. Perhaps I needed to read those as well.

Mum watched me from the couch, a slight smile on her face. Her gold hair, streaked with silver now, glinted in the sun. "Bring back memories?"

"I don't think I read many of these." I had read quite a bit growing up, but I'd been oddly furtive about it. It happens, when your little brother is onto Dostoyevsky while you're struggling to tackle *The Hobbit.* Even as an adult, I'd never read Dickens, because a little voice in my head always whispered that it was too hard for me. I was a reasonably respected lawyer in one of the best firms in the city, and I still heard it.

I think Mum understood this. She drew her feet up onto the couch, and rested her chin in her hand. "I know we covered the bottom shelf. Do you remember when I used to read you both *A Lion in the Meadow?*"

I did have to smile at that. "I think every child in the country remembers being read *A Lion in the Meadow.* That, and *Maui and the Sun*, and *Hairy Maclary from Donaldson's Dairy.*"

The yellow picture book was sitting there, next to *The Cat in the Hat.* In the story, a little boy tells his mother there's a lion in the meadow. She thinks he's making up a story, so she makes up one of her own. She gives him a matchbox, and tells him there's a dragon inside it that will scare off the lion. But it turns out to be true, and the dragon grows too big.

"That's the danger of stories," Mum said. Lydia and I weren't the only ones thinking about Charley, obviously. "They bring things into the world, and they can't be put away again."

"It all works out for the best," I said. "The boy and the lion become friends. The dragon stays where it is, and nobody minds."

"The boy, his mother, and the lion don't," Mum said. "I don't know how the dragon felt about it."

If I'm strictly honest, and not feeling sorry for myself, I don't really think that our mother cares more about Charley than she does about me. But he belongs to her, and I belong more or less to Dad. We felt that instinctively in childhood; it solidified when she was the one to go with Charley to his first few years at Oxford, when he was too young to go on his own. If he takes after anyone in our family, he takes after her—though I've inherited her temper. We spent my adolescence in some impressively blazing arguments.

"About Charley—" I began.

"Yes," she said immediately. "Where is he?"

I ignored the question—or, more precisely, I avoided it. I'm good at that, apparently. "Did you never wonder how it is that he can do what he does?"

She frowned. "What do you mean?"

"He—" I lowered my voice, though I knew it couldn't carry outside. "He fabricates living characters out of words and meaning. It's impossible."

"It's always been impossible," she said. "I don't recall you ever questioning it before."

"I'm not questioning it, exactly. I just—when I was growing up, I just accepted it. Then he was away overseas for so long—it was part of our childhood, that was all. It almost felt like something I'd imagined—the way we used to play pirates by the old tree. But since he's come back—"

"What's he done?" Mum said. Her eyes, blue like mine and Dad's, had narrowed suspiciously.

"Nothing." She wouldn't believe this, of course. "Well. There was Uriah Heep last week—"

"Oh, for God's sake." She shook her head. "I thought it was something, from Lydia's question. I suppose it could be worse. If he could just learn to *want* to suppress it..."

I don't like what it says about me that even now, fully grown and in the midst of disaster, I liked it when Charley was in trouble and not me. "He says he does."

"No, he says he *tries* to suppress it. He believes he *should* suppress it, for his own sake and most of all for ours. Not the same thing. Really, he wants to exercise his power very badly. And as long as he wants to, incidents will keep happening."

"But why can they happen at all? I assume it has to do with how advanced he always was."

She shrugged. "Oh, not necessarily. There are a lot of intelligent, precocious children—even at Charley's level. We met more than a few ourselves, over the years, raising him. There's no recorded evidence of precocity giving them the power to read things out of books."

"There's no recorded evidence of *Charley* having the power to read things out of books," I pointed out. "We saw to that."

"That's true." She sat forward in her seat and put her mug on the coffee table. "Rob—this might not be any of my business, but what does Lydia know or suspect?"

"Nothing. I mean—Charley called me up in the middle of the night to help catch Uriah Heep, so she knew something was wrong. She has no idea that something was David Copperfield's metaphorical shadow self."

"He needs to stay away from psychoanalytic theory," she said absently. "It always was a weakness. If Lydia *does* need to know about him, you know—"

"She doesn't," I interrupted. My stomach had tensed. "Why would she?"

"You're all but married to her. You must be intending to tell her sometime."

"I'm not, in fact. Why should she have to know?"

"You can't expect her to marry you and not know. It's a part of this family."

"It wouldn't be if he could just keep it under control. He could, you know. We all have things we want to do, and just *don't*. You said it yourself: he doesn't try hard enough."

"I didn't exactly say that," she said. "But I'm not talking about him right now—"

"Yes, you are. We wouldn't be talking about Lydia if it weren't for him. She wouldn't have questions about him if he weren't here providing them."

"But he is, and he is what he is, and there's no way around it. That's why you won't tell Lydia, isn't it? You're still hoping that Charley will grow into being an *acceptable* version of unusual—rather brilliant, but not actually given to bending the laws of reality—and you can have a normal life with a career and family without having to deal with Sherlock Holmes coming to visit."

Said out loud, even as sympathetically as my mother said it, it sounded stupid. "I'm trying to protect her. Charley too—it's dangerous for *anyone* to know what he can do, even Lydia, you've always said—but mostly her."

"I'd rather nobody knew," she conceded. "But you and Lydia have been together a long time now. I trust her if you do, and I know you do. And as for protecting her—from what? What Charley can do is maddening and nonsensical and inconvenient, but it isn't often dangerous."

Not until now. If we were right, it had become so in the last few days. I wasn't only protecting Lydia from the truth anymore. I might actually need to protect her life.

I fell back into the argument I would have given last week, before Uriah Heep. It still held true, at the deepest level. "If she knows, one of two things happens. She can't accept it, and I've lost her. Or she *can* accept it, or at least will try to accept it, and I've brought her into something strange and chaotic that she'll have to live with and keep secret for the rest of her life. Either way, it ruins everything."

"You can't keep trying to live in a fantasy world where everything's normal, Rob. You'll break in two."

I laughed, despite myself. "*I'm* the one accused of trying to live in a fantasy world?"

"Fantasy is relative," Mum said, with a wry smile.

"It wasn't far from my life, you know, when Charley was overseas. At least if he was summoning anything then, I didn't know about it." I sighed, just once. I knew how the question would sound, but I couldn't resist asking. "Why did he come back?"

"He got a job here."

"That's an effect, not a cause. He's brilliant. He could have got a job anywhere."

"I presume he wanted one here, where he could see us more often. Your father and I wanted him here where we could see him more often as well, I'm afraid. Did you really never miss him, the ten years or so he was in England?"

"I suppose so," I said uncomfortably. Of course I did. Things were simpler when he wasn't around, but that didn't mean I didn't feel the gap he left behind. "I didn't really know him anymore."

She rolled her eyes—another trait I've inherited from her. "You lived with him until you left home. You know him fairly well. And from someone who lived with him a few years longer, he didn't change that much in the intervening years."

"We weren't particularly close in the couple of years before I left home either."

"I know." Her face turned thoughtful—even wistful. "You know, we've often wondered if we made a huge mistake sending you two to high school together. Your father and I, I mean. We've asked ourselves if everything that went wrong between the two of you since couldn't have been avoided if we'd just made sure you weren't ever in the same classrooms."

I didn't know what to say. "We're okay," I settled on, awkwardly.

"You're both magnificent," she agreed. "But we wonder all the same. We had our reasons for doing it, which felt sound at the time. Mostly, though, we thought he'd be better where you could look after him. And that wasn't fair to either of you, especially you. I should have remembered that teenagers have enough problems of their own to deal with."

I could hear Dad and Lydia outside. They wouldn't be gone much longer: the garden isn't that big. And I still didn't have an answer to what I had really wanted to ask. "I was just wondering where he came from, that was all."

"Where he came from?" She was looking at me seriously now. "What exactly are you asking?"

What, indeed? "He just—it seems to come out of nowhere. All of it: the reading, the abilities... I know you keep telling me to stop pretending we're normal in this family, but really, apart from Charley, we are. He doesn't even look like us."

"It doesn't matter. He's still part of this family."

"I know!" I heard my own voice sounding defensive, and realized it was because Mum's was accusatory. More accusatory, perhaps, than my comment had warranted. "I wasn't trying to disown him. I'm not a monster—he's my brother. I care about him; I'm not trying to wish him away. I was just... wondering what might have caused him to be so different."

"Who says anything needs to have caused it? Why can't he just be an anomaly?"

"He can't be the only one," I said. "He just can't be."

"Why not?"

I knew why not, of course: because Uriah Heep said he wasn't. It was difficult to justify without that piece of information, and I wasn't quite ready to give it.

"Well," Mum said, when no answer was forthcoming. Her voice was back to normal. "You know your family on your dad's side. If any of them resemble Charley in any way, ordinary or extraordinary, they're keeping it very well hidden. My parents died before you or Charley was born, but I can assure you that they looked nothing like him, and I never saw them exhibit any signs of otherworldly abilities—or unusual intellect, for that matter. He might not be the only one of his kind in the world, but I suspect he's the only one we'll ever know. And that's probably a good thing. I don't think the city can hold too many more of him, do you?"

I managed a smile. "I doubt it." The back door opened; I recognized the creak, and the barking of dogs. I glanced back at the shelves. "By the way, can I borrow a few of these books?"

The sun was setting by the time we drove back to Wellington. The road hugged the long, sinuous curves of the coastline, and the waves glinted white and gold. Reflected in the water, the houses were beginning to glow with warm yellow lights.

"Whatever you're waiting for the opportune moment to say," Lydia said conversationally, "now's your moment. I've been up at five every morning this week—four that night Charley called. I'd prefer to get the armed confrontation out of the way before we get home so we can have dinner, watch a film, and get an early night."

"Fair enough." I'd been trying not to have the kind of argument that ends in fuming, silent driving for fifty kilometers, but I could accommodate. "What on earth was that all about?"

"What on earth was what?"

"You know what. You were trying to get information out of my parents about Charley."

"Well, it doesn't work trying to get information out of *you* about Charley. At least your parents don't pretend he doesn't exist."

"I don't pretend he doesn't exist."

"Rob, I was dating you for six months before I found out you even had a brother. You do so pretend he doesn't exist. That's why you don't talk about him. And Charley doesn't talk about himself around you because he isn't sure how much you *want* him to exist. This I worked out a long time ago. It isn't even disputable."

"He talks about himself."

"Not to me. Not about things I want to know."

I didn't have the emotional or intellectual fortitude to decide how true any of this was, and certainly didn't have the desire. I'd been up early this week too. "So did my parents tell you what you wanted to know?"

"No," she said, unabashed. "Not even when I cornered your dad outside. He gave me excellent tips about the passion fruit, though. You're doing it all wrong."

"I bet I am." I sighed. "My family's not like yours, Lydia. Yours is big, loud, and cheerful, and I can't keep track of all your cousins. Mine is just the four of us, plus a single set of grandparents and one unmarried aunt on my father's side, and we've been weird since Charley was born."

"I sort of thought *I* was part of your family."

"You're the normal part."

"How dare you." She glanced at me sideways. "Don't try to tell me this is nothing, Rob. I may not be a lawyer, but I know when people are hiding something. This is serious, isn't it?"

Serious. She asked the same thing about us, in exactly those terms, after we'd been dating six months. I don't have Charley's passion for words, but that one hadn't felt right to me. Our relationship—whatever it was that was unfurling between us—wasn't serious. It was important, momentous, wondrous. "Serious" sounded like something terminal. It was a word for ending, not beginning.

"It's serious," I conceded. "But I promise you, it has nothing to do with you. It's something I'm working out. I'll put it right, and it'll be forgotten. Please, just trust me."

"I do trust you. But you're wrong. If it has to do with you, it has to do with me. That's how this works."

"It'll be over soon," I said. "I promise."

I meant it—or, more precisely, I meant to make sure it was true. After dinner, after we'd watched an old film and Lydia had finally gone to bed, I sat down at the old computer out in the living room.

Eva had sent through Eric Umble's CV, as she'd promised. I opened it and skimmed, but nothing stood out. He'd moved from London in his last year of high school, he'd been through the School of Law, his grades were just spectacular enough to get him a job without rousing suspicion. It was a fabrication from start to finish, but there was no way of proving it—if I wanted to, I could try calling his references, but whoever summoned him would probably have covered that possibility. Anyway, I didn't want him exposed as a fraud. I wanted to find the summoner. More than anything, I wanted to find him by normal means, before Charley and Millie did something suicidally dangerous.

The next thing I opened was the Prince Albert University home page. I would begin with the individual pages of the academic staff;

when I ran out of those, I had access to student records. Well, to be strictly accurate, my brother had access, but I'd had his passwords for as long as I could remember. What I'd told Mum was right: we'd kept any sign of Charley's abilities out of the records. What we hadn't kept out of the records was how advanced he was, almost from the day he was born. It seemed far too much of a coincidence to think that the two weren't linked—perhaps that was even how the summoner had found him. Surely the records of the summoner, whoever he was, would show the same.

It was going to be another long night. Fortunately, I had a very large mug of coffee.

Before I started, I sent another e-mail, this one a request for an electronic copy of a birth certificate. I did it quickly, trying hard not to think about it too much. It felt uncomfortable—childish, even—trying to find out if your younger brother was adopted. But it occurred to me, for the first time, that I had not actually been there at Charley's birth; I couldn't even, racking the memories of my four-year-old self, swear that Mum had ever been pregnant. He didn't look anything like us. And unlike Lydia, I *am* a lawyer. I also know when somebody isn't telling the whole truth. There was something in Mum's evasions as I spoke to her today when I had mentioned how little Charley resembled us that reminded me a little too much of my own when I spoke to Lydia. Mine were guided by Charley's secrets, and my own guilt. I needed to know what guided hers.

XIII

We were sitting down to dinner the following evening when Charley called. We assumed it was telemarketers, and Lydia and I did our usual quick rock-paper-scissors to see who would have to deal with them. When she answered the phone, still shooting me a glare (she *always* does rock), I saw her face go to mingled relief and surprise.

"Oh, hello, Charley...No, no, that's fine...Very well, thank you. How are you?...Yes, he's here. I'll get him." She held out the phone to me, her eyebrows raised. "It's your brother. Are you going to be leaving again?"

"I hope not," I said, but my heart sank, and I knew I was.

Lydia must have suspected too. She had not missed the fact that I had been on edge all day; I had made that impossible.

"He said he was fine" was all she said.

"He's never fine," I said. "He spent the first twenty minutes of his life dead, for God's sake."

"Nobody spends the first twenty minutes of their life dead," Lydia said firmly. "Not without serious brain damage. It's a medical impossibility."

"I rest my case." I took the phone from her, and braced myself. It might be a relief, at least, to have the waiting over.

"I wish you'd tell Lydia what's going on," Charley said, before I even spoke. "She must think I'm a complete basket case, ringing you up all the time and pulling you away."

"You *are* a complete basket case," I said. Lydia, listening from the table, shot me another glare. I waved at her to keep eating. "What's up? I tried to call you this morning; you didn't answer."

"It's a little strange," Charley said. "The building in question is an office—one floor is for rent, which is where Uriah says we'll find the summoner. We've watched it all day, though, and nobody's come in or out who couldn't be accounted for. The offices have stayed empty. The Implied Reader has been watching it since the shops closed down on Lambton Quay."

"Who?"

"You know. The man with no face. But he hasn't seen anyone in the building at all."

"Well, no," I said. "He doesn't have *eyes*." Lydia's look this time was rather more startled.

"He can still see," Charley said, as if I were being very dense. "He wouldn't be much of a reader if he couldn't see. Anyway, Millie and I are going to walk down and check it out late tonight—perhaps eleven o'clock. I thought you might like to meet us there, or outside the Street. I mean, you don't have to."

I was wrong. It wasn't a relief at all. "Wait—where are you now?"

"At the Street. Or just outside it—it doesn't get cell phone reception, obviously. Darcy Two had to wait outside it all day with a phone in case the person watching the house called. He didn't mind, except that he wasted most of the batteries playing Candy Crush."

"You've been there all day?"

"Well, yes. Where else would I be? It's Sunday; I don't have teaching. And this is a bit more important than getting my chapter on Conan Doyle finished—though Beth might not agree." I heard another voice in the background. "Just a second—are you coming? Eleven o'clock?"

"I'll be there," I said. I had to be, didn't I? God knows what would happen if I wasn't. It would probably happen anyway, to be honest, but I at least needed to be there for it.

Wellington is not often dead. One of the things that had drawn me to it was how unrelentingly alive it was. It's difficult to walk down the street without people waving at you, music from buskers grabbing your attention, the wind tearing at your clothes to make sure you know it's there. At eleven at night on a Sunday, even the weather was quiet. I parked my car, and walked the near-empty streets to the Left Bank Arcade. The area around the alley was dark, and completely deserted.

Almost deserted. A tiny little girl sat against the wall; she would have come barely past my knee standing up, and her legs, crossed neatly under her blue dress, were thin as matchsticks. A massive hardcover lay open in front of her, and she held a covered mug cupped in her hands as she read by flashlight. Her dark hair fell forward, and her small, pale face was utterly absorbed. At first, I thought she looked familiar because she looked startlingly like my brother at the same age. Then I realized, and despite everything I couldn't help but smile.

"Hi," I said to her. "Matilda Wormwood, right?"

She looked up and smiled back politely. "How do you do, Mr. Sutherland?"

"Pretty good, thanks." I sat down next to her on the concrete. "What're you up to this late at night?"

"I'm on lookout," she said. "We're on alert. They tug the cable inside when they want to come out; I tug back if it's safe. If Huck Finn sees anything, he calls me on the phone, and I go inside to tell them in person. I like this time of night. It's quiet. Millie says it's all right if I read my book."

"You live on the Street?"

"Yes." Her face lit up. "I love it. I was homeless for years before, which was still an improvement on living with my family in my book, but this is so much better. I never knew there were so many of us. We can actually be secret here, and safe. I've always wanted to live in a Dickens novel, anyway."

"You wouldn't rather find a family to raise you, like Millie did?"

"I don't grow like Millie," she said. "Someone found me on the streets a few weeks after I came out of my book, and they tried placing me with a foster family. It was nice, at first—well, not nice, but they looked after me. They were going to send me to school. But then they started to be afraid of me. They said I didn't talk like a four-year-old—which was true, but I didn't know how. I moved things with my eyes sometimes, when I couldn't help it. And I didn't grow. They started to punish me, and talk about asking Child Services to take me away. I was scared that if they did tests to find why I didn't age, they'd find I wasn't real. I didn't know what would happen then. So I ran away." She smiled at my face. "It's all right, truly. I can look after myself. I'd like to go to a university, though. Charley says he'll get me into the distance-learning courses, if Dorian can get me a fake school transcript."

"I bet he will." A memory struck me. "That book wouldn't happen to be from the university library, would it?"

She looked worried. "I know I don't have a library card, but I can't get one without proof of identity and address. It isn't like in my book. I take them back after two weeks."

"It doesn't bother me," I assured her. "Take the whole library. I was just wondering if you'd ever run past my brother there. Very quickly?"

"I might have," she said. "Usually nobody goes into the stack room. When they do, I run away very fast."

"And you slam the door shut...?"

"With my eyes," she said. "Yes."

"Good for you." Well. I had been sort of right. It had indeed been a very small child in the stack room. It wouldn't surprise me one bit if she had read volume two of *The Decline and Fall of the Roman Empire* either. "Have you seen Millie and my brother?"

Matilda tugged on the cable beside her, and very shortly afterward Millie and Charley stepped through. I hadn't seen anyone come through the wall before. It looked eerie in the dark, as though they had melted into existence from the brick. Everything looks a little more eerie in the dark.

"Oh, good," Millie said. Her hair was out this time, and hung in corkscrew curls to her shoulders. She was wearing a green trench coat with voluminous pockets. Just with that, I could see the adventuress. "You're here. Ready for some breaking and entering?"

"Hopefully just entering," Charley said. He must have seen my face. "Not breaking."

"Oh, something's bound to break tonight," Millie returned. "A law. A window. The foundations of reality."

"The day," Charley suggested with a smile. "That will break. Eventually."

Me. I didn't say it, but I thought it. I was going to break.

It was just down the street from my work. We walked down the familiar street, past the storefronts with their expressionless mannequins and exotic soaps glistening in the lights, past the trees, which rustled overhead as birds settled for the night, past the closed doors of the coffee shop that saved my life most midmornings. Lambton Quay looked deeper and softer in the night, as though an outer shell had been removed.

I had been intending to persuade them not to break into an office building, even one empty and ready for lease. I knew how to persuade. I had persuaded judges, juries, and clients; on a very good day, I had even persuaded Lydia. When I saw the building in question, all arguments fled from my head.

"It can't be here," was what I said instead. "It can't."

"Why not?" Millie asked, genuinely curious.

"I work here," I answered her. "I work down the road from here. This is Lambton Quay." I couldn't quite put into words what I meant. "The Supreme Court is just down the road. Parliament is at the far end. This is all shop-front windows and offices. The summoner can't be here. It's not possible. It's not *allowed*."

"They might not be here," Charley said. I didn't like the anxious reassurance in his voice. It suggested he had picked up what I was trying to hide in mine. "We've based this on the word of Uriah Heep. He's hardly reliable."

"But you think he is here."

"Yes," Charley said reluctantly. "I think so. I think Uriah truly does know where his counterpart lives. And I don't think Uriah would lie, when it's so much more entertaining to send us into danger."

I looked at the building. It was late Victorian, probably, painted soft gray and set with ornate windows. The lower level, as with all the buildings along this way, had been gutted and replaced with a modern storefront. In this case, it was a clothing shop, with mannequins in the windows clad in summer dresses. At this time of night the models looked like ghosts behind the glass panes. The floors above had been converted to offices, according to the sign advertising them for lease. It was a lovely building, in a beautiful part of the city.

"They're up there, apparently," Millie said, following my eyes. "Though goodness knows how. Something else to find out."

"Just how do you plan to get in?" I asked. "It may be the second level you want, but the street level is a high-end shop. They're not easy to break into."

"I thought about this, actually," Charley said. "Just a second. This might not work." In the dark, I saw him open his backpack and pull out a thin green hardcover. "Um—has anyone got a flashlight?"

I was about to offer my phone, but Millie had one, of course. She whipped it from a pocket faster than a sharpshooter goes for a pistol in a duel.

"Here you are," she said. She clicked it, and gave it to him. "And I have a box of matches as well. Just in case."

"Thanks," Charley said. He started to read.

A few seconds later, there was a door in the glass plating. Its green paint was peeling, and it was overgrown with vines.

Charley exhaled with a sigh. "There. I'm not so good with objects—it's hard to find one significant enough to connect to. I was practicing that all last night."

"It's jolly useful," Millie said. "Well done. Where's it from?"

"*The Secret Garden*," he said. "And before you ask, I made sure I brought out the key as well."

Racks of designer clothing and spindly mannequins make a terrifying forest at night. I was glad to go up the stairs behind the counter to the second floor, which the light of Millie's flashlight revealed to house a perfectly ordinary open-plan office waiting for an occupant. The circle of Millie's flashlight, darting distractingly over the room, revealed nothing more incriminating than the odd yellowing phone book or mound of dust. It had the sweet, stale smell of a secondhand shop.

"I'll bet this is frightfully expensive for what it is," Millie said. "Central-city office space is at a premium these days."

"I like the view," Charley offered. "The side that looks through to the harbor, not the Lambton Quay side that overlooks the McDonald's."

"You're not here to buy it," I reminded them. "Is this what you were looking for?"

"Not quite," Millie said. "I think I was expecting something a little more like a smugglers' cave. I suppose they could have taken everything with them when they left. If the summoner puts characters back into books when they're not required..."

"Eric doesn't go back into his book," I said, against my better judgment. "Not according to Uriah Heep. And he told me he was living nearby. With friends, he said."

That could have been a lie, of course. I was used to being lied to in my line of work. But it hadn't felt like that. He had almost been asking for help.

There was enough light coming from Lambton Quay to make out shapes in the dark; the cubicle nearest me was lit by the yellowing electric glow of a streetlight. It was probably that alone that made me look at it. When I saw it, my immediate temptation was to hurry them out before either of them saw it too.

"Charley?" I said instead. "Why does this book have your name on it?"

A hardcover sat propped on the edge of an otherwise-empty shelf. A thick book, white letters on a green spine. *Dickens's Criminal Underworld*, by Charles Sutherland.

"Because it's mine," Charley replied. He said it slowly, almost hesitantly. "It's my first book. It originated in my PhD thesis. I don't... what could it be doing here?"

I remembered it now. He'd been nineteen. He'd already coauthored a book called *Dickens as Author* (I remember, because what kind of title is that?) and published a handful of papers, but this was his first glossy critical book all to himself. The copy I'd been given had seemed to glow with pride. This copy looked battered by repeated use. The dustcover had come off, leaving it naked and balding around the corners.

"Pick it up," Millie urged Charley.

"I don't understand," Charley said. He ran his hand gently over the cover, then tentatively picked it up. I half expected the world to shiver, but of course it didn't. It was only a book.

"Did the summoner leave it here?" I asked.

"Maybe." Charley let the cover fall open in his hands. "I just don't—"

And then, just like that, Charley and Millie were gone. No flare of light, no breath of air. I was alone in the room. No. Not alone. Something was in there with me.

Something spilled from the book, and now blanketed the entire room. I could see it, and feel it: a smoky haze in the air, a clammy chill on my skin. But more than that, I could *sense* it, on the level that dogs whimper at thunderstorms and cats are beside themselves in terror after an earthquake. I'd never been sensitive to earthquakes or thunderstorms; according to Lydia, I sleep through both, quite happily. I was sensitive to this.

"Charley?" I called.

My chest felt squeezed in a vise; my limbs were weak and shaky. I understood now what it meant to be beside yourself with terror. My soul was trying to leap from my body. I could hear my own voice screaming at me, and it was someone far away. Get out, it was screaming. *Get out.*

I couldn't leave. Charley had disappeared; I had to find him, and Millie too. I couldn't leave the building. But I couldn't stay either. I couldn't *breathe.*

I was in a perfectly modern office building, in the middle of central Wellington. My own office was a few doors down. There was nothing uncanny here. There couldn't be. This wasn't my brother's world. It was mine. All we'd done was open a book.

It was at that point that my phone rang.

I fumbled for it in my coat pocket. I didn't recognize the number. "Hello?"

"Hey, Rob." It was Charley. "Are you still in the building?"

"Of course I'm still in the building! Where are you? Whose phone are you using?"

"Millie's—I left mine at home. I'm right outside. Come out—I put the door up again for you."

"Don't move until I get there," I told him. I tried to pretend it was for his benefit, and not because, at that moment, I needed him more than he had ever needed me.

The fog was all the way down the stairs, through the designer boutique on the ground floor. I had to stop in the middle of the stairwell to double over and wait for a flood of nausea to pass. I could see Charley outside on the pavement once I was in the shop, but the city outside looked as though I was seeing it through a heat haze.

The green *Secret Garden* door was there, as Charley had said. I wrenched it open and all but collapsed into the street. The cool air and streetlights caught me like a safety net. At once, the disorientation dissolved.

Charley's face lit when he saw me.

"*There* you are!" he exclaimed, as though I was the one who had disappeared. "Are you all right?"

I didn't choose to answer this. I wasn't at all sure I was. "Where were you?" I demanded. "You just vanished!"

"I'm sorry." His face dimmed. I don't know why I sounded so angry. I had actually never been more pleased to see him in my life, and for some reason that infuriated me. "It must be like the wall into the Street. It took Millie and I, but not you. It took me a while to find the way back out, or I would have—"

"The way out of where? Where have you been?"

"I'll show you. It should work the same as the wall, even if—do you want to give me your hand?"

"There isn't anywhere to go. It's just a building. A building filled with smoke."

"It's not. It's quicker if you let me show you. I don't know how much time we have. Millie's gone on ahead to explore."

I didn't want to be shown anything. I wanted to go home. I don't know what I had been prepared for, but it wasn't this. The foundations of my reality had been shaken too much already this week; one more tremor could bring them crashing down entirely.

Charley offered his hand. I took it.

Hand in hand, we stepped through the ivy-covered door, and for the second time that week I found myself in another world.

My first impression was that we had traveled back in time. I felt a wave of vertigo as I stepped over the threshold, and the shop was gone; in its place, an old Victorian building blossomed around me. It seemed to correspond to the framework of the modern shop—I recognized the cornices from upstairs, and the wooden staircase was in the same place as the stairwell I had come down moments ago. Charley's green door was still mounted in the middle of the wall, but the glass storefront had been replaced by a single, dust-streaked window. I think some of the yellow light streaming through was still from the streetlight, but I couldn't be sure.

We couldn't have gone back in time. In the nineteenth century, the city was still a fledgling colonial settlement; this building would still be new, if it existed at all. We stood in a derelict. Even the air was too cold, and heavy with fog. Like the Street, it could have come from the pages of a Dickens novel.

Besides, there were the books.

The walls were covered with books. They were everywhere, teetering up to the ceiling in wobbly piles—paperbacks, hardbacks, reference books, pocket books. I had seen such a concentration of books in one place only, and that was in my brother's house.

"It's incredible," Charley said, "isn't it?"

That wouldn't have quite been my word. "What is it?"

"It's the interior of Fagin's house in *Oliver Twist*. The house where he keeps his gang of criminal youths, where he hides his treasure under the floorboards. From what we can tell so far, it overlays the entire Lambton Quay building, upstairs and down."

"It's a reading?"

"A very precisely shaped reading. It's—you know when you read about a character's house, but it's only half-described, so you fill in the blanks with memories of a house you've lived in instead? It's a little like that. It's a reading of Fagin's house, influenced just enough by this building to fit inside it. But, Rob—I don't think this was read directly from *Oliver Twist*. I think it was read from my critical analysis of *Oliver Twist*, in my book."

"This came out of that book we found? Your book?"

"When I opened it. It was waiting."

"But you didn't read it out."

"No. The summoner had already done that. This is why we can't sense where it is, the way we can the Street. It's not here, most of the time. It's hiding, waiting to come out."

"Like a picture in a pop-up book?"

Charley actually laughed, the kind of laugh that comes from a bubble of excitement bursting. "Yes. Just like a picture in a pop-up book. When you open the book, the reading is released. Only it's not quite real yet. It's a step ahead of the Street. The Street exists, but just outside of the real world. This overlays reality, but it's insubstantial. Millie and I can enter it—we can't not—but you couldn't even see it."

"I saw something," I said grimly. And I had felt it. I had nearly thrown up.

"But the pop-up book," Millie said. She was standing on the stair-case, her flashlight still in hand. "How was that done?"

"I suppose you could trap an interpretation before you've realized it," Charley said. "Like biting back a word that's on the tip of your tongue. You could form a thought, and not frame it. And perhaps it would then be trapped in the pages of the book, ready to come to life. But I have no idea how you'd go about doing that deliberately. The degree of control it would take...not even control, the degree of understanding..."

"You're actually happy, aren't you?" I said.

He caught himself. "I'm not happy about what it's being used for. I'm not happy at all, exactly. It's only the scope of what's been done here. It's exciting. I'm just—"

"Excited?"

"I'm sorry. Sometimes I forget not to be."

"Both of you need to come upstairs," Millie interrupted. Her face was unusually grim. "Charley, you need to see this. I think I've found where your intern sleeps, Rob."

The staircase we had climbed in the real world, only minutes before, was now dark and dangerously rickety underfoot. It turned twice in a very small space, leading out to a low-ceilinged room that had never seen office furniture in its life. Inside were three rough beds, made of old sacks stuffed with paper and straw. Dried crusts of bread and orange peel peeked from the folds in the blankets as they might in the nest of a burrowing animal. That explained at least some of the smell. I wasn't sure I wanted an explanation for all of it.

"It's as Uriah said," Charley said. The excitement had died from his face. "The summoner keeps them here unless they're being used, or put back in their books."

"Like tools," I said. "Or portable devices."

"The windows are barred," Millie said. "Had you noticed? And the door to this room was bolted from the outside. You can see Lambton Quay out the window, with that haze upon it; that must be what Uriah saw through Eric."

These windows, unlike the one downstairs, had been rubbed clean. I saw the clean, well-lit streets, the trees that line the center, the elec-tric glow of bookshops and boutiques and the McDonald's further down, and felt sick.

"'We talk about the tyranny of words,'" Charley said, "'but we like to tyrannize over them too.'"

"That sounds like Dickens," I said.

"It's *David Copperfield*. Except he didn't quite mean this."

"And those are the words over there," Millie said, with another sweep of her flashlight.

There they were. As below, the room was crowded with books, ringing the walls like a surrounding army. And anything could come out of any one of them.

"It's an arsenal," I said.

"It's a jolly impressive one," Millie said.

"We need to get out of here," I said. "Right now."

"Quick look," Millie said briskly. "Then we'll go."

Charley moved toward the closest wall of books. His fingers trailed the spines and sent a whisper of dust into the air. "The Dickens novels are over here," he said. "At least, a few of them."

I found more Dickens, as Millie scanned her flashlight along the wall. They were a mixture of paperback and hardback, clearly bought at different times from different places, and clearly well thumbed—nothing like the pristine bound set that I'd grown up with.

"There are some other Victorian novels over here too," Charley said. "The rest are just a mixture. A lot of crime novels."

The title on one of the spines caught my attention. I pulled out the *The Hound of the Baskervilles* and threw it to Charley. "I recognize *this* one," I said grimly.

He balanced the spine in his hand, letting it fall open where the pages naturally parted. "It's earmarked here. Look at that."

Part of the text was underlined in pencil on the page. I didn't bother to read it, because on the opposite page was a full-color illustration of a monstrous creature. Its gaping mouth glowed, and flames wreathed its head. I'd seen it before, when it attacked my brother's flat. It was now living in his kitchen.

"Is that Henry?" Millie asked, her eyebrow raised as she peered over his shoulder. "I must say I prefer him the way he is now."

"So do I," Charley said ruefully. He closed the book. "Well, we've confirmed who sent Henry. That doesn't really help much, but it's something."

"We've seen this place too," Millie said. She looked with disgust at the mildewed walls. "What a frightful hole. If there's nothing else, we need to put a stop to this person keeping characters here. We're not tools or . . . playthings for their amusement."

But there *was* something else. We were downstairs, almost out the door, when it caught Millie's eye. "I say," she said. "What's that?"

"It doesn't matter," I said. I'd begun to relax, knowing we were almost out again without anything untoward happening. I could feel reality tugging me back from the other side of the walls. "There's no time. We can't rely on the summoner being gone forever."

She ignored me, and stepped forward to investigate. Charley followed and so, after a moment's internal cursing, did I.

It was a trapdoor, in the far corner of the room. It stood out against the floorboards, and against the rest of the house: older, worn, scarred. Even closed, I could feel darkness yawning behind it.

"We're on the ground floor," Millie said. "This must go underground, to a cellar of some kind."

"This isn't from *Oliver Twist*," Charley said. He bent to touch it, then drew back his hand and folded his arms tightly instead. "At least, not directly. Perhaps it's metaphorical."

"A metaphorical underground cellar," Millie said. She ran her flashlight over the iron bolts that fastened it, then crouched down and took hold of one. "Very Jungian."

"You said Fagin kept treasure under the floorboards in *Oliver Twist*," I reminded him.

"Not through a trapdoor," Charley said. "Only in a small gap. But perhaps. It could be that. Or it's some kind of . . . I don't know, undertone. Something the summoner sees as lying beneath the narrative. Or it's just a trapdoor."

I didn't want to go down there. I knew that as strongly as I've ever known anything in my life. I opened my mouth to say something, anything, to stop Millie from opening that door. Charley spoke first.

"There's someone down there."

Millie turned, her hand still on the iron bar. "Really? Are you quite sure?"

"No." He was frowning at the door. "I don't see how I can be. But

I *feel* very strongly that there is. Sort of the way I could feel the Street was there, or you."

"I can feel the Street too," Millie said. "And the connection between us. I must say, I can't feel what you're talking about here."

"I think we need to get out of here," I said. "Honestly. Right now, if not sooner."

"You're rather nervous, aren't you?" Millie said curiously, turning her flashlight on me.

"Rob was trapped in a basement when he was six," Charley said absently. His attention was elsewhere. "And now he hates basements."

"That has nothing to do with it!" I felt unaccountably betrayed. "How do you know about that, anyway? You weren't even two."

"Well, we don't know what's under there," Millie said. She ran one hand over the pitted wooden trapdoor. "But it will probably be more of a cellar than a basement. Perhaps a dungeon."

I waved her flashlight beam away from my face. "My feelings have nothing to do with the basement, cellar, or dungeon. We've stepped outside reality. We've broken into a place that shouldn't exist. Someone could come for us at any time—Charley thinks that someone's already here. We can't go down there."

"I can," Millie said. She clapped me on the shoulder. "Buck up, Rob. We've come this far. Anyone down there must already know we're here; they'd have stopped us, if they wanted to or were in a position to do so. If we go quietly, I don't think we need to worry."

"This isn't a Millie Radcliffe-Dix Adventure," I said. "If you're caught, you're not going to be tied up in a toolshed, conveniently filled with sharp implements ready to use for escape. Whatever else the summoner is, he or she is a real person. I know what real people do to each other. It's not the sort of thing they put in children's books."

"I've lived in the real world for quite some time, Rob," Millie said. There was an edge in her voice. In the books, they called it "that fierce voice Vernon knew so well," and usually her eyes would be "blazing." They weren't doing so as literally as Heathcliff's, but I could confirm the word applied. "I grew up in foster homes—real ones, though those are usually jolly real in children's books as well. I heard things from other children. I read the newspapers. Don't think you can scare me."

"It's very dark down there," Charley said. I don't think he was listening to us. He was just stating a fact. "And cold. Whoever it is has been down there a long time."

"You're starting to worry me now," I said. "How do you know that? You're not psychic, you know. You just do a lot of very intense reading."

"I told you, I don't know." He blinked, and looked at me. "It's just coming through. Like snatches of voices in the wind."

"Well," Millie said. "We have a flashlight for the dark, if we think it's safe to use it. The rest we'll sort out as we go."

She drew back the bolts, and opened the door. It opened to utter darkness and a blast of cold air. Two steps leading down were visible, but nothing beyond.

"We'd better not risk the flashlight just yet," Millie said quietly. "Not if someone's down there. So one step at a time, and careful how you go."

She started down, Charley behind her. I followed, and the darkness swallowed me up.

I said my fear didn't have anything to do with the basement. And it didn't, in a literal sense. I was unnerved by underground spaces, not pathologically terrified. But the feeling of being trapped, of the familiar turning unknown and dangerous...those were all very recognizable from that day when I was six. Now they felt part of the space around me. The darkness was more than physical. I suppose Charley would say it was metaphorical.

The stairs were treacherous; they allowed very little opportunity to take stock of my surroundings until I was on the ground. Without Millie's flashlight, there was nothing to see. It was only when my feet left creaking wood and hit paved floor that I became aware of the whisper of the wind. And then, when I listened, I realized that it wasn't the wind at all.

It was a voice. A human voice was whispering in the dark. A man's voice, too broken for accent or personality. The words had the air of a litany, or a curse.

"...at twelve o'clock at night. It was remarked that the clock began to strike and I began to cry simultaneously. Chapter One. I am Born. Whether I shall turn out to be the hero of my own life, or whether that station will be held by anybody else, these pages must show. To begin my life with the beginning of my life..."

"David Copperfield," Charley said from beside me; I couldn't tell if he meant the name or the title. He said it very quietly, to himself rather than to us, but the cracked voice stopped.

Millie raised her voice. "Hello, there. Are you a prisoner?"

The silence lingered a moment longer, then the voice spoke. "It's you, isn't it?"

Millie frowned. "It's who?"

"Not you. Him. The one who spoke."

"That was me," Charley said. We were drowning in a sea of pronouns.

I heard a long, rattling sigh, as though a breeze had rushed through the rafters. It raised the hairs on the back of my neck, and stilled my tongue.

"I know you," the voice said. "I can touch your mind."

"I think I can touch yours as well," Charley said hesitantly. He took a step closer. "The way I can with Millie, sometimes. Did I read you out of your book?"

"I don't know," the voice said. "I don't know where I came from. I don't know where I am. All I know is the summoner, and you, and I've never seen your face."

"Have you seen the summoner's?"

"Oh yes," he said. "Yes, I have. It's a terrible face."

I heard a click, and then the flashlight flared and flickered over the room before finding the source of the voice. Millie was back in action.

The room was dank, and dark. Once again, the walls were ringed with pile after pile of books. Where the light settled, a man sat on a chair, bound and blindfolded. A prisoner, as Millie had said, dressed in Victorian garb now filthy and stained. Through his scraggly red-brown beard, the hollows of his cheeks were emaciated.

Millie, of course, recovered first. "I say. You poor thing. Hold on a tick—"

"Don't touch me!" the man said, and Millie stopped in the act of moving forward. "I can't be unbound. I can't see. I can't escape."

"But you must want to be rescued, surely?"

The man hesitated, as though encountering an entirely unfamiliar concept. "Rescued..."

Charley spoke up then. I could hear him trying to keep his voice quiet and steady. "You're David Copperfield, aren't you?"

"*David Copperfield*, by Charles Dickens," he said. His words fell back into the rhythm it had been repeating when we entered. "Chapter one. I am Born. Whether I—"

"'Shall turn out to be the hero of my own life, or whether that station will be held be anybody else, these pages must show,'" Charley finished. "Yes. That's right."

David Copperfield shook his bound head. "What does it mean?"

"It's the opening of a book. By Charles Dickens. It's the fictional autobiography of a young man named David Copperfield; Dickens based it partially on his own life."

"Uriah Heep's book," I said.

Charley didn't answer me. "I read it when I was four, I think. I started reading things out of books at four—summoning, you all call it. I might have made you, without being aware of what I was doing. It's the only reason I can think why we'd be able to sense each other. But that would mean you'd been here for years. Decades."

David Copperfield was silent for such a long time that I began to wonder if he could still hear us. His head was bowed, his dark, tousled hair falling forward around the blindfold. Then, at once, he straightened.

"You need to leave," he said. "He knows you're here now. It wasn't me; I don't know who told him. But he's coming for you."

My heart stopped.

Charley started beside me, as though his had done something similar. "The summoner?"

"Who is he?" Millie said quickly. "Can we find him?"

"I don't know who he is in your world—only who he is in ours, and that we can't tell you. I know his voice, and his face, and the feel of him in my head. I know he's taken possession of me, and twisted me. I know he means to destroy everything. I know he's been in your world for such a long time, waiting. I know he's coming, right now. Go."

"Come on," I said. My heart had started beating again, painfully fast to make up for lost time. "Quick."

"You have to come with us," Millie said to David Copperfield. "We can't leave you here."

Silence again, for an excruciating few seconds.

"Yes," he said abruptly. "Yes, please, take me with you. Quickly.

I—" His voice broke off in a sharp gasp that was almost a scream, and then he was gone. It was so quick, I almost missed the flare of light as he vanished.

A moment later, the trapdoor at the top of the stairs vanished too. Another flare of light, and then, despite Millie's flashlight, the darkness around us seemed deeper than ever.

"Oh dear," Millie said very quietly. "He's here."

XIV

We were trapped. There was no way out. My brain told me that, over and over again, as Millie instructed Charley and me to stay put, as she mounted the stairs quickly toward the ceiling where the door had been moments ago, as Charley and I waited in the foul-smelling dark. The air seemed too thick to breathe.

"I'm so sorry," Charley said to me quietly.

I didn't say anything. My throat had constricted with fear. I was perfectly willing to let Charley mistake it, as usual, for anger.

"I could put the *Secret Garden* door back," Charley said as Millie drew close. "We could still get out that way."

"I wouldn't risk it," she said. "The summoner's coming. He knows we're here."

"He might be some distance away," Charley said. "I would have to be close by to reach out and read a character of mine away like that, but in theory, if the summoner has a strong enough focus, he could do it from any distance. He's better than me. And if he were close, he could have conjured something dangerous to stop us, not just taken something away."

"We may not know how close he is," Millie said, "but we know he'll certainly be expecting us to leave out front."

"Well, we can't use any other way," I pointed out. I think I said it sarcastically. My voice does that under stress. "We're underground. It would open to a wall of dirt. In case you've forgotten."

"Rob..." Charley said. He had an uncanny knack for making my name both a plea and a reproach.

"So what you're saying is that there's no way out at all."

"We're not saying that," Charley said. In the midst of anything, I noticed that he and Millie had become "we." "I can read us out of this somehow. I promise. Just let me think…"

"I say!" Millie said suddenly. Her eyebrows raised, erasing the worried knot between them. "A secret passage."

I frowned. "What? Where?"

She waved her arm vaguely at the wall. "There, if Charley can make one! There'd be one there if this were a Millie Radcliffe-Dix Adventure. It doesn't need to go far, just take us back up to street level. Can you do it?"

"Not out of midair!" Charley protested. "I would need something to work with. All I have is *The Secret Garden*."

"Well, we're practically in a library!" Millie said. Her flashlight swept the books around us to make the point, and I saw spines and titles in a multicolored flash. "Start looking for something!"

"No, but—I don't even know if I could make one at all!" Charley said. "A secret passage—that's not a person, or an object. It's not even a metaphorical concept. It's a setting. It burrows through the earth. That would be changing the shape of the world."

"Oh, rot!" she exclaimed. "You put a door in a wall. You put people into the world. You can put a passage into the earth. I do understand it might be more difficult. But look what this summoner can do, with no more than what you have here. Just give it a go and see what happens."

"I think you probably should," I conceded reluctantly. "Otherwise we're going to be cornered here."

I'd never, in my whole life, asked Charley to have a go at summoning something. It seemed to decide him. His jaw set.

"Right," he said. "Find me something to use, and I will."

"There's a good chap," said Millie.

We set upon the books like starving orphans. Millie was the only one who had a flashlight, but I had my phone, and Charley can read print in near dark. (Mum was always nagging him to turn a light on.) One of the first I found was a thick popular thriller that I had, to my surprise, read myself last month. I snatched it up and waved it at my brother.

"There's an underground cave in this. Would that do?"

"It might," Charley said, after a quick look. "But I haven't read it."

"I have. I could find the part myself."

"Unless you can make the cave yourself, it doesn't matter. I need to interpret it. I can't use passages and phrases—well, not on this kind of notice."

I groaned, and put it back. "I thought you read everything."

"I haven't read that."

"Snob."

"There are only so many reading hours in the day!"

The ground trembled. I felt it ripple beneath my feet, and heard the walls around us creak. The noise was eerie in the dark.

"That was a shift," I said. "Like the one we felt in the Street."

"The summoner's arrived," Charley said. He said it perfectly matter-of-factly, as though an expected guest had come for dinner.

"What?" He had stopped moving, so I stopped too. "Where is he?"

"I don't know. But the room responded to someone who can alter its shape. It wasn't me, so it must have been him."

"Keep looking!" Millie hissed at us.

I pulled out book after book, heart pounding, painfully aware of the summoner approaching and the darkness pressing in around me. My hands were shaking. I hated being closed in, I hated the dark, and I *hated* this place. This wasn't my world. It wasn't even Dickens's. It was a dark corner of someone's psyche. It needed therapy, not literary analysis. And it was going to kill us.

I nearly skipped over the title of the massive hardcover at the end of the room. I think my eyes had reached the point where they just wanted to see *Millie Radcliffe-Dix and the Adventure of the Secret Passage* or nothing. At the last minute, I realized what it was.

"Hey!" I called, quietly. "What about this?"

The others turned to look.

"*The Count of Monte Cristo*," Millie read out loud.

"There's a secret passage in that, isn't there?" I said. "When he gets out of prison?"

"Well, not so much a secret passage as a tunnel," Charley said, more cautiously. "And this is a translation from French, so the words will be a bit—"

"Charley, I would rather have a nice, wide passage with secret rooms and treasure, too, but let's not be particular," Millie said. "I'll take a tunnel."

Charley sighed. "Okay," he said. "Simpler's probably easier anyway." I threw him the book, and he opened it.

"I haven't read this since I was about eight," he warned us. "I hope I can find the right—"

"You might want to hurry," I told him.

Charley turned the pages a little faster. "You do realize he doesn't actually escape using either of the tunnels in the prison, don't you? He takes the place of his dead friend and gets thrown in the sea."

"Charley!"

"I know!"

He took a deep breath, closed his eyes briefly, and then returned his gaze to the book. Some of the panic lifted, and his face became still and intent. He's always been able to do that, even under the most trying circumstances: with a book in front of him, his mind distances itself from his body. The circumstances just don't usually involve someone coming to kill us.

The summoner was here now. I heard footsteps overhead, the creak of a door that must, like the *Secret Garden* door, have been made to let his people through from the street outside. At any point now, there would be a flare of light, and the wall at the top of the stairs would part into another door. The summoner could come down, but so could anyone out of the vast arsenal of books upstairs. And anyone else walking through the shop would notice only a haze in the air, a choking sensation at the back of the throat that urged them to get out. We would be killed, or captured, behind a veil of fiction.

Millie was obviously thinking along similar lines. "Whoever comes down," she said to me quietly, "don't try to fight them off with a hardcover or anything. Just demand to talk to the summoner. He'll want to talk to us, I'm certain."

I thought she was being a little optimistic, but I nodded. "All right."

"I mean it. I saw you try to take on Heathcliff."

"That was not typical for me," I said. "I'm really far more likely to demand to talk to somebody, I promise."

Through it all I felt, ludicrously, a little proud that Millie thought I needed holding back. Before Heathcliff, I had never been in so much as a drunken Saturday-night brawl.

The noises at the top of the stairs stopped. I could hear voices, dull through the wall: one deep and apologetic, one high and whining, one—just for a couple of words—sharp with command. The summoner. I didn't know for certain, but I felt a chill.

"Well," Millie said. Her head was held high. "At least we'll find out who it is."

"Got it!" Charley said suddenly, and simultaneously there was a flare of light that seemed much brighter than usual in the darkness. David Copperfield's empty chair jumped into sharp relief, then faded again. Millie's flashlight beam swung to the wall.

There, near the floor, was the opening of a tunnel. It was small—barely wide enough for my shoulders—and the edges were rough, as though shaped by a blunt chisel. Though it was set in the gray bricks of the basement wall, the inside was a different, lighter rock, scored by toolmarks and crumbling into dust. I could see a short distance, then the passage was swallowed up by darkness.

"Oh good job!" Millie exclaimed. She dropped to her knees in front of the opening, shining her flashlight into it. "Is it clear all the way?"

"I'm not sure," Charley said cautiously. He shivered as he closed the book. "If it is, there's no way it could be stable. That fictional tunnel just displaced the real earth."

"What do you mean?" I asked.

"I mean that I didn't just pull that tunnel out. I rewrote it over the real world. Where there was solid dirt, there's now a tunnel. Reality shaped itself around it. I felt it. And I don't know if it will last."

"You mean it might just—disappear?"

"I don't know. Maybe."

"And what would happen to us in the tunnel?"

"I really don't know. Maybe we'd just vanish. Maybe we'd be—well, left in the earth."

Wonderful. I'd been so hung up on the idea of getting out of the basement that I hadn't really thought through the idea of crawling along a narrow passage in the ground. Looking at it, it seemed far smaller and darker than I had imagined. And now I was being told it might just vanish with us inside. My stomach tightened.

"That's a nasty thought," Millie said, almost cheerfully, "but I'd sooner chance it. I'd really prefer not to meet the summoner under these circumstances. Shall I go first, or would one of you like the honor?"

"I'd better go first, actually," Charley said. I saw him swallow, but a glance at the locked basement door steeled him. "If it's unstable further down, then I might be able to do something about it. Strengthen it or widen it or something."

"Have you ever been in an underground tunnel in your life?" I asked him. "The London Underground doesn't count."

"I have," Millie said, before Charley could reply. "And I declare you both honorary members of the Guild of Spelunkers, if that makes you feel any better. I'll take the rear, then, and kick off anyone who tries to follow us. Charley, go first, and Rob follows. Quickly!"

Charley pushed his backpack through the hole first and then, with a deep breath, wriggled in after it. He's a couple of inches shorter than me; even so, there wasn't space to crawl, only to slide along, commando-style. I got down on my knees and then lay flat on my stomach to follow. The entrance seemed to constrict in front of me. I almost thought I'd rather die than go in there. But then I tried to imagine telling Millie and Charley that.

I crawled forward.

Not a moment too soon either. The moment before my head entered the tunnel, I saw a flare of light at the top of the stairs.

The tunnel was dark, and tight, and it smelled of damp earth. All of these things are obvious, but at the time they were all I could think about. I couldn't really crawl; I wriggled, squirmed, and twisted, inching along with my fingers and toes, the knowledge that I could barely move chafing against the knowledge that I was technically being chased.

I must have been about halfway through when the tunnel vanished. Suddenly, there was dirt against my face, tumbling into my nose and mouth. My chest constricted, and panic shot through me. I couldn't breathe.

Then it was gone. The space in front of me was clear again. I gasped, choking on the dirt I had already inhaled. I could taste the granules in my teeth, and in the back of my throat.

"Sorry!" Charley's voice came muffled and out of breath. "I've got it back."

That wasn't very reassuring. "Did we lose the tunnel?"

"Just around the edges." He coughed. "You might want to hurry, though."

I hurried. As much as one could hurry through a tight gap in the earth, sandwiched between two people; with more in pursuit, feeling every second that the earth was going to come crumbling down, I hurried.

It had just occurred to me that perhaps the tunnel never ended at all—that Charley had pulled the tunnel out but not been able to make it lead anywhere—when the black around me lightened to gray. There was an opening ahead of me. We were nearly free.

And then Charley stopped.

"Oh," he said. "Um..."

"What?" I hadn't thought I could muster any new panic, until it flared in my chest. "What is it?"

"Nothing. Well. We're underwater."

Whatever I had been expecting, it wasn't that. "What do you mean we're—?"

"Here," Millie said from behind me. Her hand wriggled past my hip, and something poked me. "Take the flashlight."

Charley shifted a little to one side, enough so that I could shine the flashlight past him and catch the tunnel's exit.

At first, I thought I was looking into open air; it was dark, as might be expected emerging from a tunnel in the middle of the night. Then I saw how the flashlight's beam caught the surface, and distorted. My breath caught. I was looking at a solid sheet of water, as though at an aquarium without glass. It rippled and shifted with the tide. A fish darted at the beam from the light, swam through it, and then was gone.

"You see what I mean," Charley added.

"How is that even—?" I cut myself off before the final word. "Don't answer that."

"I did say," Charley said defensively. "I did say that Dantes actually escapes by sea. And you were telling me to make an escape route."

The sea was black and translucent in the dark. It occurred to me that this was probably the first time anyone had ever been *under* underwater.

"Just... tell me we're not somewhere off the coast of France," I said.

"I don't think so. At a guess, the tunnel probably comes out at the nearest body of water."

"Wherever we are, we need to move," Millie said. "They're fast behind us. Hurry up, chaps."

Charley shook his head. "But—"

"You'll just have to take a deep breath, and kick off as hard as you can," I told him. It was easy to say. I couldn't imagine actually doing so; the air already felt too stifled to breathe. "There's light, so we can't be too far under."

Charley nodded once, tightly. I could understand his hesitation. Our childhood had been populated by swimming pools, creek beds, and beach holidays, but he'd always flinched from entering the water. This was worth flinching at.

"I say, move, you two," Millie said from somewhere around my heels. "I can hear breathing right behind me. And rather a lot of clawing."

"Go!" I hissed at Charley, and almost at once, he was gone. A moment later, I realized that I was next.

Darkness. Tight spaces. Impossibility. People trying to kill me directly behind me.

I couldn't do this. It was too hard.

"Rob!" Millie's voice came.

The water was directly in front of me. The cold on my face was like a draft from a window.

I closed my eyes, held my breath, and pushed through it.

On my first week at law school, I had, with all the other idiot first years in my hall, perched on the edge of the long plank that extends over the harbor and launched myself into the water. It had been a stunningly beautiful day; even the sea breeze was warm. I was intoxicated by it all: the sun, the wind, the sea, the hills dotted with old colonial houses around the harbor, the feeling of freedom and independence racing through my blood. Just before I hit the water, I remember thinking I was in the middle of a perfect moment and that I would look back on it one day and remember it, the moment and my realization together, like a self-fulfilling prophecy. Then I hit the water, and it went up my nose, and I came up spluttering and forgot all about it.

Coming up from the bottom of the harbor was very different.

There was no glorious flight through the wind, only a miserable push into water and the feel of my lungs tightening and my heart spiking into panic. The cold shocked the air from me. My feet caught on a bend in the tunnel, halfway out; I wanted desperately to push my way back, just to take a breath and try again, but I could feel Millie pressing behind me. One quick, sharp kick, and I pulled free. Another few furious kicks, and I was floating, salt and grit and water thick about me. Another few, and I broke the surface.

At first, I was utterly disoriented. All I could see through the water streaming from my face was water, more water, and lights that could have been stars or streetlights or specks of gold dust. I gasped, and choked. The air felt cool and blissfully tangible. Then, as my eyes cleared, I saw the glowing lines of Te Papa museum, to the right, and the world reassembled itself around me. We'd crawled in a straight line from Lambton Quay out to the sea. There were the houses on Mount Vic, Frank Kitts Park, the looming cityscape behind us. Charley and Millie were beside me, both treading water to stay afloat.

"All right, chaps?" Millie said breathlessly. Of course she could swim perfectly. In the books, she and that monkey are always rowing out to islands and swimming at beaches. They call it "bathing," and when I first read the books, I had a confused image of bubble bath mixture and rubber ducks.

Charley was coughing furiously, somewhere to my left, but he nodded.

"Good show," she said. "Rob?"

I didn't answer. Down at the bottom of the harbor, beneath my feet, I could make out the entrance to the tunnel. I could make it out because there was a light coming through it. There was a light coming through it because someone carrying a light was coming through it. They were coming for us.

"Persistent, aren't they?" Millie said, following my glance.

I found my voice. "Send it back! The tunnel. Cut them off."

Charley shook his head stubbornly, still catching his breath. "They'll suffocate if I just take it away. Or drown."

"It's a book character," I said. "Whoever it is, they aren't alive. They won't die. They'll probably just go back to their book."

"Do you truly want me to risk it?" he asked, and I couldn't answer.

Truly, I did, but I couldn't bring myself to say that to his face, and in front of Millie.

Millie settled it anyway. "I think you have to, I'm afraid. We don't have time."

The hands holding the flashlight had become visible in the tunnel entrance. They clawed at the dirt—old, wrinkled hands in gray fingerless gloves—tearing their way up toward the water. I caught a glimpse of the head a little deeper in the passage: balding, dirty, a flash of white teeth and a glint of wide eyes.

"Charley!" I snapped.

"Do it," Millie said briskly.

He gave the tunnel one single anguished look, but closed his eyes. "Okay..." I heard him mutter. *"Count of Monte Cristo..."*

There was a trace of panic in his voice. I remembered what he had said about how long it had been since he'd read it, the problems with translation.

"Come on," I said. For a moment, I sounded calm and reassuring. "You can do this."

He made no sign of having heard me, but his face settled into deeper concentration. The hands were almost at the edge of the tunnel now.

There was a flash of light—not a flashlight this time, but the light that signaled the closing of another world. The water surged, as if someone had given the waves a shove from below. And then, the bottom of the harbor was clear again.

Charley's eyes flew open.

"They disappeared," Millie said, before he could ask. "That close, they'd have pushed their way out if the tunnel had just closed up around them. At least we'd see them trying. They've gone back to their books, I assume. Or they're in *The Count of Monte Cristo*, which would serve them jolly well right."

"They'd hate that," Charley said, with a rather shaky laugh. "I sent that tunnel back to chapter seventeen. They'd end up in the Château d'If."

"Can that even happen?" I asked. I wondered, ludicrously, if I could find them by opening the book and reading the chapter. But that was ridiculous. Charley took characters in and out of books all the time; it never changed the text.

"I don't know," Charley said. "I've never been clear on where exactly characters come from or go to. Can we get out of the water now, please?"

My car was parked not too far away, fortunately, as the wind was tugging and biting at my wet clothes. I checked my watch, which was somehow still working. Almost midnight. I had told Lydia not to wait for me, but she would probably still be awake. I had no idea how I would explain this to her if I went home. I had no idea how to explain it to myself.

"Are they going to come after us?" Charley asked. He was already blue with cold. "If they work out where the tunnel went…"

"I don't see how they could," Millie said briskly. "*We* didn't know, after all. They'll probably just load their world back into its book and take it elsewhere. And we'll know where. We have people in the McDonald's still, watching the shops. We'll follow them."

I wanted to avoid awkward questions from Lydia, Millie wanted to avoid awkward questions from the Street, Charley had just shifted realities, and the summoner was possibly scouring the city for us. Somehow, the decision was made to go for pizza.

Lydia

For the second time that week, Lydia lay awake and alone at night. Her feelings this time did not take a good deal of sorting through. She was thoroughly fed up.

She had more or less resigned herself to the calls that Rob got from Charley out of the blue, at odd hours of the night or on weekends. They had started only a few weeks after Charley moved to Wellington, the first coming in the evening as they sat down to watch television. Rob had sighed, unsurprised, and said this was something his brother did—and, as time proved, it was. Sometimes Rob would come back on his own an hour or so later; sometimes Charley would come back with him, pale and apologetic and looking ready to fall asleep where he was. She had accepted both apologies and lack of explanations at first, because she was determined to be reasonable. Besides, she knew Rob, and she knew that he was indeed genuinely unconcerned. She was only puzzled because, of all the many and varied causes for someone being dragged from a house to go to the aid of their younger sibling, none of them fit what she knew of Rob—or of Charley.

She had questioned Charley about it, when they were all at Mr. and Mrs. Sutherland's house for lunch and the two of them had ended up momentarily alone in a room together. Her experience of younger brothers told her that they were easier to coax secrets from than their elder siblings. Charley was quieter than any of her brothers, and knew more about Dickens; sure enough, though, he at least sighed unhappily when she broached the topic.

"I'd tell you if I could," he said. "But Rob would kill me. He doesn't want you to know."

"Whose secret is it?" she asked. "His, or yours?"

"Mine."

"So it's your secret, and I'm asking you about it. *You* can tell me to mind my own business, if you like, but I don't see that Rob has a say in the matter."

"It involves him, because I involve him in it. If he doesn't want to tell you, I can't do it on his behalf. I'm sorry. It's not illegal, if that helps."

"Is it dangerous?"

"It's a little bit dangerous. Sometimes. Not much."

"Are you a spy or something?"

He laughed. "No. I'm not a spy."

"You should have said you were. I might have stopped asking then."

"I'm a terrible liar. Probably why nobody ever suggested I become a spy."

Rob was a terrible liar too—or, more accurately, he was scrupulously honest. It was one of the things she had liked about him when they first met. He didn't try to disguise the fact that there was a secret, only to brush it away, as though it were a cloud of dust blown by the wind onto the pristine surface of their relationship. But their relationship wasn't pristine. It never had been. It was a glorious mess, as all relationships were: a mess of her large, rambunctious family and his small, tight-knit one; of her past working at hotels all over Greece and his several years living and working in Wellington; of their long, complicated working hours; of their shared love of old films and going to the beach in the rain and eating out so they didn't have to cook; of decisions about where to go on holiday for Christmas and who got to play what music on the weekends and whether to get a dog. She didn't understand what could possibly be so terrible that it couldn't fit in as everything else had. In the dark before midnight, it preyed on her mind.

As midnight came and went, she rolled over with a frustrated sigh and threw back the covers. Her phone was on her bedside table. She picked it up and tried to tell herself that she was only fed up, or even worried. It was a lot better than admitting her feelings were really more like fear.

She did know Rob. And because she did, she knew that this last week had been different from the other times. This time, something really was wrong.

His cell phone went straight to voicemail, which was unusual enough to increase her foreboding. Rob lived on his phone; they both did. Charley's rang for a while and then went to voicemail, too, which wasn't unusual. She called Rob's work phone, on the off chance that he was there, which she knew he was not.

He wasn't. But, most unusually of all, somebody answered the phone anyway.

"Hello? Mrs. Sutherland?"

"I'm not Mrs. Sutherland," she said, startled. And she never would be, her interior voice added, if Rob didn't stop disappearing at night. "I'm Lydia. I'm sorry, who is this?"

"My name is Eric Umble," he said. "I'm Mr. Sutherland's intern."

"Oh. Yes, he mentioned you. You're working late, aren't you? Don't you have a home to go to?"

"Not worth speaking of. It's no bother at all. I like working."

"I see. Well. Good for you, I suppose." Lydia frequently worked late herself, but she didn't think it would have occurred to her to say that she liked it. "Rob isn't there, is he?"

"No. He isn't here."

"I didn't really think he would be. Thanks anyway. If you do see him, can you tell him I called?"

"I could tell you where he is, if you'd like."

This startled her more than his presence in the first place. "Where is he?"

"Not here on the phone, Miss Lydia. It wouldn't be safe. But I could meet you somewhere."

"Now?"

"Not now." There was a smile in his voice, of sorts. "I wouldn't ask you to come meet me in the middle of the night. I'm not a serial killer. But you could come to the office tomorrow. Sometime when Mr. Sutherland isn't around, of course."

"I think I'll wait until Rob gets back, thanks." She let her voice turn cool, partly to hide the chill that had crept down her back. "I'm sure he'll tell me exactly where he's been."

Eric didn't sound perturbed. "If you change your mind, Miss Lydia, you know where I'll be. I'm so glad you called."

XV

Places were beginning to shut their doors, but the long stretch of pubs and restaurants along Courtenay Place were still brightly lit and buzzing. We found a small, shabby eatery on the basis of my hazy student memories. I was still wet enough to draw attention from the man at the counter; at least, his eyebrows shot up. But all he said was, "All right there, mate?"

They were closing up. Most of the chairs were stacked on tables, and I had to shout over the roar of a vacuum to ask if they could give us any pizza at this time of night. They'd turned off the ovens, but they had assorted slices left that they offered to put in a box for me. I thanked them, picked up three cans of soft drink from the freezer, and leaned against the counter to wait for my order.

I had come here as a first-year law student one night during exams week. I had been hunched over my desk, notes swimming in front of my eyes and my nerves about ready to snap, when my neighbor from two rooms down had come banging on the door.

"We're going into town to eat pizza and gelato," he'd said.

"Who is?"

"All of us. The floor. Maybe the building."

"I have an exam in the morning."

"So do half of us. The rest have one in the afternoon. Some of us have both. We're calling it an experimental trial: pizza and gelato as a last-minute study tool."

"Sign me up," I said at once, because I was eighteen and an idiot.

We had ended up here, bankrupting ourselves on pizza that was bubbly and hot and gelato that was creamy and cold, and making far too much noise about it. Afterward, we had gone to the waterfront.

It was deserted, and the lights reflecting on the water had been dazzling in the expanse. We had stood on the edge of the harbor, tried to outyell the wind, and were nearly blown into the sea in the process. I sat the exam the next day on about half an hour of sleep, came home so tired that I crashed on my bed and slept through to the next day, and somehow received an A, though I was never brave enough to repeat the experiment.

I tried to hold on to that memory, but the waterfront had already shifted in my mind, and now this place was shifting too. They were part of tonight now. They had become something unfamiliar and strange, as surely and as disconcertingly as the office block on Lambton Quay had transformed into a Dickensian nightmare around me. And I wasn't all right.

Outside the window, the streets looked bright and cold. The flare of lights from a passing car caught the glass and seemed to split the world in two.

I was walking the food back to the table when I felt the hairs rise on the back of my neck and arms. The lights overhead flickered. A faint mist or distortion was settling over the tables—the same mist, I realized, that had descended over the abandoned office, moments before Charley and Millie had vanished.

Millie had gone outside to find a payphone: the water had drowned both our phones coming up from the harbor. Charley sat alone at the booth, absently turning the pages of the summoner's book. Already, there was a faint transparence about him.

"Charley," I said. My voice was tight with panic.

Charley blinked, and looked up. His mind took a moment to follow him out of the book; when he registered what I was looking at, his face cleared. "Oh. Oh, I'm sorry."

He snapped the book shut, and closed his eyes. The mist around cleared as if in a rush of air. I could breathe again.

"Is that how the summoner was using your book?" Millie asked, with interest. She must have come back in while I was distracted.

"Mm." Charley made a face, and rested his forehead in his hand until the dizziness let him look up again. "I think so—did you get through? Is someone following the summoner?"

"No luck," Millie said. "I was just on the phone with the Artful. He says nobody came in or out the entire time he was sitting there eating cheeseburgers. We've lost the summoner again."

He stared at her. "We can't have."

"We have. However he's been entering and leaving the office, it hasn't been through the front door. And he isn't likely to come back, now that he knows we've found that particular bolt-hole."

"But...that means we're no closer than we were before! We still have nothing."

"We were a sight too close down there, if you ask me," Millie said. "And we don't exactly have nothing. We have that book."

That book. It lay on the greasy table, where Charley had pushed it away. There was a coffee ring on the green cover, and the edges were tattered. It was only my imagination that the world receded away from it, but that didn't reassure me. Imagination wasn't keeping to its proper place tonight. We all looked at it as though we expected it to bite.

"The section on *Oliver Twist* was dog-eared, with notes in the margins," Charley said into the silence. "I was just reading it, and the observations the summoner's written down. They're quite brilliant."

"Brilliant enough to create a London hovel in the middle of central Wellington?" Millie asked.

"Well," Charley said. "That's what I was just wondering."

I found my voice by putting it back on a familiar track. "You really need to be more careful about what you wonder in public. A few more seconds, and that London hovel would have been out in the open."

"I know. I'm sorry. I would have noticed before that, I promise. It's just that I was still a bit light-headed from the tunnel, and my concentration slipped. I need to practice secret passages, I think, next time we break into a building."

"Or not be up all night practicing doors the night before," Millie suggested.

"Maybe." He yawned. "But the door went really well, didn't it?"

"It was a beautiful door," Millie said, with a crooked grin. "And the tunnel was a work of art. Well done."

"Thank you." Charley smiled back. "Next time, I'll try to make it lead somewhere more dry. Like a theoretical textbook."

"Or you could just avoid summoning doors and secret passages at all," I interjected. "They don't seem to be a good idea."

"They seemed a jolly good idea to me," Millie retorted. "We got out of there, didn't we? With the book."

"It was good then," I had to admit. "But I don't think we should make a habit of this. The breaking and entering, or the summoning of passageways. For one thing, you look terrible."

"I don't feel terrible," Charley said. I believed him, unfortunately. He didn't even really look terrible. He looked exhausted, and freezing cold, but his face was glowing. For once, whatever he said, he didn't even look particularly sorry. "Or at least, if I do, it's because I need to do more rather than less. It's like when you were training to run a marathon, remember? Two or three years ago? When you push too far, you *do* look terrible. You might even collapse, and everything hurts the next day. But in the end, you can run a marathon."

"I suppose," I conceded. That had been a failed New Year's resolution—I'd worked up to one half marathon, then quit. "But it's not dangerous if people find out you can run a few kilometers. It's not a secret."

"Summoning won't be a secret if this summoner keeps going much longer unimpeded," Millie said. "He's already caused a crime wave, sent the Hound of the Baskervilles to Highbury, and turned a central-city office into Dickensian England. Sooner or later, he's bound to get noticed—and he doesn't seem to care."

I didn't answer, because it was true. But I hated this. I didn't even know, entirely, what it was that I hated: the danger that I was still shaken from, the sudden strangeness of the city I thought I knew, the sensation that Charley was tumbling deeper and deeper into a rabbit hole that I couldn't follow him down. The worst part was that the other two were enjoying it. My brother, who used to be afraid to jump into the deep end of a swimming pool, was suddenly in his element. And I didn't know how to get him out of it before he drowned.

"Here," I said, pushing the pizza between the two of them roughly. "Eat quickly. They're closing any minute."

"Thanks, Rob," Millie said. "Jolly decent of you. Can I see that book, Charley?"

"Go ahead." He pushed it across the table, and she slid into the booth while scooping up a slice of pizza.

"Dickens again," she remarked as she opened it up. "I know you're a Victorian specialist, but he seems to be a theme, doesn't he?"

"There were plenty of books there that weren't Dickens," Charley reminded her. "Thousands of them. That's more impressive than you've probably considered, you know. If they really are using that many for summoning, they would have to not just read them, but *understand* them. I bring things out from what I'm reading at the time: it's not planned. To bring people and worlds from any book, at will, and put them back, they would need to know them almost by heart."

"You always seem to know books by heart," I pointed out. I sat down in the spare chair. My clothes squelched unpleasantly around me.

"Some. But those weren't just some. They filled the entire building. I think I'd need to read for a hundred years to have that kind of knowledge."

Charley had been reading for about twenty-five years, at various levels. The thought of him with four times as much reading under his hat was disconcerting, to say the least.

"But out of all those books," Millie said, "it always seems to be Dickens they come back to—or, at least, something Victorian. The Hound of the Baskervilles, Uriah Heep, David Copperfield. The criminals, too, the ones Dorian's identified, seem to be Fagins and Magwitches and Scrooges. Is that directed at you? Or are we looking for another Dickens scholar?"

"There aren't any other Dickens scholars in the city," Charley said. "At least, nobody else at the university specializes in the nineteenth century."

"What about David Copperfield, down there in the dark?" I asked. "What was that directed toward?"

"I can't imagine," Charley said. He sobered at the memory. "David Copperfield is very important to Dickensian criticism, of course. Or his novel is. Like I told him, it's semiautobiographical. A good deal of what happens in that book is taken from Dickens's own life; at times, Dickens and David Copperfield blur so that it's difficult to tell whose voice is really narrating. Like the blacking factory."

"Are you going to make us ask?"

"It's just an example. Dickens was sent to work in a blacking factory when he was twelve, when his father was in debtors' prison. He never recovered from the experience; he was angry about child labor and social injustice for the rest of his life. Something similar happens to David—except that David is ten. The words Dickens used to describe his own experience to a friend are almost identical to those he gives David in the book. 'I know enough of the world now, to have almost lost the capacity of being much surprised by anything; but it is matter of some surprise to me, even now, that I can have been so easily thrown away at such an age. A child of excellent abilities, and with strong powers of observation, quick, eager, delicate, and soon hurt bodily or mentally, it seems wonderful to me that nobody should have made any sign in my behalf.'"

"That doesn't sound very angry," I said when Charley paused his quotation for breath. "It sounds betrayed."

"It's that as well," he agreed. "But it doesn't explain what David Copperfield was doing blindfolded and captive in a basement that shouldn't exist."

"If he *was* an old reading of yours, from when you were four or so," Millie said, "then he probably knows things about you, the way I do. Perhaps the summoner was questioning him. That might have even been how he found out about you in the first place."

"If so," I said, "he didn't seem to want him anymore. He read him away right in front of us. Could he do that, to a reading not his own?"

"I would have said not," Charley said. "But then, I didn't know I could alter the readings of someone else, until I did it to Henry. I don't know where the limits of power are anymore."

I nodded slowly. "And your book? Where does that fit into things? I assume he's using it because it was written by you, and he knows what you are."

"I assume he knows what I am too. I assume that's why all of this is happening here, now, of all the cities in the world. But I can't think what difference that would make to the book."

"What's it about, anyway?" I asked.

He looked at me, surprised. "I sent you all copies."

"I didn't read it, Charley. Mum and Dad did—well, Dad tried. He got lost when you started talking about hermeneutic traditions versus the deconstructive approach."

"I told him not to worry about that part. He said he loved the book. And Mum said it was powerful."

"Well, maybe he loved not understanding it. What's it about? In ordinary English."

Charley looked a little crestfallen, but he shrugged. "It's about the darker side of London as Dickens portrays it. You know, the world of prisons and pickpockets and thieves. It talks about Dickens's construction of the criminal underworld. There's more to it than that, but—honestly, it's not the only or even the best piece of Dickensian criticism on that subject. I was a teenager. There are other books for the summoner to use."

"But none that were written by another summoner," Millie said. She had been looking through the book as we were talking. Suddenly, she froze. "Charley, have a look at this."

On the page was a black-and-white illustration, probably a replica of one from an old Victorian edition of Dickens. It was delicately shaded, depicting a cobbled path flanked with crooked buildings. Fog writhed from the pavement, and streetlights glowed. It was the Street. It was unmistakable. I recognized Dorian's house looming in front, and Millie's farther down the road. There was the saddler's, and the pawnshop, and the pub. It could have been drawn from life. Or the other way around.

"Okay," I said. "That's very weird."

"That's from an edition of *Bleak House*, I think," Charley said. He rubbed his brow. "It's not really important to the analysis—OUP just wanted an illustration or two, and that one had the fog—"

"They've scribbled a date next to it," Millie said. "Two years ago."

"It's not quite the Street, though, is it?" Charley said. "The Old Curiosity Shop isn't there, or the bookstore—"

"No," Millie agreed. "It's the basis for an interpretation. The text fills in the rest. I suppose a little like the building we were just in."

"The summoner made the Street," Charley said.

"I think he did," Millie said. She sounded excited but, for the first time, a little shaken. "I think that's what these notes are about. He was trying to summon a setting."

"So they read out a Dickensian street," he said. "Not a street from any individual book, but a quintessential Dickensian street."

"Exactly."

"But why?" I asked, drawn in despite myself. "They haven't made any use of it. If they did bring out the Street, they haven't been back to it since. Have they?"

Millie shook her head. "It was empty when we found it."

"Perhaps it wasn't what the summoner wanted," Charley said. "Perhaps they didn't even know they'd succeeded in making it. It isn't exactly in the real world. It's stuck halfway."

"Like the *Oliver Twist* house again," I suggested.

"Sort of," he agreed. "Although that was further through. It was taking up space, of a sort; it was melded to the curves and lines of the building that housed it."

"But perhaps," Millie said, "it's still not quite far enough."

Her face had lit. It unnerved me.

"What are you thinking?" Charley asked.

"I'm thinking about what you just said about the Street." She pulled the book toward her. "If this date in the margins means what we think it means, then the summoner brought it through two years ago, and abandoned it. Let's suppose, just for a moment, that they abandoned it because it didn't work. When you read anything out, you bring it into the real world, don't you? The Street never quite came into the real world. It's stuck halfway."

"And so they left it," Charley said slowly. "They left it for you to find."

"Yes. We were drawn to it—it left a great wound in reality, and we came to infect it. But it was never meant for us. It was a failed experiment."

He considered this carefully. "And the house we were in a moment ago? *Oliver Twist?*"

"As we just said. A little further through. Still not far enough."

"Far enough for what?" Charley asked, then caught his breath. "Oh God."

I didn't like the sound of that. "What?"

"The coming of the new world," he said. "The whispers Dorian and the others have been hearing. Could they—what if it's not meant metaphorically? What if the promise of a new world is quite literal?"

"Things read out of books usually are quite literal," Millie said. "Heathcliff's eyes are made of fire. The Implied Reader is a person that lives about the saddlery. Uriah Heep can change his shape."

"Dickens's criminal underworld," Charley said. He sounded dazed. "That's what they're trying to summon. Not a street. Not a building. They want a Dickensian underworld."

"I think that's what the Street's been responding to," Millie said. "That's why it's been shifting, and growing. The summoner has been trying to bring out the rest of the city. Every time he's come close, our street has been reaching out for it."

"Just a moment," I interrupted. My head was spinning. "What do you mean by a new world? What happens to the one already here?"

"I rather think it would be supplanted by the one that comes," Millie said. "The way Charley's tunnel displaced the real earth, and his door displaced the real wall."

I thought of the Lambton Quay shops dissolving around me as Charley had pulled me through the doors.

"This is hypothesis," Charley said to me quickly. "We can't know for certain what the summoner is trying to do."

"I think we can make a jolly good guess at it," Millie said. She had no interest in sparing my feelings. "I think he wants his own reality. And I think Charley's book is his means of getting it."

Charley shook his head. "How? It's just a book of literary analysis."

"It isn't just a book of literary analysis," Millie said. "It's a book of literary analysis written by you. Another summoner—as far we know, the only other summoner in the world. And it's a book about the construction of Dickensian London. It's a written version of what you do in your head when you bring fiction to life."

"But that wasn't even close to what I was thinking when I wrote that book. I've never brought an entire city to life. Just little things. People, and doors, and paperweights."

"You almost brought a part of one then."

"That was the summoner's notes. I was just—"

"Exactly. Perhaps neither of you, on your own, would be able to bring out a city. It would be too big to hold in your mind at once. But using your work as a template, adding his own theories and interpretations—you've seen what he can do with regular criticism. Eric, and the Hound. He builds on it to shape his readings the way he wants them. Yours must fit his purpose like a glove. You couldn't help it—your minds work the same."

"Like a collaboration," Charley said slowly.

"Yes! If you like, exactly like a collaboration." She flipped through the pages of the book. "Look at all the notes through this. It's been read back to front and upside down. It's obviously taking a long time to work out—the Street was two years ago—but he thinks he can do it, with this book."

"If you're right about the Street," Charley said, "then he's getting closer. It grew an entire alley yesterday."

"I'm right," Millie said. "I know it."

"If you are," I said, "then this getting far too dangerous."

Charley didn't seem to hear me. "He'll want this book back. He can use any copy, but he's done a good deal of work in this one. I take books back to the library that I've scribbled notes in all the time. I always need to track them down. He'll come for it."

"Good," Millie said. "If he shows himself, we may be able to do something about all this. And if he goes after another copy, we might be able to track that too."

"Look, will you two slow down?" I realized I was holding half a piece of pizza, and dropped it. The sick dread in my stomach flared into anger. "For God's sake. Do you hear yourselves? You're talking about somebody trying to bring a book—not an object from a book, but an entire book—into the real world. What exactly are you planning to do if he shows himself?"

"Stop him," Millie said. "It's that simple. He's not the only one with literature's finest at his back, you know. And we have a summoner of our own."

"No, you don't. Charley has nothing to do with this. Stop asking him to fight your battles for you."

"You fight people's battles all the time," Charley pointed out. "It's your job."

"I argue for them in a court of law! Nobody's going to kill me over it."

"Would it stop you if you thought somebody might, though? Seriously? It does happen—not here, usually, but it does. Lawyers do find themselves in danger. I don't think it would stop you, if you really believed in what you were defending."

"We're not talking about me. We're talking about you."

"So why you, and not me?"

Because he was my younger brother and it was my job to be in danger, was my instinctive reply, but I knew he wouldn't take kindly to that. "Because the circumstances are entirely different."

"They are. In this case, there's nobody else that can help. There's only me."

"There's a whole street!" I turned away from Charley, deliberately, and fixed Millie directly in the eye. "Answer me this. What do you want him to do? Why do you need him, and not one of the multiple fictional heroes and villains you have cluttering up Cuba Street?"

"You know what I want." To her credit, she looked straight back at me—not that I expected anything less. This wasn't a witness for the prosecution trying to get away with something. This was Millie Radcliffe-Dix. "If this summoner keeps on the way he seems to intend, he's going to try to bring a book into the real world. At the very least, he'll expose our secret, and put us all in grave danger. If he succeeds, God knows what damage he could cause. We need to talk to him, see what he wants, and try to come to some kind of understanding. But if he isn't willing to talk—and from the looks of things, he isn't—then we need to fight back."

"And what? Kill him?"

"If we have to," Millie said, unflinching. The 1940s made children's book heroines tough, apparently. Or life in the real world did. "I hate it as much as you do, but—"

"Oh, I highly doubt that. But you don't really mean 'we,' do you? You mean Charley needs to kill him."

"I mean the Street needs to fight back. Your brother, if he's willing, is our best weapon."

"He's not a weapon! He's an academic. He's a human being, for

God's sake. He's not a figment of somebody's imagination, and he's not a part of this."

"I am, though," Charley interrupted. "I can't quite explain it, but…it's my street. It's my responsibility."

"You didn't make the Street. Just because this summoner used your book doesn't make it yours."

"I think perhaps it does. For whatever reason, I'm connected to it. It called to me, the way it called to the others. And…you know when you read a book, sometimes, and you suddenly realize that you've been missing something your whole life, and you weren't even aware, and all at once you've found it and are just a little bit more whole?"

"No," I said. This wasn't entirely true; I did know what he meant. I had felt something very like it the first time I had come to the city, as I'd looked out the window of my tiny student room and saw the harbor glittering in the distance and the skies going on forever. But I didn't know it like he knew it, so I chose not to know it at all. "No, because I'm not a nut. But I take it you do."

"That's what it felt like, stepping on to the Street. Only stronger— much stronger. The Street's a piece of my soul. I've never fit like that anywhere in my life before."

"That's how we feel too," Millie said. "All of us."

"Well, no offense, but that's understandable in your case," I said. "None of you are real. You're the accidental products of too much emotional investment in fiction."

"As opposed to what, the accidental products of a biological act?" Millie said scathingly. "Is that your argument? That we don't matter because—despite the fact I'm sitting in front of you eating pizza— none of us on the Street really exist? Because let me tell you, Robert Sutherland, if a Dickensian city bursts into the main streets of Wellington, it's going to feel real enough."

"So far, you haven't told me anything that makes me believe that's going to happen! Books don't work like that. In all the thousands of years people have been reading, nobody has ever brought through an entire city. You said yourself, even the Street doesn't actually encroach on reality."

"Not yet," Charley said thoughtfully. "It would be interesting to find out what might happen if a fictional city *does* come into existence, though. The Street will technically be part of it, or at least made of the same textual material. It's already trying to join to it."

"I *do not care.*" I felt as though I were trying to drive each word through his head like a nail. I've never understood it, how he could be so intelligent and yet so completely *oblivious.* "Charley, we've barely escaped with our lives twice. Does that not scare you?"

"Of course it scares me," he said, with more heat than I had expected from him. "All of it scares me. But I'm *tired* of being scared. I've been scared my entire life. I know you mean well, I really do. I know you want me to be safe. But I'm *exhausted* of it. Do you have any idea what it's like to grow up with everybody looking at you—scrutinizing you—and knowing that if they see what you really are, something terrible will happen?"

I hadn't thought about it, and I didn't want to now. But something about the way I saw Charley shifted a little against my will. "Well, somebody has seen now. They've found your book, and they've found you. And something terrible has happened."

"Not yet. Not if we can stop it."

"If you're right, there's a lunatic trying to bring fiction into reality. This is not going to be solved by you waving your PhD at it."

Charley flushed, and for the first time his voice hardened. "This might come as a surprise to you, Rob, but a lot of problems have been solved by people waving their PhDs at them."

"Not this one. Not by you."

"Not yet."

"You always have to do this, don't you?" The words came out before I could stop them. Perhaps I didn't want to.

"I always have to do what? What is it you think I'm doing?"

"You always have to force your way into my life, and ruin everything."

And there it was, out in the open. I knew as soon as I saw his face close up and hurt cloud his eyes that I had said it on purpose for exactly that reason; it was the one weapon I'd always had at my disposal, and I'd drawn it and wielded it like a knife. It was satisfying and sickening to watch the point plunge in. And yet I meant it. He knew that. It was why it hurt in the first place.

Millie broke in before Charley could answer. Her eyes were

blazing. "The way I see it, we didn't force you into our street, Robert Sutherland. You came to us."

"I came because Charley came."

"Exactly. Of his own free will."

"He didn't come for this."

"I'm right here, you know!" Charley snapped. He'd recovered, but his cheeks were unusually pink. "Whether you want me to be or not, I'm here. You can talk to *me* about what I want, not each other."

I crushed my guilt firmly. "Charley, you don't know what you want. You never know. Getting a straight answer out of you is like—"

"Finding an invisible street in the middle of the Left Bank Arcade?"

"All right, then, tell me what you want. Do you really want to risk everything—your life, Mum and Dad's lives, the secret we've all been keeping for you since you were born—to be involved with a conflict on another layer of reality? Do you really want this?"

"I don't—"

"See!"

"Oh, for God's sake!" He ran his hand over his face. "Look, I don't want to argue with you, okay? Not tonight. You won't listen to me anyway. I don't know if 'want' is the right word. Of course I don't want to be involved with any form of life-threatening conflict. But are you honestly telling me you think we can turn our backs on it?"

"Yes," I said stubbornly. "I am."

"Go on then," Millie said. She nodded at the door. "Jolly well leave. If you're turning your back, then turn your back."

"I just might! I never asked to be dragged into this, you know. I came because you asked me to, the same as always."

"I know," Charley said. "And I shouldn't have. Is that what you want to hear? You're right. I had no business bringing this into your life. This has nothing to do with you. If you want to get out but you don't think you can, because of me, then for God's sake just get out. You don't owe me anything. But I'm staying."

I had never meant to leave—I wanted to get out of this nightmare, but not like that. I had come in to bring Charley out with me. Beneath all my frustration and resentment, I was scared for him. He was being drawn into something from which I couldn't draw him out. He had nearly been killed; that mattered to me far more, if I was honest, than the fact that I had nearly been killed with him. I had never meant to abandon him. Not again.

And yet deep down, the parts of me I didn't want to own up to had stirred. The part that was physically ill at ease in Charley's world, with all its magic and chaos and contradictory meaning, like a poor sailor in a plunging storm. The part that, however much I had missed him, wished he had just stayed in England being brilliant where I didn't have to pick up the pieces. The part that was scared. Besides, he had *told* me to go. He didn't want me here; for the first time in our joint lives, I knew this was true. I was used to seeing him in trouble. I wasn't used to him not wanting me to get him out of it. I felt the sting of rejection, and wanted him to feel it back.

"Fine," I said coldly. I got to my feet, and walked out the door. Perhaps, I told myself, it might make him come to his senses. I knew it wouldn't.

It was cold outside. The stars above looked crisp and clear, and very far away.

Lydia was waiting for me when I came home. I saw the light in the living room as I pulled up the drive, and knew I should brace myself for confrontation. I was too tired for confrontation, though, so like a coward I opted for evasion. I was making a lot of cowardly decisions that night.

"I called you when you weren't back after midnight," she said, almost before I had closed the door. She was sitting in an armchair, her dressing gown pulled over pajamas. Her laptop was open in front of her, and her glasses were on her nose, but I suspected she had been watching the driveway more than her screen. "You didn't answer your phone."

"Didn't I?" I hadn't heard it. I pulled my phone out of my pocket, on instinct, then swore as memory came back to me. "Sorry. It's dead. It went into the harbor."

"Did you go in after it?"

"What?"

"You're clearly still drying out, and it's not raining." She took off her glasses, the better to scrutinize me. "Also, don't think I haven't noticed that you're doing that thing where you answer a question with another question to give yourself time to think."

"Am I?" I caught myself. "I am. I'm sorry. I can't really explain."

"I think I'm owed an explanation."

"You are. Look, can we just go to bed, please? It's been a very long night, and we both have to get to work in a few hours."

I must have really looked tired, or at least troubled, because she gave me a hard look but relented.

I spent a long time in the shower, waiting for the hot water to wash away every trace of the tunnel and the harbor, willing it to permeate deep enough to wash away other things as well. It was never going to happen. Apparently, guilt, fear, and memories of looks on people's faces don't swirl down the drain with soap suds. Lydia had gone to bed by the time I returned; I lay down carefully, quietly, hoping she had fallen asleep in my absence. She hadn't, but I was nearly asleep myself when her voice pulled me back from the edge of dreams.

"I called your office, too, when I didn't hear from you. Your intern was there. He said he could tell me where you were."

I blinked in the dark. "What? What did he tell you?"

"He wouldn't tell me on the phone. He wanted me to meet him. Why does your intern apparently know the ins and outs of your secret family business when I don't?"

"Don't meet him." I was wide awake now. "I mean it, don't. He's trouble."

She sounded skeptical. "What kind of trouble? He's your intern, isn't he? If he were trouble, couldn't you have him fired, or at least ask for him to be reassigned? Unless he's blackmailing you, and honestly I can't see you being blackmailed by anybody, secrets or not."

"He's not blackmailing me. I can't explain."

"Are you afraid that he'd lie to me, or tell the truth?"

I *was* afraid of her being told the truth, of course, for all the usual reasons I had never wanted her to find out Charley's secret, but also for more recent, important ones. Whatever was happening, this was not just an annoyance anymore, but real, true danger. I didn't want Lydia any deeper in it. The most shameful part of me knew that I didn't want to be in it myself. Perhaps, after all, that was why I had left Charley and Millie behind on Courtenay Place earlier.

"Neither," I answered her. "Both. I can't explain that either."

"Apparently there are a lot of things you can't explain."

She turned away from me pointedly; the mattress heaved beneath us. I lay awake a very long time after that.

E-mail exchanges of Dr. Charles Sutherland, age twenty-six

To: Charles.Sutherland@pau.ac.nz
From: Troy.Heywood@pau.ac.nz

Hi Charles,
I know you're busy this time of year, but I was just wondering if you'd had a chance to read my chapter yet? Let me know if you can meet soon.
Thanks,
Troy

To: Troy.Heywood@pau.ac.nz
From: Charles.Sutherland@pau.ac.nz

Hi Troy,
I promised to read it this weekend, didn't I? It's all my fault, all my apologies. I've been the academic equivalent of the Scarlet Pimpernel this week: people seem to be seeking me everywhere. How about Thursday? Say 4 p.m.?
Best,
Charles

To: Charles.Sutherland@pau.ac.nz
From: Beth.White@pau.ac.nz

Dear Charles,
Do you have a draft of your paper on the criminal
underworld of Sir Arthur Conan Doyle for the
Victorian volume? The publishers are after me to chase
you. You know I can outrun you if it comes to it.
Kind regards,
Beth

To: Beth.White@pau.ac.nz
From: Charles.Sutherland@pau.ac.nz

Hi Beth,
Sorry, sorry, sorry (pretend I copied and pasted that to
your satisfaction). It's on the list, I promise. Things are
happening at the moment.
I do warn you, it's turning into a paper on how Conan
Doyle doesn't really have a criminal underworld—at
least, not one that reflects Victorian social unease in
the manner of Dickens et al. Sherlock Holmes stories
glorify human intellect; his criminals are intellectual
puzzles to be solved, not living breathing inhabitants
of a world in their own right. The most dangerous
criminals—Moriarty included—are scholars and
university professors, because the threat they present is
intellectual—it's not meant to reflect real social issues,
and it doesn't really do it by accident either. Unless Sir
Arthur was trying to warn the public that all academics
are inherently untrustworthy. Which is fair.
Anyway, consider me caught. I probably won't have
time to work on it much this week, but I'll pull a couple
of all-nighters and get it to you by Wednesday of next.
Best,
Charles

To: Charles.Sutherland@pau.ac.nz
From: M.Dix1@accountswellington.co.nz

Hallo old chap,

Hope all is well after last night. I say, while you're there, do you mind seeing if anyone's taken a copy of your book out of the library? Since we have the summoner's copy, they might be looking to replace it. I'm bunking off at midday to go back to the Street— Lambton Quay is quiet, and the Artful is still watching the old office building just in case. E-mail Dorian if you have any news.

If not, see you tonight,

Millie

Sent from my iPhone

Millie

The Street was on high alert—or as high as it could manage. When Millie came back from the outside world, Matilda was sitting cross-legged against the wall with a mug of hot chocolate and a copy of *To the Lighthouse*; inside, having been duly warned of someone coming via the cord, Heathcliff and the White Witch burst from the house opposite Dorian's.

"Oh." Heathcliff lowered the lamppost, disappointed. "It's you."

"Sorry, old thing," Millie said. "But you did very well. Anything to report?"

"Not a whisper," the White Witch said. She twirled her gold wand lazily. "Are you certain you don't want me to test that this thing still works? It's been a while. Do we really need so many Darcys?"

"I think we could always use a spare Darcy or two," Millie said. "If Uriah Heep causes too much trouble, though, I might consider him. Is he being watched?"

"He's in the Darcys' attic, I believe," Heathcliff said grimly. "And should count himself fortunate not to be under my roof instead. My author's notion of hospitality was not so civilized as theirs."

The Darcys' roof was, as always, very civilized indeed. The five of them were united at least in their attempts to make their home as much like Pemberley as a Victorian London flat could be, which was not very. It was, however, clean, light, and airy, with fires burning in every room, and books and tea tables and armchairs tucked around every corner. Darcys Three and Four were at home when Millie called—the latter was nearly always so. The poor thing was the victim of one of many readers convinced Darcy's haughtiness was the product of extreme shyness, and lived much of his life holed up in the study gripped with paranoia that the others were going to organize a dance.

"Thanks for putting up Uriah Heep," Millie said to the two of them. "I know you don't like house guests."

"For a house guest, he really is quite accommodating," Four assured her, looking as usual at a spot on the floor near her feet. "He neither expects civility, nor deserves it. Unfortunately, I have not the talent which some people possess of conversing easily with those characters whose books I have not read. I cannot catch their tone of narration, or appear interested in their plot developments, as I have seen others do."

"Never mind, old thing," she said sympathetically. "At least you're jolly decorative. May I talk to Heep alone?"

Uriah Heep was hunched over a desk in the corner of the attic, writing furiously. What he was writing probably wasn't terribly important—it was just what Uriah Heep tended to be found doing. Sometimes, characters had difficulty knowing how to fill their time at first, if their authors or their readers hadn't given sufficient thought to what they got up to off page. In any case, his red eyes gleamed with pleasure when Millie entered, although he was no help at all to her inquiries.

"No, Miss Radcliffe-Dix," Uriah said, his eyes wide. "I'm afraid I still see nothing from my counterpart. I haven't since last night, when you caused all that commotion. Perhaps he's been put away? Speaking of which, where is Master Charley?"

"Never you mind," she said. "And you keep Charley's abilities to yourself, please, if you don't want to be kept under far tighter guard than you are. Thanks for the information."

"Of course," he added as she turned to leave the room, "I might be able to see more if I were given more freedom myself."

"You can go anywhere you like," she said. "As long as you're accompanied by one of the Darcys. But you must see we have to be careful. It doesn't matter if we trust you or not—there's still a danger that the summoner can use Eric to see through you."

"Surely he can create someone to see through anyone he chooses, Miss Radcliffe-Dix," he said softly. "Even you."

She'd thought of it, of course, but her chest constricted to hear it in Uriah's voice.

Darcy Three was waiting for her outside, flicking idly through a magazine. He straightened, of course, at her approach. All five Darcys were unfailingly proper, if not exactly polite.

"I take it your visit was unsuccessful?" he said.

"Rather," she sighed. "Mr. Darcy, can I ask you a bit of a personal question?"

"We love to be asked personal questions," he said, smiling. She sometimes forgot, talking to the others, that Darcy did actually know how to smile in his novel. "It really is more or less our textual function. I may decline to answer, however."

"You can all see through each other's eyes, at times. How far does it go?"

"I wouldn't quite call it seeing. It's more a form of sharing. We blend into one another momentarily."

"Right now, for instance...?"

He closed his eyes obligingly. "Five is quite clear at the moment. I can see him at a coffee shop, with an attractive young lady who has noted his resemblance to Mr. Colin Firth. He will doubtless be rude to her, and thus obtain her phone number. One is somewhere warm, white, and quiet, which I happen to know is the laundromat because it was his turn to take the cravats to be washed. Two is actually just at the pub across the street, writing his memoirs. I can't read the page, but I can see the sweep of the pen, and catch snatches of his thoughts."

"Thanks awfully."

"Not at all." He blinked rapidly, coming back to himself. "I assume you ask because of Mr. Heep?"

"Not just him," she said. She couldn't say any more, but plans were solidifying in her mind. "Is he lying, though, about what he can get from the other Uriah Heep? It doesn't seem likely that he's been put away."

"He may well be lying," Darcy Three said. "He certainly looks capable of deception, though I could not begin to guess at his motive. It may be that the other Heep is preventing him from further glimpses. We all do that to each other, at times, if we notice the touch of each other's mind. In fact..." He closed his eyes again briefly. "Five is doing so to me at this very moment. Perhaps the encounter is going better than I assumed."

"That reminds me," Millie said. "Where's Dorian?"

Dorian was in his upstairs office, lounging in his dressing gown in front of his laptop. The skull-topped crystal decanter across the desk was looking suspiciously low, as were the burning candles.

"You're home early," he observed, without looking up.

"You're awake early," Millie returned. "Or late. You're awake while the sun is in the sky, at any rate. Is there a crisis?"

"I wouldn't be awake if there was. The only thing more tedious than someone else's crises are one's own. Did you bunk off work?"

"I was worried about this place." She leaned against the doorway, unwilling to turn her back to the window overlooking the Street. "After what we did last night. If the summoner wasn't looking at us before, he will be now."

"I imagine he'll be looking mostly for your summoner," Dorian said. "You do realize what you've done, don't you? Whatever the summoner's plans were, we weren't a threat to them before. We are now. He'll be coming for us. And it isn't as though we're hidden. Any fictional person is drawn to the Street like a magnet."

"The summoners are too," Millie agreed. "At least, Charley was. But there's been no trouble so far?"

"Not a whisper from the outside world. Uriah Heep seems his usual repulsive self. Heathcliff and the Darcys are squabbling over cravats or something again, which might need your intervention. Best not make any of them keep watch together; Austens and Brontës are fundamentally opposed." He yawned, stretched, and rose to his feet. "You're right; this is far too early for me to be awake. Would you like a drink?"

"Thanks awfully, but I'd like a working liver more. We don't all have convenient portraits to take our substance abuses, you know."

"There's nothing convenient about having one's eternal soul stashed in your wardrobe." He crossed to the crystal decanter, and poured a glass. The green liquid bubbled in a way that she didn't think even absinthe was supposed to. "I want it back, Millie."

It took her a moment to register a change in topic. "What?"

"My portrait. You've given Jadis her wand back now."

"She needs it to protect the Street. I'm not happy about it—Mr. Tumnus certainly isn't happy about it—but there's no alternative. You don't need your portrait to protect the Street."

"You need *me* to protect the Street. Please don't mistake my apathy for bravery, Millie, and certainly don't mistake my service for loyalty. I'm here because the Street offers me physical protection from the outside world—or did. Risking my life for it would be rather counterproductive."

"Nobody's asking you to risk your life for it. Just to keep it secret from the outside world. We'll deal with the summoner."

"'We'?"

"I will." She knew better than to be drawn into another discussion about Charley.

Dorian sighed. "It isn't only this new summoner, you know," he said. "In fact, the summoner might have a point, if what you surmise about their goals is correct. The Street can't go on like this forever."

"It hasn't even gone on five years yet," Millie said. "I hope we still have a few anniversaries to celebrate."

"Precisely my point. Millie, do try to stop being so bloody optimistic and consider our position. The world is growing and changing too fast; we won't be able to hide in it much longer. As you say, it's my job, and I know how impossible it is. You couldn't possibly know how many threads of the World Wide Web I tweak every night to make sure that nobody discovers us. Sooner or later, somebody is going to materialize on camera. A body is going to be discovered in an alley, autopsied, and found to be inhuman. Somebody is going to find the Street, and we will be under siege."

"You can't know that."

"It's written into me to know it. Oscar Wilde knew it. Nothing stays hidden. Secrets are always found out, and the world is unforgiving."

"As I recall," Millie said, "in your book, your secret isn't revealed until you stab your painting in the heart."

He shrugged. "That's how all secrets are revealed, in the end. Either someone else betrays us, or we betray ourselves."

"Why do I end up with Wilde's most depressing creation? Why

couldn't someone have had a deep and sincere reaction to *The Importance of Being Earnest?*"

"I'm right. You know I am."

"Suppose you are. I don't see the alternative."

"Perhaps this summoner does. The Street doesn't just give us a place to hide, you know. It gives us a chance to gather, in force, for the first time. We've always been alone, and vulnerable. Well, we're not alone anymore. We have the chance of a new world. A world of our own—not a hidden world, but a world carved out of the world of flesh and blood, for us to defend, if we can. For the record, I don't know if we can. I don't know how strong this summoner is. But if we can, it might be no bad thing to strike first."

"Against innocent people?"

"There are no innocent people," Dorian said. "I know the darkness in their hearts. I'm a creature of the Gothic imagination; more than that, I'm a creature of the Internet. I don't hold it against them. I'm no better than them. But believe me, Millie, there is no happy ending to real life."

"If you feel that way, then leave." She wasn't really worried that he would, given the dangers of the world outside, but something tightened in her chest. It wasn't just that she would really miss him, or even that he was absolutely right about how much they relied upon him. The thought of Dorian on any side but their own was potentially very troubling. "When you do, I'll gladly give you your portrait to take with you. But until then, I'm not having you here at large with your soul in your possession. I know you too well, Dorian. Our White Witch actually isn't too bad, given that she's an allegory for the devil. She's mostly style and malice; she's probably from the mind of a rebellious teenage girl who didn't really understand what evil was, or wasn't interested. You're trouble."

"I'm flattered." Dorian paused. "I *could* threaten to tell them all I know about Dr. Sutherland. Your summoner. You know I'm not above blackmail."

Millie laughed. "You may as well just leave, in that case. I'd make you leave after that anyway, so it would be a sight less bother. And you don't want to leave."

Dorian smiled his lazy, soulless smile, guaranteed to thrill the hearts of all within a five-mile radius, and raised his glass. "Perhaps not quite yet. There are developments I'd like to await, I think. But—"

He broke off. The cord extending from his laptop was twitching: once, twice, three times. In the Street, Millie saw Matilda hurry through the wall, clutching her book. Heathcliff and the Witch emerged; some of the others stepped forward as well, alerted by the flurry of movement.

"Are we expecting someone?" Dorian asked slowly.

"Charley was coming," Millie said. "But not until later."

It wasn't Charley. The figure who staggered through the wall as Millie made it down was a tiny, wizened old man in a nightshirt and nightcap. He was clearly one of them: the air around him brought its own supernatural chill. Millie, standing near him, tasted frost and felt her nose tingle. His face was lean, set in crags more used to frowning than smiling. Now, though, it was stretched tight with terror.

"Who are you?" Millie asked him. "You're safe here, you know, whoever you are."

The man bent and caught his breath, struggling to speak. His limbs were fragile as old twigs.

Darcy Three spoke up first. He was standing by his own door, not far down; the magazine from earlier was still in his hands. "I know him," he said. "He's the Scrooge who told me about the new world. Do you remember, you asked me from where I had heard the rumors? I couldn't find him again."

"Is that true?" Millie asked the old man. "Are you Ebenezer Scrooge, of *A Christmas Carol*?"

The man nodded shortly.

"Did you come from the summoner?" Millie asked him.

"He read most of us away last night." The Scottish brogue was punctuated by gasps. "When you found him. He missed me. I was in the office, fiddling the accounts, and he forgot me. I escaped out the window—hid behind the dustbins. Once he remembers—or he feels me in his head—I'll be gone. I wanted to warn you..."

"We know about the new world," Millie said quickly. "We have the book. Is there anything else you can tell us? Who is he?"

"I can't. We can't speak his name. None of us can—not his real name. He reads that into us, like a spell. We don't even see him the way you would see him."

"He can do that to you?" She was almost sure that Charley couldn't—though it wasn't something that he would ever have tried. "He can make you see him as someone other than who he is?"

"I don't think so. I think—I think we see him as how he truly is. How he began."

Millie frowned. "How would we see him then? Who is he now?"

"We don't know who he is," Scrooge said. "He's a ghost to us. But I can tell you this: He knows you're here. And he knows what Charles Sutherland is."

Heathcliff frowned. "What do you mean?"

Scrooge cried out suddenly, a short sharp cry that brought him to his knees. Millie, reaching out to catch his shoulder, found him ice-cold beneath it. "No... Spirit, hear me! I am not the man I was..."

"He's fading," the White Witch said. "Look."

He was. His edges shimmered with transparency; his voice, too, faded in and out. "Assure me that I yet may change these shadows you have shown me...I will honor Christmas in my heart, and try to keep it all the year..."

"Millie, let him go." It was Heathcliff's voice, for once sharp with urgency. "Quickly."

Millie crouched down, to keep eye level with Scrooge. "Mr. Scrooge. Listen to me. Can you tell us where we might find him?"

Scrooge, with great effort of will, shook his head. "I will live in the Past, the Present, and the Future. The Spirits of all Three shall strive within me. I—"

"Millie!"

She tightened her grip on the bony shoulder. It was like trying to hold on to a fog. "Then listen to me. If the summoner reads you out again, will you give him a message from us? Tell him that we have something of his, and we want to negotiate. Tell him to stop hiding, and talk to us. Can you hear me?"

She thought Scrooge's eyes met hers, but it was difficult to tell.

"Mr. Scrooge?

"For God's sake!" Millie's hand was wrenched from Scrooge's shoulder by a grip like iron. The tips of her fingers passed through the miser rather than from him; he dissolved like ink in water, and was gone.

They looked in silence at the empty space left behind.

"You could have gone with him," Heathcliff said, at last, to her. He released her, gruff with embarrassment. "We are few enough already. We cannot afford to lose you."

"Thank you," Millie heard herself reply. "Poor soul. Jadis, Heathcliff— I wonder if you might make sure you're both around for the rest of the afternoon. Lancelot and the Scarlet Pimpernel volunteered to take a shift this evening, but…"

"I wish one of us were a Wentworth, or a Colonel Brandon," Darcy Three said, with a touch of bitterness. "Instead of so many Darcys. A war hero would be a lot more useful than a gentleman with ten thousand a year."

"I notice you don't wish *you* were a Wentworth," the White Witch said dryly.

Millie had noticed the same, but she still found the sentiment touching. Possibly because of the single lock of hair curling over his eyes. "You can all take your turn all the same," she said. "I think we'd better tighten things up around here. Just to be safe."

"That man was destroyed inside our very walls," the Duke of Wellington said. "We do have a plan, do we not?"

"The summoner can only destroy his own readings," Millie said. She thought it was true. Charley had only ever *altered* a reading not his own, and that had been Henry, not a human character. "He can't hurt us. And yes. We have a plan. You heard me: he'll come to talk to us."

"What do we have of his that he wants?"

"I'd rather not say," Millie said. "But trust me. It will bring him to us. All we have to do is wait."

Dorian was watching silently from his doorway. When she turned, she saw him, glass of absinthe still untouched in his hand. His blue eyes were not so soulless as usual.

"I do want that portrait back," he said.

"The trouble is, all we have is a book," Millie said to Charley later that evening. "It's a sight more than we had last night, but still…do you think the summoner *will* come for this book, after all? It's not impossible to source another."

"The university library copy of that book's been out for two weeks," Charley said. He had come straight from the university; his hair was still windblown from the death trap. "I checked today, as you asked. Nobody's requested it. The public library doesn't have a copy. The summoner could have his own extra copy, of course. But even if he does, I think he'll want this particular copy back. Especially if he gets your invitation."

Despite his best efforts, his eyes kept wandering, not because he didn't feel her urgency, but because Millie had made the mistake of taking him into the Street's bookshop. The walls teemed with books: not the sprawling, disorganized clutter of Charley's house, but crisp, cool, ordered. Many were new volumes, and their colors were bright against the dark Victorian wood. The faded paint over the door declared the shop to belong to "Mr. Brownlow," from *Oliver Twist*, but it was in fact occupied by a tall, brown-skinned woman. She was up on a ladder when they entered, putting a volume on the highest shelf.

"Scheherazade," Millie had introduced her to Charley. "From the *Thousand and One Nights*, of course. She understands English, but doesn't speak very much—she came into the world with only Arabic."

"I had that happen when I was reading the *Odyssey* in Ancient Greek," Charley said. "English translations came out speaking English, but when the words were in Greek, Odysseus showed up speaking Greek as well. It was embarrassing. I thought I was fairly fluent, but you realize your limitations in a dead language when you're trying to explain to a legendary hero how the coffee maker works."

Now, Scheherazade was safely out of earshot at the far end of the shop, continuing her shelving. Half the reason Millie had brought them there was that the woman cared very little about much except collecting and sharing stories, so their conversation could take place in private. The rest of the Street was terrified enough already. She had underestimated the extent to which Charley shared this trait.

"You say the library copy of your book's out?" Millie said. "Who has it?"

He hesitated before he spoke. "Well. Troy Heywood, according to the library. I asked them; like I said, I need to track down books I've written notes in all the time, so they're used to telling me who has them out. He's a postgrad. I'm co-supervising his PhD, actually... he's very bright."

"Bright enough to read out a Dickensian street?"

She had his full attention now. "He'd need to be more than bright for that—and I'd need to have firmer grounds than his intelligence to suspect it. It's not exactly suspicious that he has the book in question out from the library, you know. He's writing a thesis on Dickens and Foucault. He probably has a lot of Dickens criticism out of the library. That's what the library is for. And the Dickens criticism, for that matter."

"You said there weren't any other Dickens scholars in the area."

"He's a student."

"You were a student when you wrote most of that book. You're probably not much older than him now, for that matter. Don't be a snob." Millie sat forward. "Listen to me. Whoever the summoner is, they know you. They know your book; that might be how they tracked you down. But they also know where you live. It can't be a coincidence that they're in the same city as you; since you didn't move to be close to them, they must have moved to be close to you. They know where your brother works: they sent Uriah Heep to watch him. For all you know, there's someone watching you at your own work."

"I think I'd know. Rob recognized Eric."

"That was pure chance. He happened to have already seen another version of Uriah Heep that wasn't too dissimilar. They'd be more careful with who they sent to watch you. Certainly they know where you work. It's public knowledge. They also know where you live. They sent Henry to your house. They've almost certainly made themselves personally acquainted with you. They might not have done so from the university, but you don't strike me as having a large circle of acquaintances outside work."

"Oh, thanks."

"Am I wrong?"

"Only in the sense that I really have *no* circle of acquaintances outside work. None nonfictional or unrelated to me, anyway. I'm busy. There are a lot of books to read."

Millie snorted. "That's rather what I thought. Has your postgraduate student been to your house?"

"Once or twice. Most of the English faculty have. But—"

"So if he wanted to set the Hound of the Baskervilles on you, he'd know where you lived?"

"We probably all want to do that to our thesis supervisors, at some point... Look, I understand your argument. I know that we need to find the summoner. But we can't just jump to accusing people on circumstantial evidence. I can think of a myriad of reasons why he or anyone else in the department would be reading critical books on Dickensian London—my own book included. Troy didn't check it out this morning. He's had it for a while—before we stole the summoner's book last night."

"When exactly was he last at your house?"

"I don't remember exactly. I suppose it would have been—" He stopped. Millie waited, and behind his eyes saw a thread come together against his will. "He was there right before the Hound of the Baskervilles," he said at last. "He left just before, when Rob came. But that doesn't mean anything. There were a handful of people there—all of us on the History of the Modern Novel."

"I'll ask Dorian to look into all of them, just to be safe, of course. But the others aren't nineteenth-century scholars—if I remember the school website. They wouldn't have any reason to prefer Victorian characters over others. This fellow would. How long have you supervised him?"

"About two years. A little more. He was one of the first students I took on when I came over. I know what you're about to suggest. The Street's two years old."

"Is there any chance," Millie said, "that he came to the university because of you?"

"Well... maybe. It's not unusual to go to a university for your PhD because there's someone there who's able to supervise it."

"You know that isn't what I mean. Is it at all possible that he read your book, recognized what you were, and applied to work with you just to be by your side?"

"Maybe," Charley said reluctantly. "But if he can recognize what I am from my work, then surely I should be able to recognize him, if he were a summoner. And I don't."

"Perhaps he's hiding better than you ever have. He has, if we're right, rather more to hide. I think we should look at him more closely."

"Look at him how?"

"Well, Dorian can search his computer, for a start. Otherwise…" Millie grinned. "You haven't seen the Invisible Man yet, have you?"

"I think that would probably be something of a paradox." Meaning caught up to him a second later. "You mean H. G. Wells's Invisible Man?"

"Well, I didn't mean Ralph Ellison's. That one's in Harlem."

"Isn't he a dangerous psychopath? The Wells version, I mean. Griffin."

"A little. He's mellowed rather since 1897. And he's very good at looking at people. It's easier when they can't see you back."

Charley stared at her. "You can't. You can't set the Invisible Man on my students!"

"I can. No harm will come to him, I promise. We've done it before, when we've needed people watched. He'll just stay by the house, invisible, and keep an eye on him. If your student has nothing to hide…"

"I think everyone has something to hide. And definitely everyone has the right not to be followed by an invisible mad scientist!"

Millie cast a warning glance at Scheherazade, who was busy not deaf, and Charley caught himself.

"You saw David Copperfield tied up in the basement," Millie said. "You saw the world that the summoner had built to keep his creations locked up. Scrooge was read away in front of us this afternoon. They have rights as well, fictional or not."

"I know," he said. "I'm sorry. You know I don't mean to suggest they don't. I just don't think it's Troy."

"Truly? Or do you just not want it to be?"

"The former. The latter. Both." He sighed. It was no wonder Rob found it easy to bully him. He was too schooled in seeing other points of view to hold to his own. "If you truly trust the Invisible Man to watch him safely, then I understand it's the best course of action. I just don't want to start suspecting everybody I work with of being a criminal mastermind. I *like* the people I work with—most of them."

"I'm sure most of them like you. You just have to be open to the possibility that one of them might be trying to kill you." She paused. "Did anyone else at work seem to be paying you undue attention today?"

"How many more invisible people do you have?" He considered the question. "Well...if they did, I couldn't blame them. I suspect I was all over the place today. I know I talked too fast through two lectures, which probably drove half my students to Facebook. There was a meeting this afternoon, and I was there, but I couldn't tell you a single thing we discussed."

"You did read the world into a lot of different shapes over the weekend."

"No—well, yes, but it's not just that. I've been worried about this place, but it's not that either. It's more...do you ever get the feeling, after you've been on the Street, that the world outside is so hard and unyielding by comparison you can't get comfortable? You try to push into it, and it just pushes back at you. It's like trying to sleep on a bench."

"When did you ever try to sleep on a bench, Sutherland?"

"At an airport. Half a bench, really. I'd been flying for twenty-four hours, and I can't sleep on planes. But I'm sorry, I forgot—you probably slept on plenty of benches after you left us."

"A sight too many," she said frankly. "But it was all good fun back then. I hadn't grown into this world enough to know any different. Charley—did you mean it, when you said you thought you could learn to do more summoning than you did last night?"

"Of course," he said, without his usual hesitation. "What do you want?"

"Cross your heart? Because you were rather tired last night. You look rather tired still, if truth be told."

"I didn't say I could do it easily. Pushing the boundaries of reality shouldn't be easy, or there's something wrong. I can still do it."

She nodded. "Good man. Until Scrooge came today, I was going to ask you if you could read out anyone else like Uriah—people who had counterparts with the summoner, who might be able to tell us what's going on in their heads. It looks like the summoner's put a stop to that, but we could still try. It's the other half of why I brought us here—these books would be as good a place to start as any. If they want to stay out after you've read them, that's all well and good. Plenty of houses on the Street."

"I'll try," he said. "I also think we need to do more than that. Even if we find the summoner, we need to meet him from a stronger position. You're hoping he'll negotiate because you have me and his book, but he's better than I am. We need to know a good deal more about summoning than we know now. *I* need to know a good deal more. And that means reading, experimenting, and going deeper."

"How deep?"

"As deep and as far as it goes. The other summoner can make an entire Street. We need to understand how."

"I suppose we do," Millie said cautiously. "If you're up to it."

"I'll be up to it."

"If you do, though, we need to keep it very quiet from the rest of the Street. I don't know how they'll react."

"Even Dorian? You said he knows what I am."

She thought of the look on Dorian's face before he had withdrawn into his house. It hurt her heart, but she nodded. "Yes. Even Dorian."

"All right. It's not as though I'm not used to it." He smiled, at once shy and brimming with excitement. "I want to try something new with the *Secret Garden* door, actually. You know we were wondering how the summoner escaped the office without being seen by the lookout? The tunnel leading to the sea made me think of it. In the book, the door doesn't just go to the other side of the wall. That was a shallow reading on my part. It goes to a secret place, locked off from the rest of the world. It's a portal. It occurred to me to wonder if the summoner might know how to use portals too. And I wondered where else ours might be able to go."

"I say." She wasn't sure whether to be amused, fascinated, or nervous. "You're the literary equivalent of the scientists who split the atom."

"Books don't hurt people."

"What comes out of them jolly well does."

"Does that mean you think it shouldn't be attempted?"

"No," she said. "No, it doesn't mean that." And she knew that they were reaching deeper into something strange, glittering, and infinitely dangerous.

That night, Millie stood in the real world, at the end of the alleyway. The sky was soft and dark, only intermittently pierced by the early stars. She stood there for a long time.

At length, a shadow passed over the streetlights. A large, ungainly bird flapped across the road: a kererū, a wood pigeon. Its white chest was visible from the distance and its dark green wings fought the high wind. Millie waved at it.

The wood pigeon circled once more, then landed on the rubbish skip beside her in a clatter of claws. It tilted its head at her, and its black eyes gleamed.

"Hello," Millie said. "I say, I'm glad I found you. May we talk a moment?"

The wood pigeon indicated with a wave of a claw that it had no objections.

"We've found out what's behind the disturbances," Millie said. "A summoner means to create a new world from the covers of a book. To rewrite reality. He wants to bring Victorian England here."

In a burst of feathers, a slim, scantily clad Māori man was sitting on the edge of the skip where the bird had been. His face was shrewd and clever. It was impossible to tell from it whether Millie's news was news to him or not.

"It wouldn't be the first time Victorian England came to this country," Maui said.

"No." She knew he wasn't only talking about the Street. She wondered, once again, just how long Maui had been in the world. "But it might be the last. I know you don't like the Street being here very much, but it did at least bring our own land with it. We live side by side with you, whether inside the Street or out. The new world would rewrite everything."

"I heard the first time," he said. "It all sounds a bit postcolonial, doesn't it?"

"You warned the Duke of Wellington that the new world was coming here. It must have worried you."

"Maybe I just wanted you lot to find out what it meant. Spare me the trouble."

"Well, we did."

"Maybe I knew already." He tilted his head. His eyes were as bright as they had been as a bird; or, perhaps, they had been as bright as a human's eyes when he was a bird. "What have you come to ask from me? You want me to help you investigate this?"

"No. Well, yes, if there's anything you can do, but no. I want to know if you'll stand with us, if the worst happens, and it comes to a fight between the summoner and the Street."

Maui laughed. "And why would I help you?"

"You wouldn't. I know full well we're nothing much to you. But I hoped—you're not just a storybook character. You're a culture hero, and this is your land. I hoped you might want to protect it."

He considered for a long time. "When it's time to fight," he said at last, "I'll decide if it's my fight. If it is, you'll know. That's the best I can promise and mean it. I am a trickster, after all."

It was the best she could hope for, the best but one, and that was for the time never to come at all.

Lydia

Lydia knew Eric as soon as she saw him. It wasn't just that he was the only person likely to be in Rob's office when Rob wasn't there. She had spent the morning thinking about his voice on the phone, and his appearance matched his voice exactly. He was thin and pale—like, she couldn't help thinking, one of the wriggling white huhu grubs she and Rob had unearthed when they turned over an old log in the garden. He squinted at the laptop inches from his nose.

"Hello," she said. His eyes instantly rose to meet hers. In the yellowish light, they looked red. "I'm Lydia. Are you Eric?"

"I am," he said. His voice was even more grating in person. "What a lovely surprise. I'm so pleased to meet you, Miss Lydia."

"I'm pleased to meet you too. Do you mind if I come in?"

His head twitched in what might have been a negative. "You aren't. You're repulsed by me. But it's ever so nice of you to lie. And of course you may come in."

Lydia entered Rob's office, and closed the door lightly behind her—not all the way, but enough to keep their conversation private from the murmur of legal personnel in the corridors. She had been in Rob's office a handful of times, to wait for him to finish so they could drive home together or get lunch downtown. He had moved into it a few months ago, and it still didn't quite look like him when he wasn't in it. The sharp, corporate edges hadn't been worn in yet, and even with Eric installed at a table against the wall, there was too much empty space. The harbor looked gray and wind-whipped out the window under the clouded sky.

"You came after all then," Eric said.

"I wasn't going to," she said honestly.

"What changed your mind?"

She shrugged. "I knew Rob was in court this afternoon. I thought I might as well come meet him here. And while I was here, I thought I might as well as least come and meet you in person."

"Mr. Sutherland didn't tell you where he was last night, did he?"

"No," she said. "He did not."

"And you don't trust him."

"That's the pointed issue, isn't it?" It was something she had given some thought to, as she lay turned away from him in bed last night. "I trust him to mean well, absolutely. I don't trust him to be right."

"So you trust his morals, but not his intellect?"

She snorted. "That's not very flattering to him, is it? And it's not what I mean. You can be wrong without being either immoral or stupid, you know."

"I wouldn't know, I'm afraid," Eric said. "I know that I try not to be stupid. You want me to tell you where he was, don't you?"

She didn't answer directly. Instead, she looked at him, taking in every part, the way she always did with people she wanted to make very sure of. Very few people met the challenge of regarding her with equal frankness. Her sister had told her once that she gave the impression she was measuring them up for either a makeover or a coffin. Eric, to his credit, only twitched once or twice as she took in his pale, emaciated frame, the dark circles under his eyes, the way his eyes darted to the door at the slightest sound.

"Rob says you're trouble," she said. "He told me to stay away from you."

"You didn't listen then. Do you think I'm trouble?"

"Nobody else seems to. I asked Eva, you know; I spoke to her on the way in. She says you're nice enough, and a hard worker. Mind you, I didn't tell her what you'd said to me on the phone." She leaned back against Rob's desk. "I don't think you're trouble. I think, though, you might be *in* some kind of trouble."

"What makes you say that?"

"You're frightened of something. But whatever it is, it's not here— you wouldn't have been here after dark if it was. I think it's something at home. To answer your question: I would like you to tell me where you thought Rob was. I also want you to tell me how you know, and why you would be so invested in our lives. You must realize it's more than a little creepy."

"I do. I always realize. But I assure you, my investment in your lives is undesired on my part, and my reasons for mentioning it to you are purely self-serving. I want to help you in exchange for your help."

"My help?"

"You were right. I am indeed in some kind of trouble—or, at least, I'm in a situation that I very much need to escape. I can't say much more than that, but I assure you, I want nothing illegal."

She considered him carefully. "You must be able to say a little more than that. Are you being threatened?"

"Yes." His eyes glinted beneath his glasses. "That is exactly what I am."

"Who by? Somebody you live with?"

He laughed shortly, and bitterly. "I don't live. Not really. But yes, you could say that. Somebody I live with. At home."

"Do they hurt you?"

"Oh yes." He seemed not so much surprised by the question as resigned. That, more than anything, convinced her that he was sincere. "Always. If they knew I was talking to you right now, I would never be heard from again."

"Go to the police."

"I can't."

"They have friends in the police?"

"Something like that."

"Something." She paused. "You know, when I was working at a bar ten years ago, we used to have a young woman coming in with her boyfriend. He was a police officer—a really nice young guy, people thought. But some of us used to notice that every so often, he'd ignore her for no reason, as if he were punishing her. Her face would be so desperate and miserable. And once, he raised his hand to wave at someone, and I saw her flinch on instinct. She used to work long hours as well."

"She sounds like an unfortunate woman."

"She was. A couple of us tried to help her, but she didn't want to be helped. Not then. Perhaps she found her own escape route. What is it that you want?"

"I want to live." His vehemence startled her. "I want to live in the world, unbound, following nobody's plots but my own."

"And what's binding you now?"

"I can't tell you."

That phrase again. Her instinct was to lose her patience; just in time, she reined it in. When Rob said he couldn't tell her what was going on, he meant he wouldn't. Eric, she suspected, at least really believed that he couldn't. His waxy face had paled, and there were beads of sweat at his hairline. "Why not? What's wrong?"

He laughed through gritted teeth. "Think of it like being under a spell, Mrs.—Miss Lydia. A spell I need to work around very careful-like."

Lydia had no experience with spells. She *had*, over the years she'd worked in bars and hotels, seen people that were afraid, and who were in need of help. She was now willing to swear, whatever Rob had said, that Eric was both.

"Suppose I were to help you," she said. "What would you need?"

He drew a deep breath, and exhaled again. "Money. Not a great deal of it—enough, say, for a few weeks in a hostel, plus food. Perhaps three hundred dollars. I could take it from there. Oh, and a ticket for the ferry across the Cook Strait."

"You want to make it to the South Island?"

"I want to make it anywhere away from here. But the South Island will do well enough. It'll be summer soon. I can find work fruit picking, or anything else students won't touch."

"That doesn't sound like much to ask for. You're at the tail end of a law degree, after all—aren't you?"

"I don't need anything grand. I can be very humble. But I'm not asking. I'd be ever so grateful—more grateful than I could say—if you would help me, but I would never ask for such a thing with no return. You want to know where Mr. Sutherland went on Sunday night, and what it has to do with his brother."

Lydia blinked. "You know Charley?"

"We've not met. I've glimpsed him once or twice. Well?"

"If you're really being threatened," she said, "then you don't need to bargain with me. I'd help you. So would Rob."

"You couldn't tell Mr. Sutherland about this," Eric said at once.

"Why? He'd want to help. He's not a lawyer for nothing, you know."

"Perhaps he might," Eric said. "But it would be too dangerous for me. He's too close to it. If he tried to help me, the person I need to escape would know about it, and he'd know I'd talked. I really am not exaggerating, Miss Lydia. My life is at stake. I'm offering to help you because I need you to help me. Perhaps I didn't need to bargain, but if you'll forgive me for saying so, that doesn't accord with my experience. People don't tend to want to help me. Besides, I might think you deserve to know what Mr. Sutherland is up to."

The truth was, she did—or, at least, she desperately wanted to know. She also, having met Eric, wanted to help him—whatever trouble he was in, she believed that it was real. It was the fact that these two instincts were able to be so easily satisfied in a single blow that left her uneasy. Something wasn't quite adding up. The difficulty was, just as she hadn't been able to think of any concrete footing on which to found her suspicions of Rob's behavior, she couldn't find one for Eric. In any other situation but the one he described, it would be a terribly elaborate ploy for a few hundred dollars and a ticket across Cook Strait.

"All right," she said at last. "I'll help you. Would you want the money now?"

It was partly a test, to see what he would say—she assumed a con man would want to see cash as soon as possible. She wasn't surprised when he shook his head. "Not now. They'd find money on me as soon as I went home, and that would be the end of it. I'll phone you when it's time. I'll ask to meet; please don't be offended if I don't say anything more, or if I pretend this meeting never happened. People might be listening. But when I call, I need you to book me a ticket on the very next ferry out of the harbor, and to bring me three hundred dollars in cash. You need to be prepared to come quickly. I'll tell you everything you want to know then, I promise."

"All right." She paused. "Tell me one thing now. Is Rob in trouble?"

"Oh yes," Eric answered promptly. "Yes, I would say that is exactly where he is."

XVI

Charley's birth certificate arrived in my inbox on Tuesday morning—one of the advantages of working for a reasonably prestigious law firm. Charles Sutherland, born on the seventeenth day of August twenty-six years ago to Susan and Joseph Sutherland. So that was that. He was my brother. It didn't surprise me. I had always known that, whatever else happened. It was the rest of the world that was suddenly uncertain.

Work went by that day in a haze of conversations and paperwork and court appearances. Now that I knew, I couldn't believe nobody had noticed a fictional crime ring had been operating out of central Wellington. The firm was the busiest it had been in years. Yet I couldn't concentrate, not wholeheartedly. Every time my cell phone rang, I flinched, expecting Charley or even Millie. Twice it was Lydia saying she would be home late and asking if we needed anything from the store. The rest of the time it was work. It was never my brother. The silence from the Street felt like something holding its breath. The trouble was, I didn't know what that something was.

And all the while, Eric was by my side, observing me at meetings, following me to court, working at his table in the corner of my office. It was like having an extra shadow, one that wanted to swallow me whole.

"Have you heard from your brother lately, Mr. Sutherland?" he asked once.

"Just get on with your work," I said. I never would have spoken to a real intern like that. I wonder if he knew that—if, in fact, he was playing with me all along, knowing full well that I knew who he was.

I didn't dare to ask him, for fear he'd disappear. At least while he was by my side, watching me, I was also watching him.

I called Charley myself, while Eric was safely dispatched getting coffee from down the street. When I couldn't get him on his cell phone, I tried his office. He wasn't there, but I managed to catch Beth White.

"Charles isn't here this afternoon," she explained. "He's supposed to be working from home, though I can't get him on the phone either. I'm only in his office to get a textbook. We have a standing agreement that we can break into each other's offices if we suspect our books are being held captive there."

"Sort of a probable cause arrangement," I said. Her brisk, kind voice calmed me somewhat. "I like it. Well, I was just trying to catch him. His cell phone went to voicemail."

"It does that," she agreed. "He may be in later. Shall I tell him you phoned?"

"No," I said quickly. "No, don't worry. It wasn't important."

"Everything's all right, isn't it?" Beth said. "I apologize if it's none of my business. Charles has just seemed distracted this week."

I hesitated for a moment. I couldn't tell Beth everything, of course, but it occurred to me that if anyone would be able to help, it would be another literary scholar.

"Everything's fine," I said.

She seemed to hear my hesitation better than my words. "I'm not quite sure if I should mention this," she said, "but last week, when you came to Charles's house, I had the distinct impression that something was wrong. And I know that since then, Charles has had something on his mind. I don't expect you to tell me what it is. But if there's any way I can help…"

I don't know how Charley always manages to amass at least one or two people in any given environment who are willing to look after him.

"Thanks," I said. I meant it too. "Just—If anything happens, could you give me a call? I'd really appreciate it."

"Of course," she said. "What kind of thing?"

I almost laughed. "Oh, trust me. You'll know it when you see it."

I tried his cell phone again, in one of those classic examples of hope over experience. Voicemail. I told myself that could mean anything; he could be anywhere. I knew where he was.

I looked out the window, trying to comfort myself with the lines and contours of the city: the jumble of colonial houses on the hills, the curves of the streets, the windblown harbor. The surrounding bush, ancient and mysterious and steeped in Polynesian legend. All I could see were the old Victorian bones peeking out from beneath. Wellington had been colonized in 1840. Across the world, according to Google, Charles Dickens was writing *The Old Curiosity Shop*.

That same evening, Lydia came under fire from me when she arrived home from her late shift at the hotel and found me reading *David Copperfield*. It was the copy I had borrowed from my parents' bookshelf that weekend—probably the first one Charley had read, when he was four or so. The cover was blue leather embossed with gold, part of a set of matching volumes. Each book opened to a glossy full-color portrait of a young Dickens, seated on a chair looking into the distance, dark auburn curls tumbling around a delicate face. If not for the air of confidence, he would have looked a little like my brother.

I had started to read it for information, in a spirit of extreme bitterness, prepared to hate it. I couldn't. David's voice, from the first line, was too arresting: wry, confidential, witty, surprising. I had laughed by the end of the first page; I was lost by the second. Semiautobiographical, Charley had called it, but I doubted that Dickens's life could have been peopled with quite so many dastardly step-relatives, loving servants, and colorful aunts. It was more than that, though. He *knew* things. Things about childhood, and guilt, and suffering. When Lydia opened the door out of nowhere, I was so deep in David Copperfield's first day at school that I jumped. She found that funnier than it was.

"That's your brother's book, isn't it?" she asked.

"Why d'you call it that?" I asked, surprising myself with my own defensiveness.

I surprised Lydia too; she paused kicking her shoes off. "Shouldn't I? It's what he studies, isn't it?"

"Of course." I shook my head. "I just—I wondered why you called it that, that's all."

She shrugged. "I didn't mean anything by it. Just that when I think of Dickens, I think of your brother. He wasn't named after him, was he?"

"Charley? I don't think so." I'd never really made the connection, probably because I wasn't used to thinking of either Dickens or my brother as Charles. "Maybe. Mum always liked Dickens. I know I was named after my grandfather on my father's side. Nothing literary there."

"Unless your grandfather was Robert Louis Stevenson," Lydia said. "Is there any dinner left?"

"In the fridge," I told her. "And there's ice cream in the freezer. I picked it up on the way back."

"For that, I'll forgive you for biting my head off. And for not asking how my day was immediately."

That made me smile reluctantly, as she knew it would.

"I apologize for biting your head off." I put the book away, more regretfully than I liked to admit, and leaned back to watch her in the kitchen. "And how was your day, immediately?"

"Don't ask." She found the pasta in the fridge, and put it in the microwave. I heard the triple beep, and then the low, comforting hum. "Charley hasn't called you since the weekend."

"I thought you wanted him to stop calling."

"I wanted you to tell me what he was calling about, as a matter of fact. I still do."

"Well. I don't think he'll call again anytime soon."

"Why not?" She leaned on her elbows against the kitchen counter, so as to scrutinize me more carefully. By all appearances, she had forgiven me for Sunday night quickly—almost too quickly—but I knew it was on her mind. There was a barrier between us that was difficult to define, and impossible to break through. We'd never had real secrets before. "Have you two had a fight?"

"Not really." We had, I suppose. Of course we had. But that was the least of it. "I just...I never understand how you can both worry about someone getting hurt and want to kill them yourself, you know?"

She laughed. "That's just brothers. Trust me, I have three younger brothers, and one elder. When we get together, our friendliest interactions legally constitute grievous bodily harm. But I would kill anyone else who laid a finger on them."

My stomach twisted uncomfortably at that. It was too close to something Uriah Heep had reminded me of. I don't know why I always feel uncomfortable emotions in my stomach. It doesn't make sense, and it's not very fair. It's just a thing.

I lay awake all that night, staring up at the ceiling. Searching the university database for the summoner had done me no good; really, I had known it wouldn't, much as I had known Charley's birth certificate would only prove he was ours. If I was going to find the summoner through any rational means, the answer lay closer to home. And if I still wanted to, I was running out of time. I needed help of some kind.

When the night began to thin around me, I sat up and pulled my laptop from the dresser to my knee. I thought it would be difficult to find who I was after. In fact, I found him within three minutes on the hospital's main website. I suppose, for all their concern about secrecy, nobody would think to look for literary characters. The only reason they might choose not to use their real names would be because nobody would believe them.

Still. Victor Prometheus Godwin. That wasn't even *trying*.

The next day, I called the hospital from my office, and with a combination of bluster and legal fudgery managed to get patched down to the mortuary. When I heard the cultured voice, I knew I had the right man.

"This is Godwin."

"This is Robert Sutherland," I said. "I'm—"

"I know who you are." He didn't sound surprised, but perhaps he sounded a little cautious. "You're Charles Sutherland's brother."

"And you're Victor Frankenstein. I want to talk to you. In private."

There was silence. "I have an hour for lunch at one," he said. "You can meet me at the Bolton Street cemetery."

Many thoughts raced through my mind before I found my voice

again, the loudest being that this was a terrible idea, leave it *alone*, for God's sake.

"Fine," I said. "Which grave?"

It was one of those crisp, clear Wellington days, when trees and buildings are sharp-edged in the sunlight and the sky looks as though it would chime like crystal if flicked with a fingernail. The graveyard in question was just around the corner from Parliament, and was a piece of history rather than a working burial ground. The graves there went back to the early settlement, and over the years had grown into more of a public park. I had always liked it. It wound up the hills to the Botanic Gardens, the worn headstones peaceful in the shade of towering pine trees. People meandered through, talking on their phones or listening to music. I heard a tui piping in the distance. There was nothing in the least Gothic about any of it, except the person I was going to meet.

I followed the visitors' map to the grave the mortuary attendant had named, off the path and over the curve of the hill overlooking the old Thorndon houses. Down there, the sunlight was softer, and the grass gave off a faint warmth and sweetness. The wind rustled the branches of the trees overhead, but didn't make it to the ground.

Frankenstein was sitting on a headstone, eating fish and chips from a paper bag. His long, thin legs were stretched out in front of him, and he was waiting for me.

I haven't in fact read *Frankenstein*, but I've done everything but. I grew up watching old horror movies with Dad. I knew Dr. Frankenstein from those, as a wide-eyed black-and-white madman surrounded by crackling electricity. I met him again in one of the comic books I always got for Christmas, captured in hand-drawn lines and pastel colors. Because I'd read the introduction of Charley's copy of *Frankenstein*, I knew that his book was written by Mary Shelley, who at the time was Mary Wollstonecraft Godwin, eighteen years old and traveling with her lover Percy Bysshe Shelley and his friend Lord Byron in Geneva. Childishly, I'd never wanted to meet the Frankenstein between the pages of that book. He belonged to Charley, who managed to colonize most of the literary landscape of our house before I could reach it. My Frankenstein was the one of popular imagination, the one who cried, "It's alive!" while lightning clashed, and I liked him.

This Frankenstein was neither mine, nor exactly Mary Shelley's. He belonged to some unknown reader, who had apparently bestowed upon him a penchant for black coats, and pale skin that, in the harsh New Zealand sun, was starting to freckle. But his eyes I recognized. They were pale gray, as they had been on the silver screen, and they glittered as he looked at me.

"Dr. Frankenstein?" I said as I approached. I tried to keep my tone as businesslike as possible, as though he were an expert witness, or a client I was trying to clear of selling dodgy televisions. "I'm—"

"You're Dr. Sutherland's brother," Frankenstein said. He had a quiet, well-spoken manner; the accent was difficult to place, except as vaguely English and vaguely exotic. Swiss written by an Englishwoman read by goodness knows whom. "I know. You don't look very much like him."

"You're not the first to notice it. You two have met, then?"

"No. I don't go to the Street much. But I've heard the stories. Right now, he's the only thing standing in the way of the new world—or so they say. There are many people out there who'd wish him harm for that, and many who think he's going to save them."

"What do you know about the new world?"

"I know it's supposed to be coming. There have been whispers of it for over a year, and they've been getting louder."

"From the summoner's creations, do you mean? That's where Millie said they'd sprung from. Mr. Darcy met a Scrooge on the road one night, or something. But it doesn't make sense. It seems to imply that the summoner wants people to know he's here, and what he's planning. Why would he?"

Frankenstein raised an eyebrow. "I really have not the qualifications nor the interest to answer questions about the summoner, Sutherland. You should talk to the Street. Millie, I believe, is very keen to know his mind."

I knew this all too well. But unfortunately, the Street and I were no longer on speaking terms. "If you had to speculate."

"If I had to." He considered. "It's possible that you're correct, and as the new world draws closer, the summoner wants us to prepare for it. There is another possibility, however."

"Which is?"

"The summoner's characters are trying to warn us. As much as they can, within the limitations the summoner has imposed upon them, those poor, flat creatures of ink are trying to tell us to protect ourselves. And perhaps to save them."

I thought of Eric and his comments about my brother. I had thought at the time that he had realized I knew who he was and was taunting me—but if so, it was curious that the summoner kept him near me. I wondered, for the first time, if I had misjudged him. Perhaps Eric did, indeed, know or guess that I had recognized him, and what I had taken to be taunts were really all the warnings he could give me.

"Which do you think it is?"

Frankenstein shrugged. A veil had fallen over his silvery eyes. "Personally, I try not to listen to rumors. I'm too busy."

I didn't want to know what he might be busy doing.

"How did you know to look for me, may I ask?" he said, more prosaically. "I appreciate that once you did, I may not have been difficult to find."

"Millie mentioned you," I said. "Offhandedly. You stuck in my mind."

"I'm flattered. To what do I owe this honor then?"

I pulled my mind back to the present with an effort that seemed physical rather than mental. "I've come to you as a lawyer coming to a hospital worker," I said, in what was a desperate grab at normality under the circumstances. "I want information from the hospital, and I think you can help me."

"Once again," he said, "I would think that the Street could best help you with that. Dorian Gray is known to be a veritable fountain of information."

"I don't trust Dorian Gray," I said. "And I don't want any dealings with the Street at the moment. I can pay you for your time."

"I take it then you want information I shouldn't be giving you," Frankenstein said. "And the money you speak of would be not so much a payment as a bribe. Does the desire for knowledge often overcome your ethics, Sutherland?"

"No," I said, firmly. "Never. I'm not one of those lawyers. But this is about my brother."

"And we do extraordinary things for the people we love, do we not?" Frankenstein said. His wild eyes shone. "We pit ourselves against death itself in their names. We sell our very souls."

"Well, I wasn't exactly considering that." I kept my voice deliberately dry, and folded my arms so he couldn't see me shiver. "I was thinking maybe a hundred dollars."

Frankenstein laughed unexpectedly. "And what would you be gaining from this Faustian deal?"

"Well, first of all," I said. "I want Charley's medical records. He hardly ever goes to the doctor, so they're probably still back in England, but you should be able to access them through the hospital. Specifically, I want anything from his birth and early infancy. I know records from then exist. He was a bit of a special case."

"He could request a copy of those himself, I assume."

"I know. I'd rather do it this way, for now." I didn't want to say that we weren't speaking. It sounded childish; besides, it was none of his business. "When I find out what they say, I might have more medical data for you to find."

"I see. And what do you expect them to say?"

I thought about telling him it was none of his business, but I relented. It probably wasn't wise to push literature's original mad scientist too far. He'd see them for himself soon enough anyway. "They'll say that he was a stillbirth, who revived unexpectedly and spontaneously after twenty minutes with no heartbeat or respiration. I want to see what else they say, and then I want to see if I can find anyone else who matches it."

Two things stood out about Charley that could be tracked on paper. One was that he was highly precocious, especially at literature and language. That had been my first line of inquiry, but it didn't seem to being getting me anywhere. The other thing was that he had been pronounced dead at birth. And, as Lydia had said, nobody spends the first twenty minutes of their life dead without consequences. At the very least, I'd soon know if I was wrong. Children born dead who grow up to demonstrate brilliant language abilities have to be few and far between.

I don't think Dr. Frankenstein heard the last part of what I had said. His eyebrows had shot up at the first sentence, and stayed there as his eyes grew thoughtful.

"If you were in a certain kind of book," he said at last, "I'd say you were talking about a changeling."

I frowned. "You mean a child swapped out by fairies?"

"Exactly. A child who mysteriously awakens from death, grows up to look nothing like his family, displays a highly precocious intellect, and wields magic powers... Well, that would certainly have raised eyebrows a few hundred years ago, shall I say."

I had thought something similar, in a more literal sense. It was why I had looked for his birth certificate first—to ensure he really did belong to us. But he did. Whatever else he was, he was ours.

"I thought you were a scientist."

"I began as an alchemist. A follower of the ancient philosophers, who sought to transmute base metal to gold and bestow everlasting life. And I am one yet, in many ways. I consider myself a student of natural philosophy. I don't believe in changelings. I *do* believe there's something peculiar about your brother's origins, and that gives him the power to bestow life. Life from thought and language. That interests me."

"Leave him alone," I warned, with a sting of alarm. The last thing I needed was to set Dr. Frankenstein after my brother. "He's not your concern."

"At this point, I'm more interested in seeing his medical records than him, I assure you," Frankenstein said. "Besides, there are so many interested parties around him that I would be fortunate to catch a glimpse. What you need to understand about protagonists, Sutherland, is that we're all busy with our own plots. We can't help it; we're not used to sharing our stories. And right now, most stories are all about your brother, the other summoner, and the new world."

"And what about you?" I asked. "What's your story? What's your interest in the new world?"

"I'm Dr. Frankenstein," he said. "My story is about life and death, of course. Where do we come from? Where do we go? How do we keep ourselves from leaving? I don't care about the new world. I care about penetrating the mystery of what gives us life. That's my interest in Dr. Charles Sutherland, and the other summoner. You've increased it rather, today."

"So that's why you're here," I said, with a nod to the graves. "And it's why you work at the mortuary. You're still trying to revive the dead."

"*Your* dead?" Frankenstein said. "Forgive me, but any interest in your moldering physical forms is purely nostalgic, I assure you. I work at the mortuary because it's a job well suited to my skill set; I come here for lunch because—well, let us say it satisfies my Gothic elements. And it reminds me of simpler times, times I may not have actually lived, when life and death were human and more easily researched. It's not human life and death I'm concerned with anymore. It's ours. This life I and those like me have been so mysteriously given from fiction. I want to know how that is created, and how it grows. Where we come from, and how we can stay here."

"You come from books, don't you?"

"A book is words on a page," Frankenstein said. There was a touch of scorn in his voice. "You tell me, how does one *come from* that? I don't dispute your theory. But like most, you haven't bothered to interrogate its basic principles."

"I'm sure you have. Have you found any answers?"

"None," he said. "But I hope to, though I know that such an answer may destroy me."

"Well, good luck with that." The wind must have picked up; I was suddenly cold. "Personally, I don't want any answers that may destroy me."

"In that case," Frankenstein said, "be very careful about the answers you chase right now. Do not drink of the intoxicating draft; dash it from your lips before you taste its true bitterness. Questions are dangerous, and their answers are more dangerous yet. But you won't stop. Nor will I. Nor will your brother, I suspect, though he and I have never met. It's in our natures to chase the secrets of the universe."

"I don't chase the secrets of the universe. I don't chase any secrets."

"You told me you were a lawyer. Don't you deal with secrets every day? Did you really take up your chosen profession to not look at them? Or do you go after the facts at all cost?"

"Lately, it seems I'm going after stories."

"Well," he said softly. "I rest my case. Those are the most dangerous of all."

I hate dealing with literary characters. I really do. "Can you get the records for me?"

"I can." He ate another chip, and wiped the salt from his fingers. "And you needn't trouble yourself about payment. As I said, I want to see them too."

"Good." I paused. "While you're at it, there's another set of medical records I'd like."

"And whose might that be?"

"Susan Sutherland. Her maiden name was Walters. She's our mother."

One dark eyebrow shot up. "You suspect a genetic link?"

"I think something might show up. I don't think she has anything to do with this. But it couldn't hurt to look. I know Dad's side of the family. I don't know hers."

And she had been hiding something. However hard I tried, I couldn't twist that into something I had imagined. She really had been startled by my question. It was Mum who had made me suspicious of Charley's birth in the first place when I asked her about our family history. I had thought she might be reacting to the idea that Charley wasn't a member of our family at all—that was how it still read to me, in my head. But it wasn't what I had asked. I had asked if anyone else in our family had been a summoner. I had said that his ability must come from somewhere. I had never seen Mum read anything out of a book, of course. But she was the one whose family history was a blank. She was the one from whom Charley had inherited his love of books, and reading, and Dickens.

It couldn't hurt to look.

"It always hurts to look," Frankenstein said. It startled me, until I realized I had used the phrase earlier. "Sometimes it even blinds. But I'll see what I can do."

I left him sitting on the headstone, the trees rustling and creaking above him against the cloudless sky.

The following day was our father's birthday. I phoned him to wish him the best—late in the day, because it was the first chance work had given me to so much as breathe—and he told me Charley had already called. To be accurate, he had phoned at six in the morning, and though Charley had been purposefully vague about it, Dad suspected he hadn't been to bed. It was still better than the hours he rang when he was in England.

"I'm sure he's fine, Dad," I said, although he hadn't really suggested otherwise. I could hear the question lurking around the edges. "I mean, he's Charley. You know how he is. He gets obsessed."

"Oh, I know," he said. "And I know you're both old enough to take care of yourselves. Still. It's good you're in the same city, to look out for each other."

And of course, I felt a guilty lurch, because I wasn't looking out for my brother. At most, I was looking into him, the way I would a murder suspect. I hadn't even seen him. As far as I was concerned, it was as if he'd disappeared from the face of the earth.

Millie

A re you sure?" Millie asked. "Not a whisper?"

The person to whom this question was addressed was a fearful man, all in coarse gray, with a great iron on his leg. A man with no hat, and with broken shoes, and with an old rag tied round his head. A man who had been soaked in water, and smothered in mud, and lamed by stones, and cut by flints, and stung by nettles, and torn by briars; who limped, and shivered, and glared, and growled; and to whom Charley had already apologized profusely for his current state.

"I should have gone from the last third of the book," he said, "when you've come into a fortune, and you look a bit better. It's just that I think the Abel Magwitch the other summoner has, if he indeed has one, would be from the opening of chapter one. And I thought that might make the connection between the two of you stronger."

"No, young miss," the Abel Magwitch in front of them now replied. "There's nobody as to who I can 'ear. More's the pity, if I'm to believe you're telling the truth—which I does."

"Bother," Millie sighed. "We did hope—they have a Magwitch, you see, according to Dorian. And we hoped that if we brought you out, you might be able to share glimpses of what they were seeing or hearing. We've tried it with Fagin from *Oliver Twist* as well, earlier tonight, but he couldn't hear anything. And Uriah Heep claims he's told us all he can."

"Would you like some refreshment before you go?" Charley asked. "We have tea and—actually, I have no idea. It's Millie's house."

"You've been here often enough over the last few days," Millie reminded him. "You ought to know what I have by now."

"Thankee my boy," Magwitch said. "That's right noble of ye. I'd like some wittles, if ye've got 'em."

Millie found him some sponge cake and some orange juice in her cupboard, without lighting a candle or the gas lamps. They were keeping her living room dark so the Magwitch of the summoner would see nothing through the eyes of their own Magwitch; only the fire glowed dimly, so that Charley could read the text of *Great Expectations* sitting cross-legged in its light. Henry lay stretched out by the warmth, his tail thumping peacefully. Literary figments coming and going held no concern for him, apparently.

"You're sure you can't sense another one of you?" she asked Magwitch. "Perhaps he's asleep, or in the dark?"

Magwitch shook his head. "'E might be, miss. But I can't sense anybody." He shoved the cake in his mouth, chewing noisily, and gulped down the juice. "Excellent wittles, thankee both."

"You're welcome," Millie sighed. "I think we'd better send you back, assuming you don't mind. Charley?"

"If you'd hold still, Mr. Magwitch, or even give me your hand," Charley said, "it would help."

Magwitch held out his hand obligingly. "Thankee, my boy," he said. "For the hint that I come into a fortune later in the story. I'll enjoy that, I will."

It was the second time that night Millie had seen somebody disappear back into their book. The flare of light was sudden and sharp, and she thought she heard a faint gasp from the criminal before he vanished.

"Do we believe him?" Charley asked as the smell of smoke and marsh drizzle faded from the room.

"I think so," Millie said. "Magwitch always seemed a decent sort. And they all say the same story, the people you've brought out over the last few days. Nobody can see anything. I think the summoner's gone dark after our expedition into his lair, just as Scrooge said. To stop us seeing him."

"Scrooge also said that they didn't see the summoner the way he would look to us. If that's true, it wouldn't matter if we found a character looking at him directly. We wouldn't recognize him. I still don't know how he can do that."

"They see him as he really is, Scrooge said. As though he spends the rest of the time in disguise. Would you like some of this sponge cake, by the way? I'm having some. It's important to keep your strength up on adventures."

"Thanks." He put aside *Great Expectations* and stretched as Millie went to the kitchenette. "If the summoner *has* recalled all his characters, you know, that means his criminal activities aren't important to him anymore. He's entirely focused on reading out the new world. It also means he's probably unlikely to want to talk to us. I think we're running out of time."

Millie didn't argue. Everyone could feel it. It was a hush on the wind, a whisper in the dark. The Street shifted and creaked at night as they lay in their beds, and walls and sky shimmered. The quiet was that of a waiting ambush.

"I don't see what more we can do," she said. She handed Charley a piece of cake on a plate, and leaned back against the couch with her own in hand. It was sweet and slightly stale, and it crumbled when she bit it. "We have the Street on high alert. The Invisible Man has nothing to report from your student's house, by the way. Perhaps you're right, and that's another dead end."

Charley winced. "I still find it a little discomforting that he's there at all."

"Needs must, old thing. Dorian's been watching your student's computer. That's probably an even greater invasion of privacy."

"Yes, but Dorian isn't doing it naked."

"Never assume that."

A smile flashed across his face, before it settled back into seriousness. "Dorian doesn't know about the book, does he?"

"Nobody here should know about the book," Millie said. "But it's never wise to underestimate what Dorian knows."

"Do you think he'd give it to the other summoner if he could? Does he really want to join him?"

"I think Dorian will do what he thinks is best for him, and nobody else," Millie said. "That's always been true, and usually it makes what he's going to do rather obvious. These are strange times, though, and what that might be isn't obvious anymore. I don't think he's done anything—I'm still sure I'd be able to see that on his portrait. But his soul's been troubled lately."

"That's probably true of a lot of us," Charley said. He picked up the book they'd taken from the summoner's house, and turned it over in his hands. It looked dark in the firelight. "What about the other Uriah? The one with Rob. Do you think he's been sent back?"

"I don't know," she said. "Our Uriah says he can still feel him. But he might just be trying to make sure we don't break the deal and put him back. I trust Uriah Heep about as far as you could throw him."

"As *I* could throw him?"

"I'm jolly strong. Are you worried about Rob?"

"Why do you ask?"

"You asked about the other Uriah. Besides, I'd be worried about my brother, if I had one and if he had a twisted version of a Dickensian villain on his tail."

Charley shrugged uncomfortably. "Rob can take care of himself. Honestly, I mean that, he can. You should have seen him in school."

Millie rolled her eyes, but refrained from further comment. "Well, if he doesn't need our help, I'm sure we could find a use for his. Call him."

"I'm not going to call him," Charley said firmly. "I've done too much of that already. It's good he's out of this. It wasn't fair for me to put him in it in the first place."

"None of this," she said, "is exactly fair to any of us. Oh, bother!"

The room rippled, just once, like a shiver across the skin of the world. Millie stumbled as the couch moved away from her, and caught herself. The fire flickered and died. The Hound of the Baskervilles whined piteously.

"That was only a tremor," Charley said in the dark. "It's okay, Henry..."

Millie drew a deep breath, then released it, trying to calm her heart. "Still. There have been a sight too many of them lately. Clearly not having the annotated book isn't too great an inconvenience after all. Can you get a light?"

"Just a minute," Charley said. She heard him whisper something; the cadence of poetry, too low to hear. A moment later, the room filled with stars. Not real stars, but poetic stars: tiny orbs of gold that danced and spun around the room like particles of dust in sunlight. The fire kindled too, with the same golden light, and the glow lit the room.

For a moment, Millie forgot the shift and the summoner. She forgot everything. "I say," she said, and felt the inadequacy of Jacqueline Blaine's prose. "Those are rather nice. I meant switch on the gas lamp, or something."

His smile, again, was somewhere between shyness and excitement. "I didn't quite mean all that. I only wanted the fire. I suppose they follow each other, though. They're from Yeats. "When You Are Old." I've made them before, sometimes, by mistake."

She reached out for one, on instinct, but it fled from her touch. Its loveliness pierced her like a knife. "They're rather nice," she repeated. "But they're rather sad too. I can't quite say why."

"They're lost love—rejected love, really. Mythic love. That's why you can't touch them."

"That *is* rather sad, for a light source." She tore her eyes away from the stars and looked at him more closely. "Are you all right? You're frightfully pale."

"I know, I know," he sighed. "People are starting to tell me that at work—in a more modern vernacular, obviously." She made a face at him, and he smiled. "It's not the stars, it's just the putting back—I'm still not very good at it. Give me a minute before I try anything else."

"We're doing well, you know. You've come an awfully long way. We could spare a few hours."

He shook his head. "It's not enough. We know what the summoner wants now, but we can't find him. I can't get any fictional door to work as a portal, even though I'm still certain the summoner did. And I still don't have a clear idea of the Street. The summoner created it based on an interpretation of my book and Dickens's novels. I can't find that interpretation. When I try to reach out for it, hold it, and change it, it slips through my fingers. And that's what I'm going to need, if it comes down to war between us. Doors and stars are all very well. But they won't stop the summoner's new world."

Millie didn't argue, because she agreed. The other summoner was, to put it frankly, better than Charley. His control over what he brought out was more focused and deliberate; he was able to sculpt his creations with greater precision; he had made an entire street, while Charley's greatest shift of reality had been an erratic tunnel. Apart from the fact that their lives might at any moment depend on being able to meet the other summoner at his level, Charley, Millie had discovered, did not like being inferior at something he loved. She appreciated that. Neither did she.

"Besides," he added. "I don't *want* to stop."

"I know," she said, because she did.

A knock at the door broke the quiet. Charley closed his eyes briefly, hurriedly, and the stars vanished.

"Come in," Millie called, and the Artful Dodger's ugly, old-young face loomed into the room. His usually mischievous expression held a hint of worry.

"Thought youse would like to know," he said, with a quick glance at Charley. "Someone's at the wall. The White Witch has him at wand-point. He says he's come from the summoner. He's ready to negotiate."

At that moment the Street shifted again.

This time, the shifting showed no sign of slowing as Millie and Charley fought their way down the stairs and out into the Street. The effects were mild enough to allow them to walk, but the sky and buildings and streetlights swirled about them like a Van Gogh painting.

There was a crowd gathered at the Darcys' flat. Even from a distance, it was obvious why, and that it had nothing to do with the news that a new person had come through the wall. The building was more than shifting; it was writhing. It flickered, split in two, then reformed again. Stone and wood and glass melted together in a horrifying mess.

"What's happening?" Millie demanded as she and Charley drew near.

It was the Scarlet Pimpernel who turned to answer her; he was in the back of the crowd. "The Darcy flat is shifting," he said. "Truly shifting—I fear it's going to sink."

"Are they all right?"

He shook his head. "They were on their way out of the house to see the newcomer when it started—four of them got out, but the door disappeared after them. Three is still in there."

Darcy Three. The quiet, practical Darcy, who spent his time reading in coffee shops, and actually knew how to smile. She didn't want to think she had favorites on the Street, but her chest tightened.

"Can't we get the window open?" she asked. The answer was obvious by looking at it.

"The others are trying," the Scarlet Pimpernel confirmed. "But it's phasing in and out. We can't get a hold of it."

"There's an ax at the back of the public house," Millie told him. "See if you can find it. We might have to smash the window."

The Scarlet Pimpernel nodded, and turned to push his way back through the crowd. Millie didn't hold much hope, though. The Street was still shifting. The ax was part of the Street—it would be as malleable as the house.

"Can you do something to stop it?" she asked Charley.

He didn't answer, and she realized, of course, that he already was. His face was deep in concentration.

The two of them had tried to steady the shifts before when they came over the last few nights. Those had been shorter and faster; it was difficult to tell whether Charley had made any difference to them, but he had thought not. Even with the textbook, the Street was too elusive. And this time, they had left the textbook back at Millie's house.

Millie could see Darcy Three at the window now. He was tugging frantically at the catch, but the walls themselves were wavering and vanishing. For that matter, though it was difficult to be sure, Millie had a sickening suspicion that Darcy Three himself was wavering. The glimpses of him behind the glass flickered like a light.

"Come on!" she called to the others. "Quickly!"

And then, at once, the house froze. Half in and half out of reality, it stood still in the midst of the shifting Street. Millie glanced quickly at Charley. His face was pale and remote. Inexplicably, she felt a chill. He scarcely seemed to be behind it at all.

It only lasted a moment. In the next, Charley caught his breath with a gasp, and the house collapsed. It split down the middle, fell to the ground in two halves, and kept falling as the ground gaped open to receive it. Behind it, and through it, a new alley splintered out into the distance. New shops and houses unsheathed from it like the folds of a fan.

Millie's heart stopped; then, almost at once, she saw the uncharacteristically disheveled figure of Darcy Three being helped up from the cobblestones. Clearly, in that one moment of stability, he had managed to open the window and tumble out to the ground outside. The other four Darcys stood in a cluster, looking at the space where their house had once stood.

"Get back!" she ordered, pushing them away.

She didn't need to worry. Already, the Street was quieting, settling back into its usual lines with creaks and shudders. The new alley shimmered once, then stilled. Millie breathed a long sigh of relief.

"Are you all right?" she asked Darcy Three. He nodded wordlessly and managed a very small smile. She gave his shoulder a comforting squeeze and then, for the first and possibly last time, gave in to the impulse to smooth his single lock of hair back from his forehead. "Good show. It's over now."

"It can hardly be considered over," Darcy Five said, with none of his usual hauteur. All of them looked shaken to the core. "The house has gone. We barely escaped this time. What is to become of us the next time, or the next?"

"One thing at a time," Millie told him. "We'll get you a new house. What about Uriah? Did he get out?"

"Dorian offered to take him for the evening," Darcy Five said. "I must say, we offered no very strong protest."

Millie frowned. "Why on earth would Dorian take him?"

Darcy Five might have replied, but he never got a chance. An unfamiliar voice cut across the Street.

"Good evening, Dr. Sutherland."

Millie turned. A man was coming to the front of the crowd, and that man was another Uriah Heep. His blood-red eyes were shielded by glasses, and his bright red hair was smartly cut. In some ways, he looked more real than their own Uriah. In others he looked less.

"You're Eric," Charley said slowly. He was standing where Millie had left him; but for his increased pallor, there was nothing to show he had played any part in what happened at all. "The other Uriah Heep. The one who came to Rob's work."

"How kind of your brother to mention me, Dr. Sutherland," the other Uriah Heep said, with the convulsive wriggle she recognized. "And how kind of you to remember. You don't look very like your brother, if you don't mind my saying. No offense meant, of course. Both very distinguished-looking gentlemen."

There was no hint of sarcasm in the wheedling voice, but given that Charley was currently wearing a jumper with holes in it and had forgotten to shave that morning, Millie wasn't surprised that his hand went automatically to smooth his hair.

The White Witch burst through the crowd. Her eyes blazed, not so literally as Heathcliff's but more terribly; her face was white as her leather jacket, and she towered above Eric as she pointed the length of her wand directly at his head.

"Minion!" she thundered. A chill shot down Millie's back. "You dare to disobey me! I forbade you to enter this place!"

"He got through the wall when the Street shifted," Heathcliff told Millie, more calmly. He had his pistol drawn at the intruder, and was enjoying the opportunity to glower ominously. "We had him before that. Do you wish him disposed of?"

The White Witch laughed shortly. "*I* may wish him disposed of."

"Steady on, old thing," Millie said. She stepped in front of Eric, arms folded. "Did you have something to do with that shift?"

"Me, miss?" he asked, his red eyes wide. "I'm sure I could never do something requiring so much power. The one who sent me may have, of course. Very fortunate, I am, to be in the service of someone who can bend the world."

Millie gave Heathcliff and the Witch a quick nod, and they reluctantly lowered their weapons. "Look here," she said to Eric. "I'm sure it's very nice to meet you, but what are you doing here? We've already got one of you, you know. That's probably all we need."

"I'm sure it is," Eric agreed. "More than you need. I haven't come to stay long, and certainly someone as umble as I am expects no hospitality. No, I have dared to venture here only to convey a message from my master, he who summoned me and raised me above my station to the real world."

"Do you like the real world?" Charley asked curiously.

"Oh, I like it very much, Dr. Sutherland," he said at once. "The parts I see of it are admittedly very umble, being mostly a basement and a law library, but there is such potential here."

"Potential for what?"

"What's the message?" Millie interrupted. Bitter experience had taught her that Charley could chase a point of inquiry around the world and back, if allowed.

Eric turned to her. "Well, if I might be so blunt, it concerns the Street. This Street, and Dr. Sutherland. My master feels that this Street, and Dr. Sutherland, have been working against him. He would like to warn you to stop."

"We've seen what your master would like to do," Millie said. "Where is he, by the way? You must have got our message that we were willing to talk, or you wouldn't be here."

"He did receive your very kind message, thank you. Mr. Scrooge was happy to pass it on, the next time he was in the world. You indicated that you had an offer to make?"

"Not to you, if you don't mind. To the summoner. In private."

"I understand completely. You don't want all these people to know the terms." Millie didn't give him the satisfaction of looking at the Street, but she knew his barb had found its mark. They wouldn't be happy with the idea that she was keeping them out of things. "Well, I myself am fortunately authorized to make an offer of my own. My master intends to bring forth a new world. It would be a world where characters the likes of you could be safe, and free, no longer hidden and fearful of discovery. He would protect you. If you hand over the book, and leave him to summon it forth, he invites you to join him there. Otherwise, if you continue to hamper him, he will have to put an end to it."

"We've seen his new world," Millie said. "Stunted readings like yourself sleeping on filthy mattresses amid old books, or read in and out on a whim to do his bidding. No thanks."

"Those like me, the readings you speak of, were read out for no other purpose," Eric said. "We don't mind. It fits our umble stations. It wouldn't be like that for you. You would be citizens of the new world."

"A world built on slavery."

"As I said, Miss Radcliffe-Dix," Eric said, "the slaves don't mind. I can say that, speaking as one myself. And once the new world comes, there will be no need for us. This is just a beginning."

"And what does it look like in the end?"

Eric licked his lips. "It's really more like the old world, in the end." He almost seemed to be reciting. "Some of you lived through the nineteenth century. You might remember what it was like when it was easy to hide in plain sight, to move across borders and countries without fearing detection. Some of you came from a fictional nineteenth century, or thereabouts, the old world that only really existed on paper. The world that the Street embodies."

"'In those days Mr. Sherlock Holmes was still living in Baker Street,'" the Witch said unexpectedly. They were the words that opened the first of her books. The invocation of an early London that never really was, built from the pages of other children's stories. "'And the Bastables were looking for treasure in the Lewisham Road.'"

"Yes." Eric's eyes gleamed. "Exactly."

The Witch tossed her head, recovering her equilibrium. "Fool. What do I care for your master's new world? Do you think it is in me to be the subject of another ruler? In my book I was a queen. I crumbled entire cities into dust. I cloaked a world in eternal winter."

"And you can again," he said. "But not here. Not in their world. In their world we are nothing—you, if you'll forgive me, Your Majesty, were working as a bouncer in a nightclub in Hong Kong before the Street arrived. You'd fled from England, where the authorities had sought to commit you to a psychiatric facility because you believed yourself to be a queen and tried to turn them to stone. What they might have discovered had they examined you too closely, we don't know."

She stiffened. "How could you possibly know that?"

He ignored her. "The Street keeps you safe, but at a price. You're trapped behind this wall, fearing detection. Imagine a world of our making. Imagine the Street, but as one of many streets, going on and on and on until it covers the world. Twists and turns and cobbled roads, all yours for the taking. You don't need to fear discovery anymore. You'll be under protection."

"And under control too," Millie pointed out. "You say that he has his own slaves, summoned forth for the purpose. But what's to stop him rereading us as well?"

"It would be very difficult, with such complicated readings as yourselves." This, Millie suspected, was flattery, but it sounded sincere. Certainly, the Witch would believe it, as would several others. They wanted to believe themselves to be real. "He may not even be able to manage it. Certainly there would be no point. He doesn't want slaves—he could have those in abundance. He wants citizens."

"Well, as I said," Millie said. "No thanks."

"Suit yourselves, of course." He looked at the surrounding characters—some of whom, Millie saw with unease, were listening with more interest. "All of yourselves. But my master does want to tell you that if you don't intend to join him, then from now on, there will be repercussions for anyone attempting to thwart the new world—repercussions for the entire Street."

"Why can't he tell us that himself?" Millie asked. "Why won't he meet with us? Perhaps we could come to some arrangement."

"He said to tell you that there can be no arrangement as long as this street is allied with Dr. Sutherland. My master and Dr. Sutherland are archnemeses."

"What?" Charley half laughed, half frowned. "I don't have an archnemesis."

"With all due respect, Dr. Sutherland," Eric said, "I don't think you get to choose."

"Possibly not," he acknowledged. "But I think I should probably have been informed."

"My apologies, Dr. Sutherland. A terrible oversight, to be sure."

"This is nonsense," Millie cut in. "We'd be your master's archnemeses with or without Dr. Sutherland. What he's doing threatens all of us. It threatens you, if you could see it. You can't, because you've been read not to, and that's a jolly shame. But we can."

She spoke for the benefit of the Street rather than for the Uriah Heep who called himself Eric. She thought he was probably beyond reach. But the Street's inhabitants were capable of being swayed, and she wanted to make sure that it was by her. She hadn't forgotten the expression on the portrait of Dorian Gray.

"You're quite right," Eric said, shaking his head sadly. "Of course, I am too umble to understand what you understand. But I do understand this. The new world is very close. It's come to the time of choosing sides. Choose the right one."

"We have," Millie said.

He ignored her. "You're not used to doing that, are you? Some of you have been in this world for such a long time. A century, perhaps even more. You've seen wars come and go. You probably think you can wait this one out in the same way. They're not your wars. It's not your story. It's what his brother's telling himself, isn't it? Mr. Sutherland. But this is your war. As long as Dr. Sutherland is here, you're fighting already. His brother might find the same, if he's not careful."

"Don't you dare threaten my brother," Charley said. For the first time, there was a note of warning in his voice. "He has nothing to do with this."

"Me, Dr. Sutherland? I'd never threaten anyone. You asked for a negotiation. I'm only passing on what my master sent me to tell all of you."

"Your master sent the Hound of the Baskervilles to kill my brother and me. He took him from his book, twisted him into a monster, and launched him at us. And I took him back, and reread him, and now he's here at my side. I'm not afraid of your master."

"Perhaps you should be, Dr. Sutherland," Eric said. "Just a little."

With a start, Millie realized that the Street was growing darker. It was the quirk she had noticed earlier, and at which Dorian had hinted: the way Charley's mood seemed to change the lights and shadows of their written world. It could have been illusion before, but it was unmistakable now. Clouds were rolling in. Millie looked up at the sky, and felt the first specks of rain on her face.

Of course, it made more sense now. It was his street. He may not have summoned it, but he had written the words from which it was grown. On some level, it was listening for him.

"Get out," Charley said to Eric flatly. At his side, Henry growled. "I have no idea if I can read you into your book, or into a lesser version of yourself, or into a Christmas pudding, but I can promise that if you stay any longer, I'll give it my very best shot. And the same goes for anything or anyone else that your master sends to intimidate this street. Get out."

"May I tell my master that, then, Dr. Sutherland?" Eric said.

"Please," he said. "Maybe not the bit about the Christmas pudding, but otherwise, yes. Do."

"Keep the bit about the Christmas pudding," Millie declared. The rain was falling harder; her curls were darkening into ringlets. She felt, illogically, that part of it was hers. She gloried in the power of it. "I liked it. And add that we did not appreciate being threatened. Any of us. Did we?"

"We certainly did not!" Heathcliff spoke up, to her relief. He aimed his knife-gun squarely at the stunted version of Uriah Heep. "Get out. Or I swear from the depths of my stormy soul you shall feel my wrath."

Eric seemed neither affronted nor worried, although his eyes flickered to Henry.

"You know, Copperfield," he said, and his voice changed. At once, Millie could hear the grating wheedle of the other Uriah, stronger than before. It was a quotation. She recognized the tone of a character turning without warning into a caricature of themselves. "You're in quite a wrong position. You can't make this a brave thing, and you can't help being forgiven. I'm determined to forgive you. But I do wonder that you should lift your hand against a person that you knew to be so umble!"

Guilt crossed Charley's face; then, just as quickly, his eyes flashed with anger.

"Oh, you want to do chapter forty-two?" he said. "Very well. Here's chapter forty-two." He paused, and gathered himself. "'Heaven knows I write this, in no spirit of self-laudation. The man who reviews his own life, as I do mine, in going on here, from page to page, had need to have been a good man indeed, if he would be spared the sharp consciousness of many talents neglected, many opportunities wasted, many erratic and perverted feelings constantly at war within his breast, and defeating him. I do not hold one natural gift, I dare say, that I have not abused. My meaning simply is, that whatever I have tried to do in life, I have tried with all my heart to do well; that whatever I have devoted myself to, I have devoted myself to completely; that in great aims and in small, I have always been thoroughly in earnest—'"

The Street heard him, and knew him. It was the only way Millie could describe the shiver in the world around her. The houses rippled, flexed, with a groan of wood and stone. The pavement trembled. Rain poured from the sky. In the lamplight, it was a cascade of gold.

There was a flash of white.

Millie blinked at the man now standing in the middle of the Street. An older man, with a wide mouth, expressive eyebrows, and dark hair swept flamboyantly across his head. Victorian, no doubt—the waistcoat and cravat gave that away, as did the utter confidence with which he wore them. Something about him was familiar, though she couldn't think where she had seen his features before.

Eric peered at him too. "Master Copperfield?" he said uncertainly. Then his eyes widened. "No—"

"Hello, Uriah," the man said.

Eric took a step back, his red-brown eyes wide behind his spectacles. "No. You can't—not from that book. Not him. It isn't possible. Not Mr. Dickens."

Millie's eyes widened. "I say," she breathed.

The man who was, somehow, Charles Dickens cast a quick glance at the Street. In that one look, he seemed to take in his surroundings, buildings and inhabitants alike, and make himself perfectly at home. His eyes were very large and dark.

"As you can see," Charley answered Eric, "I can."

Eric had recovered his composure, but his shoulders twitched. "It's very impressive, Dr. Sutherland. My master will be very interested to hear of it. I'm just not certain it will be enough, if you'll forgive me."

"Get out," Charley said.

Eric looked Millie and Charley in the face, one by one, then inclined his head. He didn't look at Dickens. "I'll give your regards to your brother, Dr. Sutherland."

He stepped back. The gray wall took him, and swallowed him up.

"Put Dickens away," Millie said to Charley in an undertone. "Quickly."

The words seemed to take a few moments to reach him; when they did, he shook himself and nodded.

"I'm sorry, Mr. Dickens," he said. "We'll talk another time. May I have your hand?"

Dickens gave it, his eyes twinkling, and Millie saw Charley start a little at the touch. Then Dickens disappeared in a flare of white.

The sudden burst of rain had faded, quietly and without drama, to a drizzle, and now the stars overhead were shining between wisps of cloud. The Street was still once more.

In retrospect, Millie wondered if she hadn't done more harm than good. Her instruction had been an impulse, guided by the feeling that it would be easier for the shock to die down without Charles Dickens standing in their midst. Instead, she might have just added the shock of seeing one of their own kind disappear. Too late now.

Charley seemed to feel the same. She saw his eyes sweep over the crowds of characters.

"If you want me to go," he said, raising his voice above the growing whispers, "then I'll go."

"Don't be silly," Millie said quickly; her heart had leaped at the offer. "Nobody wants you to—"

"Can you in fact protect us?" Darcy One interrupted. The five of them were clustered together much more tightly than usual. Darcy Three, though he had gotten to his feet, still looked pale and unsteady.

"I can try," Charley said. "I want to try."

"In that case," Two said, "I do not see how you can possibly contemplate leaving us with your honor intact."

"I don't want to," he said. "Obviously. But if you don't want me here, now you've seen what..."

"We do," Millie said firmly, before he could do any more well-meaning damage. "We need you."

"But what about that man?" Miss Matty said, almost too quiet to be heard. "What's going to happen when he tells his master—?"

"We'll deal with that when the time comes," Millie said.

"And who are you to make that decision for us?" the Witch said, her voice dripping ice. "I think we need to know more about this book that little worm spoke of, and what exactly it is we've agreed to stand against."

"I'll tell you all tomorrow," Millie said. "But what we're standing against is simple. Goodness, everybody, you saw Scrooge read away in front of our eyes—how frightened he was, and how hopeless. Those are the people Eric says are happy to be enslaved. Whoever the summoner is, he's either deluded, or a monster. And there's nothing to stop him treating us the same way."

"He said he couldn't." Uriah Heep's voice spoke up: tentative, apologetic. Millie wondered where he'd been until that moment. "He said he wouldn't want to—that he wants to build a world where we could be free."

"We *have* a world where we can be free!" Millie snapped, with what she knew was too much temper. Uriah Heep had that effect. "We're not alone anymore, and we're safe behind these walls—as long as we stay secret, and support each other. What the summoner wants to do will expose us. And frankly, I don't believe that anyone who manufactures slaves out of pen and ink cares very much for anybody's freedom."

Nobody replied. She let the pause grow just long enough; when it was at the right length, she broke it.

"We'll talk about this tomorrow," she said. "Come on, the show's over. Time for bed."

As usual, her bossy Jacqueline Blaine voice seemed to do the trick. The crowd dispersed—reluctantly, with many glances over shoulders.

Dorian was one of the last to go. He leaned against his doorway, watching Millie from glorious blue eyes, until it became obvious that she was not going to move until he did. Then he gave a tiny smile, and straightened.

"Good show, Millie," he said, with just a trace of irony. "I cannot wait for the curtain to rise again."

"Dorian," Millie called sharply, before he could disappear. "Do you have Uriah Heep in there?"

"I do," Dorian said. "He had nothing to do with this interesting arrival, if that's what you were asking. As soon as he heard of it, he hid himself. I believe he feared being noticed by the summoner through his counterpart."

"What was he doing with you in the first place?"

"Talking." His young, guileless face was utterly sincere. "I have to amuse myself somehow, when you're not around. Don't worry, he'll be going back to the Darcys soon enough. Uriah Heep is rather one of those guests who cause happiness whenever they go rather than wherever they go—as you made so abundantly clear."

He closed the door.

Charley stood next to her, his hand still on Henry's collar. He showed no signs of having even heard her conversation with Dorian.

His eyes had darkened, and seemed to be seeing something either very far away or deep inside his own head. Surprisingly, Millie felt a touch of unease; all at once, she found herself unwilling to touch him or attract his attention. It was foolishness, but she felt it anyway.

She made herself punch him lightly on the arm. "Good show, Dr. Sutherland."

He shook his head, and came back to himself. "I'm so sorry. I can't believe I did that. I knew we needed to keep it secret—I've been doing it my entire life. I just didn't care anymore. I was so angry at him."

"The time for secrets in the Street is over, I think," she said. "We needed to make a stand. We made it. There's nothing to be sorry about."

"I've never talked to anybody like that in my life."

"Clearly you've hidden depths."

"I think I'm just tired, actually. Come to think of it, I snapped at Brian by the photocopier today as well."

She snorted, then hesitated. "Was that really Charles Dickens?"

"I think it was the Dickens of *David Copperfield*," Charley said. "Have you heard of an implied author?"

"Like the Implied Reader?"

"Exactly. The implied author is the character a reader may attribute to an author based on the way a book is written. It might have nothing in common with the author as a real, historical person, or it might be very close—that's completely irrelevant. What matters is what's on the page."

"So that was the Dickens that we imagine when reading *David Copperfield*?"

"I think so. I just...did an autobiographical reading."

"And we had Dickens on our street." She wasn't sure why she was so unnerved. She'd thought herself fairly hardened to the way Charley's abilities worked. "Well, it certainly scared Eric."

"It did," he agreed. "I thought it might."

"What could it do to him?"

"I don't think he could do anything, really. I think an implied author is no different from a character in a book—it's just a collection of words and interpretations on legs. It's the idea of it that frightened Eric. It was the author who brought him to life—not even the historical man, whom I could have brought from a biography, but the author of his book. Nobody likes to be reminded of their own fictionality."

It was true. She knew it was true.

"I shouldn't have done it," he added. "I was angry and scared, so I lashed out. I knew it would scare him. And he was right. It wasn't fair of me to threaten him. He has no power in any of this."

"Oh, rot," Millie said dismissively, back on firmer ground. "He deserved it. If there's one thing I took away from *David Copperfield*, it's that Uriah Heep deserves a lot more than he ever gets."

"He can't help it. He's designed to. Dickens wrote him that way. You must have noticed the reaction our Uriah Heep always receives, even from people who'd usually be kinder—nobody can stand him. He makes their skin crawl, even when he's doing nothing at all. That's probably another reason Eric was so scared of Dickens. He's the man who wrote him to be hated. Uriah Heep is a scapegoat, so that David can achieve what Uriah wants to achieve without being dangerous himself. That's how happy endings work. For there to be a restoration of order, there has to be a sacrifice."

Millie didn't really care about Uriah Heep, in or out of *David Copperfield*. This was perhaps evidence of Charley's theory in itself. "The way the Street responded. The rain, and the tremors. Was it responding to Dickens?"

"No," Charley said. She realized that he wasn't as calm as she had thought. He was trembling with barely suppressed excitement, like a divining rod in the presence of water. "It was responding to me. I had it. Just for a moment, I had it. I could feel the shape of the reading, the way I've been trying to do all week. I held it in my mind, perfect and complete. It has to do with anger."

Millie remembered the ripple across the world, and a shiver went through her. She was soaked through, of course. "Whose anger? Yours?"

"No—well, I don't think so. Not exactly. Dickens's, I think. Perhaps even the summoner's. Whatever it is, I tapped it for a second, when I lost my temper at Eric."

"You made it rain," she said, and felt very cold.

"Yes! I didn't intend that. That was just pathetic fallacy. But..."

Millie, if I could get there again, I could do anything with this place. I really could. I could stop the shifts, properly, not just for that one second I managed earlier. I could shift it myself. I could alter it, reinterpret it, maybe even read it all the way out into reality."

"Could you read it away? Back into your book?"

He didn't hesitate. "Yes. If I could ever understand it completely. I could. I was so *close* just now..."

"And what would happen to us?" This, Millie realized, was what was bothering her. It was the same thing that was frightening everyone else on the Street. The appearance of Dickens, and the change in the Street, had been too much. It seemed to touch on things that were unknowable and unspeakable. In all their efforts to make Charley's abilities more powerful, it had somehow never sunk in that he was gaining the power to shift her reality at its core. "If you were to read away the Street with us still inside it?"

"I don't know. I—I suppose you would disappear." The glow on his face faded as his words caught up to him. "The way the characters in the tunnel disappeared by the harbor. You'd be read out of existence. I wouldn't do it. I didn't mean that."

His sudden uncertainty made her feel guilty. "Of course you wouldn't. I know that. But you've read people back before, you know, who didn't want to go. You read back Uriah Heep the first time you met him."

"I know I did," Charley said. "And it was wrong. I knew that, even then. I would never do it now. I just meant...if the war the summoner promised comes to anything..." He shook his head. "It might be something worth knowing. Possibly. I'm sorry. I'm not thinking straight these days. I'm sorry I couldn't save the house before too."

"Don't be," she said. "Mr. Darcy escaped. You saved him. I don't care about the house."

"I care," he said. "I want to save all of it."

Henry took the opportunity to shake himself suddenly, and pelted them both with droplets of rain.

"Henry!" Charley complained.

Millie laughed, and snatched at the sudden release of tension. "Come on," she said. "Let's go back to my place and get warm and dry. We still have cake to finish too."

Charley sneezed, and made a face. "Oh, wonderful. I'm going to catch cold from a pathetic fallacy. I'd love to come in. But is that a good idea, after what I've just done? The people here would rather I go home, wouldn't they?"

"I think," she said, quite seriously, "that going home wouldn't be a good idea right now. I think most of the people here would be very nervous if you left; a few want you gone. They'll all be watching out their windows to see just where you do go. I think it's best to tell them that you're not going anywhere."

He nodded slowly. "This street's complicated, isn't it?"

"Thousands of years of the written word, filtered through countless readerships," she said. "How can it not be?"

When they reached Millie's apartment, a window was open, and rain had blown through onto the table. A few minutes after that, they realized that the summoner's copy of *Dickens's Criminal Underworld* had gone.

XVII

On Friday after lunch, Eric came into my office. I had found an excuse for him to spend the morning in the archives, just to give me breathing space.

"I have the files you wanted, Mr. Sutherland," Eric said. "I know you said I could take all day if I needed, but I really couldn't bring myself to waste so much of your valuable time."

"Fine, thanks, Eric." It might have been my imagination, but the dark circles under his eyes looked deeper than usual, and his hair was a little less smooth. "Just put them over there."

"Of course, Mr. Sutherland," he said. "Is there anything else?"

Perhaps I should have kept my mouth shut. It was his last day as my personal assistant; as of next week, the interns would be rotated around the firm, and I would probably be able to stay out of his way. I doubted he would be back in November with the other two. But something Frankenstein had said had been niggling at me. They were trying to warn us, he said. The creatures the other summoner had made—the creatures like Eric, the ones sent to do his bidding. If he was right, then Eric's method of trying to warn me was very peculiar. So far, he had done nothing but offer oblique taunts that may or may not hold meaning. But they *were* strange, the things my brother brought out of books, and the ones the summoner made were stranger still. And as long as we kept up this pretense that neither of us knew who the other was, I would never get anything more.

"Last weekend, I saw where you live, Eric," I said as casually as I could. My heart was pounding. "Or rather, the place where the summoner keeps you. You can't like being there."

He stiffened, then straightened slowly. With a twitch, he pulled his glasses from his face, and his red eyes gleamed. "I'm not, anymore. We've shifted now, thanks to you and your friends, Mr. Sutherland."

So I was right. He did know I knew. And both our masks were off now. "And where you are now is better?"

"Oh, *much* better, Mr. Sutherland," Eric said. "The new place has rats as well as spiders. And the damp is ever so much more penetrating."

"You could actually mean that seriously and I would believe you," I couldn't resist returning. What was it about Uriah Heep that made it so difficult to speak to him civilly? "But assuming you're being sarcastic, and you're half as miserable as I would be—why would you stay? I could help you, you know."

"You couldn't." The obsequiousness had dropped from his voice. For once, he sounded almost human.

"Why not?"

"Because he would know. Believe me, Mr. Sutherland, your movements are being watched very closely."

"Not that closely," I said. "The summoner doesn't know I've recognized you, does he? You knew I had—you've known from the beginning—but you never told him. You never told him about the other Uriah Heep either, even though you must have felt him in the world. Your summoner thinks I believe you're a regular intern, and that you've done nothing to make me think otherwise. If you had, he'd have pulled you out of here."

"That's true," Eric said. "If he knew we were having this talk, he would read me away right now, this minute. He can do that, you know. I've been beside people when they've disappeared, with the summoner ten miles away. The only thing that's saved me this far is that he has no idea I'm capable of deceiving him. He thinks I'm here doing what I'm supposed to."

"What *are* you supposed to be doing here? What does the summoner want with me? If you tell me, I might be able to stop him."

"He can't be stopped," Eric said. "He's too powerful."

"You don't know my brother." I forgot, for a moment, that I'd told Charley to stay out of this. "He's pretty powerful too, you know."

"I know exactly what he is," Eric said. "And it won't be enough. My master means to see to that."

"How?"

Eric didn't answer. Perhaps he couldn't.

"I don't care what your summoner does to the Street," I said. "That's between you and them. But you tell your summoner that if any of you lay a finger on my brother, then it won't be him you need to worry about. It'll be me. Understood?"

"Perfectly, Mr. Sutherland," Eric said. "Interestingly, Dr. Sutherland said something similar to me, last night. Only about you, of course." He bowed, his thin arms and legs like a spider's, and headed for the door. "Let me know if you need anything else, Mr. Sutherland."

After the door closed behind him, I sat in my chair without moving. I felt hot and cold at once. Last night. Eric had seen Charley last night. And he had threatened him. Eric had told me so; it had indeed been a warning, in the only way he could give it. Whatever that breath held, it was about to be released.

By sheer good fortune, Frankenstein picked up the phone on the first ring when I called. Presumably I'd caught him on a lunch break. Or a graveyard break, or whatever.

"Tell me you've found something," I said. "Now."

He seemed unsurprised by the force of my command. I think the creations of the Romantics expect emotional registers to be high.

"I have the records you requested," Frankenstein said. "I received them only this morning. I was about to send them to you. I've just been looking over them myself."

I was past caring about any threat Frankenstein might pose. He was, after all, far from the most dangerous Gothic hero I had met that fortnight. "And? Does anything stand out?"

"Such as?"

"Anything unusual. Anything I could use to find the summoner."

"Apart from the fact that your brother did indeed come back from the dead? Your mother did not, by the way. If you were expecting that to be a family trait, you are bound for disappointment." He paused. "I found one thing interesting. His eyes changed color."

I blinked. "They what?"

"What color were your brother's eyes, in infancy? Dark or light?"

"Dark." I didn't need to think about it. "They've always been dark. Black, in some lights."

"When he was born, they were light. Or should I say, before he came to life. It was noted by the midwife, though nobody took it very seriously. I can only imagine she insisted it was put in the folder. She claimed that he was born with light blue eyes. When he came to life, when they came to weigh him and record his details, they had darkened."

"That happens with children's eyes, doesn't it? They darken?"

"As they grow older. Not in the space of twenty minutes, ordinarily."

"So what might it mean? Why would the midwife want it noted?"

"Perhaps she thought he was a changeling as well."

"Do you?"

"I don't believe in changelings. But it might be useful in giving some hint to the exact nature of what he is." He broke off suddenly, and when he spoke again his tone had changed. "If you want to know. Let me try to warn you again. Knowledge is dangerous. You might not want to investigate your brother any further."

"I'm not investigating Charley." A chill had shot down my back; I was determined to ignore it. "I'm trying to find the summoner before Charley gets himself killed. And I think I'm running out of time. Can you send those files through already?"

I hung up without waiting for a reply. I was shaking.

The e-mail came through with a chime like a death knell. My brother's file didn't take long to look through. Summoning aside, my brother was a healthy twenty-six-year-old; like a lot of men his age, myself included, he avoided going to doctors until he was basically on his deathbed. In the three years since he'd returned to New Zealand, he hadn't been at all; in England, only a handful of times, mostly in his midteens. I scrolled past these quickly, looking for the very first entry. Somehow, I thought this was probably what the summoner had been looking for.

It was the same story I had always been told: stillborn, resuscitated unexpectedly after twenty minutes, no noticeable cognitive impairment. The midwife's comments about his eyes were there, as Frankenstein had said. I didn't know what to make of them, except that my brother had always been peculiar.

Almost on a whim, I opened my mother's.

Frankenstein was right. My mother's birth was perfectly ordinary.

There was another early note, though, that was less usual. Franken-stein hadn't paid it any mind. It wasn't the kind of thing he was look-ing for: no miracles, no transformations, no returns from death. It wasn't what I had been looking for either, this time. But I had seen it before, far too often in my line of work. It was the code doctors used to flag suspicious injuries in children. The kind that indicates poten-tial abuse.

Susan Walters had been four years old. She was brought to the local emergency doctor by her mother, bleeding profusely from a series of cuts across her back. Her mother—the grandmother I had never met—was unable to satisfactorily explain them, except to say that Susan had been playing in the paddock outside and perhaps a wild animal of some kind attacked her. The doctors were presumably skeptical. This wasn't the plains of Africa. There was nothing further noted on the file.

Some kind of wild animal attack, in a place without dangerous animals.

Charley had been four the first time he read out the Cat in the Hat.

No wonder my questions had shaken Mum. She was indeed hid-ing something. She had been hiding something, it seemed, for all our lives, and most of hers. She was a summoner.

Dad answered the phone on the third ring. He sounded pleased, yet surprised, when I announced myself: they didn't usually hear from me during the day. "Hello, Rob. What's going on?"

I didn't answer—it was too big a question. "Is Mum there?" I asked as calmly as I could.

"She's been at the animal shelter all morning—it's her week to vol-unteer. She should be back for lunch soon. What on earth is all this about?"

"I don't know yet. Look, when Mum gets back, can you ask her to give me a call? Please?"

"Of course," he said slowly. "Of course I will. Is everything all right?"

I didn't know that yet either. "Fine," I managed. "I'll talk to you later, all right?"

I had to call Charley. It didn't matter what had passed between us. I had to call him right now. And if he didn't answer, I was going to get in my car and find him. This had gone on long enough. He was my brother, for God's sake. And he was in trouble. Probably more trouble than he knew; definitely more than he could deal with. He needed me.

As it happened, I didn't need to call. Before I had steeled myself to pick up the phone, it vibrated noisily on my desk. It was Beth White. Charley had collapsed in the middle of a lecture on literature and the British Empire, and she was wondering if I could give him a ride home.

XVIII

I was surprised at how bright the English department looked in the light of day. Perhaps it should have been obvious, but in my mind, it was the backdrop against which I had chased Uriah Heep in the dead of night. My memories were of corridors and shadows, of knives and transformations and the city glittering far away.

Now, I could see that those same corridors were cream yellow, and tree branches clustered outside the windows. As I stepped out of the elevator, I nearly collided with a cluster of chattering adolescent girls, clothed in colorful summer dresses despite the bite in the air. From behind a closed door I could hear the soft murmur of a tutorial taking place, and somewhere the whir of a photocopier. It was a dreamy, daytime building. It did not look as if it ever had the kind of nightmares I had seen in its rooms.

"Hello," I told the woman at reception, who was probably wondering why my business suit and I were here. "I'm looking for Charley Sutherland."

"Charles?" It was the voice I spoke to on the phone when I called to chase down my brother. I had paired it, unconsciously, with an older lady in tweed; in fact, she had a ginger crew cut, and a leather jacket. "I think he's just finishing a lecture right now. Is he expecting you?"

"I doubt it," I said. "I'm his brother."

Her face cleared. "Oh, of course."

I wondered how she'd been picturing me.

A man working the photocopier beside her paused in the act of leaving. "Rob, right?" he said. "I'm Troy. We met at Charles's place, last Thursday."

"Of course—I remember." I shook his offered hand on reflex. Up close, he looked to be in his midtwenties, with the kind of lanky physique that seems to require twice the usual number of knees and elbows. He was strikingly tall; by way of compensation, he had combed his hair as flat as possible. "Is he all right?"

"I just saw him on the way to his next class," Troy said. "He said he was feeling much better. He looked all right. Well, embarrassed."

That didn't sound too dire. Charley spent half his life embarrassed, and the other half not noticing he should be. "What actually happened?"

"Well, I wasn't there," Troy said cautiously. "But apparently he just lost consciousness for a few seconds in the middle of taking a lecture. On Kipling, I think. He woke up right away."

"Beth should be in her office," the receptionist put in. "She doesn't teach on Fridays. Do you want me call her?"

"I'll take you, if you like," Troy volunteered. "I was going to drop by on her anyway. She borrowed a book from me a few days ago, and I need it back."

From what I'd seen, this seemed to be the perpetual state of the English department.

We found Beth sitting at her computer, in an office both larger and neater than my brother's. Troy knocked perfunctorily on the wall outside, but she'd already caught sight of me and got to her feet. Her cardigan was green this time.

"Thank you so much for coming." The firm, precise voice steadied me somewhat; I'd been more worried, in truth, than I'd let myself realize. "I hope you didn't mind my calling? It was only that after what we discussed on the phone..."

"No, thanks," I said. "I've just been hearing about what happened."

She shook her head. "It was a bit of excitement for the students, I must say. I was hoping you could drive him home. I'd take him myself, but I have a class this afternoon."

"Of course I'll give him a lift." There's a difference between driving someone home and giving them a lift. I didn't want to pick at that difference too closely, but I heard myself reach for it. "Is he willing to go, though?"

"Not precisely," Beth said, with a smile. "I must admit, Robert, part of my reason for calling was that I thought he would be far more willing to go home if you were there to take him. I know he listens to you. He's a good deal more stubborn with his colleagues."

"He's pretty stubborn with family as well," I told her, managing a smile. "I'm starting to realize he just doesn't tell us what he's up to, so we can't stop him."

"Oh, we're used to that here as well," Beth said dryly. She took me by the arm, a surprisingly old-fashioned gesture. "Come; his class should be finishing any minute. Troy, you wanted your book, didn't you? It should be on my desk. Help yourself."

Frankly, I was sick of the sight of books. They were starting to look like grenades lying about to be triggered.

We took the stairs. As I passed the storage closet near Charley's office, I couldn't resist a quick look inside. The pile of books that Charley had kicked over was still half on the floor, and, to my annoyance, a long sword that had to be Excalibur lay along the bottom shelf. I'd have to do something about that. It did look like a prop sword, but not to those that knew, and they existed now.

I heard my brother's voice a second before Beth opened the door.

I'd never seen my brother in a lecture hall. I saw him lecture once. He'd been back in the country for a conference, when he was about fourteen, and our parents insisted we make a family outing of it. The room here was larger—and draftier—than that glossy conference room, but Charley was older now, and far more confident. He stood in front of the lectern, and if he had any notes, he seemed to have abandoned them a long time ago.

"So, the two most important figures in Pip's life turn out to be linked by blood," he was saying. The projection above him displayed the cover of *Great Expectations*. Another one I had to read, after I finished *David Copperfield*. "Magwitch, the criminal he meets in the marshes, and Estella, the aristocratic woman he loves, are in fact father and daughter—yes? Waving hand at the back?"

The hand belonged to a bespectacled Asian boy. "Charles?"

"Jacob."

"Isn't that a massive coincidence?" he said. "That just about every-one in the book turns out to be related?"

Charley smiled. "Well…yes, you're right, is probably the short answer? The Victorians don't mind coincidence—they wanted the world to make sense. They love people turning out to be related, especially people with titles. Seriously, if you bump into a kind aris-tocrat in a Dickens novel, he will turn out to be your uncle by chapter fifty-seven, so aim well."

There was a scattering of laughter, and the boy—Jacob—smiled.

"Forget about the short answer, actually," Charley added. The light that kindled in his face was the one I'd always resented. "It's a good observation. Let's chase it for a while. There are coincidences in life, not in books. Everything in a book is placed there for a reason. What's the reason for this one?"

Silence greeted the question. Then, one by one, hands started to raise.

"It's more satisfying," someone hazarded.

"Satisfying just means something works," Charley said. "Why does this work?"

A dark-skinned girl in the front row put her hand up. I knew, before she spoke, that she had found it. Her face held the same glow that I'd seen on my brother's. "Because they're connected," she said. "Aristocrats and criminals. What Pip wants to avoid and what he wants to be. The child of a criminal looks like an aristocrat when you dress her up."

"Exactly." It was as though a new country had been discovered. "Pip's gentlemanly clothes are bought with a convict's money; the great lady he wants to marry is a convict's daughter. They're entwined. It's not just a coincidence. It's a moral precept. And it's a radical one, for the nineteenth century. It's the darkness at the heart of Dickens's world. Underneath all the fun stuff—and that fun stuff's important, don't misunderstand—these books are angry: about children being forced into workhouses and indentured servitude, about people being hanged or transported for stealing to feed their families, about igno-rance and cruelty and complacency. About failure to recognize com-mon humanity."

They were listening; I could see that. Charley obviously saw it, too, because he almost bounced from the lectern to the whiteboard. "What are some of the things *Great Expectations* is angry about, specifically? Anyone?"

There was silence for a moment, then someone called out, "People getting hanged?"

"Okay," Charley said, writing it on the board. "How do we know that?"

I listened to the responses grow louder and more confident. Charley's scribble began to cover the whiteboard. Injustice. Public execution. Magwitch's death. Poverty. Transportation. Newgate dust. Hypocrisy. Betrayal. Perhaps I was too attuned to Charley's particular brand of wordsmithery, but I had a sudden impression of the darkness at the heart of Dickens as a real and tangible thing. I hadn't read *Great Expectations*, but I could see it creeping through *David Copperfield*, in children cast away to work in factories, and women used and betrayed. And in Uriah Heep, who wanted revenge on a world that tried to keep him down. This, right here, was how Eric was born.

I resisted the urge to put up my hand. That would have been embarrassing.

"Okay, we'll talk more about this next week," Charley said finally, with a glance at the clock. He raised his voice over the rustle of students packing up their notes. "On Wednesday we're starting on Victorian poets, so read the Tennyson and the Arnold in your course books over the weekend and impress your friends at parties."

The girl from the front half raised her hand to catch Charley's attention, and went to talk to him as the rest of them began to stampede around us. I found myself hanging back. This had been my university, not even a decade ago; suddenly, though, I felt as alien and unwelcome as I always had on the Street. Given half a chance, I would have turned and left.

Beth, though, didn't give me that chance. As the room emptied, she started forward, beckoning me to follow. "Charles?" she called.

The lingering smile from talking to his student fell away as he caught sight of me. Despite knowing what was behind it, that hurt.

"Rob, what're you—?" he started to ask.

"I invited him," Beth said firmly. "Charles, you need to go home."

"I will." He turned back to the lectern, and started to gather the papers there. "I just have one tutorial at three, and then a supervision. Look, honestly, I'm fine. There's nothing wrong with me."

I could see what she meant, though. Without the adrenaline surge from being in front of a hundred teenagers, he didn't look good. I was used to him being pale and interesting after a reading; this time, he looked almost transparent.

"Brian's offered to take your tutorial," she said. "And I saw Troy in my office only moments ago; he knows not to expect a supervision meeting. Anything else you need to do—particularly if it's that paper you promised me—you can do from home. And I wanted someone to take you there. You're not riding on that death trap of yours."

Apparently, my opinion of Charley's moped was universal.

"That's my decision, isn't it? I'm not a child, Beth. It's not your job to send me home from school."

"I can't make you go," Beth concurred. "But I think I speak for the entire department when I say we're concerned about you. And since your brother's here—"

"He's only here because you called him here!" Charley glanced at me quickly. "I mean—sorry, Rob, thank you for coming, but—"

"Come on, Charley," I said. Charles. They all called him Charles here. Dr. Charles Sutherland. It made him into a slightly different person, and one I felt suddenly less comfortable shoving into my car and telling off for being an idiot. "I've come all this way. You may as well let me drop you off."

"You had no right to call anybody," Charley said to Beth. "Especially not my brother."

"Not as your colleague," Beth countered. "But I have every right as your friend. You can be as angry with me as you like tomorrow. All I ask is that you humor me for this afternoon. Go home."

Charley sighed, and I saw him give up. "Okay." He rubbed his forehead wearily. "I'm sorry, I'm not angry, I know what you're trying to do. I just wish you hadn't... Tell Brian I'll do one of his tutorials next week, okay? I'll do them both if he wants—he hates Tennyson anyway."

"I'll tell him," Beth said. "But he told you not to worry about it.

You're something of a celebrity, you know. We've never had a lecturer collapse in a lecture hall before."

"God, it'll be all over social media by now, won't it?" Charley said, with more of a smile. "There were about two hundred students there. No wonder that class just now was suspiciously full for a Friday lunchtime..."

He glanced at me, and his smile died again. I don't know what I was projecting, but it probably wasn't terribly amused.

"I'm sorry," Charley said as soon as I got in the car beside him and slammed the door. I'd stopped to put Excalibur in the trunk of the car.

"I'll bet." Already, he seemed smaller than he had in the lecture hall, and a good deal more defenseless. "Tell me you didn't actually summon anything in the lecture hall."

"No—it was this morning. Before I came to work; I didn't even put them back. It just knocked me out more than I was expecting, on top of everything else that's been happening. At least I missed teaching the rest of the Kipling section. You know the worst thing about Kipling's poems? They stick in your head, and it's as though you have a racist bigot following you around talking to you about Mandalay."

"Charley—"

"I've actually been to Mandalay, for a conference. It was very nice. And I know Kipling was a genius, and his influence over twentieth-century literature is about as far-reaching as any writer in the canon. I just wish that either his speaker were less of a racist bigot, or his meter were less earwormy. That's all."

I was still catching up to the start of the explanation. "Charley. What do you mean by 'them'?"

"Someone stole the summoner's book last night," he said. "And it had to be someone on the Street."

"Probably Uriah Heep," I said. "I told you, you can't trust him."

"We don't," he said. "But we don't know it's him. That's what I was trying to find out. Whoever it was needs to leave the Street if they're going to pass the book back to the summoner."

"So stop people leaving the Street."

"We don't want to stop them. This is the closest thing the sum-moner's made to a mistake since we broke into Lambton Quay—he's revealed that he has someone in the Street. We want to follow them. That's what Millie and I arranged this morning. I read out a host of butterflies from *Aesop's Fables*, and asked them to wait outside the wall and follow whoever leaves. If one of them meets the summoner, we should know about it by the end of the day. I had to go to work— Millie's stayed home, but she still thinks the summoner's from the university, and if that's the case I should be here so as not to arouse suspicion. And to keep an eye on things."

I pinched the bridge of my nose. "You're using fairy-tale butterflies as spies?"

"Fable, not fairy tale. I needed something simple. There had to be a host of them—people come and go from the Street all the time, one or two wouldn't be enough—and I wanted to make sure I could read out enough. These were just basic allegory. They have the power of speech, really, and that's it. I—"

I backed the car out of the lot, and he broke off and closed his eyes as we started to move. He really did look pale, even by his post-reading standards—no wonder Beth had been alarmed.

"Deep breaths," I advised him, and he nodded tightly. I did a quick calculation in my head. "Before you came in—that has to be at least four hours now. You're still not recovered?"

"I'm just dizzy," he said. "It's nothing. It's mostly the motion of the car, I think. And it's a bit stuffy in here."

I rolled down the window on his side for him. The wind roared in, speckled with rain. The clouds had rolled in while we were in the building.

"There you go," I said. "Do you want to come back to my place, or am I going to yours?"

"You can just drop me off at home." He opened his eyes, and straightened in his seat. "I don't need anyone to keep an eye on me, honestly. Beth only said that because she didn't know about—"

"*Aesop's Fables*?"

He smiled a little. "Exactly."

"Okay." I turned the corner, and the university disappeared from

my rearview mirror. I might have argued once. For now, I was more
concerned about what he'd been doing than what it was doing to him.
"I heard about last night, you know. Eric told me. He said he paid a
visit to the Street, and he told you to back down."

He frowned. "Why would he tell you that?"

"I don't know." I didn't mention the fear that had been on his face.
It would only give him something else to chase. "Is it true?"

"Did he tell you I brought out Charles Dickens? Because I did.
Well, Dickens the implied author of *David Copperfield*, not the historical person. But still, he was there. I didn't even need the book. I was
face-to-face with your Uriah Heep, the one from the office, and—"

"What are you doing experimenting with that stuff?" I demanded.
I didn't care about Charles Dickens; I didn't care about a host of
bloody butterflies. All my pent-up worry and frustration of the last
few days was threatening to break its dam. "Is this really what you've
been up to all week? Deliberately using the abilities you're supposed
to have been suppressing all your life?"

"It's important," he said, which answered my question.

I groaned. "Was this Millie's idea?"

"The butterflies? No. Some of last night was. Not Dickens, but
earlier—we tried calling up Magwitch and Fagin, just in case they
could glimpse the ones with the other summoner, but the other summoner must have put theirs back. They had nothing—or said they
didn't, and I don't think they were lying."

"If Mum and Dad knew about this—"

"You haven't told them, have you?"

"Not yet. I'm about to. Tonight. I think this concerns them too. I
think—" I hesitated, then resolutely pushed on. "I think Mum might
be a summoner as well."

"She is," Charley said. "Well, sort of. She summoned something
once, when she was four. She hasn't done anything since."

I almost drove the car off the road. "What—how on earth do you
know that?"

"She told me. A long time ago, when I was small—how do *you*
know that?"

"Why didn't you tell me?"

"I was six. She asked me not to."

"Didn't it occur to you that it might be relevant now? Considering we're searching for someone else who can read things out of books?"

"Someone trying to bring about a new world and possibly kill us in the process," Charley reminded me. "It's not likely to be *Mum*, is it? And she's the only one in her family who can summon. She told me that too."

"And you just decided to leave it at that?"

"Not quite. It's been in the back of my mind. So far it hasn't sparked anything. For all we know, she's one of the many people who summon one thing in their lives, usually without knowing it, and never do so again. I mean, yes, there's the possibility that it runs in the family, some long-lost relative has tracked us down, discovered I existed, and proceeded accordingly, but if that's the case, they've done so under Dorian's radar."

"Dorian is looking for our family?"

"Dorian's looking for a lot of things. Too many, probably. It's difficult to keep him from knowing more than Millie wants him to know."

Now I felt like an idiot. I was so tired of feeling like an idiot around my brother, when I knew I wasn't.

"You can't tell them," Charley said. It took me a while to remember what it was we had started to argue about. "Not now. We're so close."

I grasped at the familiar argument almost with relief. "That's more reason than ever that they need to know. We're not kids anymore, Charley! This isn't me trying to get you into trouble. This is serious."

"Yes." There was nothing childish in his face now. "It is. And that's why I need to understand. I need to know what can be done, and what can't. I need to know what these things are, the things that I can make and that somebody else can make too. And I can't know anything if I don't try things out."

"Don't give me that," I said. "You're enjoying it. You don't care how dangerous it is to you; I don't think you even care how dangerous it is to anyone else. There's a threat to the Street, fine, but that's an excuse. You've been wanting to push deeper into your abilities for years."

"All my life," he said immediately. "And I've been holding back all my life. I don't know if I'd still be holding back under other circumstances—probably—but I'm not sorry I've stopped, no. I want to understand. I need to, but I want to as well."

"You and bloody Frankenstein. You're two of a kind."

Charley frowned. "Who?"

I hurried past that. "You know what your problem is? You don't really believe you can fail. How could you? This kind of thing—books, reading, critical thinking—it's always been easy for you. You don't realize what's beyond you, because you've never been there. You're headed there now. You can't do this."

"Someone out there can, and is."

"It's going to kill you. I don't even mean the summoner, though he may well get to you first. This isn't right. People aren't supposed to play around with story and reality. You can't live in two worlds like this indefinitely."

"I won't *let* it kill me," he said. "I just won't. It's too important."

"You don't get to decide things like that. You're talking about the complete unknown."

"And do you know how rare that is?" he said. "The complete unknown? Even if nothing else was at stake, that should be enough to justify any amount of risk."

I didn't know how to answer that. I never do, when my brother gets that look on his face. It's like part of him is already somewhere else entirely.

"I'm missing lunch with Lydia, to come pick you up," I said instead. I knew it was a mean, guilt-tripping tactic, and I knew I said it partly to see the light dim in his eyes, which made it worse.

"I know." He sounded very quiet suddenly. "I told Beth not to call you."

And now I felt terrible. "Look, it's all right," I said as carelessly as possible. "That's not important. But you've got to be more careful."

He nodded, without speaking, and I knew I'd blown it.

We had almost reached the house when Charley's cell phone rang. He snatched it up quickly, grateful, I suspect, for the break in the silence.

"Hello—Millie, hey," he said. "Is everything okay?" I was watching the road, so I didn't see his face, but I heard his voice tense.

"What? Seriously? Okay, don't worry, we'll be right there...Rob's here too; we've got his car...Ten minutes? Look, I know, just try to distract it. We'll be there as soon as we can."

"What is it?" I asked, alarmed now myself.

Charley ended the call, and turned to me. "The Street's under attack."

"But—what kind of attack? As in with weapons?"

"Sort of," Charley said. "As in by a Jabberwock."

XIX

The Street was on fire. I felt the heat even before I was completely through the wall; when the Street came into focus, the buildings on both sides were awash with green flame. It glowed with the eerie phosphorescence that had spilled from the mouth of the Hound of the Baskervilles, and colored the fog that wreathed the ground. One of the houses, halfway down, had been torn open at the seams. In the midst of it all, there stood a Jabberwock.

I knew the poem. I remembered the old Tenniel illustrations from my childhood copy of *Through the Looking-Glass*, showing a comical, bucktoothed dragon in a waistcoat. I remember being read the book, sitting in my parents' laps before Charley was born. I remember giggling as Mum reached the fourth stanza and tickled me playfully.

> *And, as in uffish thought he stood,*
> *The Jabberwock, with eyes of flame,*
> *Came whiffling through the tulgey wood,*
> *And burbled as it came!*

It hadn't been enough to prepare me—at least, not for this one. The Hound had been the size of a carthorse; this was bigger than any creature I had seen alive. It towered above the two-story buildings that lined the Street. Its claws were half the length of its body, its jaws as large again: not surprising, I suppose, when the "jaws that bite, the claws that catch" were the only features Lewis Carroll described. Oh, and the "eyes of flame." There was certainly flame. Green fire gushed from beneath its eyelids and spilled from between its teeth.

It *was* wearing a waistcoat. But it wasn't so comical in person.

"Oh God," Charley said quietly. He had been brimming with reckless urgency on the other side of the wall; now, surveying the destruction and the monster in the thick of it, he was very still.

"If you can't do this," I said, "then we can just go. It hasn't seen us yet."

Charley gathered himself. "No, I can do this. I have to. Where's Millie?"

It was a good question. The Street looked deserted. I scanned it for a while before a flicker of movement caught my eye.

"There!" I pointed. "Rooftop."

"Oh, of course." Millie must have climbed out the upper window of the pub. From the slope of the roof, she waved at us, her curls bouncing. Charley waved back before I could stop him. Fortunately, the Jabberwock ignored both.

"She'll keep it away from us until I can read it into something harmless," he said. Millie had stood, and was climbing back through the window. "Or at least, away from me. You don't have to stay, Rob, really—"

"Oh, shut up," I said. "Quick—it'll see us if we just stand here."

There were limited hiding places along the narrow Street, but we ducked down outside Dorian's front door. Smoke was choking the air. Through it, I saw the pub doors open; the glint of armor showed beyond it. Lancelot, presumably. They had the Scarlet Pimpernel too. What happened when characters from different books clashed? If both were written to be undefeatable, what decided the victory?

"Do you need the book?" I asked Charley. "You don't have it, do you?"

"I don't need the book. I know the poem by heart—I have for years. I love the poem. That's not going to be the problem."

"What is the problem?"

"The problem is that the poem's nonsense! It's a semiotic nightmare. People have tried to read all sorts of things into it, but I've always maintained that it's just pure, perfect gibberish. The Jabberwock is just a word."

"Well, can't you just twist it to mean something? Something harmless, preferably? If the summoner can—"

"I'll try, obviously. But I don't think I'll convince myself. Um— you don't happen to have a piece of paper and a pen on you, do you?"

Astonishingly, I did. I had a tiny notepad in my coat, and a stub of a pencil. I'd put them there one desperate day when I forgot to charge my iPad before a meeting and needed something to write with. I handed them to Charley, and received a look of such astonished admiration I felt as though I'd casually pulled a sword from a stone.

"There," I said. "Go wild. But hurry up. It's looking at us."

"Don't *tell* me that." He was already scribbling, as fast as he could. The poem was taking shape on the paper in scrawled handwriting. I had a feeling, as he drew tighter into himself, that he was trying to forget he existed.

("Beware the Jabberwock, my son! / The jaws that bite, the claws that catch!")

"Okay," I heard him say to himself, very quietly, "what *does* make sense? There's a quest structure, to start with..."

I looked away, and kept my eyes on the Jabberwock. It hadn't moved, but it knew where we were. We were in the open out here. The Street, which I'd found claustrophobic before, now seemed to expose us for all to see. My heart was racing so fast it hurt to keep still.

("And, as in uffish thought he stood, / The Jabberwock, with eyes of flame...")

I almost missed it, when it happened: a shiver ran through the Jabberwock, and then a quick blink of movement I can't explain. Like the flicker of a light, or the ripple of wind across grass. The creature gave a sharp, startled sniffle, and its head whipped in our direction.

("Came whiffling through the tulgey wood, / And burbled as it came!")

"Charley." I grabbed his arm, and hauled him to his feet. "Come on, we've got to get under cover."

He blinked as if I'd pulled him up from underwater. "Where?"

I gave him a push in the direction of the ruined saddlery. It was ripped open, but the Jabberwock would never fit inside, and I had a vague idea that the rubble might afford us something to use as a weapon. "There. Move!"

The characters inside the pub had seen it too. Lancelot and the Scarlet Pimpernel burst from the door; their swords flashed as they jabbed ineffectually at the creature's legs. It ignored them entirely. It was after us.

We were almost too late. I had just thrown myself against the door to wedge it shut when I felt the Jabberwock's weight crash against the outer wall. The whole building shook; I ducked instinctively and covered my head. Outside, I heard the creak of rafters and the concussion of bricks hitting the ground, and then screams.

Charley had turned amid the rubble, horrified. The building next to us had collapsed.

"Don't look," I told him fiercely.

"But—were Lancelot and Sir Percy under the—?"

I didn't know. I couldn't hear them anymore. "Don't think about it. Keep reading."

He nodded, pushed his hair out of his eyes, and looked back at the notepad. Somehow, he'd managed to keep his place.

("One, two! One, two! / And through and through / The vorpal blade went snicker-snack!")

The claws that catch were scrabbling at the broken wall. I could feel the Jabberwock's hot breath in waves through the gaps, and hear the mad, incessant burble as it dug. The stones were already flying; it would be through in a moment.

I searched frantically among the bits of wood on the ground— this was a saddlery, there *had* to be something deadly and sharp *somewhere*—but found nothing. Plainly, this was a saddlery in name only; nobody was forging horseshoes. I found a particularly sharp piece of wooden scaffolding, ripped from the wall, and seized it in desperation. A stick, basically. I had a stick.

"If you can't read it away," I said to Charley, "can I at least get a vorpal sword?"

"If you can tell me what a vorpal sword is," Charley replied, without looking up, "then you can have one."

"I assumed a really sharp sword."

"Everyone assumes that. But there's no textual evidence."

Blinding light. The boarded window had smashed in. I saw the glare of a flaming eye, then felt the heat of real, true flames. I strongly suspected the building was catching fire.

"Charley," I said, as calmly as I could. "You'd better read faster."

"I'm trying," he protested. His voice was tight with panic. My own calm, really, was only a different kind of panic. "It's a bit hard with all this going on. I can't think."

"Are you telling me you can't do it? *Now?*"

"No! I'm not! I'm just—Rob, please, just let me read, will you?"

"It was working for a moment. I think I saw it start to change, right before it came at us."

"I nearly got a New Historicist reading to take, but it doesn't hold up. I'm trying to see if I can get it to be a rather sinister bildungsroman. But—"

"What has the summoner made it?"

"Honestly? I think this is an archetypal monster. It means nothing, so it means whatever you take a monster to be. That's why that green flame's left over from the Hound of the Baskervilles, I think. It's plugging the gaps in description. Rob, I really, *really* need to think here."

I heard a shout ring out from the fog. Outside, the Jabberwock turned from the wall, and snarled. Curiosity pulled me forward against my will. Tightening my grip on the stick of wood, I stepped forward, just enough to see through the holes in the damaged walls.

It was Heathcliff. The Brontë hero was approaching the Jabberwock at a walk, his knife-gun raised. Against the green flames, the black flames of his own eyes burning, he looked striking and powerful: a creature made of human passions, as the creature in front of him was made of suggestion and wordplay and fear. He fired. The bullet bounced harmlessly from the Jabberwock's waistcoat; it gave no sign of having been hurt by the shots, but it clearly felt them. Fire spilled from its eyes, and it roared. Even Lewis Carroll would have had to describe that sound as a roar: deep, elemental, furious. It chilled me to the core.

Heathcliff only laughed. "Do you think to frighten me? I am a demon, too, you know. You may best me, but we are the same."

It towered over him, tall and lithe and ridiculous. The claws snatched for him; the head with its grasping jaws came for him. Heathcliff, his teeth bared in a grim smile, threw the pistol aside and struck it, hard, on the snout.

The Jabberwock let out one startled cry, then its eyes flared. As Heathcliff drew back to hit again, its fangs flashed, crunched down on his torso, and flung him to one side like a rabbit.

I gasped. I couldn't stop myself, even though I knew it would catch Charley's attention and pull him out of the close-reading trance he was trying to enter. Heathcliff hit the ground, hard, and lay there limp and broken as an old doll. I thought I heard him groan.

"What's happening?" Charley demanded from behind me.

"Heathcliff. He just hit the thing in the face. Don't look," I added sharply as he started forward. "Keep reading."

"Is he safe?"

I looked again, dreading the answer. The Jabberwock slunk toward the prone body, burbling green flame. The Street was a crumble of crushed stone and acrid smoke. There was no sign of the two swordsmen. There was no sign of anybody.

At once, the door to the pub crashed open. Matilda Wormwood stood there, her thin legs braced determinedly. Her head was beneath the level of the doorknob, and her face looked very pale and remote. She reached out her hand; Heathcliff, on the cobblestones, gave a convulsive twitch that wasn't his own.

I swore quietly.

"What?" Charley demanded. I didn't answer. The Darcys were at Matilda's elbow now, one crouched, waiting. She narrowed her eyes, and reached out further. Heathcliff's limp body gave another jolt; then the invisible force spilling from her eyes wrapped around him and lifted him up. He rushed forward, jolting over the cobbles. One of the Darcys scooped him up, hand under Heathcliff's arms. The Jabberwock curled back its lip in a shriek.

"Rob..."

"The others have got him," I said, but that wasn't answering the question. They had him, but they had drawn the Jabberwock's attention. It would be on them soon. It would be on all of them, those hidden out of sight in the pub. Heathcliff, if he wasn't dead already, would almost certainly be torn apart; so would the Darcys, and little Matilda. Millie would, too, if she was still inside, along with God knows who else.

Unless someone distracted it long enough to buy Charley more time to save them.

I couldn't do it. I couldn't. It would be monumentally stupid, not to mention reckless. Probably it would eat me in the blink of an eye without any good being done at all.

"Definitely an Emily Brontë," Charley said, with a very quick, very shaky smile.

"What?"

"She used to punch her dogs in the face."

I had no idea what he meant, and had no intention of stopping to ask. I was about to do the stupidest, most reckless thing I'd ever done.

"Stay right here," I told him. "And for the love of God, if you can't read it back soon, then get out."

I didn't wait for him to reply. I ran. It occurred to me as I did so that he couldn't both stay there and get out, but too bad. He was smart enough to work it out.

The Jabberwock was lunging after the retreating characters, its great claws scoring the cobblestones. I saw Heathcliff's head bump against the ground as the Darcys dragged him. The Witch fired a spell from the door; it hit the Jabberwock and glanced off harmlessly. Little Matilda still stood on the pavement. Her head darted sharply to one side, and a chunk of debris tore itself loose from the rubble and flew at the Jabberwock's head. It bounced off; the creature shook itself with a snarl, and roared.

"Hey!" I called loudly.

The monster turned. Its nostrils flared in a shower of sparks as it took me in. I wanted nothing more than to run, but I didn't. I stood there, braced myself, and tightened my grip on the stick.

No time for second thoughts, or even for panic. It was on me before I had time to see it move, the burble of its motion filling the air. I lashed out with the stick, and the mighty jaws caught it and wrenched it from my hand. The impact knocked me down; the cobbles jumped up to meet me, and my elbow jarred the ground. It was just a fall, no worse than tripping over on the pavement, yet the momentary shock of pain knocked the breath from me.

Above me, the Jabberwock was a mass of leathery skin. I saw the wet gleam of its teeth as it crunched down on the stick and splintered it in pieces. God. I was actually going to die.

The gun. Heathcliff's gun. Where was it? It wouldn't do much good, probably. But I could try. It had a knife attached. Who said that knife couldn't be a vorpal blade?

"Stop it!" Charley's voice came, sharp with command.

The Jabberwock's head snapped around to look at him. I turned as well, on reflex. Charley had come out of the ruined shop; he was a few feet from us. It was hard to see through the haze of fog and smoke, but I could make him out.

"'You're nothing but a pack of cards,'" he said. Through everything, I dimly remembered the lines from the end of *Alice's Adventures in Wonderland*.

The Jabberwock flickered, distorted, and screamed. The cry cut through the air, so deep I wondered if they could hear it out on Cuba Street, across the lines of reality. Then... it's difficult to describe what happened next. The Jabberwock folded in on itself, a flurry of claws and flashing teeth.

Yet it was not gone. Where it had once stood as flesh and blood, a void gaped. It was a great hole in the sky, cutting through air and brick and fire. It wasn't black, but I couldn't say what it was instead. I could see suggestions of color, suggestions of form, nothing my mind could catch hold of and name. It was unnatural, even by the standards of story. It made no sense. I felt cold and sick at the sight of it and yet, at the same time, I couldn't look away. I knew I was seeing something impossible, and powerful, and wondrous.

Around the mass in the air, the Street itself was beginning to alter, to *shift*, like the interlocking parts of a kaleidoscope. The air was superheated and sparse. I caught my breath, and the Street did the same.

The void that had been the Jabberwock vanished. It was there in one eyeblink, and gone in the next. I felt the rush of a breeze, and on it the rustle of paper.

Charley made a sound somewhere between a gasp and a cry, and stumbled. I scrambled to my feet just in time to see him hit the ground. Now I knew how his students had felt.

"Whoa." I bent down, and caught him by the shoulders; he was already blinking furiously, trying to wake up. "Careful."

"Is it gone?" He pushed himself to sit, with my help. I could feel him shaking. "Did that work?"

"It's definitely gone; that definitely worked," I said. "Relax. It's over. You did it."

My own words caught up to me a second later. The danger had passed so quickly, I still couldn't believe it. Flames still licked some of the buildings; people ran to put them out. Buildings lay in rubble, and the road we were on was furrowed from the marks of hooked claws. But it was over.

"You did it," I repeated, more quietly. "What did you do? What did you read it into?"

"I couldn't make it mean anything. I tried. But it was meaningless. That was the point. So I just—I read it into nonsense. I made a complete absence of meaning. I think that's the most difficult thing I've ever done. It was more dangerous then than as an archetypal monster; I'm not sure what it could have done if I hadn't been able to..." He shook his head.

"What *did* you do? I thought you couldn't read back other people's readings."

"So did I. I can't, technically, but—I just thought that if I could truly reinterpret it, then it would be my reading, not theirs. I could take possession of it. And then I could read it back, the way I always have my own."

"It worked." The import of that sank in a moment later. "Which means that the summoner can read away your readings, or anyone in the Street, doesn't it? What else can the two of you do?"

"I don't know. I didn't know I could do that, until a moment ago. I just had to do *something*. It—did it hurt you?"

"No, I'm fine." Now that the shock had worn off, my body was aching from the fall; my elbow and probably other less mentionable places were going to be bruised later. I was grubby, and shaken, and sore. But I knew how lightly I'd escaped. "Nothing broken. You okay?"

He nodded unconvincingly. "Just let me sit down a second."

He was already sitting, technically, but I helped him settle on the curb of the road, where he drew up his knees and buried his head in his arms. I felt a quick tug of worry, but was distracted by the crowds gathering around us. The fog had lightened, and the last of the Street's inhabitants were beginning to limp from the houses.

Millie pushed her way to the front, to my relief. When the second house had collapsed and I'd heard the cries, my terror twisted them into hers. Despite the tension between us, I realized, I had been almost as worried for her safety as I was for Charley's.

"All right, chaps?" she said to us breathlessly. "Close one, wasn't it?"

"Yes," I said. That was the understatement of the year. "Very."

"Is everybody all right?" Charley asked, raising his head. He didn't quite look at her; I suspected his vision wasn't yet in focus.

"Not quite." Her face was tense and dirt-streaked. "Heathcliff's in a very bad way; I have him in the public house, and the Duke of Wellington's with him. We're still digging Lancelot and Sir Percy out of the rubble. But we're all still alive. How are you?"

He managed a smile. "Fine. Just my head's spinning. What happened? Where did it come from?"

"We don't know," Millie said. "Not from outside. It just appeared, in the middle of the Street. Started tearing everything apart. Flames raging, doors flying, the whole thing. Yet another thing we didn't know was possible. It's good to see you again, Rob," she added, giving me an affectionate punch to the shoulder. It made me smile a little. "I told Charley you'd be back."

I thought about explaining that I didn't have much choice, under the circumstances, but I didn't. For one thing, I was very aware of the crowd of people getting close enough to hear what I was saying; for another, I didn't think it was necessary to be a complete bastard *all* the time.

"I don't understand," I said. "Why did the summoner do that? I thought they had the book back already?"

"They do," Millie said. "Or at least, somebody does. I intend to find out who. But this—I can't say what they wanted. Perhaps just to threaten us, after we refused to give in to them last night. Perhaps this is just for show."

"Quite a show," Uriah Heep said. It was the first time I'd seen him since the morning in Charley's house. Of course, he'd pushed to the front. "From you as well, Master Charley."

"What's that supposed to mean?" I snapped. I really had no time for whiny little Dickensian villains at that moment.

To my surprise, it was Dorian Gray who spoke up. His hair was attractively rumpled, and a smudge of dirt accentuated one perfect cheekbone.

"I believe it's obvious," he said. "I believe you said, Millie, that your summoner here was only able to send back those characters or objects he had already read out himself? Clearly, that's not true— unless you're saying that he was the one who sent that thing in the first place."

"Oh, dry up, Dorian!" Millie said, more resigned than angry. "Obviously, we underestimated how far a rereading could go. Under the circumstances, I think you should probably be a sport and thank him."

"Thank him?" Dorian said, with the rise of one perfect eyebrow. "As you just said, it was almost certainly sent here because we refused to listen to the warning we were given last night. That warning was against having anything to do with Charles Sutherland. He and the summoner are archenemies. He's putting us in danger just by being here."

"He *wasn't* here! He was at work. He came just now because I called him to help sort out our problem."

"Our problem," Dorian said, "is that I'm not entirely sure we're on the right side."

"I'm not trying to put anyone in danger," Charley spoke up. "I'm just trying to help."

"Why?" Dorian said, turning to him. "Why would you care what happens to us? Why would you not take care of yourself?"

Frustration crept into his voice. "Because I love this street! And because there's more than just the Street at stake, if the other summoner has their way. It's the whole world."

"As Millie keeps telling us," Dorian shot back. "But it seems to me it's the other way around, isn't it? The rest of the world is at stake, if the other summoner took control. The Street would thrive. We won't be in hiding anymore, tucked away in a crack in the world that doesn't technically exist. We'll open up and spill out across the city. We'll be real people, with a real place."

"And what if the real world objects to our spilling over half the city?" Millie demanded. "What if they see that as an invasion, and try to get rid of us?"

"Let them try!" Dorian exclaimed. For the first time, I saw his beautiful face alive with something like passion. "We have an arsenal born of thousands of years of literature. Imagine what we could summon in our defense? They have planes and guns; we can have those alongside starships, dragons, black holes, monsters. Fictional magic might not work in the real world, but teeth and claws and fire do. You saw what the summoner can do with a book of Victorian children's literature."

"You're talking about a war," Millie said.

"The war's already begun," Dorian said. "That was the first volley. We just need to make sure we join the right side before we find ourselves in the line of fire again."

"So far, the other summoner seems to have declared war on us as well."

"He's declared war on Dr. Sutherland. If we were rid of him, we'd be free to choose whatever side we so desired."

I broke in then. "Nobody is getting rid of anyone."

"Tell that to the Jabberwock, Mr. Sutherland," Uriah Heep interjected. He said it placidly.

"What exactly is that supposed to mean? Your evidence that Charley is dangerous is that he just *saved your lives*? He did, you know. You'd all have been killed if he hadn't been here."

"As Mr. Gray says," Uriah said, with one of those writhing shrugs, "we wouldn't have been under attack if he'd never been here."

The crowd was stirring; I think in confusion, rather than agreement, but I didn't like some of the undertones. Neither did Millie. She glanced at them, then moved toward me.

"I rather think you two had better go for now," she said to me quietly. "Leave me to calm them down."

"Nothing I'd like better," I retorted. "Come on, Charley."

I expected him to argue, but he stood unresistingly as I grabbed his arm and pulled him toward the crack in reality. The crowd parted to let us go. Dorian was the one exception. He stayed leaning against the wall, watching us with cool hostility.

There was a parking ticket on my windshield when we returned to the car. I ripped it off and crumpled it up, still brimming with righteous indignation.

"Dorian Gray." I didn't feel the need to add an epithet. It sounded like a bad enough word in itself. "Seriously, why do you want to help someone like that?"

"He's not responsible for your parking ticket," Charley said. "Just for information."

I threw it at him, not in the mood to smile. "Shut up and get in the car."

The road was beginning to fill up with afternoon traffic; it took a while to get an opening, and when I did I realized I was going in the wrong direction and would have to swing around. It didn't improve my temper.

"Ungrateful bastard," I muttered. "After what we did—what *you* did—"

"Dorian's all right," Charley said. "I shouldn't have lost my temper at him. He's just scared."

"Well, yes, a Jabberwock just tore through his street. But that's not your fault. You just saved his life."

"I just reduced that Jabberwock to nonsense and made it disappear. It wasn't even mine, and I did that. What could I do to him? To any of them? What could the other summoner do? Their entire reality is under threat. How would you feel if you watched that, and knew it could be you next?"

I hadn't thought of that. "Could it be? Could you do that to Dorian?"

"I don't know." He closed his eyes. "Neither does he."

I looked over at him. His face and hair were damp with perspiration.

"Hey," I said belatedly. "Are you okay?"

He blinked, and opened his eyes with a worrying amount of effort. "Um. I think so."

"You *think* so?"

"I don't...I feel a bit strange, actually."

"Strange how?"

"I don't know. Just..." He trailed off. I realized, for once, that really was all he had to give me.

"Okay." I tried to sound reassuring, and not at all as though my stomach had jolted. "Well, you *are* a bit strange, so that's understandable."

He laughed a little, then shivered. His eyes were drifting closed again.

I shouldn't have been too worried. It was probably reasonable to feel not quite normal after banishing a Jabberwock to textuality. But... when you ask Charley if he's okay, he always says he is. He was that one motion-sick kid on bus trips who would keep quiet so as not to be a bother, no matter how often you tell them that it's a far greater bother for the driver to have someone be violently sick in the back of their bus. I'd never heard "I think so" before.

"I'll be fine," he added, as if reading my mind. I hoped he wasn't. I'd had about enough magic from him for now. "I think I just need to lie down or something. I haven't slept in a while. Listen, I'm sorry you were brought into all this."

"It's no problem." I forced myself to go on. "I shouldn't have made such a fuss earlier. It's a good thing Beth *did* have an afternoon class. Imagine if she'd been the one driving you when that call came through."

Charley frowned. "Is that what she told you? That she has an after-noon class?"

"Something like that. Why?"

"I don't know. I'm missing something. But..."

"Hey." Something definitely wasn't right. I'd seen Charley wrangle plenty of literary characters, and I'd never seen him like this. His words were coming too slowly, as if he was having trouble finding them; his breathing was coming too rapidly, as if he was having trouble finding air as well. "Don't worry about it. We'll be home in a minute, all right? Just... maybe try to stay awake for now."

"Mm."

"No, not like that!" I cast a quick, alarmed glance in his direction. "Come on, you can do better than that. You're Dr. Charles Sutherland. You just told a Jabberwock where to stick itself. You can do anything."

"You don't actually think that." He said it perfectly matter-of-factly, without accusation. He could almost have been talking to himself.

"What do you mean?"

"You don't. You don't think I can do very much at all. Apart from read. It's all right. I don't mind. I was just... saying."

I wanted to tell him that wasn't true. I couldn't quite bring myself to. Because it was: I had told him that, after all, over and over again, in different ways. I thought I believed it. But on the other hand, I really did think he could do anything, and resented him for it. And it occurred to me, suddenly, how contradictory those two thoughts were.

"If that's what you think," I said instead, "then you'd better prove me wrong, hadn't you?"

"I'm trying," he said. He was white as paper.

Lydia was waiting outside when I pulled up in our driveway.

"What's happened?" she asked as I got out. "Your message just said you had to go pick your brother up because he'd passed out in a lecture hall, but it was nothing."

"You're supposed to be at work," I said foolishly. That message felt like a hundred years ago.

"So are you," she countered. "I came back at lunch, to make sure everything was all right, and you weren't here. I phoned you, but it went to voicemail. What happened?"

"Look, Lydia—" I started to say, with no idea how I was going to finish. It turned out I didn't need to. By then, she had seen Charley in the front seat, and her eyes widened.

"God." She opened the door, and crouched down to his level. Her voice was suddenly gentle, though very firm. "Charley? It's Lydia. Can you hear me?"

He stirred, and his eyelashes flickered. Otherwise, he made no response at all. He hadn't for the last couple of minutes, even though I was pretty sure he could still hear both of us. That didn't count as unconscious, did it? He'd fainted a few times before with these things, when he was much younger, but he always woke up as soon as he hit the floor. It was never an actual problem.

"What happened?" she asked, in a rather different tone than before. She put the back of her hand to his forehead, then took his wrist between her fingers. Lydia had done some first aid training, I remembered, when she got her hotel job. She wanted to be able to help in case of emergencies. This was, I had to admit, starting to look like an emergency.

"Is he all right?" I asked, and received exactly the look I deserved.

"His pulse is going mad," she said. "And he's like ice. Are you going to tell me what happened?"

"Well. It's sort of—you know the family stuff I keep—?"

"Rob," she said. "You need to forget this stupid family matter business, and you need to get him to a hospital."

Millie

It might have been all right, had Heathcliff not died. Despite how badly injured he was, Millie hadn't been expecting it. Perhaps she'd thought, despite all she'd ever said, that none of them were alive enough to die.

They didn't have any surgeons among them. They tried to call Frankenstein, but he wasn't picking up. And they felt they couldn't risk taking Heathcliff to the hospital, not with his eyes of dark flame. Millie would have taken him anyway, at the last, but the last came so quickly that it was over before she recognized it. Besides, Heathcliff himself wouldn't allow it. He was filled with glorious, Brontë-like exultation as he lay on the floor in the public house.

"Last night I was on the threshold of hell," he said. "Today, I am within sight of my heaven. I have my eyes on it: hardly three feet to sever me!"

"That's all very well," Millie said, rather helplessly. She recognized the words, but she didn't know *Wuthering Heights* well enough to speak in its language to him. As his strength failed, he seemed to be sinking deeper and deeper into its pages. "But I do think we should find you a doctor, at least."

"Perhaps Master Charley can read one from a book," Uriah Heep said blithely, from the corner of the room. Millie gave him a hard, cold look, and he blinked back without a trace of guile. His suggestion wasn't even a bad one, she had to admit, in practice. But it made the others stir uneasily. The entire Street was watching at this point, those who could not fit in the shop peering through windows or just standing outside the open door trying to see over people's heads.

Somehow, Uriah had ended up in prime viewing position. The Darcys should have been watching him, of course, but she could hardly blame them for having other things on their minds.

Heathcliff tossed his head in what might have been a negative, or just an attempt to shake off pain. His brow had furrowed. "But you may as well bid a man struggling in the water rest within an arm's length of the shore! I must reach it first, and then I'll rest. I'm too happy; and yet I'm not happy enough. My soul's bliss kills my body, but does not satisfy itself."

"All right," Millie said soothingly. "Absolutely. You just stay quiet. You were jolly brave, you know. We all owe you our lives."

"The Sutherlands certainly do," Uriah said. This time, the look he gave Millie was not quite so placid.

The Duke of Wellington gave his very best attempt at battlefield surgery, bravely assisted by Miss Matty, who knew little about medicine but a good deal about stitching. When Wellington cut back Heathcliff's shirt, the wounds on his body were so unexpectedly deep and bloody that Millie's throat caught and her stomach heaved. Gasps went up from those around her, and she steeled her face into calm.

"It's not so bad," she said out loud.

She didn't believe it. Of course it was bad. All the same, she did not expect to lose him. Miss Matty was only just beginning to stitch, her hands trembling, when a gust of rain-specked wind blew through the open window. Heathcliff gave one gasp. His eyes opened wide, and his teeth bared a keen, fierce smile. Then he stopped breathing. His breath had been coming ragged and harsh before that; if it hadn't been for the sudden quiet, Millie would have thought him still alive.

"He's gone," Wellington said. Miss Matty gave a little cry of distress. "Oh, the poor man," she said.

He couldn't be. Millie stared at his face, still so triumphant and so vital, and thought she couldn't believe it. It was only when her vision blurred that she realized tears had sprung to her eyes, and she knew it was true. One of them had been killed. And it was Heathcliff. In his book, of course, he had died, his soul lured from his body by the ghost of his dead love to roam the moors. But that was a different Heathcliff; Brontë's Heathcliff. This one had died to save them.

"He always hated it here," Darcy Three said, into the silence. "Not on the Street, precisely, but out of his book. The world he came from was too alluring."

There was a butterfly drifting about his shoulder. The only one that had come back from the outside: it had followed Darcy Three to a café on Cuba Street, where he had eaten his breakfast in relative peace and had a cup of coffee before returning. Their plan, it seemed, hadn't been very successful. And now Charley was gone, and they had no more ideas.

"This is really about to happen, isn't it?" Miss Matty said from beside her. Her quiet voice seemed to speak for all of them. "The new world."

"Not if we stop it," Millie said. She turned to face the others, and spoke so they could all hear her, even those outside on the cobbles. "No."

"But if we try to stop it," Darcy One said, "the summoner may try to kill us."

"It's no longer a 'may,'" she said. "Heathcliff is already dead. Yes, they will try to kill us unless we submit. Which strikes me as precisely why we should refuse to do so. I don't intend to be frightened into submission."

"Hear, hear," the Duke of Wellington said firmly. "And they won't kill us without a good fight. We still have Charles Sutherland."

"It's all right for you," the Artful retorted. He was standing by the door, arms folded and cap jaunty. "It weren't *your* author Dr. Sutherland pulled from a book last night, were it? If he can do that, he can do anything. How can we trust him to do the right thing by us?"

"And you trust the other summoner?" Millie said. "The one who pulled a monster from a book and sent it to our doorstep?"

"How did that *happen*?" Darcy One said. The Darcys were sounding uncharacteristically helpless today. "It didn't come through the wall. It came from here. Is the summoner here?"

"No," Millie said firmly. "He couldn't be. But someone must have helped him. The same person who stole Charley's book from my kitchen table last night. The same person who—"

And then she knew. The shock of discovery stopped her breath; the corresponding flare of anger dried what was left of her tears.

"Dodger?" she asked slowly. "Where's your butterfly?"

He frowned. "My what?"

"When you left the Street this morning, a butterfly should have followed you. Where is it?"

"I dunno know what you mean," he said. "Who says I left the Street this morning?"

"You always do. Every day. It's your job to pick up the supplies; I expected it. But a butterfly should have followed you there today. Why didn't it follow you back?"

He didn't answer.

"It was you, wasn't it?" A number of things were catching a different light in her head now, and she could see them clearly for the first time. "You took the book to the summoner. You helped him bring that monster here."

"Dunno what you mean," the Artful said again. The universal plea of the guilty. It was convenient, sometimes, to deal with people so bound to literary conventions.

"The Jabberwock couldn't have come here itself. It didn't come through the wall. It materialized in the middle of the Street. I'm not sure how. At a guess, I'd say it was some arrangement similar to the *Oliver Twist* house in Lambton Quay. But it had to be brought by someone who passes from this world into the other on a regular basis. There are only a few of us who do that: me, the Darcys, Dorian Gray. And you."

"Talk to Dorian then. He don't want Dr. Sutherland here neither."

His voice was more convincing this time, but she knew. In the presence of death and her own certainty, she felt stronger than she had in a long time. The missing piece of her, locked in her book, was calling to her. She was Millie Radcliffe-Dix, girl detective. She knew she was right.

"No, he doesn't. And I have to admit, I thought that if it wasn't Uriah Heep, it might be Dorian Gray. But Dorian was in the doorway of his house the whole time Eric was here, and there was no way he could have got past me to steal the book. You did that, didn't you? You did that after you came to tell us that Eric was coming through the wall. The Street shifted as you were standing there; we all ran out. You took the book then, and gave it back to the summoner this morning when you went out. And somehow they gave you a monster to unleash."

"Good God," Darcy One said.

"You haven't got any proof," the Artful said.

"No," she said. "But there's a telling *lack* of proof. You were followed this morning, when you left. By a butterfly, one from *Aesop's Fables*. It never returned. If we count them outside, I'm certain we'll find one missing. The summoner realized what it was, didn't he? Did he read it back, or just kill it?"

The Artful looked around, then shrugged. She could see the moment his story changed. Suddenly his face looked a good deal less young.

"It was your fault, really." He didn't sound at all repentant, but he may have sounded slightly defensive. "You said you could keep the summoner's creations out. You never thought that some might have been here from the start."

"Who are you talking about?"

He gave his cocky, infuriating smirk spasmodically, like a twitch. She remembered the first time she had seen it, the day she came to the Street. He had been one of the first here, just after Darcy One and Heathcliff. She thought, at the time, how well he had matched this place.

"He likes Victorian criminals," Millie said slowly. "We asked you if you had heard or seen anything from another Artful Dodger, one the summoner might have read out. But we were talking to that Artful Dodger, weren't we? You were read out by the summoner."

"He felt the Street grow too," he said. "He was probably the first to see it. After a bit, he saw you lot starting to trickle in to infest it. He sent me to watch you. Did a better job on me than on most of those poor saps with no free will—I'm the same as one of you lot, except that I'm bound to him. He weren't overworried about you, but he wanted to make sure you didn't turn into a problem. Which you did, the minute you let Dr. Sutherland through your doors."

Despite herself, Millie couldn't resist a quick glance at Dorian. He gave her a very small smile back.

"I did warn you that you had made us a target," he said.

"Did you know about the Artful?" she demanded.

"I suspected. I knew he had come into the world much earlier than he claimed. I suspected who had brought him in the night you found the hideaway on Lambton Quay. I thought I would wait to see what happened."

"I trusted you."

"No you didn't," he said. "You aren't a fool. You just trusted that you were cleverer than me. You may be, yet, but we have a lot of story left in us. Or perhaps only one of us does."

"Oh shut up. Just shut up, Dorian." She turned back to the Artful. "You were the one on lookout, that night at Lambton Quay. You were the one who called the summoner back, after we'd entered—as soon as Huck Finn had left, and you took over. That was how he knew we were there. And that's how he was able to leave afterward, without us seeing where he went. You did see him leave. He didn't have any particularly secret means of exit. He read the rooms away from memory, and walked out the front door. You just lied about it."

"I'm the Artful Dodger," he said. "You couldn't have thought I was honest."

"No," she conceded. "But I thought you were on our side."

He glanced away. "Now you know I'm not."

"Who is he?"

"You heard Scrooge, that day. We don't know who he is in your world, or what he looks like. We know who he *really* is, but we can't say. Not even me." He paused. "But I'll tell you this. He's one of us."

Lady Macbeth spoke up from one of the barstools, her black eyes sharp. "How now? What mean'st this?"

"I mean he's our kind." He turned to her. "A character. He was read out of a book, a long time ago. That's why he hates them so much—the people out there. He's as afraid of them as we are."

"Thy master art a summoner and a creature of fiction in one?"

"That's right. I don't know how, but he is. He's on our side."

"That doesn't mean he's on our side!" Millie retorted, over the murmurs of surprise from the rest of the room. She was shaken herself, but there was no time to wonder at new impossibilities. There was no time for a lot of things. "Where is he now? You can say that, can't you?"

"You think he'd tell me? His world can go with him in the pocket of a coat. I have no idea where he is now. But he knows where I am.

He found me yesterday. He told me about the book you stole, and he told me to get the book back while you were distracted and bring it to him. Which I did last night, and this morning. He said he needed it for the new world."

"But that wasn't all he needed, was it?" Millie asked flatly.

The Artful shrugged again. "He gave me *Through the Looking-Glass* this morning. Asked me to bring it in. He said the Jabberwock was trapped halfway between the words and the world. If I opened it, that would let it out. So I put it in the middle of the Street, and I scarpered. And you're right, by the way. He saw your spy at once. He said he knows Dr. Sutherland's work when he sees it. He crushed it with the book I gave him. One blow."

Millie shook her head. She should have seen it earlier. Of course she should have. She was Millie Radcliffe-Dix. But Millie Radcliffe-Dix, she remembered, didn't solve cases until the book was almost over.

"Why? Why would you listen to him? You could have come to me."

"You?" the Artful retorted. "You think you can protect me? You saw what he did to Scrooge, right here in the Street. He could do that to me, easy as winking. The Street's not yours, Millie. It's his. Once the new world comes through, he's not going to let you keep it."

"Then we fight for it," she said.

"With what? Dr. Sutherland? He did all right with the Jabberwock, I'll give him that, but that was a game, and it nearly finished him. He won't stand a chance in a real war. The more he tries, the worse it will be for all of youse."

Millie looked out at the Street. She saw the shattered buildings, the still-smoking houses, the claw marks scored on the road. The red smear on the cobbles, just outside, where Heathcliff had lain before they'd dragged him away to die.

"I swear, Dodger," she said. "I'll—"

"What?" the Artful said. "Hurt me? Kill me? See me in the dock for my crimes? Plenty have tried that, and I'm still here. My summoner could look at me, and I'd be gone. There's nothing you can threaten me with that worries me like that."

"You do realize that your summoner could do that just as easily once the new world comes? He doesn't seem to have a good deal of respect for our kind."

"I told you, he's one of us. He's on our side, in his way: us against the outside world. I'm not like those half-formed things he uses to do his bidding and puts away again—nor are you lot. You heard that Eric, when he came—he was right about that. We're fully written characters. There'd be a place for us in the new world. Besides, how can you say that *your* summoner won't do exactly the same thing to you? To any of you?"

"Of course he won't. Don't be ridiculous. Dr. Sutherland doesn't put people away against their will."

"That's not what Uriah Heep says. And he speaks from experience, don't he?"

"That was different! He didn't know about this place then. He didn't know about any of us."

"So what's changed now that he does? What's he after? I know what my summoner wants: a new world, where we don't have to hide anymore. I don't know what yours wants."

"None of us do," Dorian Gray spoke up.

All eyes went to him, Millie included. He was perched on one of the piles of fallen rubble, as lithe and graceful as a cat. His curls were battle tousled about his perfect face. He looked magnificent. He was at his most dangerous.

"He wants to keep us safe, and hidden," Millie returned. "As we've always been. He wants to stop the summoner from revealing us to the world, and threatening our lives in the process. What do you want, Dorian?"

"I want to *be* safe and hidden," he said. "But I don't think Dr. Sutherland can accomplish the task. Even if he successfully defeats the other summoner and protects our secret, it's only a matter of time before somebody else finds us. The old world is no longer feasible. We need a new one."

"Well, here it is," Millie said. She waved her hand to take in the broken public house, Heathcliff's body still warm on the floor. "Welcome to it."

"This isn't the new world," Dorian said. "This is the old one burning down. Heathcliff chose to burn with it. Very well, that's his narrative. That's good, that's aesthetically sound, I admire him for it. But I have no intention of burning. And I'm tired of hiding here, trapped like the

Artful's monster friend between the pages of a book, neither in one world or another. I'm tired of watching your summoner, wondering what he'll do; I'm tired of watching you struggle to keep everything the same; I'm tired of lurking in the shadows of the World Wide Web. I'm tired of the Street. I want the *world*. And it's coming."

Millie looked at the faces around her. They weren't all hostile, or angry, or in agreement. Many of them, she suspected, didn't know what they felt. But she could see echoed in them the expression that had been on the face of the picture of Dorian Gray for a long time now. They were all afraid. Everything had changed, when for so many of them nothing had changed for a hundred years. They didn't know what to do. The other summoner, with his whispers of the new world, was promising permanent safety with him even as he also promised death for standing against him. And she couldn't promise anything in return except the fragile safety of the last two years: the safety that came from secrecy, and could never be maintained if the summoner were to win. That and, perhaps, the dangerous prospect of doing what they ought to do in spite of fear.

"There is not going to be a new world," Millie said. She said it as firmly as she could. "Not if I can help it."

She somehow was not surprised when it was Uriah Heep who spoke in reply. "But you see, Miss Radcliffe-Dix," he said apologetically, "you can't."

Charles Sutherland, age eight

Extract from diary (yellow sun on cover)

I only did it to try to get Rob to play with me. Rob never plays with me anymore, now that he's in high school; he says he's too old for imaginary games. I try to be too old for imaginary games, too, and sometimes I succeed, but I miss being pirates in the old tree by the creek. I like the way the tree branches swing low to enclose us in leaves, and the hills slope up around us so the rest of the world doesn't exist. And I like how the wind creaks the branches and turns them into masts, and the leaves rustle into sails, and the grass swishes into waves and salt spray, for miles and miles and miles. This is all just pretend, of course. I thought perhaps if it wasn't all pretend—if I could make some of it real—then Rob might like it better. So I read *Treasure Island*, as deeply as I could. And unfortunately, the most real part of that book is Long John Silver.

And unfortunately, Rob wasn't there to help me catch him.

And unfortunately, Mum was.

She came into the room, took one look at Long John Silver, and yelled at me to put him back right now. He didn't want to go back, and I didn't know the book well enough, which was my fault. When I did get him back, I felt so tired and dizzy and sick that when Mum turned to me, I lost my temper. Well, I'm not sure if it was my temper I lost or something else, because I was furious but I was crying too. Something burst and spilled out. I lost that, whatever it was.

I said it wasn't fair. It's not fair I have to put everybody back all the time. They don't want to go back, and I don't want to put them back; it hurts and it's mean and it's not fair.

She said don't bring them out at all, and then you won't have to.

I said they want to be real, and I want them to be real, so why shouldn't I? I don't hide that I can read or write well; even when I want to, you say doing your best is important. So why isn't this important too? And why doesn't Rob ever have to hide himself?

She said because life's not fair.

I was angry because she wasn't taking me seriously, and worse because I knew I didn't deserve to be taken seriously. I could hear myself sounding like a child. But I also thought I was right. So I ran to my room, and jumped on my bed, and buried my face in my pillow so deep the tears and the whirling in my head didn't matter. I wanted to slam the door, like Rob did last week, but I didn't dare.

After a while Mum followed me. She wasn't angry anymore. She sat me up, and gave me a hug, and some chocolate biscuits from the tin in the kitchen.

I said, "I'm sorry."

She said, "It's okay," and did that thing where she sort of smooths my hair back from my forehead. I know I should be too old for that, too, but it felt nice. I hate fighting. Rob fights with our parents sometimes, especially lately. I hardly ever do. I hardly ever cry either. This was all very anomalous.

Then she said, "When I was four years old, I brought something out of a book. I think maybe that's where you get it from, your ability. I gave it to you, without meaning to. And I'm so sorry for that."

I sort of forgot how terrible I felt, because I never knew that. It was interesting. I said, "Is it everyone in our family? Can we all do it?"

"No," she said. "Just me, and now you. I only did it once."

"What happened?"

She said, "My own mother told me to hide it away, and to never do it again. She told me if people found out, they would take me away and hurt me. She was scared for me. She made me scared too. I know what it's like to hide something, Charley. I don't want you to be scared, ever, but I want you to be safe. Because I love you and your brother more than anything, and I never want any harm to come to you. Do you understand that?"

I nodded.

She smoothed my hair back again and kissed me on the forehead, and told me not to tell anybody else what she had told me, not even Rob or my father. I nodded again, because she had said she was scared of people finding out, and I didn't want her to be scared either.

Now I'm writing this before Rob gets home from rugby practice and Dad gets home from work. I can feel the gap inside me where whatever it was I lost used to be. It's not like a gap where a loose tooth was. It's more like a spot on the lawn where a weed's been yanked up. Bare and tender and ready for something else to take root, only I don't know what that something is.

The trouble is, I was right too. It's not fair. It feels good to write it, even if it doesn't change it. It's not fair. It's not fair it's not fair it's not fair it's not FAIR.

It's.

Not.

Fair.

I know that life isn't.

But stories are. Or if they're not fair, they're not fair with purpose.

I wish I could tell better where stories end and life begins.

XX

The drive to the hospital had taken fifteen minutes, even flooring the accelerator, and in that time it became undeniable that Charley was extremely sick. His face was bone white and drenched in perspiration, his breathing was coming shallow and rapid, and by the last set of traffic lights, his shivering had deepened to near convulsions and then abruptly stopped, which was worse. I couldn't pretend he could hear me anymore. He was obviously somewhere very far away.

Lydia had phoned ahead from the back seat on the way, and I was both reassured and scared by how quickly the medics wheeled him out of sight.

"Can you tell us anything about his medical history?" a red-haired woman asked me briskly, and I had to bite back a laugh. I had after all read it very recently. The trouble was, as I'd ascertained, none of it was at all helpful.

"He was born dead," I offered in the end, and they looked at me as though I were mentally deficient.

That was the last Lydia and I heard before we were swept into a waiting room on the floor above. It was a small room, with a single window overlooking the gray, windblown streets. An elderly couple sat on a sofa clutching hands, a pale woman in track pants lay stretched out across three seats, and a broken vending machine took up space in a corner. The air was thick with other people's anxiety, and my own.

Like most people, I hate hospitals, but until now it had been a theoretical hatred. Nobody I'd known had spent any substantial time in one, so thankfully neither had I. I knew now that I hated the antiseptic smell, the overbright corridors, the artificial heat, the buzz of fear and sickness that permeated the walls. Charley had spent even less time in hospitals than I had—he wasn't even born in one—and he would hate it even more than I did. It was the exact opposite of everything his cluttered, Victoriana-saturated, book-infested life was. It was definitely a million miles from the Street, which had cobblestones and probably the plague.

If the Street was still standing. We'd left at a bad moment. For all I knew, it had erupted into civil war.

I must have looked pretty grim, because Lydia frowned at me.

"You're not one of those people who faints in hospitals, are you?" she asked. "I've got a cousin who does that."

"No," I said, although actually I wasn't sure. "No, I'm pretty sure my brother holds the copyright on fainting in our family."

She gave me a critical look. "Why don't you step outside and get some air? They're probably doing tests and things now—it'll take a while. I'll get you if there's any news. And you can phone your parents. They'll want to know this is happening, right?"

That thought wasn't making me feel any better. They would kill both of us if they found out what was actually happening. But Lydia was right, I did need to call them. I also needed to call Millie.

The gray, windy afternoon outside was like a welcome dash of cold water on my face. For a moment, I just closed my eyes and let it revive me. My cheek stung, near my left eye, and I remembered that it had been cut in the rubble chasing the Jabberwock. I was probably covered with dust too. Lydia hadn't mentioned it, but there was no way she hadn't noticed. There was going to be trouble when things settled.

When things settled. Right now, things seemed to be roaring about me in a hurricane. I supposed they had to settle soon, but I was scared of where they would land, and what shape they would be in when they did. Things that happened because of Charley's abilities had always been something of a dream before. They happened, we dealt with them, and then I went back to reality. This was painfully real now. There were forms to fill out and everything.

And the summoner was poised to make a move. According to Victor Frankenstein. God, how did I get here?

Millie wasn't answering her phone. I knew she wasn't likely to do so for a while. She'd be in the Street, outside cell phone reception, and she would likely be busy there for some time. I phoned twice anyway, frustration bubbling hotter each time. It wasn't just that I needed to know what was happening with her, or she needed to know what was happening with Charley. I wanted to blame her. I wanted to tell her this was all her fault. He was all right before he found her and that bloody street. Why couldn't she have left us both alone?

I *needed* to tell her it was all her fault. I needed to tell her that before I rang my parents, because once I rang them, I would know it was mine.

Her phone went to voicemail. I had to give up. I couldn't unburden my anger on a voicemail. It wouldn't take it.

My father answered on the third ring.

"Hello, Rob," he said. "We were just about to call you. Is everything all right?"

I had to swallow hard before I spoke. "Not really."

They reacted to the news that Charley was in the hospital better than I had feared. Dad was notoriously uncomfortable around illness, and Mum was fiercely protective of Charley. I had expected to have to try to calm them down. In fact, once their initial shock was over, their instinct was to try to calm me instead.

"It's going to be fine, Rob," Dad said. "Really. Your brother's much tougher than he looks."

"That wouldn't be difficult," I said, on reflex. But I thought of his face aglow as he had banished the Jabberwock to unreality.

"Do they have any idea what's caused it?" Mum asked.

I braced myself. "They don't," I said. "I do."

I don't think I explained very well. Words tend to trip over themselves when my brother is concerned, and language certainly wasn't quite built to explain the Street. Or perhaps it's more accurate to say that *my* language wasn't.

"How can there be a street filled with fictional characters?" Dad said. "Where do they come from? Wouldn't Charley have to read them out?"

"They're from all over the place—but the Street, it turns out, was read out by another person. A summoner, they call them. Another summoner. And it looks like—well, it's turned into some kind of war."

"A war between whom?" Mum said slowly. Mum, who was possibly a summoner herself. "Is that how he ended up in the hospital?"

"Not directly. I think he's just been doing far too much reading. But...he's in danger. I should have told you earlier, I know, and I should have stopped him..."

"What do the doctors say?" Dad interrupted. "How is he?"

I had to pause to take a breath. "I don't know. They've just taken him in. Lydia's waiting while I phone you—she'd have come out if there was any news. She thought you'd want to know as soon as possible."

"She was right," Dad said. "Never mind the rest of it for now. We'll get in the car and come as fast as we can. Phone us on the cell if anything happens between now and then, won't you?"

I nodded tightly, then remembered they couldn't see me. "Of course. Look, I'm sure he'll be fine."

"Of course he will," Dad said. I knew, seventy kilometers away, that he and Mum were exchanging those wordless glances they perfected over our childhoods. "You get back to your brother. We'll be right there."

I hadn't even made it back into reception before I was stopped by Victor Frankenstein. His skin was ghost white in the hospital lighting, behind the freckles.

"Is it true?" he demanded. I caught the faint scent of disinfectant as he gripped my arm. "Is Charles Sutherland here?"

"I'm not in the mood, Victor," I said, which effectively answered his question. His eyes gleamed. I shook him off, too sick with guilt and worry to rally more than mild irritation. My phone was still in my hand. My parents' shock was still painfully sharp in my mind. They would be here in an hour, and I would have to face them in person. My brother could be dead by then. I had no time for fictional people. "Look, leave him alone. He can't help you with your little quest into the nature of fictional life at the moment. Though I'm sure if he were awake, he'd love to. He has no idea when to stop chasing knowledge either. The two of you would get on perfectly."

"I'm certain we would. That wasn't what I meant. I simply meant to watch him closely, especially if he's not in a position to watch out for himself. I started to wonder why his records were already on file with us, given that you expected them to need to be requested from overseas. We hadn't treated him, after all. I went to follow it up this morning."

"Are things slow in the mortuary today?"

He ignored me, which was a fair response. "Someone else had requested them only weeks ago. The request came from the university's School of Medicine, according to the computer. They have offices in the building, and a branch of the health center operates from there. But I would stake a good deal that they weren't the ones who received the records. Anyone from within the university could have made that request, assuming a certain degree of duplicity."

My brain started to catch on to his words. I frowned. "Did they request my mother's as well?"

"There's no sign of that. Should they have?"

If they were looking for a summoner, then yes. The fact that they hadn't meant either they didn't know about her, or they didn't care. "But why? What's in them?"

"Beyond what I've told you, I've seen nothing. I have no explanation for it. But things are starting to move."

"Don't I know it. The Street was attacked, did you know that?"

He shook his head. "Then things are moving even faster than I thought."

"Where are these files?" I asked. "I need to look at them again."

His laptop was in the mortuary, of course. Frankenstein swiped me through the glass doors that separated the private section of the hospital from the public, and I followed him, ignoring the curious glances of white-coated hospital staff as we passed through. I ignored, too, the probable contents of the massive steel fridge doors that lined the room Frankenstein ushered me into, and the purpose of the gurney that lay waiting, draped with a maroon blanket, in the center of the room. At least the gurney was empty.

"We should be left alone in here for a little while," Frankenstein said. He swung his long limbs up onto the empty gurney, and snatched up the laptop from beside him. I stood over his shoulder, trying not to touch anything. The air was chill. "There are no autopsies scheduled this afternoon, and I'm supposed to be taking a break. I don't take many—they won't come looking for me. Here's the file."

There wasn't much to see: I had read it, after all, only an hour or two ago. A lot had changed since then. The file wasn't one of them—though, I supposed, it was now growing out of date as we spoke.

"They had given up trying to revive him," Frankenstein said. His long fingers scrolled down the touch screen. "Really, I don't see how he's alive at all."

I saw the section he indicated. But now, perhaps because I was still thinking about Mum, I was struck by something else.

"They recommended he go to the hospital for an overnight observation," I said. "And it says that our mother refused his admission. He was checked up on the following day at home instead."

"And found to be perfectly healthy," Frankenstein said.

I shook my head. "No. I mean...why would any parent, Mum included, refuse to have their newborn child admitted to the hospital when they had nearly died? If it were my child—God, I'd insist on it. So would Lydia."

"People can be superstitious about hospitals."

"Not our parents. Not usually."

I was four years old then. It had never occurred to me, then or in the years since, how odd it was that my fragile, dark-eyed little brother who had barely survived his entry into the world was waiting for me when I came home a few hours later. Now I wondered how I could have failed to ask. Mum had always been protective about his abilities—she was reluctant to take him to the doctor at times as a child, because they tended to have books in waiting rooms, and Charley with a raging fever and a copy of Dr. Seuss was a lethal combination. But that didn't make sense when he was a few hours old. We didn't know there was anything to protect him *from*.

At least, Dad and I didn't. My words caught up to me.

"She knew," I said. "Even back then, she knew. But how?"

"Perhaps you were right." Frankenstein was a disconcerting companion to have at a moment like this. His interest was too piercing, to the point where it became painful. "Perhaps she was indeed a summoner, and she suspected he had inherited the gift."

I knew I was right. It still didn't make sense. "But *I* didn't inherit it. She never showed any sign of worrying that I had."

"She had, after all, just seen him return from the dead. Perhaps that told her. Perhaps that is what whoever requested it was also looking for."

"But even if that's true, so what? So what if she knew he'd grow to be a summoner? Why would that stop her from letting him be taken to the hospital as a newborn? He wasn't going to perform close analysis in the infants' wing. He couldn't *read.*"

"Might there be some other physical sign she was worried they would detect?" He answered his own question. "Foolish. There would be nothing to indicate a summoner in any physical exam—a brain scan, perhaps, but they would be unlikely to perform one of those. And even then, they wouldn't know what they were looking at. Sutherland?"

My breath had caught. All at once, I knew. I knew what must have happened, and what my mother had known. And I thought I'd felt sick before.

Frankenstein pounced on me. "What? What is it?"

With great effort, I pulled shattered fragments of myself together tightly enough to say words. They weren't particularly good words. "Nothing. Look, thanks for showing me this. I'll ask Mum about it when they get here, all right? It's probably nothing."

I don't think I fooled Victor Frankenstein—I don't think "it's probably nothing" fools anybody—but perhaps a man who built a monster in his attic has some degree of respect for personal secrets. At least, to my eternal gratitude, he nodded. "Very well."

I rubbed my eyes, trying to collect myself. "I owe you a hundred dollars still, don't I?"

Frankenstein snorted. "I care for knowledge, not money. I've had payment enough. I need but one more thing, and I will consider myself in your debt. If your brother did indeed return from the dead, and you find out anything more about it, will you promise to tell me?"

"He didn't," I said. "At least, not in the way you mean."

"Disappointing. But thank you."

"I'm sorry you didn't get any closer to the secret of your life." In the wake of my gratitude to him for not questioning me further, I actually meant it.

"No. Don't be." He closed the laptop, stood, and paused. "Will you permit me to tell you something?"

"What is it?"

He seemed to be groping for words, as someone might for an unfamiliar door handle in the dark. When he spoke, he was uncharacteristically hesitant. "There used to be a Nancy who lived homeless around Vivian Street. Nancy of *Oliver Twist*, I refer to. We would help each other now and again. I'm not sure why she never chose to go to the Street when it came. Perhaps the idea of living on the fringes was too deeply embedded in her character for her to overcome. She should have gone. She was a lovely young woman. Too kind to be on the streets."

"Were you friends?" There was a note of grief in his voice, but I wasn't tactless enough to ask if he was in love with her. Still, he *was* a Romantic.

"If I were," Frankenstein said, without change of expression, "I should have known better. I don't exactly have luck with friends. One day she told me about a dream she kept having, a glimpse of a dark place that changed sometimes to a glimpse of thievery or prostitution or blackmail. She was the first person I ever heard speak of the new world."

"She was seeing through another Nancy," I said, with a rush of realization. "One belonging to the other summoner. As Uriah Heep was seeing through Eric."

Frankenstein didn't ask about Uriah Heep, or Eric. "I believe so. It's rather difficult to verify."

"Why? Where is she? Millie would like to talk to her, I'm sure."

"As would I." His gaze was fixed carefully on the steel fridges. "Two weeks after she told me of her dream, she was found dead in an alley. Her skull was caved in. I had the honor of viewing her body right here in the hospital mortuary."

"God." My brief excitement turned cold in my stomach. "She was killed for talking to you?"

"I doubt it. I doubt the summoner knows or cares that I exist. I would imagine she was killed because, willingly or not, the other Nancy revealed her existence. Through no fault of her own, she was a person who could be eyes in the summoner's camp. Had Nancy—the Nancy I knew—been more protected, the summoner would probably have merely stopped using her own. But she was a nobody, and easy to dispose of. And that is how I know that the summoner's promise to respect the lives of freeborn characters is a lie. It's how I know that the summoner, whoever he is, is driven not by that desire for knowledge which might supply a reason for experimenting with one's powers, but something altogether more monstrous. It's the reason why I am, despite my general disinterest in politics, quite glad to have been able to aid you. And it's also why I think it's perhaps time to absent myself from this city before the new world comes. I have no desire to be a part of it."

"And go where?"

"Anywhere. Preferably some lonely castle or vast snowy wasteland, but in this country I may have to make do with a beach. Don't leave your brother unwatched, Sutherland."

At that moment, I wanted nothing more to do exactly what he was doing: retreat, as far and as fast as I could. A beach would be fine. More than fine. He'd been right about knowledge. I never wanted to see or know anything, ever again. But at the last sentence, I nodded.

"I won't," I said.

I went back through to the waiting room, after a while. I had to; I couldn't stand in the mortuary forever. Perhaps I should have stayed there longer, though, because when Lydia saw me, I wasn't ready to talk to her.

"I was just about to come out and find you," she said. "Are you okay?"

I nodded. Obviously, my nod was a lie, but it was an expected one. "Mum and Dad are on the way."

"Good. A doctor stuck his head in the door. They still don't have anything definitive about Charley, but they've got him admitted to intensive care and wired up to things I can't pronounce, and they said he's stabilized. He's not a medical emergency anymore. More of a puzzle, they said."

I laughed, painfully, before I could help it. "They have no idea." The rest of her words caught up to me a second later. "That sounds hopeful, anyway. Can we go see him?"

"We can go in anytime, they said. The doctor wants to talk to you properly, when he has a moment. Rob…"

My heart sank at the look on her face. I should have known I wasn't going to get away with this for much longer.

"Rob, what the hell is going on?" She must have been dying to ask this for the last hour; really, it's amazing she held out this long. "What kind of family business puts your brother in a coma that you won't even explain to the hospital?"

"I told you, I don't know why he's in a coma," I said, knowing how lame it sounded. "I'm not a doctor."

"And I'm not an idiot. I know you requested his birth certificate last week, after we got back from your parents'."

"What...? Have you read my e-mails?"

"I don't have to read your e-mails. You downloaded the form on our home computer. You never remember to clear the search history."

"I'm not usually trying to hide things from you."

"Is Charley adopted?"

"No." I ran a hand over my face wearily. My head was pounding. "I thought he might be, but no. There are a few things I need to ask my parents, though, when they get here."

"What sort of things?"

"Family things."

"And when do I get to become family?" She folded her arms. "Because we've been living together four years. We've bought a house together. We've been...I *thought* we were thinking about having a family of our own. I've met your parents. They're lovely. You've met mine. They love you. And I've just helped you rush your brother, about whom I happen to care deeply, to an emergency room in a coma. I think I'm entitled to know a few things."

"You are," I said. "I just—look, can we have this conversation another time? I can't really deal with this right now."

"And by 'this,' you mean...?"

"Lydia, please, for God's sake, just leave me alone."

That sounded a lot more irritable out in the open than it had in my head. From the look Lydia shot me, I knew she thought so as well.

"Okay." She took a deep breath. "Look, I think I'd better go home. I'll call you tomorrow morning from work, and see where we're at. Call me if anything happens with Charley, won't you? I can know that, at least?"

"Yes," I said. "Of course. Lydia, I didn't mean to sound—"

"I don't mind how you *sound*, Rob," she interrupted. "You're worried, you're upset; you can sound however you like. But you don't want me here, do you? You don't want me part of this, whatever this is. Tell me you do, and I'll stay. But you don't."

I desperately wanted her to stay. The trouble was, I needed her *not* to stay. There was a hurricane raging, out of control, and there were too many things flying around—Millie, the Street, the summoner, Eric, Dorian Gray, Uriah Heep, Charley—to risk adding Lydia to the mix. I didn't want her to collide with any of them. At best, it would break the last thread of normality I had left. At worst, it could put her in terrible danger, and I couldn't bear the thought of that, not when I had just come from seeing the Street in tatters and my brother on a hospital gurney, struggling to breathe.

I was still thinking of something to say when she shook her head.

"Well. I'll call you tomorrow. We'll see where we go from there. Give Charley my love when he wakes up, all right?"

I managed a nod.

She hesitated, then touched my arm briefly; it might have been a compromise between a hug and nothing at all. Then she was gone.

Lydia

L ydia had gone as far as the parking lot when she realized she was more or less trapped in the hospital suburbs. They had come together. Even if she'd wanted to take their car—and while she was frustrated enough to leave Rob stranded, she wouldn't have risked it when Charley was in intensive care—he still had the keys. She liked walking, but it was a long way from Newtown to their house, and she was wearing her very highest heels, the blue ones that Rob had thought would be impossible to walk in. He was wrong, but not for several kilometers. That left a bus, and she had no spare change. She could have screamed.

She bought an unwanted bottle of water at the nearby convenience store for the sake of getting five dollars cash out, and managed to squeeze into the aisle of an old bus that was rapidly filling with afternoon commuters. Over the rumbling of the engines, she almost didn't hear her phone ring in her handbag. An unknown number. She didn't think it would be anyone from the hospital, if it wasn't Rob or his parents, but her heart still pounded and her fingers fumbled as she answered. "Hello?"

"Miss Lydia?" She recognized the voice at once. "This is Eric Umble, Mr. Sutherland's intern. I was so sorry to hear about his brother."

"Thank you," she said reflexively, to give herself a chance to collect herself behind the pleasantry. The bus turned a corner; she lurched sideways and mouthed an apology at the harassed-looking woman next to her. "Can I help you?"

"Actually, I was thinking I might help you." She had to press the phone tighter to her ear to hear his voice. It buzzed close to her skin. "I said on Sunday night that I might be able to help you. I don't know if you remember our conversation—"

"Of course I do," she said. She remembered more than that, of course. He had told her that he couldn't speak freely on the phone: he was being listened to. This was the call he had promised her. The timing, though, sent a chill down her spine. It wasn't a coincidence. Somehow, Charley's collapse and Eric's escape were connected.

"Then you remember what I said," Eric was saying. "That I could tell you what was going on. I still can. If you meet me in town in an hour, I can tell you everything."

Trouble, Rob had said. Lydia wasn't afraid of trouble. She had worked in hotels since she was in her early twenties; she had worked part-time in bars before that. There weren't many species of trouble she hadn't served drinks to or booked a room for in her time. Still...

"Can't you tell me right now?" she asked, just to test the waters.

"I'm afraid not, Miss Lydia. It's the sort of thing that really needs to be told in person. Face-to-face. I could meet you at the café outside your hotel, if you have the time. It should be convenient."

"How do you—?" She cut off the question. How did he know any of this? Where she worked was the least of it.

A boat ticket, and a few hundred dollars. It wasn't a good deal to ask—it wasn't a good deal to give. It wasn't as though any harm could come to her, in a public café right outside her own hotel. It was just all deeply, troublingly strange.

He clearly heard her hesitation. "Please," he said. He said nothing more, but the sincere note was back in his voice. Perhaps it was that note that decided her. Perhaps it was just that she couldn't bear not to know for a moment longer.

"All right," she said. "The Black Finch, right? I'll be there in an hour."

XXI

There's something very naked about intensive care wards—not that I'd ever been in one before, but that was my impression when I was escorted through the door to find Charley. The industrial-looking machines displaying heartbeats and respirations for all to see, the tubes and pipes snaking from bodies like plastic intestines, how small everyone looks suspended in a swathe of blankets and equipment. I had a sick flash that the patients had been turned inside out, their organs on display, and wondered if perhaps I was one of those people who fainted in hospitals after all.

Charley was in the third bed down. I was relieved to see him wired to less machinery than many of the other patients. Drips piped liquid into his veins, as Lydia had said, and a couple of monitors beeped rhythmically above his head. But he was breathing on his own, and more easily than he had been in the car. That had to be a good sign.

The doctor came through quickly, as the nurse who'd shown me in had promised, looking extremely harried. It was getting late in the day, and the hospital had been bustling as I stood outside. Also, from what he told me in his kind, professional way, Charley was a stress-inducing patient.

"Frankly, Mr. Sutherland," the doctor said, "your brother makes no sense at all. His blood sugar levels are almost nonexistent, and yet he has no history of hypoglycemia. He's suffering severe exhaustion, and yet has no sign of muscle fatigue or even physical exertion. When he came in he was mildly hypothermic, which we can't explain. There's no trace of any foreign substance or infection. Most puzzling, based on what the university told us when we phoned, his condition has managed to go from slightly run-down to critical in the space of about two hours. We were hoping you could shed some light on what exactly he's been doing to himself."

"I really can't." It was true. "Look, how is he? Can you do something?"

"We can, and we are," the doctor said. "We're calling this a hypo-glycemic coma for now, and pumping him full of glucose; he's also on a saline drip, to counteract dehydration. He's responding well already. We were concerned about the strain on his heart, but his pulse is slowing right down. As far as I can tell, he could wake up at any time. We hope he will. But if we don't know the cause of all this, we don't know how to stop it from recurring."

I did know the cause, and I knew exactly what would cause it to recur. Unfortunately, I didn't know how to stop it either.

"Thanks," I said. "My parents should be here soon. Can I wait here, in case he wakes up?"

"We have no idea when that will be," he warned. "Even if all's well, it may not be until tomorrow."

Tomorrow. The world could be over by then. I thought of Victor Frankenstein.

"I don't mind," I said. "I think I'd better be here."

The sun was starting to crawl down the sky when my parents finally arrived. It surprised me when I went out to reception to meet them. I had lost track of time in that timeless, sterile room.

"How is he?" Mum asked as soon as she saw me. Her eyes were wide and anxious. I noticed, irrelevantly, that she was still in the old jeans and wrap she must have worn to volunteer at the animal shelter, and Dad wore his gardening trousers. Neither had bothered to put on a coat.

"He's okay," I said. I had meant to rush to reassure them, but at the sight of them my throat closed up. "He's still unconscious. There's a doctor waiting to talk to you. But he's alive."

That was the least reassuring reassurance ever, but Dad managed an encouraging nod. "Well... good." He squeezed my shoulder. "It's going to be all right, you'll see."

I looked at Mum's face, and knew I was in trouble.

Sure enough, as soon as the three of us were alone, it started. The doctor had talked Charley's condition over with Mum and Dad kindly, as he had with me, and then found us a room to wait in not far down the corridor. This one, unlike the emergency admissions waiting room, was abandoned; we thanked him politely, and waited for the door to close.

"What on earth is all this about a street from Dickens populated with fictional characters?" Mum demanded. Her arms were folded tightly across her chest, pulling her gray wrap close. She seemed to have shrunk several inches since the weekend—or, more probably, since my last phone call. "For God's sake, Rob, you know he's supposed to be staying well away from anything like that."

"Calm down, you two," Dad began, without much hope. He'd been on the sidelines of too many fights between us.

"And it's my job to stop him?" I returned, as if I were fifteen years old. "He's an adult, you know."

"And that's exactly what adults do," Dad said dryly, unable to help himself as usual. "Go through walls into fictional streets."

"You should have told us," Mum said. Her eyes were now bright with tears. "We needed to know."

Because I wasn't in fact fifteen, I bit back my defensive instincts. My own eyes were suspiciously hot, and my throat ached. "You're right. I should have told you. But there are things you should have told me too."

"Such as?"

I felt exactly as I had on Sunday night, when I gathered myself to plunge through the harbor waters above my head. "The night Charley was born. Who was there when he came back from the dead?"

Dad frowned, pulled out of his role as conciliator. "What do you mean? What's this about?"

"Just—tell me who was in the room with him. Please. Were you?"

"Well—no. I'd stepped out to talk with the doctor. Your mother was there, of course. He woke up in her arms. Probably the midwife was with her. Why? How could that possibly matter now?"

I turned to Mum. "*Was* the midwife with you?"

There was a pause, which may have been down to surprise. If I were wrong, it would be an unexpected change in subject.

When she spoke, I knew it wasn't.

"No." She sounded, suddenly, calm. It was as though she'd been waiting to give that answer for a long time. "Nobody was with me. Your father and the doctor were talking in the corridor. The midwife had stepped out to get a blanket. I was alone in the room with him."

She seemed to be waiting for the next question. I asked it. "What did you do? What is he?"

"Rob—"

"What are you talking about?" Dad interrupted. He was looking from Mum to me; he might have been asking either of us. "What does it matter who was with him? What does that day matter at all right now?"

I kept my eyes on Mum. Her face was very still. "What did you do that day?"

"If you're asking that question, Rob," she said quietly, "then I suspect you already know."

"He's not really my brother." I said it as bluntly as I could, but I still felt the words torn from me. "Is he?"

"He is your brother," she said. "In every way that matters. But he wasn't the child that was born dead on that day. No."

Dad stared at her. "What do you—? He had to have been. You *were* alone in the room with him at that moment, but not for very long. There's no way you could have—"

"Replaced him," she finished. "I did. It's exactly what I did."

"How? You couldn't—you can't just pull a newborn out of midair!"

"Charley could," I said. "Given a few minutes alone with a book. And so could you—I think. Please tell me I'm wrong."

She shook her head, and my world came crashing down. "You're not wrong."

("In another book," Frankenstein had said, "I'd say you were talking about a changeling.")

Something was roaring in my ears. It took a while for me to realize my mother was asking me a question, and when it did, it came from a long way away.

"How did you know?"

I had to swallow twice before I could speak. "About you, or Charley?"

"Either. Both."

"I knew what you were when I saw your medical records. You

summoned something when you were four, didn't you? It attacked you. And Charley—little bits of things. I saw his medical records. Physical details didn't match from before and after the midwife returned to the room. You wouldn't let them take him to be examined in any detail. I may not be a literary specialist, but I *am* a criminal defense lawyer. I know how to recognize *something* going on."

"I didn't want the doctors to look at him too closely," she said. "Not then. I wasn't sure enough what he was."

"I told you it would be best to let them take him to the hospital for the night," Dad said slowly. He looked dazed. "You said you couldn't bear it."

"I couldn't," she said. "If they'd found anything strange—I hadn't looked at him myself yet. I didn't even know if he had a heartbeat. I still don't trust what hospitals might find—I'm terrified that he's in there. I'm reasonably confident that nothing about him stands out that a routine medical check would flag. But if they look too closely— if they start taking blood work and X-rays and scans—"

"What?" Dad demanded. "What might they find?"

Mum turned to him. "Did you really never suspect anything was strange? In all these years?"

Dad threw up his hands. "He was a strange child! Even without the magic, that was commonly accepted. He read Dickens at three. I didn't suspect he wasn't *human*, no. Perhaps that was naive..."

"Still. You must have seen things you couldn't explain."

"I saw there was nothing of me in him," Dad said bluntly. "Of course I did. I'm not an idiot. But I didn't let myself suspect anything at all. The natural explanation was that I was not his father, and that's not something I would ever believe of you. You hadn't conceived him with anyone else."

An involuntary smile escaped. "'Conceived.' That's exactly the right word. And no. Not with anyone else. I didn't have some sordid affair with another man. I know other people must have accused me of it, at times. They just...I suppose nobody could have suspected where he really came from."

"Which is a book," Dad said. "Rob's right, isn't he? You read him out of a book. The way Charley does."

"Not quite the way he does," Mum said. "At least, not for a very long time. But yes. I did that." She fell quiet.

"It happened when I was four," she said at last. "Just like Charley. I didn't have the gift for reading that he had, of course, but I was learning. I was sitting out in the paddock on a Saturday morning, at the back of the house, while my mother worked in the garden. It was one of the first times I'd ever read entirely on my own. I remember the excitement of the words making sense."

"What came out?" I asked.

She smiled a little. "A lion. A roaring, whiskery lion in the meadow."

"The picture book from the shelf?"

"That exact one. I wasn't old enough to control it, or interpret it. It was just fear, and excitement, and the joy of being scared. It lunged to get away; its claws glanced me as it went. I don't think I even felt the pain at first. I was just filled with the wonder and the terror of it. My mother, on the other hand . . ."

"I can imagine."

"She had no idea what I'd done—neither had I—but she was beside herself. The lion had escaped over the fields—there was nothing she could do about it. She packed me in the car and hauled me down to emergency, where they gave me a handful of stitches and a tetanus shot. I don't know how my mother explained it."

"They thought you were being abused," I said. "At the hospital."

"I wasn't then. The abuse came later, if you could call it that. They were trying to protect me. I understood that when Charley was born, but at the time I hated them. I was already hurt, so they didn't beat me. They only yelled at me, repeatedly, and then when I was crying so hard I couldn't hear them anymore, they took every book out of my room and locked me in there for a month. They brought me food, and water, and changed the bandages. They didn't neglect me. After a while, when I showed no signs of calling up any more lions, they let me out. But I never saw or heard a story for the next three years. They schooled me at home, and they made sure I came nowhere near the written word until the magic, or whatever they thought it was, had been entirely driven out of me. They told me, again and again, that nobody could ever know what I had done, or I would be taken away and experimented on. It was the 1960s: I suppose they believed it. Perhaps they were even right. At any rate, as far as I was concerned, they needn't have bothered."

I couldn't form the question, but she took my silence as an invitation. "I had felt what happened to my lion. My beautiful lion, the creature of imagination, whom I loved. A few days later and a few miles away, a farmer shot him. It caused a stir, as you can imagine. It was assumed someone had been keeping one illegally as a pet, but nobody knew who or how. My parents told me when it hit the papers, but I had already felt him die. I was terrified of what had happened to him, of what had happened to me, of what might happen still if I was ever to be discovered. By the time I was eight, I could read again, but I had no intention of ever summoning. I didn't even think I could. That part of me had been squashed flat. Until that night, when our child died."

Their child. My real little brother, the one who'd had blue eyes like me.

"I didn't think we could survive that," she said. "It felt like the tear in my heart the day the lion died, only worse—much worse. I can't describe it. There are some things too big for words."

"God," my father said slowly. "He's still dead. I thought all this time...but he's still dead."

Mum was still speaking to me. She didn't even look at Dad. "It was just before midnight. The doctor and your father had left the room; the midwife left me alone to get another blanket. She shouldn't have done that, poor woman, but she was crying too. She was so young— we all were. I sat there with my dead child in my arms. He was so beautiful. I just—I kept thinking of you, and how we would have to tell you that you wouldn't have a brother after all."

"Is that an excuse?" I snapped, before I could stop myself. "A child isn't a new toy. You can't just swap one out for a new one."

"Do you think I want an *excuse*?" Paradoxically, I much preferred the flash of anger to the raw grief it replaced. I had never seen my mother cry before. It tightened my stomach. "Nobody was swapped out. I loved that child as much as I love you and Charley. I still grieve for him, every day, and I've never been able to tell anyone why there's a part of me that died twenty-six years ago. But I'll never regret bringing Charley into the world, however it happened. You can blame me for not telling you all—you have every right to. I'm so sorry for that. I'm not sorry for a single moment of your brother's life."

"None of us are," Dad said, but as if on reflex. His own eyes were glittering. "But—bloody hell, Susan."

She drew a deep, shuddering breath. "I know. I must have been mad. I just wanted—I don't know what I wanted. I just know that the book I needed was right there, on my shelf. I opened it, and I started to read the first paragraph. It wasn't really a reading, not the way Charley does it. I didn't interpret, or frame, or analyze. I just poured everything—my love, my grief, all the hopes I'd had for the child that was dead—into that book. And then there was a new child on the bed in front of me. It didn't even sink in, what I was really doing, until the clock struck twelve and the baby—"

"—'began to cry, simultaneously,'" I finished. One of the most famous opening paragraphs in history. I'd read it only a few nights ago. My stomach tightened further. "*David Copperfield.*"

"You knew that too?"

"That was how I knew. I've been reading it lately—your copy, the one I borrowed from your house on the weekend. It wasn't the words, though. It was the frontispiece. It has a picture of Dickens in his twenties."

"The Daniel Maclise one," she said. "Yes. I know. I saw it at the National Portrait Gallery in London. It's starting to look like him, isn't it? Or rather he's starting to look like it. Not precisely, but enough."

"I didn't notice at the time. But then I saw the medical records, and it fell into my head. Like Dad said. He's never really looked like us. He had to come from somewhere."

"I don't really know where he comes from," she said. "Me, originally, but I've had control over how he grows. I don't know what he is now. A little bit of David Copperfield, maybe, a little bit of Dickens, but so much that seems to come entirely from himself. Or perhaps it's from all of us. Perhaps we've all made him up over the years, without realizing it. I can't explain him. As I said, he was a miracle. I never thought he'd grow up—how could he grow up?—but he did."

"I know," I said. "I was there."

I was there the day after he was born. I'd seen him in his crib, all enormous dark eyes. I was there as he started to talk in complete sentences while the others in his playgroup were still learning to recognize their own names. I was there when he came to high school and sat quietly at the back of my classroom getting everything right and learning not to be noticed. The weird kid, whom everyone regarded with fascination and unease.

Was that why he had been such a prodigy? Had he been born with our mother's knowledge and abilities, just waiting to develop as soon as his brain was ready for them? Did he really never need to learn, but only to remember?

"I couldn't tell you," Mum said—to Dad, I think, this time. "It was before Charley's abilities had manifested—I had no idea they would manifest. I had no idea how you'd react to the idea of things coming out of books. I thought—if you had made me put him back—"

"What about our first child?" Dad said. The words came out too calm, as though they were being strangled. "What did you do with the—what did you do with him?"

"I wrapped him and put him in the clothes chest, under the bed," she said. "Then I called out. When you all came in, I was holding a child that was alive, and crying. Of course you had no reason to suspect it wasn't the same one. The following night, I buried him under the oak tree outside."

At that, of all things, bile rose in my throat. I knew that tree. Charley and I had played under it, a hundred times, in the early years before I grew out of games and he started to be tutored so intensely. We'd never thought there was anything dark or haunted about it. There hadn't been.

Dad shook his head. He looked about as sick as I felt. "I can't handle this." He picked up his coat from the back of the couch.

"Joe—" Mum started to say.

He held up a hand. "I'm not leaving. I'm going to go see how Charley's doing. But I can't be in here with you at the moment."

"Don't blame him," Mum said. She blinked, just once, and tears spilled down her face. "Be as angry at me as you want. But please, don't blame Charley for being what he is."

"I'd never do that," Dad said. "It's not his fault. I just don't know how to think about him right now. And I have *no* idea how to think about you."

As Dad left, I drew a deep breath and leaned back against the wall, fighting dizziness. Perhaps this was how Charley felt when he put something back. The world opening, and changing, and things forced into place that didn't want to fit.

My brother wasn't real. He wasn't my brother. And he wasn't real.

"Rob?" My mother was watching me, anxious, drawing herself together. "Are you all right?"

"Does he know?" I managed. "Charley?"

"I don't think so—though I never quite know what Charley knows. He knows about what I did as a child, or he did once—I told him when he was small. He might have forgotten. I certainly never told him where he came from."

"Don't tell him." I could hardly tell what was real anymore, but that seemed important, so I grabbed at it. "It would destroy him. He can't know."

"I don't want him to," she said. "I wanted him to feel he belonged with us, and to this world. But there are a lot of things I wanted for both of you that are impossible. And your father is absolutely right that your brother is much tougher than he looks."

I wasn't listening. Another thought had just struck me. "You said that he needed to stop wanting to read things out into the world," I said. "Back at your house last weekend. I thought you just knew him. But you *knew*, didn't you?"

"Do you know when I stopped wanting to?" she said. "The day you were born. I hadn't read anything out for years, but on that day I decided I never wanted to again. It just wasn't as important as keeping you safe."

I don't know what I would have replied. At that moment, Dad came back in.

"I think you two should probably come." His voice was calm again now, the kind of calm that implies a storm beneath the surface. "Charles Dickens has arrived to pay a visit."

XXII

It wasn't the Charles Dickens of popular imagination, with his wise, bushy-browed face and wiry beard; nor was it the younger Dickens in our family's books, with his delicate chin and tumbling curls. This was a middle-aged Dickens, no more than forty. His hair had thinned into an extravagant comb-over; his mouth was wide and expressive; his dark eyes twinkled with intelligence and humor. Presumably, this was the Dickens who had written *David Copperfield*. He stood beside Charley's bed, entirely unfazed, even as Dad drew the curtains around us all to hide us from view.

"This kind of thing," Mum said, very calmly, "is exactly why I didn't want Charley to have his tonsils out when he was fourteen."

"I understand that now," Dad said.

Dickens didn't give them more than a passing glance. His dark eyes focused directly on me. In that movement, I saw Charley in him.

"I've come from your brother," he said.

"But—" I cast an uncertain glance at my parents. "He's not awake, is he?"

It was a stupid question: I could see him there, in the bed, as still and unresponsive as before. Fortunately, other than the shadowy unconscious figures on the other side of the curtain, the room was empty. No nurses or doctors had seen Dickens's arrival, or we would probably have heard about it. I wondered about security cameras, but consigned it to the list of future worries.

"He is not awake," Dickens confirmed—patiently, under the circumstances. "His body is still unconscious. His mind is awake, and fighting to get out. I, perhaps, am the part of his mind that made it. He fears you are in terrible danger."

"Danger?" Mum repeated.

Dickens seemed to see her and Dad for the first time. "Forgive me." He inclined his head to Dad, then took Mum's hand in his own and bowed over it extravagantly. "Mr. Sutherland, Mrs. Sutherland. I am delighted to see you here. I'm certain Dr. Sutherland will be as well, when he awakens."

"Don't be too sure about that," Dad said dryly. "I'm sure he knows full well the trouble he'll be in."

"How is Rob in danger, Mr. Dickens?" Mum asked.

"I'm not," I said firmly. "I'm really not. The Street might be in danger—"

"Of course the Street is in danger," Dickens said. "Your brother knows that very well. He left it on fire. His fears are for you."

"Why? I have nothing to do with this. This is about his world, not mine. It always has been. What possible cause could he have to worry about me?"

"As usual," came a familiar voice, "you have seen, but you have not observed."

I have no idea how long he had been there. He might have come into the world at the same time as Dickens, while my parents and I argued outside in the olive-green waiting room, or at that very moment. But the curtain surrounding Charley's bed swished back with a flourish, and Sherlock Holmes peered around it. Next to Dickens's yellow waistcoat and flamboyant hair, he looked as sleek and dark as a jaguar. The animal, not the car, although that would fit too.

"Oh, for God's sake!" I was determined not to be shaken. "Not you too."

"Rob," Mum admonished me. She rubbed her brow, but kept her voice calm. "Just... be polite to Mr. Holmes, won't you? He can't help being here."

"Thank you, Mrs. Sutherland," Holmes said graciously. "It's been a very long time since we've met, has it not? I believe not since Oxford. And longer yet since I've seen Mr. Sutherland."

"Not since that time you came for Christmas," Dad confirmed. Strangely, the sight of the new arrival seemed to settle him. He'd always got on with Sherlock Holmes. "Good to see you. No offense, but there aren't any more of you gentlemen, are there?"

"I doubt Dr. Sutherland will be summoning any further apparitions," Holmes said. "He's very tired."

This, after all, must be what it feels like to be mad. "He's in a coma. Why are either of you here at all? I suppose I understand you," I added to Holmes. "He always calls you. But—"

"Yes," Holmes agreed. "When you do not hear him, he does."

I ignored this. I was talking to Dickens now. "I don't understand what *you're* doing here. Charles Dickens. What was he *thinking*?"

"He was not thinking, Mr. Sutherland," Dickens said. "He was dreaming. Dreams, after all, are the bright creatures of poem and legend, who sport on earth in the night season, and melt away in the first beam of the sun, which lights grim care and stern reality—"

"Dreaming of what?"

"He knows who the summoner is."

My heart quickened. Beside me, I felt Mum put her hand on my arm—for support or to warn me, I'm not sure. "Who? Who is he?"

Dickens gave me a look of exasperation. "I cannot read his thoughts as though from a page. I have only partial knowledge of the landscape of his brain, and right now it is a peculiar landscape of ideas and thoughts and notions half-remembered. I only know that he knows, and that his last conscious thought was that he needed desperately to tell you. That is why we're here."

Mum's grip tightened on my arm. "Rob? Do you know who he's talking about?"

"I have no idea!" I turned to Holmes and Dickens, mostly so I didn't have to look at my parents. I was so tired of feeling inadequate, and knowing that I was. "If Charley's trying to tell me something through you two, I don't understand it. I don't understand *you*. I've never understood you."

"Calm yourself," Holmes said, not unkindly. "Emotions are antagonistic to clear reasoning."

"That's not what Charley says," I returned. I felt, illogically, that I was scoring a point. "He says that feelings are a mind picking up on things it doesn't always understand."

"Perhaps. But if so, they are a poor substitute for true understanding."

Dad stepped between us and held up his hands, as he might if I were fighting with Mum or Charley. In a way, I suppose I was. "Okay, steady. Let's back up and calm down. Do we really need to know who this summoner is right now? Isn't that a problem for another time? Rob's right here. He isn't in any danger at the moment. None of us are. We just need to sit tight, and try to get through this."

I felt myself calm against my will, as I had that day in the basement when I was six years old. Dad's voice has always been able to do that for all of us, even Charley. Unfortunately, I wasn't six years old anymore.

"I think we are in danger, though," I said with a sigh. "I think the whole city is. And so does Charley, clearly. I do want to find the summoner—I've been looking myself. But I don't know who he is."

Holmes sat in the plastic foldout chair opposite me and steepled his fingers. Dickens watched him with mild curiosity.

"Sutherland," Holmes said. "We do not know what deductions your brother has made about the summoner: he is not conscious to communicate them. But we know he has made them. Therefore it must be possible to deduce the summoner's identity from the information available."

"There is no information. We don't know anything."

"We do. We know, for example, that it is someone widely read, with an extensive knowledge of literary theory. We know that whoever it is knows where Dr. Sutherland lives, and knew that he would be at home the night they sent the Hound of the Baskervilles to his door. It is probably, then, someone who knows him, possibly someone from the university."

For God's sake. "They certainly have some connection to the university," I said. "Frankenstein said that someone at the university requested Charley's medical records recently."

In truth, I hadn't thought about that fact since I was told it earlier that day. Too much else had been happening, and had happened since. But I wasn't about to be outdone in detection by Sherlock Holmes. And yes, I do realize that could be considered ambitious.

Holmes didn't seem irritated by my interruption. His eyes gleamed. "Interesting. Why should they do that?"

"Well, I requested his records to find the other summoner," I said. "I thought there might be something that marked Charley for what he is. Perhaps there is, and the summoner was looking for it too."

Holmes dismissed that. "But they have been using his book for at least two years. The thought must have entered their head that he was a summoner before now; it more than likely originated their use of his book in the first place. If they wished to confirm it by such means, they would have done so long ago."

"Does it matter?" Dickens pointed out. "Surely the clue to take is that the summoner either is hiding in the university themselves, or has someone there who can work for them as Rob's intern does. Millie believed the former, given that the summoner would likely wish to observe and work with Charley directly. She suspected Troy Heywood."

"The postgraduate student?" That startled me. It cast my meeting with him earlier that day in quite a different light. "Why him?"

"Troy had in his possession a copy of the textbook the summoner is using. He has had it for some time."

"Which should be a very good argument for his *innocence*," Holmes said, with a trace of impatience. "Given that the summoner was using a different copy entirely."

"I know that Dr. Sutherland is fond of Troy Heywood," Dickens said. "But—"

"Fondness does not cloud *my* reasoning," Holmes said, "even if it were to cloud Dr. Sutherland's. Sentiment is foreign to me. It is grit in a sensitive instrument. I leave such things to your novels."

"Are you describing my novels as sentimental?"

I felt the need to interject. "Well, everyone sort of does that. Even I know about the death of Little Nell."

He dismissed this. "They are also intricately plotted, and a plot is exactly what you are trying to uncover. I believe Troy is a part of it."

"I have no doubt that you are a very clever man," Holmes said, "and very skilled at your own trade. But your trade is fiction."

"As is your own!" Dickens retorted. "You are fiction. Your cases are fiction. The London you know like your own mind is fiction. The world we seek to prevent is fiction. What the summoner is planning is an act of story."

"Stop it!" Dad ordered, before Holmes could respond. "What are you two doing fighting? Aren't you both parts of Charley's mind?"

Mum laughed. "Joe. Have you *met* Charley?"

"Apparently he wasn't who I thought he was," Dad replied, and Mum's face went quiet.

Something inside me went quiet too. Involuntarily, my eyes flickered toward Charley: not the parts of him that were awake and arguing, but the body lying in the hospital bed. I tried to see him not as my younger brother, but a figment pulled from thin air in infancy and overlaid with years of growth and experience. Unfortunately, this was completely counterintuitive. He looked like Charley. I was used to his face: the details of it weren't unfamiliar, or even interesting. He *was* real. It's hard not to feel someone's physical reality when they're lying hooked up to machines monitoring every beat of their heart and fluctuation of their blood, and when you're watching them intently for every tiny sign of movement or discomfort or life. And I could hardly convince myself he was only a physical shell, when he was usually all thoughts and visions and ideas.

And words. Always words.

David Copperfield. Chapter One. I am Born. Whether I shall turn out to be the hero of my own life, or whether that station will be held by anybody else, these pages must show.

"What is it, Sutherland?" Holmes asked. He was watching me carefully.

I drew a deep breath, then released it. The sharp, chemical air of the ICU filled my lungs. "Nothing," I said. "It's nothing."

"I'm sorry," Dad said to me quietly. He still didn't look at Mum, though, and he hadn't once looked at Charley. "I didn't mean that."

"Dr. Sutherland did not believe the summoner was Troy Heywood, or that Troy was connected with the summoner," Holmes said. If I didn't know better, I would say that he was helping me. "Was he likely to have been wrong?"

"Charley's not usually wrong," I said, with only a touch of bitterness. "Not like that. He sees things, when he's not off in a dream. If he was actually looking at Troy, then he would probably have seen him clearly. He's more likely to overlook someone else."

"Now," Holmes said quite softly. "Think. What did your brother discover before he fell unconscious? What was he saying?"

"I wasn't paying attention."

"He believes you never pay him attention. If there were ever an opportunity to prove him wrong, Sutherland, this would be it."

I gritted my teeth, but I closed my eyes. Because of course I paid Charley attention. Everybody did. He was difficult to miss.

And he had, as Holmes said, been falling unconscious. He had nearly died. Of course I had been listening to him.

"I told him it was lucky Beth did have an afternoon class." My eyes flew open. "Or else I wouldn't have been called to the university. That was what was bothering him."

Holmes nodded. "And why would that bother him?"

The answer came almost while I was still speaking. "Because she doesn't have an afternoon class. She doesn't have any classes. The receptionist said she would be in her office because she doesn't teach today. She *could* have taken him home."

"But instead," Holmes said, "she called you. And because of that, you were with him when the Jabberwock attacked the Street."

It was true. It was the *only* reason I was with him. I hadn't even spoken to him for a week before that. "That's why he thinks I'm in danger. Because Beth didn't just send Charley to deal with the Jabberwock. She made certain I was there as well."

"Could she have requested Charley's medical records, and sent Uriah Heep to your work?"

"I don't see why not. Not under her own name, perhaps, but if she took the time to get to know the system..."

"She might be one of the summoner's creations," Dickens said. "Like Eric."

"I looked her up when I was searching the university database for anyone with skills like Charley. For that matter, Dorian was keeping an eye on the English staff before we found the Street. I would swear her career at least was real. She isn't like Eric. She's been working and publishing for years; people in the community know her. She has all the right skills. I think it's her. It's always been her."

"Very good," Holmes said.

I didn't even have it in me to resent being talked to like a student who'd made a clever answer. I could see it. Facts were lighting in my brain, and they made a pattern, stretching out across the past week like points on a map of the city. This must be how Charley felt the moment he called something into being. It would have been exhilarating if what I could see by their light wasn't so terrifying.

"Troy said Beth had borrowed a book from him a few days ago," I said. "It was Charley's book, wasn't it? *Dickens's Criminal Underworld.* We took her copy on Sunday. When I phoned on Tuesday, she was searching for it in Charley's office—clearly, she didn't find it. She resorted to borrowing the library's copy from Troy. Last night, she took her own back. That's why Troy was taking the library copy back from her today. She had no further use for it."

"Largely supposition," Holmes said. "But not unlikely." He cast a glance at Dickens. "There is his place in the plot, Mr. Dickens. A supporting character, not a protagonist."

"Every supporting character is the protagonist of his own story," Dickens replied, somewhat haughtily.

I ignored them. "They said he was male. David Copperfield, Eric... they always referred to the summoner as 'he.'"

"So they did," Holmes said. His eyes were unreadable. "These are very deep waters."

"Wait a minute," Mum said. "Are you talking about Beth White? At Charley's work? An older woman, with a cardigan?"

"That's her. Do you know her?"

"She called at Charley's place when we were visiting him, a few weeks ago. Do you remember, Joe? She said she'd heard a lot about us. About all of us."

"God." Beth White. She had been there at the house the day the Hound of the Baskervilles came too. She had been there from the first. "I'm an idiot."

"You are not entirely to blame, Sutherland," Holmes said generously. "Nothing clears up a case so much as stating it to another person."

I chose not to dignify this with a response. "It's happening tonight, isn't it? The new world."

It was Dickens who replied. "She has the book now. And she almost certainly knows that your brother is powerless to stop her after her attack on the Street. Yes. I imagine she won't wait very much longer."

I checked my watch belatedly. The sun would be setting out there.

I don't know if that mattered: there wasn't, after all, a deadline for shifting reality, and it didn't need to be done under cover of darkness. It could be any moment.

"I need to phone Millie," I said. "At least, I need to try. Whatever state the Street is in, she needs to know this."

Dickens nodded. His face was still and grave. It could almost have been the frontispiece from the book I'd seen. "Go. We will keep vigil here."

It took me a moment to realize what he meant. Vigil, because Charley was at the heart of this all, and he couldn't be left unguarded while I left the ICU to phone Millie. I glanced at him, motionless and remote in a swathe of machinery. Between Charles Dickens and Sherlock Holmes.

"We'll stay too," Mum said. "Be careful, won't you?"

"I'll be right back," I said.

I went all the way to the edge of the car park this time, almost to the road. Cars rushed past, the roar of their engines mingling with the wind. The hospital was in an old, run-down part of the city, but I could see the lights of Courtenay Place down the far end of the road. In the cooling dusk, it was a long, glittering stream of traffic and nightclubs.

It had been dusk when the Hound of the Baskervilles attacked, dusk on the Street when we fell through the wall for the first time. The time between day and night. Liminal space.

Millie still wasn't answering her phone. It went straight to voice-mail, a clear indication that she was outside reality. I tried three times, with increasing fury, as though how hard and fast I dialed would make the slightest bit of difference. I just didn't know what else to do.

I was about to go back inside when it came to me. Beth had phoned me that afternoon, mere hours ago. She had called the same phone I held in my hand. She might, of course, have been calling from her office, in which case it was not of much help. But when I checked the call log, I saw that the number was that of a cell phone. I called it.

I didn't expect her to reply. After all, she had quite a lot to do this evening, if she was indeed planning on unleashing a new world. To my astonishment, she answered almost at once.

"Hello?"

I was so startled, my voice disappeared. I'm not sure how I found it again. "Beth, it's Rob."

"Hello, Rob," she said calmly. "How's Charles?"

"Well, not good, actually." There was a note of distraction in her replies, perhaps as though she was driving at the same time. Otherwise she sounded perfectly normal. "You heard he was taken to the hospital, right?"

"I did. The entire department did. The hospital phoned to ask about his collapse earlier today. I'm so sorry. I thought something wasn't right—that was why I phoned you."

"Yes," I said. "Thanks for that, again. Um. What did you tell the hospital? Did you—?"

"I'm so sorry, Rob, I'm afraid I can't speak right now," she said. "May I call you back in ten minutes?"

"I know what you're doing." It was the only thing that came to mind to keep her talking to me. I had the feeling, as I had had with Eric, that she understood very well the game we were playing.

"I'm sure you do, Rob," she said, almost kindly. I pictured her, as I'd seen her that afternoon: the round, pleasant face, the neatly cut gray hair, the green cardigan. I had heard a note of steel underneath the surface of her brisk common sense, and I'd liked it. I was hearing it now, and it scared me. "And I suspect I also know what you're doing. You want to find me. You've been trying to find me for a while. It will be obvious where I am, in a moment. Do, please, come when you can."

Dear God. It was happening right now.

"Why don't you come here?" I countered. "I mean it. We've been dancing around each other long enough. Let's talk."

"We will talk. The three of us, I mean, of course. Tell Charles I'd love to see him too."

"You nearly killed him." I like to think I loaded it with enough bitterness to poison an elephant.

"Yes." She sounded somewhat regretful. "Yes, I'm sorry about that. When I see him again, I possibly will kill him. It's a shame. I like and admire him very sincerely. But it had to be done."

"Why? What could you possibly have to gain by this?"

"I really can't explain it to you, I'm afraid," she said briskly. "You wouldn't understand. I may explain it to Charles Sutherland, when our paths cross again."

"I might understand. Try me."

"But I have no need to be understood by you, and I certainly have no time. I've been planning for this moment for so many years, and it's here. Goodbye, Rob. It was nice of you to call."

"Wait—" I heard the dial tone in my ear. The call had ended.

A moment later, the world split in two.

Lydia

The café doors were closed against the wind when Lydia got there. When she opened the side door, a gust chased her in with a rush of dust and noise, ruffling through her hair and stirring the menus on the counter. She saw Eric Umble immediately. It wasn't just that he sat alone, when nobody else did, or even that she knew what he looked like. Here, as at Rob's offices, he stood out. In the bright, upmarket café, with its coffee smell and trendy furniture, he looked like a ghost.

He saw her at the same time and got to his feet. She hadn't seen him standing before, and was struck by how long and thin his limbs were.

"Miss Lydia," he said as she approached the table. "So nice to see you."

"You too," she replied.

His mouth twitched. "I do like the way you bother to lie. Won't you sit down?"

Once they were sitting, he lowered his voice—almost, she thought, as though what he'd said earlier was for somebody else's ears. But there was nobody there except the other diners, and none of them had glanced in her direction.

"Did you manage it? The money, and the tickets."

"I did," she said, just as quietly. If there was one thing her job had taught her, it was how to get people last-minute tickets. "The ticket's booked online, in your name. It leaves in twenty minutes. They'll let you on. And the money—"

"Don't bring it out. Under the table."

She pulled the envelope out from her purse in her lap, and held it out. Eric's fingers brushed hers as he took it; reflexively, without knowing why, she wiped them on her skirt.

"Thank you." It was the most sincere she had heard his voice yet. "I won't forget this. You'll regret it soon, but know that I mean that most humbly."

"Good luck," she said. "Now what was it you promised to tell me?"

"About Mr. Sutherland?"

"And Charley. You said they were in trouble. I really think they are."

"They are." He hesitated. Something flickered in his peculiarly colored eyes, and he leaned toward her. She resisted the impulse to pull away. "If I may, I'd like to tell you something. Think of it as a story, or a metaphor. It may make little sense to you, but please humor me, if you can find it in your heart."

"All right," she said warily.

"Imagine this, if you can. All at once, you exist. You don't know where you were the moment before—you don't know if you were anywhere. You have in your head a memory of a dirty London street made of meandering sentences, and of yourself, perched on a stool with a book open in front of you and a small, hated boy at your side. You remember smog and scheming, ink and toil, and always aching, burning resentment masked behind a servile smile. You remember wanting to destroy the world.

"That London is gone. You're in a new city, halfway across the world, a hundred and fifty years forward in time, a reality away. The room you're in is dark, but not so dark that you can't see the figure standing in front of you. A tall figure, male, old, with sunken eyes and a domed forehead. You know the name, but you will never be able to unlock your tongue to say it. It just drums in your head, through your veins, coded into your cells. When he talks, you obey. You're filled with his meanings, and his voice. That, and hate, is all you have.

"And perhaps that's all you would ever have, except that one night, the night before you're sent outside to do your job, something flickers on the edge of your awareness. All at once, another presence, one that both is and isn't you, is in your head. You feel his fear, his anger, his determination to escape. You see a figure opposite him, who both is and is not the hated boy you once knew. It fires parts of your brain left purposefully dark. When the presence is gone, those parts remain, the parts that can scheme, and dissemble, and yearn for escape.

"And so you wait. You plan. You work around the conditions placed upon your life. This is what you did in your earlier life, if you had an earlier life, so you know it well. You make yourself indispensable to those above you, so that when you lie, they have no choice but to accept your vision of reality. You use this to manipulate a battle between your master and the child you once knew, all in the hopes that you will be able to use it to escape. And perhaps you will. But without money, without travel, you know you have no chance of surviving the real world. And then, one night, you receive a phone call that might be your only opportunity."

She seized on the last sentence. "Are you talking about the night I phoned the office?"

"I am," Eric said. "I know you won't understand the rest. It was an indulgence on my part. But I wanted you to understand something of why I did what I'm about to do."

"And what," she said slowly, "are you about to do? What does this have to do with Rob and Charley?"

He raised his voice. "You were a little late, Miss Lydia."

She checked her own watch, out of habit and to cover a cold flutter of nerves. Something in their conversation had shifted. All at once, the taunt was back behind his words. "I suppose I was. Does it matter?"

"Not in the end. But it's a shame we didn't have longer to talk."

"Well," she said. "I'm here now."

"You're here now," he agreed. "But time's up."

She frowned, and opened her mouth to ask him what he meant. Before she could, something caught her eye. It was a shadow on the wall. Nothing unusual about that, perhaps, it was the end of the day, and the sun was beginning to set. But this shadow was creeping across the wall fast—very fast. And there was nothing there in the room to cast it.

Other people had noticed it too. Two women sitting at a table were pointing and remarking to each other in low, interested voices that didn't yet betray foreboding. Another group got to their feet to stare. Outside, Lydia realized, the sky, too, was darkening, as if a shadow was passing over the sun. The darkness on the wall was spreading like a tea stain.

Lydia turned back to Eric. He looked at her with something chillingly like regret. "What the hell is going on?"

"The new world," Eric said. "It's here. And I'm sorry. There is no place for any of you in it."

In that moment, Lydia realized that Rob had lied, after all. He had told her Eric was trouble. This wasn't trouble. Trouble was the time a drunk had pulled a knife at the bar she'd worked at as an undergraduate. Trouble was her first week in Athens when she'd foolishly gone out alone after dark and almost had to pepper spray an overenthusiastic stalker. This was danger.

Lydia kicked off her shoes slowly under the table, and got to her feet. The door was behind her; a few of the diners, unnerved, were gathering their coats to head for it. She could back out, then turn and run. This was Wellington. He couldn't do anything to her in a public place. And if he did, his arms were like twigs—she was solidly built and strong.

It was then she noticed the diners at the other tables. A handful of them were still looking at the shadow on the wall, looking about in confusion for any explanation. A waiter had come out, his face furrowed. But others were drawing slowly to their feet. She had taken them in at a glance, looking for Eric, and seen nothing surprising: a tall elderly man in black, a short pug-faced man in a suit, a handful of pale businesspeople drinking coffee. Either she had not seen them properly, or their features were somehow, impossibly, rippling and changing. The elderly gentleman turned to her, and his old, wizened face drew back in a grimace. She had seen enough old films with Rob to recognize what she was looking at. The vampire drew back its red lips, and its fangs gleamed.

"Hold still, Miss Lydia," Eric said. "Count Dracula won't touch you if you don't try to run. We will none of us touch you."

Lydia was too busy to be a prolific reader these days, but her childhood was rich with story: the same picture books that Rob had grown up with, but also Polynesian tricksters and gods and creation myths from her Māori grandfather, Olympic gods and heroes and monsters from her Greek mother. She knew spirits and fairies and shape-shifters. She knew, although she had never expected to see, the mark of unworldly things in the world. It was perhaps because of this that while her mind reeled with shock and terror, her hands seized the chair in front of her and hit at the approaching vampire as hard as she could. Fortunately, the chair was a sturdy one, industrial in design; the metal glanced off the creature's head, and it fell back with a snarl. She threw the chair after it, snatched up the fork from the table, and turned to run.

A small, muscled figure in a torn suit stopped her. She had a quick glimpse of a brutish face, red eyes, a snarling grin before he grabbed at her arm and threw her to the ground. The fall tore her stocking at the knee and knocked the air from her lungs; she half sobbed with the impact, but she scrambled out of the way. When he came forward, she flung her arm up and stabbed with all her strength with the prongs of the fork. The man howled; blood, more black than red, dripped from his cheek. She hauled herself to her feet.

Eric stood between her and the door. It was only him and the nightmare things left in the restaurant now—she was alone with them. He stood calmly, but his long limbs twitched.

"Steady, Mr. Hyde," Eric said. His voice was almost a croon. "We don't want to hurt Miss Lydia."

"Get out of my way," Lydia ordered, not because she thought he would, but because she needed to hear her own voice, and Eric, at least, was human enough to be talked to.

"I'm afraid I can't do that, Lydia," he said.

It happened in a flash. She lunged for the door, heart in her mouth; Eric lunged, too, and grabbed her. The back of her head collided with the wall with the force of his tackle, and stars winked before her eyes. His fingers locked about her wrists, ice cold, iron fast, stronger than any brittle human fingers could be. She twisted in his grasp; her foot made sharp contact with his shin. His face contorted in pain, but his grip didn't slacken and his footing didn't shift.

"Not much longer now," he said.

The darkness had spread across the floor, the tables. As it touched the monstrous nonpeople, they disappeared inside it. Her hand, pinned flat to the wall, was stretched toward it. The thought of that darkness was more terrifying than any vampire, than any Gothic monster this strange new world could throw at her. Whatever happened, it couldn't take her. It couldn't. She fought with all her strength to pull it back.

"I'm sorry," Eric said. The terrible thing was, he meant it. "Everything I told you was the truth. I am a victim, and I need you in order to escape. But I'd never have been able to meet you at all without giving you to him."

She wouldn't scream, and she wouldn't cry, but she could so easily do both. "To who?"

"Don't worry," he said. "You'll never have to see."

Outside, the streets were turning gray. Through the window, if she twisted her head, she saw people looking at the sky, and pointing. A green wood pigeon sat perched on a street sign. It struck her as strange to see one outside the bush that ringed the city. It took one look at her, and flapped away. It was the last thing she had the chance to see.

The touch of the darkness on her fingers was like a plunge into ice. Her lungs contracted; her vision darkened. She had no breath to scream. Somewhere, at the dim edges of her hearing, her phone was ringing.

The darkness took her.

Dr. Charles Sutherland, age nineteen

Extract from Dickens's Criminal Underworld. *Oxford University Press, 2012*

The idea that there is a darkness at the heart of Dickens's most loved works is not a new one: the most cursory of readings reveals it. It peeks through in the caustic humor of the beginning of *Oliver Twist*, and reveals itself in that book's climactic scenes of Nancy's violent death. It shadows Pip in *Great Expectations* as he enters a London begrimed with Newgate dust and finds aristocracy inextricable from criminality. It haunts David Copperfield, first in the form of his childhood injustices, and then in the form of Uriah Heep, who acts as the novel's conscience and its scapegoat. It is a darkness born of anger: anger at what Dickens perceived as the injustices of his own society, injustices that he felt firsthand at the age of twelve, and struggled against for the rest of his life.

I want to examine the nature of this darkness, and the role it plays in the construction of Dickens's criminal underworld. In doing so, I wish to argue that Dickens's depiction of criminality is not merely a social statement, but central to his conception of humanity.

Charles Sutherland, age twelve

Notes extracted from diary (dark blue) by Associate Professor Beth White. Prof. White's annotations in square brackets.

- "And I don't really know what I felt then. I can't understand it. I was alone, I was scared, I was suddenly furious, my heart was racing, and even Rob didn't want to protect me. Somehow, all those contradictory feelings surged in one big wave. [...] And then, I pushed that feeling, and I directed it at them."
- [This is it.]

XXIII

A shaft of light shot up from the hills behind Courtenay Place, spearing through the night sky and up into the clouds. It might have been a firework, had it not been so bright—too bright for mere chemical reaction. It was blinding. Instinctively, I shut my eyes against it.

When I opened them again a second later, the light had gone, but a purple-green afterimage haunted my vision. I thought at first that was what I could see, overlaying the hills and shadowing the buildings immediately in front. But it was moving. No, it was *growing*. A thick, dark cloud rose from the ground and rolled down Courtenay Place like a wave coming up a beach. It was as though the light had cracked the sky, and this was what was spilling out.

I knew what that light was. It was the flare that signaled someone's arrival from a book; I had seen it a hundred times in my childhood. Beth's city had arrived. It was ghostly and insubstantial—more mist than solid structure. But it wasn't mist, any more than what had spilled from a book in Lambton Quay was mist. It was here.

My heart stopped.

Lydia. She should be well out of the way, at home. She had said she would be. But what if she were coming back, or she had stopped in town? Her hotel was on Courtenay Place. She, like me, tended to work when she was upset. What if...?

I fumbled for my phone yet again, my hands shaking as I dialed. It couldn't happen. It just couldn't, not to Lydia. I had done everything I could to make sure this never *touched* her.

Her phone rang once. Then twice.

"Come on, come on, pick up..." I muttered.

She might want to ignore my call, given the terms we had parted on, but she wouldn't. Not when Charley was in the hospital. She would pick up immediately, for his sake if not for mine.

All at once, my phone cut off.

Oh God. No. No no no.

"Lydia?" I raised the phone to my ear, and heard nothing. "Come on, please, pick up."

She was inside the cloud. It had taken her, right then. I could see it now, extending down the street, and her hotel was nowhere in sight. Any hopes I had that it might be like the *Oliver Twist* house, only vaguely disorienting to anyone real inside it, vanished with the dial tone in my ear. My phone had worked from within that mist. It was not penetrating this one.

No. Please no.

Dimly, I was aware of people around me, stopping on the streets to point to the growing shadow. In a moment I would hear sirens, and see the lights of police cars. The army would probably be mobilized for this; it was too big to hide. They wouldn't be able to do anything.

It was my fault. Not all of it, maybe. But I moved too slowly and too reluctantly from the very beginning. I should have helped earlier. I shouldn't have tried to ignore what was happening. And Lydia. Lydia was all my fault. I had pushed her away, for reasons all to do with me and not her, and now she was gone. I had to fix this. I had to *be able to* fix this.

Someone was calling my name. I heard it, recognized, even as I turned around, the sound of my mother's voice. All four of them—Mum, Dad, Holmes, Dickens—were hurrying toward me. My parents and two figments of Victorian imagination, blown toward me in a hospital car park.

I blinked stupidly at them as they drew close. "But—is Charley alone in there?"

"The doctor came in to see him," Mum said, without looking at me. She was staring at the cloud in growing horror. "He asked us to step out. He—this is it, isn't it? The new world?"

"You saw it arrive?"

"We felt it," Dickens said. "Like a tearing of the curtain between the realms of fiction and the realms of mortality."

I expected Holmes to challenge this melodramatic description. He didn't.

"I'll go in to Charley," I said. Somehow, my mind was assembling plans while the rest of me panicked. I don't how it was doing it, but it made me feel better. I'd take it. "I'll stay with him. You need to tell Millie about Beth as soon as possible. Holmes, Dickens—do you two know how to get to the Street?"

Holmes nodded briskly. "Of course. It was I who directed you toward it in the first place. I know it better now, through Dr. Sutherland. And Mr. Dickens was there only last night."

Neither of them had passed through the wall before, but I would have to trust the world's greatest detective and the world's greatest novelist to manage that between them.

"Then go. If things are as bad there as I imagine they are, she'll need you. And take Mum and Dad with you."

"Wait a minute!" Mum protested. She tore her eyes from the shadow. "There is no way we're leaving you or Charley when the world is ending. Forget about it."

"She's right," Dad said. "God knows I'm still trying to work out what else we are, but we're a family."

My family believes in family. I went through phases in my teenage years when that was embarrassing beyond words, but at that moment my throat tightened. Now, of all times, my eyes felt hot. Again.

"You can't stay here," I forced myself to say. "Mum, you're a summoner. A reader, like Charley—even if the last time you read anything out was twenty-six years ago, that was a pretty powerful reading. Beth met you. She knows Charley's a summoner. There's a very high chance she knows that you are too—and she definitely knows full well that taking Charley out would draw you to the hospital. You're a threat to her. You're in danger here."

"I don't care," she said fiercely. Her eyes looked suspiciously bright as well, but they were also burning.

"You'll put us all in danger too, if you stay." I wasn't sure if it was true—Beth would probably come for Charley regardless, if he didn't come to her—but it didn't matter. I was fairly certain I could make Mum believe it. "She won't just leave you at large. She'll send someone or something to come for you. The Street's the safest place to be right now, at least until the shadow reaches it. I'll bring Charley there as soon as I can, but please, please go on ahead of us."

Dickens spoke up. "Forgive me, Mrs. Sutherland, but if you are indeed a summoner, even a fledgling one, your protection is desperately needed. Without Dr. Sutherland, the Street is very vulnerable right now—doubtless exactly what Professor White intended. Anything you could muster would be greatly appreciated."

I wasn't sure I liked the idea of my mother defending the Street rather than being defended by it, but I took it up anyway. "There, you see? If you want to protect us, you're more use there."

"More use to *them*," Mum corrected, but she was wavering. She ran a hand through her hair. "You really think I'm putting you in danger by being here?"

"If Beth knows who you are," I said firmly, "then definitely."

"She knows. I remember the look on her face. I thought at the time—but I don't want to leave you both."

"I'll stay," Dad said. "Rob, you go with your mother."

"That doesn't make sense. You don't know what to look for if Beth sends anyone here. You don't know enough about any of this. Look, I realize I haven't done a very good job of looking after him so far—"

"Who says you haven't done a good job?" Mum said. She actually sounded surprised.

"Well, you did," I reminded her. "I should have stopped him from going to the Street in the first place."

"I never said that. Neither of us did. You should have told us what was going on, definitely, but—for God's sake, Rob, nobody ever stopped Charley doing what he was determined to do for long. It isn't your job to do it. It isn't your job to look after him, for that matter."

"You used to say it was."

"When he was six, perhaps! Not anymore. He's a grown-up. That's one reason I was angry at you. You shouldn't have tried to deal with this on your own. You should have told us. Your job is to look after yourself—and Lydia. Where is she, by the way? Is she safe?"

"I don't know." My throat ached with trying to keep my voice from breaking. At that moment, I wanted nothing more than to be looked after, as if I were a child. But I wasn't a child. "I can't get in touch with her. She might have been at her hotel when—"

"Dear God." Mum stared at me for a moment and then, without

warning, hugged me tightly. We didn't hug very much in our family. The unexpected rush of warmth almost broke me. "I'm so sorry."

"She'll be all right," Dad said. He squeezed my shoulder. "Probably the reception's just on the blink, with all this happening. You'll see. She'll phone when she can."

"Right." I swallowed hard. "But that's another reason why I need to stay out here. Because if she phones and I'm in the Street—"

"Of course." Mum took a long, shaky breath. "Well. We'll go then. But please, Rob, follow as quickly as you can."

"I will," I promised. I turned to Sherlock Holmes and Charles Dickens. "Look after them, okay?"

"I give my word," Holmes said very gently. "No harm will come to them."

Mum gave me one last embrace. "I know I never thanked you for saving your brother's life," she said. "I just blew up at you. But you know how proud I am of you, don't you? Both of you?"

"Oh God, don't," I said. "I sort of liked it better when you were blaming me." It wasn't true, but it made her laugh.

Holmes lingered behind as Dickens led Mum and Dad back to their car.

"Sutherland," he said quietly. "We have not yet addressed the question of why the summoner—why Beth White—requested Charley's medical records."

"Is this the time?" I asked. "Do we have to?"

"I suspect you do not. I suspect you already know exactly why, or at least believe you do."

"What gave you that idea?" I knew, before I had finished speaking, that I was too defensive for him not to know he was right. "Can you read the marks on my left shirt cuff or something?"

"Of course, but that's of no matter. I know your brother, and he can read you. You are an intelligent man, Sutherland, in your own way. You would not dismiss an important point of inquiry unless you already had the answer."

I still didn't have the complete answer, but Sherlock Holmes was right. Of course he was. I knew exactly why the records had been requested.

Charley's medical records, first and foremost, said that he had returned from the dead. I knew now that he had not returned from the dead. He had come from somewhere else, the same place as Holmes and Dickens and Millie and the Street itself. And to the right reader, that was what his records would reveal. Not that he was a summoner, but that Mum was, and that Charley was her invention. Somehow, Beth had wondered if he were real, and had gone to his records for proof he was not. I didn't know what she could do with this information, but it had to be dangerous.

"This isn't the time," I said. "Just...keep watch over him until I get back."

Holmes nodded.

I hesitated just a moment longer. "Is that what Charley thinks of me?" I asked, against my will. "An intelligent man in my own way?"

"Of course not," Holmes replied at once. "It is what I think of you. Your brother thinks you the best and wisest man in this world. As I said, emotions are antagonistic to clear reasoning."

It had been minutes since the light split the sky, and the city was in a panic. As I entered the reception area, the two women at the desk were talking on phones in low, urgent voices; many in the waiting room were making calls of their own. The television mounted in the corner displayed the news channel. Too soon for news of the shadow city yet, but already people were clustered in front of the screen. Outside, I heard the whine of a siren.

"It's too late now." Eric's voice came out of nowhere.

I spun around, pulse racing. There he was, standing apart from the other spectators a few meters away. Something had shifted in him, or in the way I was looking at him. At the law firm, he had looked passably human. Now he was an evening shadow in the hospital reception, all elongated limbs and insubstantial menace.

"He's done it," Eric said. "The summoner. The new world is here."

I'd known it. But part of me must have held out some faint, stupid hope that I was wrong, because hearing it from the lips of Uriah Heep hurt beyond measure.

"Why do you say 'he'?" I asked Eric. "It's Beth White, isn't it? The summoner? From the university?"

"Is it?" Eric said. "How interesting. I wondered if it might be somebody at the university, on account of my placement in the internship program. And on account of your brother. You've seen him then, in the flesh? How does he look to you?"

"Beth? A perfectly ordinary, gray-haired, cardigan-wearing academic. How does she look to you?"

"It's not really a question of looks," Eric said. "We see what we know is there. A spider in a web. A—no, that's as much as I can say. You should mention that phrase to your brother. He might understand. Either way, I'm afraid I won't be coming into work on Monday, Mr. Sutherland. The summoner doesn't care about you anymore. He might kill you, if he can be bothered. Probably not."

"Did she want to kill me with the Hound, and the Jabberwock?" I asked. "Was that why she made sure Charley and I were together when they struck?"

Eric laughed. "Kill *you*, Mr. Sutherland? All that mattered was your brother. They need each other, you see, or at least the summoner needs Dr. Sutherland. He didn't want him dead, or not yet."

"Then why did she send the Hound to kill him in the first place?"

"I'm afraid that was my fault. I was sent to your firm to find out how much you and Dr. Sutherland knew—about the summoner, about the threat to your world. I might have given the impression you knew more than you did."

"We didn't know *anything* at that point."

"Yes," Eric said. "I said that you did. I convinced the summoner to send Dr. Sutherland a calling card. It's never a good idea to listen to a Uriah Heep, you know. We lie. He didn't think I could, the way he read me. Probably I couldn't have, except for one thing. I'm sure you can guess what that was, Mr. Sutherland, being so clever."

I was about to say I had no idea, but all at once I did. "The other Uriah Heep," I said. "Charley brought him to life, completely by accident, the night before you were due to start at the firm. That was it, wasn't it?"

"My mind touched his," Eric said. "Our thoughts merged—not much, but enough. Enough for him to see my master's plans. And enough for me to glimpse some of his cunning, and use it for my own. It gave me some ideas. Just one idea, really, at first: to bring your brother and my master into open conflict, as soon and as often as I could. I need Dr. Sutherland to kill the summoner for me. It's the only way I can be truly free."

The idea of Charley killing anybody was so preposterous I almost laughed. But I didn't. "And me? What do you need me to do?"

"Oh, it's the summoner who needs you, Mr. Sutherland," Eric said. I swear, if I heard my name one more time... "The summoner doesn't want to be killed by Dr. Sutherland, you see. He doesn't want to kill him either; he needs to deal with him. But he wants him weakened. And Dr. Sutherland is always weaker around you."

Once again, I felt a chill. "No he isn't. Don't say that."

"He is. You know what he is now, don't you? I knew the first time I saw him through the eyes of the other Uriah Heep. We know David Copperfield when we see him. Perhaps we knew even before our master did."

So I had been right. Beth knew too.

"He's very subject to interpretation, Mr. Sutherland, just like the rest of us. And you see him as small, helpless, hopeless. You tell him that often enough. He believes what you tell him."

"I don't tell him that."

"He's a reader," Eric said. "Do you think he can't read you? Everything you do tells him that."

"I don't," I insisted, but the cold deepened. Because I did tell him that. I never meant to. I never realized. I just wanted to protect him. No, I wanted him to *need* me to protect him.

"I'm not a summoner," I said. "However I saw him, I couldn't alter him."

"You're not a summoner," he agreed. "But he is. And he trusts your opinion more than any other, including his own. When he sees himself through your eyes, he reinterprets himself, against all evidence and experience, as your irritatingly helpless little brother. Or that was the summoner's theory, anyway. You can tell yourself it was wrong, if you like. But that's the other reason, when the summoner realized your importance to your brother, I ended up at your work. Not just to find out what you knew about the new world. I was meant, where possible, to keep track of you so that the summoner could draw you into this mess at your brother's side."

"Why? How did she know what I could do to Charley? We'd never even met when you arrived."

"I don't know. But I'd be careful, when you go in."

I was looking back at the sprawling shadow over Courtenay Place. It took me a while to catch his words. "What—when I go in?"

"When you and Dr. Sutherland go in. To the new world. You're supposed to go with him, you know. That's why Miss Lydia was taken in there. To make sure you didn't decide this wasn't your problem."

I didn't feel cold then. My heart opened, and heat spilled into my veins. In that moment, I could have killed him. "What have you done?"

"The summoner wants you in there. I told him you might not go in just for your brother. But you would definitely go in for her. And she would come to meet me, at the right time, if I promised to tell her what you and your brother were doing."

"She had nothing to do with this."

"Of course she did. But she might have been left out of it. My master wasn't very interested in her; I had to persuade him that she was worth using at this late stage. It was me. I needed her. I needed someone to bring me things, to help me escape. I was ever so relieved, when she phoned our work that night, and I realized I could use her. But my master would never have let me meet her if he hadn't thought I was doing it for his purposes."

"Where is she?"

"If it helps," he said, "I'm sorry I had to do it. She was kind to me, even though I revolted her. Not many are. I'm not written for people to be kind to."

"Where is she?"

"She's nowhere. Now. I invited her to the heart of the darkness, and I held her there until the darkness touched her. Then I let her go, and it took her. You really should have told her about your brother, you know. She had no idea what she was walking into."

He was right. Of course he was right.

"Why are you telling me this?" I managed.

"Because I want you not to fall for it." Eric was deadly serious now. There was no trace of the half-ingratiating, half-mocking lilt. "If you want to help anybody, including Miss Lydia, leave your brother alone. He doesn't need you. All you do is make him vulnerable."

"Stop saying that."

"Do you remember that day by the bike sheds? When you were both in your last year of school?"

He could have been talking about any day. I knew he wasn't.

"Yes," I said. "I don't know how *you* know, but I do. I let him down that day."

"You did," Eric said. "You abandoned him. And he was more powerful on that day than he had ever been when you were at his side."

That wasn't a conversation I wanted to have. "He's still unconscious."

"Oh, I doubt that," Eric sighed patiently. "I never heard of a story where the main protagonist just slept through the climax. This story has been between your brother and my master. I was sent with an invitation from him—my master. He wants Dr. Sutherland to come find him in the city. Give him that message, will you? I was supposed to give it to him, but I thought I'd give it to you. As we have such a relationship. I have a boat to catch, before they cancel them."

"Why would I give Charley a message from you to come and be killed?"

He shrugged. "It doesn't matter if you don't. He'll come anyway. I told you, it's his story—his and my master's. They both need to see it through. You're not a literary character, though. You need to think about what part you should play."

"And what part are you playing?"

"I'm nobody, Mr. Sutherland." He sounded almost tired. "I'm not like the other Uriah. I was made to be without autonomy. I'm not supposed to rebel. The schemer in me is downplayed as much as possible, given the materials the summoner had to work with. But I'm still Uriah Heep. I hate the people who tell me what to do. I hate you, but I hate the summoner more. I want to be free of all of you."

"You're not going back to the new world, are you?" I said. "This is what you've been planning all along. You're going to make a run for it now, with whatever Lydia's given you, while Beth's distracted with the new world. You're hoping that we can deal with her before she realizes that you're missing; because as soon as she does, she only needs to think of you and you'll be read out of existence. You need us to win."

"I don't know if your brother can win," he said. "I haven't been very impressed so far, I must admit. Perhaps this was all impossible from the beginning, and we're all of us doomed. But if you *can* win, Mr. Sutherland, I would be *ever* so umbly in your debt."

I didn't have time for this. The world was ending. The last person I wanted to be with was Uriah Heep.

"You people are all insane," I said, and went to find my brother.

The television screen cut to the studio in a flash of color as I started toward the stairs. The broadcaster's immaculate voice followed me down the corridor.

"Reports have come through of an explosion in downtown Wellington. Police are warning residents not to approach. Nobody within the affected area has yet emerged, or made contact with teams of rescuers waiting for permission to move in."

XXIV

Charley's bed was empty when I entered the intensive care ward. The first thing I saw was crumpled blankets, with equipment and IV tubes hanging limp to the side. A second later, I saw him in the aisle, a ghostly figure in pale hospital pajamas. In that moment, pure, perfect relief washed everything else away. He was alive. Whatever else he was, he was awake again, and he was alive.

"Hey, idiot," I said.

Perhaps Eric had a point. You might be considered a little hard on your brother when that was the most affectionate term that came to mind.

Charley didn't seem to care. His face lit at the sight of me, as though I were a new metaphor he'd uncovered. "*There* you are."

"You're awake," I said, redundantly. He was so awake it was exhausting.

"They took my clothes. I think it's to keep me here."

"That happened to me once at the swimming pool," I said. "When I was twelve. You could say hello back, you know. Before I get the impression that I'm not welcome."

That did raise a smile, though a quick one. "Hello. Sorry—you are very, very welcome, believe me. It's just that nobody will tell me what's going on. There was a doctor here for about a minute, then something started happening outside. He told me to lie back down and stay quiet."

"Well, that's probably standard business in hospitals."

"The instruction, perhaps. I don't think doctors usually run out the door immediately after giving it and not come back. It's here, isn't it?"

"It's here," I said. "There was a flare of light, and now Courtenay Place is filled with smoke. It looks like a great cloud spilling down the road. Like the *Oliver Twist* house, only more tangible."

"It's even further through. I felt it come into existence, I think. At least—something jolted me awake, like when you open your eyes to the blinds swinging and know an earthquake just hit. Does that make sense?"

"Yes." I felt my stomach tighten, but kept my voice normal. I knew then that what Mum had said was true. "I suppose it was like when the Street came into being. It called to you then, didn't it?"

"Characters from all over the world will be flocking to this one. I can still feel it, the way I can feel the Street, and it's far stronger. It's not just calling them, it's pulling." He shook his head restlessly. "I need to be there. They can't legally keep me here, can they?"

"Why? What can you do?"

"I don't know. Something. Where's Millie?"

"The Street, I assume. I can't get her on the phone. I sent Dickens and Holmes to her."

He frowned. "You sent whom?"

"Charles Dickens and Sherlock Holmes. You made them—don't you remember? Dickens said he was the part of your mind that made it out."

"Did he?" He pinched the bridge of his nose. "Okay. Sorry, I didn't mean to do that. What did they tell you?"

"Just that you'd worked out who the summoner was. After that, we put it together ourselves."

"The fact that she doesn't have a class this afternoon?"

"That, exactly. And a few other things." I sat down on the edge of the bed, mostly in the hope that he would too. He was wearing me out. "Look, calm down. They can't legally keep you here, no, and I will make sure they don't. Take a breath. I know this is urgent, but— why Beth? How did you know it was her?"

"I should have known earlier, really. But—it doesn't make sense. Why would she do something like this?"

"I don't know. It's insane. But she's definitely done it. I was practically on the phone with her when she made the city. How did you—?"

"The archetypal monster," he said. "It was a paper Beth gave at a Victoriana conference at the National Library, last year. 'The Claws that Catch: Lewis Carroll's Jabberwock as Archetypal Monster.' She isn't a Victorian specialist really, or not officially; she only came to do me a favor, because I was on the committee and we were short on submissions."

"Still," I said. "The summoner might have used her paper."

"Unlikely. It was never published. Besides, it was too perfect. The Jabberwock was her work, and so was Henry. The critics she uses, the interpretations she favors...they had her brushstrokes all over them. I can't *believe* I didn't realize sooner."

"Maybe you didn't want to. She was your friend."

"She started at the university about the same time as me," he said, after a pause. His face had gone quiet. "From London. She took a lower pay grade to be here. She came because of me, didn't she? She knew what I was."

"That sounds likely," I had to agree.

"I should have realized," he repeated. "It was only when you told me, in the car, that she lied about having a class this afternoon. I could see it then, but I—I don't know, I just couldn't focus. I was so cold. Did I talk to you? I can't remember."

"We nearly lost you," I said.

"I'm sorry." I knew he had heard more than my words, and that he meant it this time. "You were right. I thought I could do this. I didn't believe it could kill me."

"*You* were right," I corrected him. "You didn't die." He didn't respond, and after a moment I moved on. "I told them I'd bring you back to the Street, if you're up to it. It would probably be safer there."

"I wish I could go," he said with a sigh. "I promised to protect it. But this isn't about the Street; it's about the whole city—maybe the whole world. And it's about Beth and me. She made it about us when she sent the Hound of the Baskervilles to my door. I need to find her."

"She's waiting for you," I said. "Eric was outside the hospital just now. He told me. He also said you'd go."

"He was right." He looked at me. "You don't have to come, though. I know you don't want to."

"Of course I do!" I said, stung despite myself. I tried not to think too hard about what else Eric had said. I didn't take advice from any variation of Uriah Heep. "Have to, not want to. I'm not letting you enter a nightmare version of Dickens on your own. And besides—"

Charley waited.

"Lydia's in there." It hurt almost as much to say it as it had to realize it. "In the city—in the cloud. It swallowed her up."

His eyes went round. "I'm sorry." He finally sank down onto the bed beside me, and I realized I hadn't wanted him to. The frantic energy I'd come into drained away at once. It was frightening how quickly he could shrink back into the person I usually thought of him as. "I should have asked—but the doctor said you two had both come in, I just…"

"She left," I said, without further explanation. "And now she's gone."

"We'll get her back," he said. "I promise. God, I'm so sorry…"

"What for?" It was that kind of apology: an admission of guilt, not an expression of sympathy. "You didn't do it."

"I did," he corrected. "I didn't bring out the city, precisely, but…I know I ruined things when I moved here, Rob, even from the first. You had your whole life here; you didn't want me in it. I knew that, and I came anyway. Uriah Heep, the Street, the new world—I brought it all with me, and I brought it to you."

The terrible thing was, that was almost exactly the narrative that ran through my own head—at the worst of times, in the dark hours, but still, it was there. It was startling to hear it repeated back in Charley's voice.

"Why did you come back from England?" I asked. This wasn't the time for that question, but there might not be another. In the three years since he'd arrived, I'd never asked him.

"I don't know." This time, I waited for him to continue. "I was homesick, I suppose, but it wasn't just that. It was just…I was thirteen when I went to Oxford. I never even thought about it. It was just planned for me, and I was happy to go along with it. I loved learning, and I wanted to make people proud. I did both, and it was fine, for a while. Then—I don't know. I wanted something more. And I realized I didn't know what more there was."

"I think you wanted this." I gestured, which was pretty stupid, since we were in an intensive care ward. But he knew what the gesture encompassed. "The Street. The written world."

"I did," he said. "And I knew that was ungrateful. You were right. I've always been given everything I ever wanted, in terms of my normal abilities, even when it did nothing but inconvenience the rest of you. It was stupid to want more. But I did."

"It wasn't stupid," I said. "And it wasn't ungrateful—I was stupid to say that. I've always wanted everything."

He shrugged. "Anyway. I went through a month or so when I didn't do much of anything—I could barely read, much less research, and certainly much less summon. Oxford's a suffocating place when you're in the wrong mood, and I was. I had enough old material that I could keep working, but still—I think a lot of people who knew me over there started to get disappointed in me, which frightened me, because I'd never disappointed anybody before. A few more started to get concerned, which frightened me more, because people looking too closely at me means they might find out what I could do. Right at that point, a job came up here. I didn't know what I was looking for, but I knew it wasn't in Oxford. I thought perhaps it might be at home."

"I'm sorry," I said.

He looked surprised. "What for? I was fine, really. But that's why I came, since you asked. I knew you didn't want me, and I was being selfish. I promised myself I would leave you alone. But somehow I broke that promise, again and again—whenever something came through that I was having a hard time dealing with on my own, I picked up the phone and called you. I *could* deal with it on my own— I did for years, over there. I don't know why I kept calling you."

I remembered at once something I had overheard my parents say, when Charley was preparing to go to Oxford. They didn't know I was listening; I *wasn't* listening, until I heard my name. Mum was talking about how she wasn't convinced Charley could cope with going to the university emotionally, even though the work had probably been within his capabilities for quite a while. He was still painfully unsure of himself.

"He'll be fine," Dad said. "Honestly, part of what you're talking about is just called being a younger brother. I was one myself, you know. He'll be a different person without Rob there all the time."

A different person. Those were the words he used. He didn't mean what Eric had meant, of course—nothing that literal. He hadn't known what Charley was any more than I did. It didn't mean Eric was right. But still...

"You can't do this," I had said to him in the car, only hours ago. "It's going to kill you." And almost at once, it nearly had.

I felt sick.

"I didn't *not want you* here," I said to Charley, as firmly as I could. I'd thought it was a lie when I said it, but I realized it was true. Funny how words do that. "I just—I didn't know you anymore. I still don't, perhaps. We've been on opposite sides of the world since we both left home. I saw you grow up in glimpses, a week every Christmas. We both kept changing in between times."

He smiled, very slightly. "'We changed again, and yet again, and it was now too late and too far to go back, and I went on.'"

"I assume that's Dickens."

"*Great Expectations.* He wasn't really talking about that kind of change. But sometimes I think he was. The book is."

As usual, I had no idea what to say. "This isn't your fault," I said finally. "This isn't your city covering mine, like your stuff encroaching on my side of the room when you were seven. It's Beth. She did this. You tried to stop her before, and you're going to stop her now. We both are. Right?"

He nodded.

"So let's stop wasting time, and go find her."

I stood. Charley stayed seated.

"Thanks for sticking up for me," he said hesitantly. "With Uriah Heep, back in the Street. I was fading in and out, but I do remember that."

"No worries," I said. I didn't want to dwell on that, so I changed the subject. "Eric said something else outside—about Beth. He said that her characters couldn't see her as we do. They see something else."

"I know. We had one of her characters come to the Street—he said the same. But they can't name what it is they do see."

"Eric tried. He said it was a spider in a web. Does that mean anything to you?"

He frowned. "No. That is—I don't know what it might mean to Eric. It's not an uncommon phrase."

"Well. He said to mention it." I paused. "We have another problem, you know."

It took him a moment to pull out from his thoughts. "What problem?"

"Mum and Dad are here. Dickens and Holmes have taken them to the Street."

For a second, Charley looked completely, genuinely horrified. Then he laughed, tried to stop himself from laughing, and ended up giggling so infectiously I smiled myself. I hadn't heard him laugh in a long time.

"Oh God, they're going to be so mad at me," he said.

"They're never mad at you. They'll say this is all my fault."

"That settles it. We should both go into Beth's world. It can't be more dangerous than facing Mum and Dad in the middle of the Street."

"I agree," I said. "So come on."

Millie

When the new world came, it cut through the Street like a knife through paper. Wind roared. Cobblestones rippled like scales underfoot. Walls breathed in and out like the sides of a monstrous serpent. It was the shift that everyone had been building toward.

Millie and the others were still in the public house, where Heathcliff's body lay on the floor behind the counter. Night had fallen early, for no reason that they could fathom, and all the lamps in the building were lit. The room had been alive with their arguments. In the wake of the shift, the silence was devastating.

Darcy One was the first to speak. "It's here, isn't it?"

"It's here," Dorian answered. The light from the lamp gleamed on his hair, as light was wont to do. He looked as though he were posing for a portrait.

Millie found her words again. "Wait here," she instructed the room. She looked at Dorian, and forced firm bossiness into her voice. "I mean it, Dorian. I won't have you causing a commotion in the pub like a common drunk. It's beneath you."

"You'd be surprised," Dorian said, "what may or may not be beneath me."

He didn't say it with much fire, just as Darcy One had spoken with neither pride or attractive haughtiness. Everyone was very quiet.

Millie slipped through the wall, out into the dusk of central Wellington. The air was warm out there, despite the breeze. She went down Cuba Street, and turned onto Courtenay Place.

To a point, the street stretched out as it usually did: grand old theaters, restaurants, redbrick walkways lined with metal sculptures and leafy green trees. After that point, it just stopped. Instead of the hills in the distance, Millie found herself looking at a wall of darkness. It was moving, inch by inch, toward them.

"I say," she said, very quietly. It was all she had been given to say.

She was still standing there when the others began to come through the wall. Dorian came first, followed by a handful of characters: the Artful, Uriah Heep, Lady Macbeth, and the Implied Reader. Normally it would be dangerous for so many to leave the wall at once, at this time of the evening. Now, the Left Bank Arcade was deserted. Everyone had flocked to see the shadow spilling across the city or flocked just as fast in the other direction. Nothing was dangerous now, or everything was.

Dorian had sighted her too. He motioned to the others to wait a little distance apart, and came toward her. She saw a covered square tucked under his arm, wrapped in a cloth, and knew immediately that her suspicions had been right. Her heart tightened.

"Hello, Millie," he said as she drew near. In the darkness, he was a little less glowing, a little less larger than life. "Come to say goodbye?"

"That's your portrait, isn't it?" she said, with a nod at the covered frame under his arm.

"The agreement was that you would hold it for as long as I resided in the Street," he said. "I'm taking my soul back now. You were fortunate I didn't ask you to hand it over. A soul is such a heavy thing when it passes from hand to hand."

"I didn't realize you had a key to my wardrobe."

"I have no key to anything concerning you, I assure you. The Artful picked the lock. He's coming too, you know. And the Implied Reader, for some reason, although what he expects to find waiting for him out there..."

"You don't have to go."

"It's here, isn't it?" he said. "The new world. We all felt it come."

"Yes," she said. "It's here. It's devouring everything."

He smiled a little. "Glorious."

"Dorian..." She paused until she could trust her voice. "What's this about? Don't give me all that posturing out there; I want to know what's really going on. I don't understand."

"Oh, Millie. Of course you don't. You're Millie Radcliffe-Dix, girl detective. Always strong, always loyal, always brave. I'm Dorian Gray. I'm frightened for my own life. I'm sorry to disappoint you, but that's all this is about. I want to stand with the strongest party, because I'm afraid to stand against them."

"You can't think you'll be safe with the summoner. He let a Jabberwock loose on the Street, and didn't care whom he killed in the process. If he really cared about the lives of freeborn characters, he wouldn't have done that. At worst, he's lying about everything. At best, he's ruthless to the point of cruelty."

"I never thought he'd be kind," Dorian said. "I'm not kind myself, you'll remember. I don't mind if he wants to kill me one day—he can try. I may kill him one day, if it comes to it. But he'll kill me more certainly if I oppose him. Besides, he'll make things happen. He already has. I have no doubt, Millie, that Charles Sutherland is a very kind person—so are you, underneath Jacqueline Blaine's penchant for outdated idioms and bossiness. Kind people don't make things happen. They try to prevent bad things from happening, and they fail, and they live in fear of that failure. So do those under their protection. Perhaps if we're out in the open, with an army at our backs, I will finally go a day when I'm not frightened of anything." He smiled, very slightly. "Unfortunately, Oscar Wilde knew too well what it was like to live in secret, consumed by concealment. And equally unfortunately, he gave me all of his vices, plus a few more, and none of his virtues. It's so boring to be afraid all the time. I find one can live so much better without kindness than one can live with boredom."

"Don't give me that," Millie said. "The summoner could read you away with a thought. Have you considered that?"

Dorian shrugged. For a moment, his seventeen-year-old face looked uncharacteristically tired. "Oh, I don't think so. I think he needs us. But even if he does . . . well, there are worse places to go than one's own book. At least I'm the main protagonist there. It's so difficult, isn't it, to realize that one is not always the main protagonist?"

"Not really," Millie said. "No. But then, I went to high school."

A flicker of a smile crossed Dorian's face. "Goodbye, Millie."

"Dorian—"

"One final thing," he interrupted. "Your Charles Sutherland. He isn't what you think he is. I'm not even certain he's what *he* thinks he is."

Millie frowned. "What do you mean?"

"He's one of us, Millie," Dorian said. "A reading. Conjured out of thin air. It's my job to find such people, remember. People who appear out of nowhere, without real explanation. Who can walk through our walls, when no real person can. Well, I was suspicious, so I looked. I looked at his medical records. I looked at his birth certificate. I think you would have looked, too, if you hadn't been so close to him. I can't be certain—there's no proof, of the kind I can usually find—but there's enough that I feel confident about it. He's one of us."

"That can't be true," Millie said. Something inside her was reeling in shock, but it was very deep down. There was too much else happening on the surface. "Why are you telling me this?"

He shrugged. "Why not? I was going to save it for blackmail purposes, but I have my soul now. I need nothing from you. I thought about taking it to the other summoner—I still will, perhaps—but I'm almost certain he already knows. So take it as a gift from me—a parting gift. You *have* been fun, you know. So have I. You'll miss me."

She was still thinking of Charley. "But I met him as a child—he summoned me as a child."

"And then you both grew up," Dorian said. "You really do need to open your mind to what can and cannot be true. You're not in a children's book anymore, Millie. The truth here is rarely pure and never simple."

"It isn't so simple in a children's book either."

"Very likely." He leaned forward, adjusted the painting under his arm, and kissed her very gently on the lips. It was a kiss from Dorian Gray, so it was light and soulless and utterly thrilling. She held herself perfectly still as he pulled away. "Goodbye, Millie. I hope I don't have to kill you one day."

"Oh, stop being so bloody Gothic," she said. She ignored the sudden rush in her heart and the lump in her throat. She was ignoring a lot of things at the moment. "It's not going to cut any ice with the summoner, you know."

"I should hope not," he said. "I may not have morals, but I do have standards."

And with that, he and the others walked away. Five of them. She was thankful it was no less—at least, not yet. The Artful and Uriah

Heep had not really been theirs to start with; the Implied Reader was a startling loss, but not a devastating one. But she wished that it had not been Dorian.

Cuba Street was already deserted. Courtenay Place was lit by people taking photos on their screens from a safe distance. When a car pulled up on the road in front of her, she didn't pay any attention until she heard her name called.

Four people were climbing out of a blue Mitsubishi. Two of them were Sherlock Holmes and Charles Dickens—the latter she recognized from last night, the former was recognizable anywhere. The other two were a man and woman, perhaps in their early fifties. The man was tall, with a square, comfortable face; the woman was smaller, slightly built with her graying hair cut short. Both looked familiar, as though from a memory of an old photograph. She didn't think she'd ever met them, so she assumed the memory came from Charley. It took a moment of fumbling around in her own head, as though through a chest left in the attic, before she unearthed it.

"Mr. and Mrs. Sutherland," she exclaimed. "How nice to see you. You're looking well."

"Thanks," Mr. Sutherland said. His brow furrowed. "I'm sorry, have we met?"

"Millie Radcliffe-Dix, girl detective." She held out her hand. "How do you do?"

"We've come from the hospital," Charles Dickens interrupted. "I'm afraid we have something of a problem."

Millie nodded. "Tell me."

The Street was waiting for her. Nobody else had moved from where she left them. The Darcys were seated at their table; Miss Matty, the Mad Hatter, and the Duke of Wellington were standing by the window. Lancelot and the Scarlet Pimpernel stood behind the bar, both battered and bruised from the rubble but still on their feet. Scheherazade had arrived, clutching two or three of her most precious books to her chest. The witch stood near Heathcliff's body, tall and imposing. Matilda sat at the bar, swinging her legs. It was a friendlier room, she knew, without Dorian, and Uriah Heep, and the Artful.

And yet she felt horribly alone without them. It took her a moment to realize why. All the people who remained believed in her.

She reached deep inside herself, and found the part that belonged to Jacqueline Blaine. She was acting it at the moment, but that would have to do for now.

"All right there, everyone?" she said. "Because I think we've found ourselves in the middle of an adventure."

XXV

The city was in a state of emergency. The staff at reception were talking quietly about evacuating the hospital, although the cloud was still some distance away. The television screen now displayed a windswept news anchor, colored by emergency floodlights. I heard only snatches of the report, but the tone matched the gravity given to news of natural disaster.

As we drove nearer to the shadow, we saw the flashing blue lights of police cars and fire engines; closer still, there were orange traffic cones and barricades marking the danger zone. Police clustered around them in droves.

"We'll have a job getting through," I said.

"If it helps," Charley said, "I can do the *Secret Garden* door without the book now. I practiced it with Millie Tuesday evening until I couldn't see straight. I was trying to turn it into a portal."

I didn't ask. "Good. Then the easiest thing might be to get through a building that's half-swallowed-up. They might be guarding the doors, but not the walls. And you're a little conspicuous at the moment."

I had looked for someone to give us back Charley's clothes, but everybody was busy, and we couldn't afford to wait. I had a pair of my old running shoes in the car, so he wouldn't be barefoot. Otherwise, he was apparently going to meet the destiny Eric had spoken of in pale blue hospital pajamas and a gray dressing gown that couldn't have been much protection against the raging wind. He didn't seem to mind one way or the other; as he pointed out, he'd been in pajamas at many a stupider time. I minded. He looked far too vulnerable, with the hospital logo printed on his chest and the plaster from the

IV still on his wrist. The walk out to the car had made him dizzy again, although the brisk wind had revived him.

We got in through an alley that bordered the back of a Chinese restaurant. As we stepped through the familiar green door, we nearly walked right into the dark cloud. It hung in the air halfway across the kitchen, engulfing pots and pans and benches up to a point and leaving the rest untouched.

"That's weird," I said flatly.

"Very," Charley agreed. "Don't touch it. It's swallowing everything up—you might go with it."

"What about you?"

"The Street accepted me. I hope this will too—or else all this is for nothing."

He reached out and let his fingers brush the edges of the cloud. Straightaway, they vanished, as they had passing through the wall in the Left Bank Arcade. It looked even stranger without a solid wall to see them disappear through.

Because I was real, and Charley wasn't. The simplest explanation for his ability to enter the Street, and now this place, had never occurred to either of us. We had never even thought to ask. Perhaps we were just too used to Charley being able to do things I couldn't.

"Do you feel that?" he asked, pulling my thoughts back. "That faint breeze?"

I thought I could, now that he mentioned it. It was cool on my face. "Like a draft."

"Exactly." One corner of his mouth twitched. "A draft from another world."

"Someone left reality open."

He laughed a little, and lowered his hand. "I think I'll have to take you through. The way I did the Street."

"Right." I hesitated. "So—is Lydia in there? And the others? Will we find her?"

"Perhaps," Charley said cautiously. "But, um—I actually think everything that cloud's taken has just been overwritten. It's not like the Street, or even the *Oliver Twist* house—it's taking up real space. Two things can't exist in the same place at once. That's why nobody's come out. They're just—nowhere. I'm sorry. We'll get her back, I promise."

For a moment, I felt too sick to speak. I really had lost her. She wasn't just somewhere else. She was *gone*.

"How do you *know* all this?" I said with a welcome flash of irritation. "Why do you always know everything?"

"I don't," he said. "Not even close. I'm just keeping my eyes open, and making this up as I go along. But it makes sense."

He held out his hand. I took it.

"This might be more difficult than before," he added. "This world is further through, and the edges are still growing. It might help if you could try to concentrate very hard on a story."

I frowned. "What kind of story?"

"Any story—an important one. It might help you make sense of the reality in there—or help it make sense of you."

I instantly forgot every story I'd ever known.

"Ready?" Charley asked.

In that moment, I would rather have died than pass through that thick black cloud and out of my entire world. But Charley stepped forward, and so I followed him.

A rush of air, a rush of words in my ears, a roar of vertigo. My eyes went dark. Every particle of my body screamed, separated, and then dissolved. It wasn't like passing into the Street. That had just been a jump, like stepping down from a pavement in the dark. This was a leap across a canyon, or a plummet into one. I could no longer feel Charley's hand in my own.

Then, at once, I was back. It was daylight, though the sun was low in the sky. The air was chilly and thick with fog; my nose filled with the sharp, pungent smell of mud and smoke. Charley's hand was back, solid and tight around mine, and cold. He was usually a little bit cold.

And I was in another world. I could almost have mistaken it for the Street at first, albeit on an unusually dismal day: the same cobbled road, the same streetlamps burning dim in the fog, the same tight-packed houses. The difference was that it didn't stop at one street. Down what would usually be the length of Courtenay Place, Victorian roads and shops and houses went on as far as I could see.

"This is incredible," Charley said. He caught my eye, and shrugged defensively. "I don't mean I *approve*. It's terrible. It's dangerous. But it *is* incredible."

At that moment, the city gave a groan. The cobbles beneath my feet shifted, as though in a minor earthquake; the sky darkened simultaneously.

"What on earth was that?" I asked. "Another shift?"

"As I said," Charley said, "this is—well, definitely not a safe place to be. We need to get it under control, and quickly." He released my hand and stepped forward. Fortunately, I didn't disappear, as I had been worried I would. I really hoped he had thought of that first. "Do you know where Beth was in the real world? It might help to find her there."

"The light started behind the Embassy Theatre," I said. "Which would be further up this high street, I assume. What's wrong?"

Charley was frowning; it took him a second to recall himself. "Just a thought," he said. "Where is everyone?"

"What do you mean? The summoner's people?"

"No—well, yes, but I'm sure they'll be along. I said that this place would be calling everybody. Dorian Gray and the others were ready to answer that call. They should have been here before us. Where are they?"

"Perhaps Millie talked them out of leaving," I suggested, without much conviction. Much as I respected Millie, it didn't seem likely.

"Perhaps," Charley agreed doubtfully. "Well. Where did you say Beth might be?"

I started to answer, then nodded at the street instead. "You might want to ask them."

From the distance, a horde of characters was approaching. They were moving slowly, but they were unquestionably moving toward us. Dorian Gray was not among them, nor was anybody else belonging to the Street.

"Hold still," Charley said to me. I didn't really need the advice. I wasn't going anywhere.

Still, I found myself wanting to flinch away as they came to a stop near us. There was an unmistakable threat in their stillness and quiet. It wasn't like being among the characters in the Street. Those were individual, unique; they moved and muttered and tried to kill you with lampposts. These were oddly homogeneous, as if they'd been shaped from the same bland dough on a production line and baked to the same pale, half-done crust.

"What's wrong with them?" I kept my voice low without quite knowing why.

"Nothing's wrong with them," Charley said grimly. "They're meant to be like this. They're meant to do what the summoner wants them to do and nothing much else."

Their eyes were blank as pebbles underwater. "Beth made them, didn't she?"

"I'm always telling her that her readings are too reductive," Charley said. "Brilliant, but reductive."

"What do they want?"

"I think they want to make sure we get to where we're going," Charley said. He started to move toward a side street, experimentally, and at once one of the characters moved to block him. It was a young woman, her hair caught up in a messy plait and her face painted with makeup. Charley backed away, raising his hands.

"It's okay," he told her. "We'll follow, if you lead."

"We're supposed to lead you to the house," the woman said, much to my surprise. She looked barely capable of speech. Her accent was thick Cockney, and her face brimmed with sudden feeling as she looked at us. "But you should run. Just run away from here. Don't let us stop you."

"It's okay," Charley repeated. For a moment I couldn't think who he reminded me of, then with a start I realized. It was the way I spoke to him sometimes, on the increasingly rare occasions I was trying to be a good elder brother. "You're Nancy, aren't you?"

The woman nodded. It gave me a start. This was the woman Frankenstein had spoken of; or, at least, it was the echo of her that she had glimpsed in dreams. Her gaunt face took on new significance for me. I could see the lines of kindness in it, waiting to be read out.

"You're not betraying us," Charley said. "We want to go to the house. Please do take us there."

Nancy gave him one last, anguished look, then her face smoothed over. She drew herself upright, and what personality there had been on her face was already draining away.

"Follow me," she said.

The house was tall, old brick, and derelict. Many of the upper windows were boarded up, and all the lower were barred with iron; I had the unusually metaphorical impression of a blind creature grinning at me with rusty teeth. A wrought iron fence surrounded it, encompassing a deserted courtyard, and the gates were barred.

"Satis House," Charley said, almost to himself.

"You know, I've read *David Copperfield* now," I said conversationally. "Apart from the last two chapters, and that slow bit in the middle. I mention this because the rest of Dickens's works are still a complete blank to me."

"Sorry. This is from *Great Expectations*. It's the house where Miss Havisham lives. She was jilted on her wedding day as a young woman—part of a scam—and keeps the house and herself in exactly the same state as it was the moment she found out she was betrayed. Wedding dress with one shoe, cake still on the table, clocks stopped—that kind of thing. Oh, and she raises Estella to wreak revenge on men."

"Estella being the aristocratic young woman who turns out to be Magwitch's daughter."

He turned to me with a frown. "How did you know that?"

"It was in your lecture this morning. The bit I heard. I did listen, you know. Why would Beth bring you here?"

"I don't know. I wrote about it in my book as a place where the rich and the criminal collide. But I've talked about Satis House with Beth, once or twice. To her, it's about the past slowly poisoning the present."

"You academics and your metaphors."

He didn't get the chance to reply. The doors to the house had opened, and two figures were coming across the courtyard. They were children.

I say children, but one of them was really a young man, well built and strong jawed. He wore his hair the way I had worn it at fifteen or so, only much smoother, and his eyes as they looked out of his face were as blue as mine. In fact, he would have been the mirror of me at fifteen, if I had been a little better looking, a little cooler, a lot more sure of myself. And the smaller boy...

"Oh," Charley said quietly.

I blinked, and felt cold. It *was* me at fifteen. A confident, mature, perfect version of me at fifteen. And the boy—he must have been ten or eleven, logically—was my brother. In some ways he looked older than ten—the pale, pointed face was older, indefinably so, as was the way he carried himself. But he was tiny, even for that age; his limbs were thin and stunted, like those of a bonsai tree.

"That's us," I said flatly.

"Yeah," Charley said. "That's...I'm sorry."

"Do you have something to do with them?"

"My...um. My old diaries went missing from my house a few months ago. I got them when Mum and Dad moved, mostly because they were too horribly embarrassing to risk anybody seeing. I assumed they were somewhere about—I never know where anything is. But... Beth was at my house the day before they vanished. She asked what they were. In retrospect, given what she is, it would have been very easy for her to have someone break in and take them. I think those are from my first day at high school."

"How do you know that?"

He nodded at the younger boy unhappily. "He's just had his hair cut. I never had it that short again. And...that was my new watch. It broke on that first day, when a couple of the kids tripped me up and I landed on it wrong."

"You never told us that."

He shrugged.

I looked at them critically. "I did not look like that at fifteen. I was pudgy, and had spots."

"You probably still do, on other pages. When I was mad at you."

"And your ears never stuck out like that."

"Okay, just shut up. This is so embarrassing."

"Why do you even have diaries? That's such a girl thing."

"I liked words, okay? I was ten. I didn't know someone was going to steal them sixteen years after the fact and bring them to life."

The two figures came to the gate. They each carried a candle, and it illuminated their faces. In the case of the elder, this cast the perfect features in a forbidding light; in the younger, it made the cheekbones too sharp and the eyes too large and dark.

"Hey," I said, trying to make my voice sound something between friendly and firm. It was hard, when what I felt was something between terror and revulsion. "I assume Beth sent you?"

They looked at me.

"They don't talk?"

"Well, they're from my diary entries," Charley said. "Those weren't exactly masterpieces of eloquence and erudition. I only vented a few paragraphs, most days, and not usually with dialogue."

"Next time, write more or not at all. Why are they here? She could have sent anybody. Why them?"

"She's trying to unnerve us, I think. Or show off. Or both. Try to ignore them."

The older boy—the one who was me—reached out and unlatched the gate. He pushed it open, loosely, and beckoned to us with one hand.

"Looks like we're supposed to follow them," I said.

The characters who had walked us here had disappeared. It was just us, and our peculiar echoes.

It was dark inside the house. The smaller boy held back and closed the door behind us, just to make doubly certain of that. By the lights the children carried, I could make out corridors and rooms, but they all were unlived-in, and they all were cold. Intellectually, I knew they had only come into being an hour or so ago. They looked as though they had been neglected for years.

Straight ahead was a staircase. The little boy tried to get up the stairs at the same time as the older; the older coldly shoved him to one side, and he stumbled back. On instinct, I caught him by the shoulder, but he flinched away. He shot me a fearful glance, then quickened his pace to catch up with his brother.

"What did I *do* to you on your first day of school?" I asked. That one look had hurt more deeply than I wanted to admit.

"Nothing," Charley said firmly. He looked as uncomfortable as I was. "Ignore them. You didn't do anything."

"Was that the problem?"

"There was no problem. I was young, that's all. So were you."

But I hadn't been, I realized. Not to him. To a ten-year-old, fifteen is ancient.

I was desperately glad that I had kept no journals or diaries while I was in high school, or ever. I would hate for Charley to see either of us through my eyes.

We went up one flight of stairs, down a corridor, then up another. Still, there was no sign of life but the two figments leading the way, and they weren't exactly alive. And then, at last, we stopped at a door, and the other Rob opened it.

It wasn't like the other rooms in the house. Those were musty, stifled with cobwebs and old furniture. This room was gray and bare. Although we were indoors, I could feel rain in the air, the heavy damp of a rural winter. The floor beneath my feet was harder and more unforgiving than the wooden boards in the corridor, and when I looked down, I saw it was shimmering intermittently into tarmac. Shadows danced on the walls, and from somewhere distant there came voices and the harsh, mocking laughter of children.

"This doesn't look like Dickens," I said.

"No," Charley said. He looked sick. "No…this is me."

It was only then that I saw the young boy standing by the window.

It was Charley again, a little older than the one who had shown us in, with his face starting to lose some of its childhood roundness and his hair grown out again. Like the other, he was in a school uniform, but this one was wearing the dark trousers and blazer that marked the privileged ranks of Year Thirteen. He seemed clearer than most of Beth's readings. The waxy, unfinished look was still there, but there was more feeling in his face.

"Hey there," I said to the boy uncertainly.

"Hey," he replied. His voice was as young as the rest of him; given that, it was startling to hear it so hard and bitter.

"So where are you from?" I asked. "How old are you?"

"Twelve," he said. "I'll be thirteen soon."

"Oh," the real Charley said quietly, beside me.

"What?" I started to ask, then looked closer. Charley's birthday was in August, toward the end of winter, which meant this one was probably from June or July; that would account for the chill in the air. Year Thirteen. His trousers, I noticed, were torn at one knee.

"Oh," I repeated.

Somehow, it wasn't a surprise. It seemed as though things had always, inevitably, been circling that day.

Diary Charley spoke before either of us could say anything more.

"Why did you have to come here?" he demanded. It might have been my imagination, but I felt the room tremor.

"Beth invited us," I said. I nodded at Charley. "At least, she invited him."

"That's what I meant!" It was the tone I'd sometimes heard lurking in Charley's voice when someone was being frustratingly slow. When *I* was being frustratingly slow. "Why did you have to come? She'll send me back now. It's not fair. I did everything she asked. I don't want to go back."

"Back where?"

"I don't *know*. Death. Oblivion. Some kind of postmodern textual unreality. I don't care. I won't go."

"Why would she send you away?" Charley asked his younger self.

"Because she doesn't need me anymore! Not if she has you." His skinny shoulders rose and fell as he caught his breath. "I'm not going back. I'll kill you first."

The room definitely rippled this time. I saw the windows flex and crack. The cellar in Lambton Quay had trembled as we waited for the summoner to come, I remembered. It had shivered exactly like this.

This wasn't the summoner, though. This was a preteen boy. More than that, it was *Charley*, in some shape or form. And God knows what he had been through, if the basement room in the *Oliver Twist* house was any indication. Belatedly, I took in how painfully thin he was, and the dark circles under his eyes.

"Calm down," I said to him. "Look, you don't need to kill anybody. We can help—"

"Get *away* from me!" I'd put out a hand instinctively; the child had shied away as if from a blow. Hurt and anger were brimming in his eyes. "I don't want your help! I *hate* you!"

I flinched back, despite myself.

"Don't listen to him," the real Charley said to me. "Of course I don't hate you."

"He does," I said, with a nod at the diary child. He glared at me. "And he's you, isn't he?"

"He isn't me." I could hear some of the child's vehemence in his own voice. "Neither of those two diary fragments are me. *I'm* me. I'm right here. This is Beth's reading of my writing—it's a character, or an implied author, or some combination of both, I don't know. It isn't me."

"You're saying there's no truth in him?"

"There's truth in anything! It's the truth of a single moment in time. It's... it's as if someone made a painting of you, based on a photograph. The photograph would be an accurate picture of you; the painting would be a valid interpretation of that photograph. Nobody's lying. But that painting isn't you, not all of you. It's just a picture."

"Unless it's the picture of Dorian Gray. Then it's a picture of your soul."

He shook his head. "Does this really matter?"

"You tell me. Why is Beth doing this?"

Charley opened his mouth to reply, but I never heard what he would have said. At that moment, Beth came into the room.

XXVI

This is what happened on the day that Beth had pulled from Charley's diary. It's not that exciting, or that terrible. I tried to tell myself Charley had forgotten all about it. I suppose what I had hated most about Uriah Heep knowing about it is that it meant Charley remembered very well.

It was during our last year of high school, when I was seventeen. Thankfully, that year we only shared history together, at which he was only a moderate genius; he was in a different English class, and I did my best to take as many non-arts subjects as I could so I would find myself sitting across the classroom from him as infrequently as possible. (This is why I have fourteen credits in economics, and never learned French.) Most people didn't talk to me about him, unless he'd done something particularly brilliant that week. He'd been with us for two years already; the novelty had worn off. But still, everyone knew who he was, and who he was to me.

Up until then, he'd been picked on a bit, but he was too young, I think, to feel like a fair target to the other kids. At twelve, he was the same age as the new Year Nines coming in, and some of them that year were vicious. I chased them off, when I saw them, but I didn't always see them. I didn't hang around with my little brother at lunch or anything—I mean, who does?

One day, I saw a bunch of them ganging up on him behind the bike shed. It was just kid stuff—they had him cornered, clutching his books to his chest as they snatched at his backpack, and when one of them shoved him, he overbalanced and went down. He wouldn't put out his hands to catch himself, because it was raining and he was trying to keep *The Adventures of Sherlock Holmes* from going in a puddle, so it must have hurt. I heard him start to cry out and then bite it back. He caught my eye, and I knew he saw me. I saw mingled relief and shame on his face, and I knew he thought I was coming for him.

But I didn't go to him. I don't know why. I would have, normally, without thinking. He had just got full marks on a test I had done badly in, which might have had something to do with it. People had been teasing me about him lately, for reasons that really had nothing to do with him, but with a feud between me and Jono Maxwell over First XV rugby team. I was a teenager. I really don't know the reason. I just know I felt a surge of anger, and that surge carried me right past him. I felt his eyes on me the whole time, even when I had turned the corner and I was well out of his sight. I wanted to go back with every step. I didn't.

Later, I found out that before things had gone any further, a tall, sharp-eyed man had appeared on the scene, dressed in old-fashioned clothes, and broken things up. The Year Nines swore that he had materialized out of thin air, but nobody believed them, obviously. After break, Charley came back to history with the rest of us. His trousers were torn at the knee, he was limping a little, and I could tell he had been crying. But he sat down, did his work even more quietly than usual, and never said a word to me about what had happened. Nobody else ever noticed a thing.

There was nothing much to notice. It *was* nothing. Just stupid kid stuff. Everyone gets into fights at high school. But I always hated it when Sherlock Holmes came, after that. He had protected Charley that day; I hadn't. And we all three knew it.

XXVII

She came through the same door we had entered, silently flanked by teen Rob and ten-year-old Charley. By the window, twelve-year-old Charley took a step back.

I don't know what I had been expecting. I suppose, now that Beth had been revealed as the mysterious other summoner, I thought she would look a little more like a villain from a story. Perhaps I thought that now, in her own world, we might be able to see her as Eric and the others saw her, however and whoever that was. But she looked exactly the same as she had when I saw her a few hours earlier. Short and plump, the edges of her crisp haircut just brushing the collar of her green cardigan. Her blue-gray eyes now seemed hard to me, glittering in her kindly face, but that might have been my own imagination. She was not a monster. I shouldn't have been surprised. Charley, after all, is her rival summoner, and I couldn't quite see him as a hero at this moment. He was in pajamas.

"Hello, Charles," she said. Even her voice was the same as it had been. "It's nice to have you finally see me. And Robert, of course."

"It's a bit different from the last time I came to your house," Charley said. "You know, when I came to drop off the last of the honors essays, and you offered me tea."

"I could do the same here. I have plenty of books hereabouts. One of them is bound to contain a kettle and some tea bags. The cup of tea is an English tradition. Steeped in symbolism. Served with irony."

"Actually, I don't want to be flippant about this," Charley said. "Not here. Not in front of him."

Twelve-year-old Charley glared at him, but didn't speak.

Beth smiled a little. "Very well. I don't need to introduce you, do I? You've met young Charles Sutherland?"

"I have," he said. "Put him away. He's grotesque."

"He's yours," Beth said. "So are the other two. I read them from your words. I'll put those two away, if you like." She didn't wait for an answer. There was a flash of light, and at once cold, perfect Rob and tiny, fearful Charley were gone. I felt a weight lighten on my chest. Perhaps it was guilt.

The other diary Charley, the one by the window, stayed quiet. But I was watching him, and I saw him give a tiny convulsive shudder.

"I only brought those two out to be hospitable," Beth said. "But *this* one... he's the key to it all, isn't he? Charles Dickens in the blacking factory. Charles Sutherland in the playground. The anger of a brilliant, sensitive twelve-year-old at being thrown away."

"I wasn't thrown away," Charley said. He glanced quickly at diary Charley, then away again. "It was one time. One day."

"And for Dickens it was one year," Beth said. "It doesn't matter. It only takes one moment. One moment of realizing that you are alone, and that survival requires both strength and power. I'm still using this one. Not for much longer, I trust."

"Using him for what?" I said. I heard my voice tight with anger. "He's a child."

"He's a good deal more than that," she said. "He's angry, and hurt, and dangerous, and he wants to destroy the world. But you're quite right, Robert. He's not enough for what I need. Helpful, but not perfect."

"I never wanted to destroy the world," Charley said. "Not even... I never did. I can't remember what I wrote in that diary, but that's a complete misreading."

"Is it?" Beth said. "Feel free to try to correct it. I don't care about it anymore. It's served its purpose. It's you I want, Charles."

"You tried to kill him," I said, bluntly. "Twice. Once with the Hound, once with the Jabberwock."

"Those weren't true attempts to kill him," she said. "I knew he would be too strong for that. Frankly, I was surprised that the Jabberwock managed to put him into a coma. Surprised, and most concerned. For both of us." She turned to Charley, and her voice became softer, less dismissive. "I was never going to kill you like that, Charles. I simply had to distract you until I could bring this city about."

He shook his head. "You had to distract me with Victorian monsters."

"You would have tried to stop me. Out in that world—the old world—you might have succeeded."

"So why wouldn't you kill me? Kill me, or talk to me. We saw each other most weekdays—neither would have been difficult."

She ignored the first question. "I wasn't quite ready to talk to you. It's taken me so many years to get this far. I meant to spend at least another month perfecting this city, more likely two. I must admit, too, that part of me wanted to see how good you were, even to push you to become better than you thought you could be. You're very good, Charles, but your technique still needs work."

"I helped," the diary Charley spoke up, almost defiantly. "I couldn't see through your eyes, but I could guess what you'd do sometimes. It helped."

"I saw you once." The memory struck me suddenly. Of course. I might have recognized him, even through hat and glasses, if I had had any notion that such a thing were possible. It was before Eric came to work, but even afterward, I would never have expected to see an adolescent version of my brother in the streets. "You were outside the courthouse, the day it all started. You were watching me."

Diary Charley cast a quick, guilty look at Beth. "I just wanted to see you," he said. "That's all. I just wanted to know what you looked like."

"And I made quite sure he never did it again," Beth said smoothly. I saw her jaw twitch. "It wasn't exactly this one you saw. He's been read in and out several times since then. This version is rather more pliable."

Dear God. "You really do think you can do whatever you like to these people, don't you?" I said. I didn't bother to wait for an answer, or to keep disgust out of my voice. "So you sent the Hound to attack us when Eric told you we were onto you; you sent the Jabberwock to tear up the Street when you were ready to make your final move. Didn't you care that it might mean turning the Street against you?"

"It pushed some of its inhabitants *toward* me," she said. "Fear is a wonderful recruiting tool. But I don't care about the Street. The Street was an experiment—an accident, if you prefer. Its inhabitants are literary misfits, figments of undisciplined imaginations. I've watched it grow for the last two years, and learned to factor it into my equations, but I have no desire to make an alliance with it. I gave its inhabitants that impression at times, I know. It was a lie, to keep them at bay. I've only ever cared about this city."

"I understand that," Charley said. Even now, he sounded hurt and bewildered, rather than angry. "Not all of it, but enough. I understand how you've made this place. I understand how I could be a threat to you. I think I even understand what my diary version is doing here. I just don't understand *why*. Why would you do any of this? What do you want?"

"Have you never wanted to escape into a good book, Charles?" she said.

"Often. I try not to let that book escape into downtown Wellington. Really, Beth, why? I thought we were friends."

"We were much closer than friends," she said. "We still are. We are nemeses."

Charley shook his head. "Real people don't have nemeses."

"No," Beth said. "They don't. I think it's time you stopped calling me Beth, or at least stopped thinking of me as such. There was a Beth, but I am not she—well, not really. Not entirely."

"Would you like to unpack that sentence a little?" Charley said after a brief pause.

She gave a small smile. "It might help if I told you who Beth was. Could you bear with me, if I did? It may take a while."

"I'm not going anywhere."

"No," she agreed. "You're not." She nodded at diary Charley. I saw a shadow pass over his young face briefly—it might have been pain, or just reluctance—before he turned his head sharply toward the door we had entered through. It closed over and vanished without a trace or seam.

I blinked, startled, but Charley didn't seem surprised. "You could have just locked it," he said.

"Shut up," diary Charley said. His voice was tight—with anger, I thought, until I looked a little closer, and realized how white he had become. Whatever Beth was making him do, it was draining him like a battery.

Beth paid him no attention. She was already talking to us. "Beth

White was born in 1856," she said. "The elder daughter of a Glasgow merchant. Her father was the kind of man Dickens would have loved to write about: extravagant, florid, filled with amusing quirks of depravity, and entirely worthless. Her mother was too weak to oppose him. Beth grew up in a soup of fog, near poverty, and fear."

"Who was she to you?" I asked.

Beth didn't answer directly. "When she was four, Beth began to bring things out of books. Little things, then bigger things. I'm sure it was the same with you, Charles. Her father tried to make her stop, but she loved it so much. They were an unhappy family; book characters were her friends, her playmates. When her father was drunk and unruly, she could call upon them to defend herself. Perhaps she did so one too many times. One day, when she was barely thirteen, her parents put her on a train to London and sent her away to find her own living. It was common enough practice in those days."

"Thrown away," Charley said, almost too quiet to hear. And the walls sighed around him.

"I don't know what happened to them," Beth said. "Such things were difficult to trace, in those days. I never saw them again."

"You mean Beth didn't," I said.

She nodded. "You're quite right. Thank you for the correction. Beth didn't."

"What happened to Beth then?" Charley asked.

Beth laughed. "Oh, a good deal happened to Beth then. She learned to take care of herself. She was very gifted, of course—as you are, Charles, but unlike you, nobody was rearing her for Oxford. At first she made her living on the streets, picking up what work she could. For a long time, she gave up summoning entirely; she had learned her lesson about standing up for herself, and in any case she didn't love books anymore. She didn't love anything. Her entire life was a means to an end, and that end was so very...meaningless." She shook her head, with a note of impatience. "What happened to Beth isn't important, apart from this. One day, she began to bring people out of books again. Her readings weren't particularly skilled—more feeling than scholarship—but they had a certain life that I've never been able to replicate. When they were good enough, she began using them to commit criminal acts. Nothing large scale that would attract attention—certainly not in London, that cesspit of humanity. It was profitable, to an extent, though she cared less about that than she should; for the most part it just amused her to set Daniel Quilp loose in Piccadilly and see what happened. And then, one day, she made me."

"Moriarty," Charley said. "The Napoleon of crime."

The woman who wasn't Beth smiled. "Yes. And may I say, Dr. Sutherland, that it is a dangerous habit to finger books in the pocket of one's dressing gown."

Charley looked at her for a moment, then reached into his pocket and drew out a book. It was a small paperback, well-worn. He laid it faceup on the table between us. *The Memoirs of Sherlock Holmes.*

I stared at him. "Where did that come from?"

"I had it in my bag, in the back of your car. I got it out just before we came in. It was what Eric was trying to quote: "He sits motionless, like a spider in the center of its web, but that web has a thousand radiations, and he knows well every quiver of them." It's about Moriarty. I wasn't sure—it isn't the only place to use that phrase—but I had suspicions it might be useful to have. The irony is, I only put it in there this afternoon because Beth asked me to write that essay on the criminal world of Sherlock Holmes. I was going to do it tonight."

Beth-Moriarty's smile stayed in place. "How did you know?"

"You started with the Hound of the Baskervilles. That might have been directed at me—I've talked about my early reading experiences with that book often enough, but it wasn't, was it? We wondered all along why all your readings were Victorian: Conan Doyle, Dickens, Lewis Carroll. It wasn't because of me. It wasn't because you were a Victorian specialist. It was because you were a Victorian. A Victorian university professor, well respected in your field, secretly running a ring of criminals that nobody would ever be able to trace to you..." He shrugged. "I said Conan Doyle was trying to warn the world about academics, didn't I?"

"You're quite right. I congratulate you. You're always such an intellectual treat, Charles. I say, unaffectedly, that it would be a grief to me to be forced to take any extreme measure."

I felt as though I were in yet another world again. I didn't know how much longer I could take these constantly shifting realities. "You're Professor Moriarty?"

"I was summoned forth as Professor Moriarty," Beth-Moriarty confirmed. "Yes. Beth waited a long time to do it. She encountered Moriarty in print, in the last month of 1893. Beth was thirty-six years old, bitter and angry at the entire world. Victorian London did not bend over backward to accommodate women from the poorhouse who understood the nuances of the written world. She perhaps gave in to anger too easily and without purpose, but that's understandable. I doubt you can imagine, Charles, what it is like to have all your gifts— intellectual as well as magical—and be relentlessly denied the use of every single one. That month, Sherlock Holmes died in the pages of *The Strand*, and Moriarty was the man who killed him. The allure of him, to Beth, was almost overwhelming: the man who could defeat everything that Sherlock Holmes represented. Order, empire, masculine intellect. But she held back from summoning him. Perhaps she was afraid of him, on some level. She held back as the Victorian age came to an end, and everything began to change. She held back for years. Until one night, when bombs were falling and the world seemed drawing to an end. That night, her fear and despair were great enough to overcome any fear she had of the Napoleon of crime. She wanted the old world back. She was alone, and powerless, and she summoned the most powerful creation she knew."

"The First World War," Charley said. "That's what you're talking about, isn't it? That's what you were born from. The longing for a simpler kind of evil."

"The Great War, it was called then. It sent shockwaves through the world. Certainties broke down. Stories that had already been changing were now changed forever. Dickensian sentimentality passed out of fashion; so did villains, and so did heroes. The birth of the modern world. Everything became so much more complicated."

"'Always 1895,'" Charley said.

I was still trying to keep up. "What?"

"It's a poem. About Sherlock Holmes and Dr. Watson, and 221B Street. It begins:

Here dwell together still two men of note

Who never lived and so can never die:
How very near they seem, yet how remote
That age before the world went all awry.

"That's rather sentimental, isn't it?" I heard my mouth say, as if quality of verse were an all-consuming issue at present.

"I didn't say it was a *good* poem. But it's a poem that confuses history and story. It's about longing for an age that never actually existed. Like Sherlock Holmes's London. Or Dickens's."

"Beth longed for Moriarty," Beth-Moriarty said. "She was afraid, and she reached for him. But Moriarty is a vague figure in the Sherlock Holmes canon, isn't he? All we know of him, beyond his career as an elderly professor, is that he is, as you said, the Napoleon of crime. The spider at the center of the web. A brain of the first order. A genius, a philosopher, an abstract thinker. What we think about when we think about a criminal mastermind."

"Like the Jabberwock," Charley said. "Archetypal evil. The shorthand for absolute terror."

Beth-Moriarty inclined her head. "Beth, foolish woman, invested herself in him very heavily. She had been lonely for a long time. Perhaps she thought she was in love with him. She didn't really want him. She wanted to *be* him."

"She got you instead," I said.

"She did. Her exact doppelgänger, in many ways: in appearance, in knowledge, in skills. But also Moriarty. So much more ruthless and ambitious than she knew how to be. It frightened her. She tried to put me back."

"You didn't want to go back?" Charley asked.

"There *is* no back!" Beth-Moriarty snapped. It was the first trace of anger I had seen on the mild face. "There's *nothing*. We're not summoned from anywhere. We're created, of pure thought and idea, from the words on a page. When we're dismissed, we're destroyed. We go nowhere. I had just been called into existence. I was not going to be destroyed."

"Do you know that?" Charley asked. "Truly? I've been wondering about it, and that sounds logical, but I know Millie feels—"

"Feeling doesn't matter," Beth-Moriarty said. "I am a logician, a scientist, a philosopher, and a scholar. I know the world. I know it is impossible to be taken from or put back into a book. A book is paper and words, nothing more. She was going to destroy me."

Her face rippled; for just a second, someone else looked out from behind the round face. Then it passed, and she spoke again with perfect calm.

"That is where Beth's story ends," she said. "I killed her as the bombs fell. I hid her body in the rubble, and I took over her life. It was her fault. She should not have tried to take mine."

"But you're a summoner," Charley said. "That was what confused me. Is it possible for a literary character to be a summoner as well?"

I held my breath at that, but Beth-Moriarty only smiled.

"Oh yes," she said. "They have what their reader can give them. If they're created by a summoner, and that summoner pours enough of themselves into them, there's no reason they can't inherit that particular quirk. You've seen a little of what your diary self can do. I can summon perfectly well. It served me well, over the years. I studied the burgeoning fields of literary criticism, and I honed my skills. I studied the literature of the new age, and kept my affiliation with the old to myself. Time passed by, but I never aged along with it. Times changed; when necessary, my identity changed with it. I became one of the first female professors of literature at Oxford, when it became inconspicuous to do so. I kept reading. By the turn of this century, I had a network of unreal criminals that spanned most of London. It was not enough. I did not believe I had a book to return to, as I said, but I also had no desire to live in Beth's world. Victorian London is my city; not the sordid reality of Victorian London, but the literary version, as interpreted by Sir Arthur Conan Doyle. Moriarty's world. The world of Victorian fiction. You'll understand my interest in your work."

"You read my book," Charley said. *"Dickens's Criminal Underworld.* That was when you noticed me."

"Quite. I read it three years ago. It wasn't my field, as far as the universities knew, but I retained a private interest in Victorian London. I recognized what you were at once. There's a certain style to the analysis that is very pure, very organic, yet utterly sound—Beth, without the benefit of your education, had it in her readings. You wouldn't recognize it in mine anymore. It's the mark of an immature summoner, before they learn to exert the control I've perfected over the years."

"Before you start manipulating words to your own ends, you mean."

"You would call it that. I visited your colleagues and old professors at Oxford, and what they told me about you confirmed my deductions. But, of course, they also told me you had accepted a post in New Zealand. I was fortunate the opportunity came to follow you here so quickly."

"My book was about Dickens, not Conan Doyle," Charley said.

"Yes. I've been urging you to write on Conan Doyle's criminal world, you remember, but you never have. You're meant to be writing a paper at the moment, of course. I might have waited for that, but since you told me I was likely to be disappointed..."

"Conan Doyle doesn't *have* a criminal world, not the way Dickens does," Charley insisted. I had the feeling this was an old argument, and also that this was a strange setting to be having it in. "Sherlock Holmes stories are logic puzzles: his criminals are problems that only exist to be solved. Moriarty is a product of intellect, not of Victorian social evils. Beth, I'm not just saying this as a point of academic dispute. I'm saying it because I don't think you realize what you've created here. There's a darkness in Dickens's city that isn't there in Conan Doyle's. This place is alive, and it's dangerous. There isn't a great criminal mind in control of all the evil here; evil is *everywhere*."

She ignored him. "I wasn't only trying to create this city for the years I've been here, you know. I was investigating you. This isn't only Dickens's city; it's also yours. In order to understand it, I had to understand you."

My heart skipped. In my decision that Charley shouldn't know what he was, it had, stupidly, not occurred to me until this moment that of course Beth-Moriarty might tell him.

"This doesn't matter," I said.

Beth-Moriarty looked at me, and her lips curved very slightly. I saw the world's greatest criminal mind then. It was as monstrous as I could have wished.

"I learned quite a lot from your book itself," she went on. "I learned far more from working with you in person. But there was still something missing. That was why, that day at your house with your postgraduate student, I was interested to hear of the existence of your old diaries. It was an easy matter to have them stolen; the Artful Dodger has broken into far more secure homes than yours. You just didn't seem quite *right*. Charles Sutherland, linguistic prodigy, born to Susan and Joseph Sutherland...It was just a little too simple. I found a lot, from those diaries. Finally, I found what I was looking for."

"Found what?" Charley asked.

"You aren't Susan's child," Beth-Moriarty said. "Nor Joseph's, but I'm more interested in Susan."

"Shut up!" I cut in. "I'm warning you—"

"Oh, Robert," Beth said, with a mock-fond sigh. "I found you in those diaries as well, you know. I hadn't realized your importance until then; it was why I sent Uriah Heep to watch over you, so late in the game. Hush now, though. This is strictly between people who aren't real."

"He *is* real," I said. "He's not like you."

"He's exactly like me, and I suspect you know it," Beth said. "Charles—"

"Stop it!"

"You are not Susan's child," Beth-Moriarty said. "You are her creation."

There was a silence then, so heavy that I began to understand metaphors about cutting silence with a knife. If I'd had a knife, I'd have taken it to this one.

"I don't understand," Charley said finally. It came to me, inconsequentially, that I hadn't heard him say that since he was about four.

"I think you do," Beth-Moriarty said. "I think this is the last piece snapping into place for you. You know the feeling of the last piece snapping into place well, don't you? The feeling of seeing the whole world, and knowing that it makes sense. I think you're seeing yourself for the first time, right now. You've always known you never quite made sense."

He didn't say anything.

"I didn't suspect it myself for quite some time," she said. "Your mother told you she read something out of a book once, a long time ago. When she was a child. She was punished, like Beth, and unlike Beth she stopped. I started to wonder, then, if you were not a good deal more like me than I had imagined. I reread your diaries then with a different purpose, and it began to make sense. I requested your medical records, and discovered the peculiar story behind your birth. I knew I had been right."

"You met her at Charley's place," I said. "She said you did."

"I did," Beth-Moriarty said. "And it was interesting. Nothing more. She doesn't truly come into this story. She's a mere human being, a flesh-and-blood summoner, as Beth was. Perhaps she could have been powerful in her way, but she turned her back on it. After she grew up, she came into her power once, and once only: the day her second child was born dead. She brought you to life that day. It took me a while longer to work out what she had brought you to life from. You're almost unrecognizable. You grew with Susan's gifts, and her knowledge, and you made them your own. But not all your gifts are from her. Some of them belonged to Charles Dickens. Do you really need me to tell you to whom he gave them?"

"Leave him alone," I said.

"He's been alone his entire life, Robert. He's been a creature of words in a land of flesh and blood. You know, don't you, Charles?"

She reached into her own coat. Not the pocket, it would never have fit, but the lining. From it, she drew an enormous thick hardcover. As Charley had done a moment ago, she laid it on the table faceup, almost reverently.

David Copperfield.

Charley made a tiny, convulsive noise, then swallowed.

"This is why the Street lets you through," she said. "It's why the city welcomes you—it wouldn't welcome your mother. Do you remember the first time you read Dickens? I do. You wrote about it. You said it was like finding yourself."

"Yes," he whispered. He was frighteningly still. The stillness that means he is very, very frightened. "Yes, I remember."

"It doesn't matter," I insisted. "It doesn't change anything."

Charley looked at me. The moment his eyes fell on me, I knew I had betrayed him.

"You knew," he said. It wasn't a question.

"Not for long." It sounded weak to me. "I suspected. Mum told me for certain right before this city spilled out. When you were in the hospital. So what? It doesn't matter."

"You don't mean that."

He was right. I didn't. Of course it mattered. And I know he was reading it on my face.

Charley drew a deep breath and, to my relief, finally looked away. "Oh God," he said, almost conversationally.

"If you're going to be sick," Beth-Moriarty said calmly, "please do so in the fire grate."

"I'm not."

He was, though; or at least, if he wasn't, it was out of sheer stubborn willpower. I recognized the signs. It had been my job to recognize them, a couple of decades ago, on long car trips.

"Just as you please. Some of that nausea is from overwork, of course. It isn't so much the summoning itself, though that does require a degree of pacing oneself. It's the emotional energy. You need to put less of yourself into fictional creations. Keep it simple, and intellectual. For an intelligent man, you have a remarkable lack of ability to puzzle out the simplest life skills. I've been watching you wear yourself out all week."

"That was why you sent the Jabberwock when you did, wasn't it?" I said. "He'd just collapsed. You knew he was at a low point."

"It seemed the right time to act," Beth-Moriarty said. "I had the knowledge, I had the book you stole from me, I had the diaries. I needed him out of the way for the time being; I thought he was weak enough that I could achieve that. I admit, it worked a little too well. I had no intention of killing him."

"So you said. Why not? I can't think it would trouble your conscience."

"You don't seem to understand." She looked at Charley. "Charles, I am the world's greatest criminal; you are my nemesis, as Holmes was to Conan Doyle's Moriarty. Moriarty doesn't exist without Sherlock Holmes. He's a mirror, a shadow, the underside of a very bright coin. I need you to define myself against, and vice versa. That is how literary villainy works. You are my equal, my opposite, and we are the same. We were destined to be enemies."

"You weren't destined to be anything," I said. "Real life doesn't work that way."

"But we are not real people," she said. "And this is no longer the real world. This is my world."

"And it's mine," Charley said. It was the first time he had spoken for a while. "Whatever else I am, I'm the person who wrote this world. You didn't take it from Dickens, not directly. You took it from me. My interpretation, my writing, my book. It's mine."

"Yes," she said. "It's yours as much as mine. A collaboration. And we find ourselves at the point now where we must grapple with each other for control over it, or take control of it together. Our stories, as I read them, say we must do the former. We are enemies, and must fight as enemies. If we follow my story, that of Moriarty, we will probably destroy each other."

"I thought Holmes defeats Moriarty and comes back," I said.

"Not in the first story," Charley said, without looking at me. "Conan Doyle was forced to bring Holmes back later; he was too well loved to be allowed to stay dead. But he died. It was how the story was intended to be read. He and Moriarty fall over the edge of the Reichenbach, and they die."

Beth-Moriarty nodded. "But we need not die. This may not be the real world, but neither is it *David Copperfield* nor *The Memoirs of Sherlock Holmes*. We are authors as well as characters. We write our own stories now."

"What are you suggesting?" Charley asked.

"This is *our* world," Beth-Moriarty said. "Your writing, my reading. We've made it together. Our control of it will be stronger together. You know we've worked well together in the past, Charles."

"That was before I knew you were Professor Moriarty."

"And it was before you knew you were David Copperfield."

"I'm *not* David Copperfield," he insisted. "I'm not. Maybe I began as him, but I'm not him."

"'Chapter One. I am Born. Whether I shall turn out to be the hero of my own life, or whether that station will be held by anybody else, these pages must show.'"

Charley shivered, just once. He was as pale as he'd been in the car on the way to the hospital.

"Do you remember what you wrote about those lines, once? You called them the most perfect opening lines in the history of literature.

Because they are all our opening lines. They are how our stories all begin. It was how you began."

"Stop it."

"But you're quite right. You needn't be bound to his story, just as I needn't die at the Reichenbach Falls. We're in our own story now. And it can be greater than anything dreamed of by Dickens or Conan Doyle. They were only writers, after all. We *are* the stories."

"Charley—" I started to say, and he turned.

In all my life, I had never seen Charley truly angry with me. I have now. I felt something in me curl up and die.

"Why didn't you tell me?"

"Did you want to know?" I said. "*I* didn't want to know."

"It doesn't matter what either of us wanted, Rob! I needed to know. I need to know everything. I don't need you to *protect* me."

"He needed you not to know everything," Beth-Moriarty said. "He needed you to be protected. He's needed you to be less than you are for your entire life, Charles, because you're more than him. You know that. You know you don't belong with him, and those like him. You are better than them. You are words, and thought, and memory."

"Stop telling me what I am!"

"You know what you are. And you know what Robert Sutherland is. Do you remember the day he abandoned you, when you were twelve years old?"

"Why does everyone keep talking about that day?" I snapped. "We were both young. He didn't get hurt, not really. I never did it again."

"You never had to," Beth-Moriarty said. "Nobody ever touched him again. He came into his power on that day. You did, Charles. You unleashed Sherlock Holmes upon your tormentors. You were alone, and strong, and indomitable. Then you went away and cried because your own brother hated you and you didn't fit. You had no need to. He was never your brother. You were never supposed to fit there. You were supposed to be here."

"You're just saying that because you need him to be here," I said. The realization wafted by me unexpectedly, and I grabbed it. "That's what this is about, isn't it? That's why that... thing... is here."

"Don't call me a thing," diary Charley said. "I'm not a thing."

I felt a stab of guilt, but I couldn't stop to talk to him. "You can't manage the city alone after all. It's too big for you—and you want it to grow bigger still. You've brought Charley from a diary to help— from the point where he's angry enough and scared enough to do it—but he's not powerful enough. You need the real Charley's help to stabilize it. Your copy can't manage it."

"I can!" diary Charley insisted. "I can so manage it. I just need more time."

"No, he can't," Beth-Moriarty said calmly. "I read him to be a summoner, but he hasn't been very successful. He's a limited inter-pretation of a child's diary, after all, and of course he's a child. Even were he a more detailed reading, he would be years away from the author of *Dickens's Criminal Underworld*. Rather like collaborating on a science project with a twelve-year-old Einstein: one could set him some basic background sums, but he's hardly going to crack relativity. So yes, Charles." She turned to him. "I don't *need* your help. But I do not deny I want it. Nor do I deny that if you do not either join me or stand aside, I will rain destruction down upon you and everyone you hold dear. But that is not the point. The point is what you will do. What you could be, for the first time in your life."

She was talking to Charley, but I answered. "Which is?"

"Whole," she said.

The word hit me like a blow to the stomach. Because she was right. He'd said it himself, back in the pizza place after we'd escaped Beth's house, and I hadn't wanted to listen. The Street was a part of him he'd been missing his entire life. It was part of what frustrated me so much about him when we were growing up: that he never seemed to fit in the real world. He belonged here. I could see the resem-blance between him and Beth-Moriarty, as the two of them stood there, and it was the resemblance that strangers had never been able to see between him and me.

Charley blinked suddenly, as if waking from a dream. "Wait—are you both actually waiting for me to answer?"

"I think we both are," Beth-Moriarty said.

He started to laugh, then broke off as though it hurt. "You really don't know me at all, do you? Either of you."

"Do you know yourself?" Beth-Moriarty said. "Really?"

"No," Charley said. "No, I don't. But I know you. You're *Professor*

Moriarty. I know who you are, and how your story goes. I know how Holmes replies when you make a similar offer to him. Do you really think any self-respecting Victorian scholar would do differently from Sherlock Holmes?"

Beth-Moriarty smiled tightly. "You stand fast?"

"Absolutely."

"I have no need to threaten you explicitly. As you say, you know the offer I made to Sherlock Holmes once, on paper. Here is one thing, though, with which I did not threaten Sherlock Holmes. I will kill Robert Sutherland in front of you, right here, right now, and I will paint the walls with his blood."

"Do you really think," Charley said, quite seriously, "that I would ever, ever let you do that?"

At that moment, there was a sound: a single gunshot, short and sharp. Beth-Moriarty's head whipped toward the window, as did mine. Footsteps and shouts were coming from the courtyard outside.

Charley didn't turn to look with us; he didn't need to. His eyes widened.

"Millie..." he whispered.

Millie

The occupants of the Street had gathered in the public house as the world shifted. Outside, the cobbles spasmed; buildings creaked, and the sky grew dark. They clustered together for safety. Predictably, this meant they argued.

"The new city is coming for us," Darcy One said. "That's why it appears to be traveling in a straight line down Courtenay Place. It's reaching for us. And the Street is reaching back. The road has extended a quarter mile since that great shift. It's no longer safe."

"It's no longer safe anywhere!" Millie protested. "Do be sensible, Mr. Darcy. The new city is spreading over everything. If we leave this street, we'll lose it, and any tactical advantage it might give us."

"They'll take it from us if we stay," Darcy One said. "Mr. Gray was right about that, at least."

The Witch laughed. "Then we take their new world from them first! Dorian was right about one other thing, fool though he is. This is a war of magic. We have strength of our own. Whatever the rest of you may be, I am a queen. My enemies will crumble before me."

"Your wand had no such effect against the Jabberwock," Darcy Two pointed out.

She tossed her head. "That strength came from its author. It was written to be practically invulnerable. I doubt the summoner has many more such weapons in his arsenal."

"He can have the same one back again and again, if he wants to," Matilda said sensibly. "We need Dr. Sutherland to come back."

"I'll duck outside and phone Rob," Mr. Sutherland said to Millie, in an undertone. He had been looking increasingly overwhelmed; she suspected he was glad of the excuse. "If Mr. Holmes doesn't mind getting me through the wall."

She nodded her thanks, and turned back to the others.

"There's little use in our defending the Street," Darcy One was saying. "The purpose of the Street was to give us a place to hide. A place of refuge, and secrecy. That is lost to us forever. The summoner has made sure that everybody knows we exist, and his actions have put us at war with the world. Before long, the people out there will find the Street, and they'll find us. The only prudent course of action is to withdraw and hide."

"Or," Millie countered, "to fight back."

"Fight back for what reason? This war isn't between the Street and the new world anymore. It's between the real world and the summoner. We have nothing to gain by fighting in it."

"It isn't a war yet," Millie said. "And perhaps we can prevent it from becoming one. The summoner's attentions are still focused on creating the new world. If we strike now, before the world is solid, we might have a chance. Charley might still be able to read the new world away. We might still stay secret. And even if we can't, we can jolly well save some lives. If the new world is anything like the Street, we're the only ones who can. The army, the air force—none of them will be able to cross the boundaries of reality. We can."

"We would have no chance," Darcy One said flatly. "They would kill us at once."

"The we die with honor!" the Scarlet Pimpernel declared.

"Aye," Lancelot agreed. "For once shamed may never be recovered."

"What does Mr. Dickens think?" Darcy Three spoke up. He had been quieter since his escape from unreality the night before. This was not surprising, given that day had included a Jabberwock attack and a new world arriving, but even that morning Millie had caught a faraway look on his face. Mr. Darcy did many things; he didn't characteristically dream.

Dickens considered the question carefully; one could, uncharitably, say self-importantly. For once, the pub quieted to listen. "I think," he said slowly, "that it is worth sacrifice to rid the world of a shadow. This threatens reality, and not only us. Those people out there are our readers. I think to die in their defense would be a far, far better thing than we have ever done."

"That's from *A Tale of Two Cities*," said Matilda.

"Yes," Dickens agreed. "It doesn't mean it isn't for us too."

The discussion was ongoing when Mr. Sutherland and Holmes slipped back in. Millie, seeing the looks on their faces, went to join them and Mrs. Sutherland in the corner.

"I can't get hold of either of them," Mr. Sutherland said, before she could ask. "I tried Charley's phone, when I couldn't get Rob. To be fair, Charley hardly ever answers, even when he's not in a coma. But Rob lives on his phone. And it's not just not picking up. It's coming up unavailable."

"Did you try the hospital?" Mrs. Sutherland said anxiously. "Perhaps the signal's down."

"Thought of that. I got the hospital straightaway. They're in chaos there, but they said Charley was still officially checked in."

Millie knew then. It made sense, but it wasn't just that. She knew. She thought of Darcy Three, and the connection he had explained with the other Darcys. She and Charley were creator and creation, not different incarnations of the same character, but they shared a similar connection. Experimentally, she closed her eyes, and reached out for the part of her mind that sometimes felt what Charley was feeling. It wasn't, as Darcy had said, strictly an image she received, but something came to her nonetheless. Darkness, and fear. Clouded skies, and uneven pavement underfoot. The Street, but not the Street. It turned her stomach.

She opened her eyes and saw Holmes looking at her.

"He's gone in, hasn't he?" she said. "Into the new world."

Holmes nodded. "I believe so. In fact, given the evidence, I would strongly suspect they both have."

Millie found it difficult to swear—it went against all her Jacqueline Blaine vocabulary. But she felt she could have managed at that moment.

"Why would he do that?" she demanded, exasperated.

"What do you mean?" the Scarlet Pimpernel called from the counter. He had unfortunately sharp hearing. "Who's gone?"

"There is no other place where he can go," Dickens answered Millie.

He had obviously overheard too. "I am an author, Miss Radcliffe-Dix. I understand his story. The only way it can be brought to conclusion is for the two of them to meet."

Dickens had misunderstood her question. Millie knew perfectly well that Charley had to go. She had been asking why he had not taken her with him. It was her fight as well. They were one and the same, him and the Street and herself and the summoner. They were part of the same world, and they had been made part of the same war.

She might have been willing to follow him right then. But it was the Artful Dodger who, in the end, pushed her to make the final step. He came at that moment, hurtling himself through the door with such force that he almost knocked over the Duke of Wellington. Darcy Five caught him securely as Millie hurried over to them.

"What happened?"

"What do we care for what happened?" the Witch demanded. Her wand was already pointed at the urchin's head. "Hold still, traitor!"

"No, wait," Millie ordered. Up close she could see that he looked ashen and trembling. For him to come running back to the street he'd half destroyed, something terrible must have been close behind him. "Dodger, what is it? Where are the others?"

"He took them," the Artful said. His voice was smaller and younger than she'd ever heard it. "My master. The summoner. He just read them away."

"Into their books?"

He shook his head. "He put them in a room. He told them to wait there a moment. Then he locked the door from the outside, and he read the room away. I don't know where they are. They're just... gone."

Millie's breath caught. She thought of the tunnel under the sea, that night less than a week ago, and the hand reaching from its depths. "Dorian?" she heard herself ask. "Did he escape?"

The Artful shook his head. "He went in last. He looked at the summoner, and then he closed the door behind himself. It was as though he was daring him to do it."

"But they were going to join him," Darcy Five said, as if the Artful needed to be reminded. He'd been with them. "Or her, if Mr. Holmes is correct. Dorian and the others were going to help the summoner."

"He didn't need them," the Artful said. "He doesn't need any of you. I thought he did, I swear. I thought he wanted—I knew he had people of his own, people who weren't real people, just as blank as he could make them. But I thought those were just the tools he was using to bring the new world about. I thought there'd be a place for other characters there. I thought—"

"You thought there'd be a place for you there," Millie finished.

The Artful sniffed. "I thought I was different. He made me to be like you lot, to fool you, and I thought you were different. But you aren't, not to him. We're all just tools. And you lot—Dorian's lot—are just tools with minds of your own, ones he can't use. The new world isn't for us. It's not for anybody but him."

Millie stood still for a moment. The Street stood still, too, around her.

Like tools, Rob had said. Or portable devices. Taken out and put back as needed. But it was worse than that this time. Beth—or whoever she was—could bring her own interpretations out again and again—maybe not quite the same, but continuous, nevertheless. She could never bring back Dorian and the others, not as they were. They were gone. It didn't matter where; that was a question that might never be answered. They would never be here again.

The part of her that belonged to words, to adventures and smugglers' caves and eternal summer, was very strong now. Out the window, the butterfly spies—the ones from *Aesop's Fables*—were fluttering about the rubble. They were blue with white tips on their wings. In the streetlight, it looked unexpectedly beautiful.

"Everyone who wants to leave," she said, and marveled at the calm in her own voice, "can leave now. If you head out of town, as fast and as far as you can, you might escape all this. I promise, I understand. But those who want to follow me, I'm going into the city."

"It might be a trap," Darcy One warned. "To lure us in."

"I don't care," she said. "As far as I'm concerned, we are at war."

Scheherazade rarely spoke at these kind of gatherings, though her dark eyes followed every word. She did so now, in her lilting English. "I think," she said, "it's time for a story of our own."

"What about Dr. Sutherland?" Matilda asked.

"We'll meet him there," Millie said.

Susan Sutherland stepped forward. Her chin had the determined tilt that Charley's had at times. "And in the meantime," she said, "you have me. I don't know what I can do now, but I was born a summoner. I'll do what I can."

The roar of a motorcycle engine greeted her words. Turning, Millie was just in time to see the silver Harley pull up outside the open door, the Witch astride it. Her hair gleamed black in the lamplight, and her skin was pale as ice.

"If anybody intends to come with me into battle," she said haughtily, "I might even deign to let them ride on the back. But they had better earn such a privilege."

Heathcliff's knife-gun was strapped to his belt. Millie took it in his name. Other than that, they had few weapons. The Scarlet Pimpernel and Lancelot had their swords, and it turned out the Artful had been stashing a good few knives and shotguns in the Old Curiosity Shop that Millie would have certainly made him dispose of if she had known about them. The Witch had her wand; Matilda had her powers. Many of them would be without weaponry at all. But somehow, one by one, they all agreed to follow her.

Cuba Street was deserted in the evening. The sounds of sirens wailing and shouts drifted down the redbrick footpath. As Millie strode out of the alleyway at the head of her army, though, a green-and-white kererū drifted in on the breeze. It carried the last of the sunlight on its wings.

"Stop," Millie said. They waited as Maui lit on the ground, shook off his feathers, and stood. The jawbone clutched in his fist gleamed white.

"I thought you weren't coming," he said.

"We had to decide if it was our fight too," she said. "Have you come to stand by us?"

"It's my land," he said. "But I might let you stand by me."

"Thanks," she said. "I think there's room for all sorts of stories in this."

There were policemen at the barricades when they went to meet the city. They saw them, and tried to stop them. But the dark fog reached out to welcome them, and they entered its embrace. The time for secrecy was over.

At the gates of the crumbling house at the heart of the city, Millie stood at the head of her army as Maui flew in pigeon form overhead. They looked back at her: gentlemen and knights, witches and urchins, Victorian spinsters and powerful children. The keeper of a thousand and one stories. Charles Dickens. Sherlock Holmes. And the parents of Robert and Charles Sutherland, whose children were in there and, not incidentally, one of whom was a summoner. Those two looked rather lost and bedraggled, the only real people in a world of fiction.

"Are you ready for this?" she asked them, in an undertone.

"I don't think we could be," Joseph said, but dryly. "Only a few hours ago I was gardening. We haven't even had dinner."

"I'm ready," Susan said. "But I don't know what I can do."

"You're a summoner," Millie said. "Something will come to you."

"I said that before we came in. But now that we're here...I haven't read anything out of a book in twenty-six years."

"You hadn't for some years before that," Millie reminded her. "And you created Charles Sutherland."

Surprise flickered across her face, but below the surface. There was too much else going on. "You know about that?"

"Dorian told me. It was his job to know things."

"I never knew how I did it, though. It was just an uncontrolled rush of grief, and decades of suppressed magic came out at once."

"You have decades of suppressed magic locked up in you again," Millie said. "And your sons are in danger. I rather suspect you'll feel a rush of something."

Maui lit on the gate above her head. "The place is locked up," he said. "There might be a way in the back. Where's your summoner?"

"He's in there," Millie said, without needing to check. The connection between them was very strong at that moment.

"He is," Susan agreed. "I can feel him there too. I can do that, sometimes, with him. I've always wondered if that was real magic, or just my imagination."

"It's both," Millie said. She closed her eyes, and concentrated, the way she had seen Darcy Three do on request. She saw a dark room, and the face of a woman. A light glowed; when she opened her eyes and looked up, she saw that same light burning in the window.

"There are few ways we could get in without their seeing us," Maui said. "We could take them by surprise."

"There's no time," Millie said. She could feel that too.

"In that case," Maui said, "just break the gate down."

Millie didn't wait any longer. She aimed Heathcliff's knife-gun at the lock on the gate, and fired.

The shot would draw the attention of anyone inside; they would be thrown into open assault. But that, to be honest, was all she reasonably expected from the entire venture. There was very little any of them could do to Beth. Charley would have to do it. Their attack, if it did anything, would have to be to buy him time and space to act. Making noise and trouble was a battle plan in itself under those circumstances—though she hoped other plans would unfold in due course. The Duke of Wellington was with them, for goodness' sake. And Charles Dickens, though he had no experience in war, had a good deal of experience in plotting.

Against odds, the shot hit the lock, and when she rattled the gate, it began to give. It seemed that only the long wooden planks nailed across it were left to hold it closed, and they were rotting. The whole city was rotting, as far as she could tell. This was nobody's new world.

"Come on, chaps," she called. Her voice was fierce and jaunty; that of the girl adventuress despised by critics and loved by children who should have been doing their math homework. "Let's get this down. When we do, fan out into the courtyard, and hold your ground. Make them come out to us."

"Watch the windows," Wellington advised. "Good position for riflemen to fire from a distance."

"Those with weapons share with those that don't," Millie added, "and if you have any bizarrely literal metaphorical traits that might come in handy, this would be an excellent time to use them."

The doors to the house opened as the gates came crumbling down.

XXVIII

The noise outside was getting louder. It sounded as though an army had arrived; knowing Millie, it wouldn't have surprised me one bit if one had.

Beth-Moriarty was still looking out the window, her gray eyes hardening. I, stupidly, was still doing the same, although from where I stood I could see nothing but the sky and rows of chimneys.

"Should I kill him now?" diary Charley's voice came. He didn't care about Millie. He wasn't built to. He only wanted to please, and to destroy. "You said that—"

Beth-Moriarty never looked his way. "Go ahead," she said. I didn't realize, until he attacked, that they meant me.

I felt the floor rock under me, and then a burst of searing heat. My muscles reacted, the way reflex kicks in when your hand gets too near a hot stove. I flinched away. The chair behind me went up in flames.

I didn't have time to say anything, or even to feel. But I looked to diary Charley, instinctively, and I remember the shock of the expression on his face. I had seen naked hatred like that only once before, and that was on the face of Uriah Heep.

The next burst rippled the entire room. It was more luck than skill that I fell to the ground as a second ball of fire flew. I felt the heat over my head, and on the back of my neck.

"Stop it!" I heard Charley's voice snap; the real Charley, who was actually no more real than anyone here. The room twisted dizzily around me; then, at once, the fire retreated. I heard a terrible scream, a cry of agony and loss that went to my heart like a knife. When I looked up, diary Charley was enveloped in flame. Fire rose almost to the ceiling. His tiny form was lost in a mass of hungry orange light.

I could only stare, horrified. Charley, for once in his life, moved quickly; or perhaps, not unusually, he thought quickly. All at once, there was a door set in the floor. I recognized it: the green-painted wood, entwined with ivy that looked even more peculiar growing from the floorboards. The *Secret Garden* door.

Charley lunged forward, grabbed the paperback from the table, and wrenched the door open.

"Quick!" he said to me. "Jump!"

I understood what Charley had meant, that day last weekend when he'd said that if he stopped to think about breaking and entering, he wouldn't act. I couldn't stop to think about this. As Beth moved forward, I sat down, swung my legs over the new opening in the floor, and jumped.

I know, because I measured during a fit of early-home-ownership DIY, that the height from the floor to the ceiling of my house is eight feet. The ceilings of old Victorian mansions are much higher. Until that point, I'd forgotten the bruises from the Jabberwock earlier today; as I hit the ground, the wooden floor reminded me, forcibly. My vision flared white. The air shot from my lungs. I couldn't breathe. My chest burned, and I fought to subdue panic as I gasped. I knew, from my experience playing high school rugby, that I would draw breath again soon, but I hadn't had the world's greatest criminal mind trying to kill me on that particular rugby field. For a moment, everything just hurt.

You can't do this, something in my head whispered treacherously. It's too hard.

Then my chest spasmed, air flooded back, and I sat up, still gasping. Everything still hurt, but it was no longer the only thing on my mind.

"Charley!" I snapped, almost before I could.

He was still dazed, but his face cleared at the sound of his name. He caught his breath sharply, and looked up at the door in the ceiling. I could see it as a rectangular hole, through which the orange glow of flames was burning. Almost at once, it vanished.

The room was very dim, and quiet but for the sound of our ragged breathing. From the other side of the wall, I could hear shouts and footsteps. The ceiling was streaked with ash.

"Are you okay?" I asked Charley.

He nodded, and winced. "Ow. Yes. Yes, I'm fine. Just—you know, fell through a floor."

"Know the feeling." Beth-Moriarty could follow, of course, at any time. I had no idea why she hadn't. Maybe she thought we'd both broken our necks. Maybe, judging from the noise outside, she was distracted by other things.

Things like fire raging, and the child she was using to keep this world together transformed into a pillar of flame.

"Is... Did you kill him?" I asked Charley. I didn't need to clarify whom I meant, and he didn't pretend to ask.

"I think so," he said. "I didn't mean to. I thought he'd stop me. I just wanted..." He shook his head. "No. I was going to say that I just wanted to stop him from killing you. That's not true. I wanted him to go away. I wanted to burn him up, the way I always meant to burn that diary entry. But I didn't mean it to be like that."

I felt a shiver. "What did you *do*?"

"He read the fire that burns up Satis House, the fire that destroys Miss Havisham. He flung it at you. I just read him as the Miss Havisham of this house. The parallel works: it's his house. He's the one living in a frozen moment, trapped in a memory of a betrayal, who creates weapons to wreak vengeance. And so he burned, just as Miss Havisham did in the novel. Though I suppose in this case he's also Estella. The weapon without a heart. The—" He took a deep breath. "I didn't mean it to be like that."

I didn't know what to say.

"Good job with the door," I said finally, in that effusive way I have.

"It's easier in here." Understandably, he sounded distracted. "This reality's more malleable."

"Couldn't you have made the floor softer?"

"I think I did," he said. "Or we probably would have both broken every bone in our bodies."

"Softer still next time, okay? Let's not break any." My ankle was throbbing fiercely. If it wasn't broken, I at least wasn't going to be running any half marathons anytime soon.

As we got to our feet, Charley's eyes widened suddenly at something over my shoulder. "Oh..."

I turned, my heart quickening. At first, I saw only what I expected to see: a rotten, moth-eaten sitting room, with floral sofas and cob-webs. A broken chandelier hung from the ceiling, and a pile of old clothes moldered on the floor.

I looked again. It wasn't a pile of clothes. It was a man, his eyes wrapped in a blindfold, curled up only a few feet away. I'd never seen a dead person before, but I'd seen enough crime-scene photos at work to recognize that this one was indeed dead. His throat had been cut. I remembered the dark, sticky feel of the floor beneath me, and recognized the iron tang of blood in the air.

"It's David Copperfield again, isn't it?" I asked.

Charley shook his head, too briskly. "I don't know."

"Yes, you do," I corrected him.

I approached the dead man carefully. It wasn't as horrible as it might have been. The blindfold over his face obscured most of his features. Apart from the wound at his throat, he looked almost peaceful, as if death had come as a release. His hands and feet were bound, so perhaps it had. Something about the dark, tousled hair looked familiar.

Oh.

My breath caught. I understood why Charley was trying so hard, for the first time in his life, not to think.

"He's here because of you, isn't he?" I said slowly. "He's here because he *is* you."

"I think so," Charley said. The words seemed to hurt.

"That's why you could sense him through the door that night. You didn't read him out. You were read from the same character. He's the Eric to your Uriah Heep. That's why he lived his life blindfolded, and in the dark: so you couldn't see through him."

Charley nodded tightly. "But I wasn't blindfolded."

For a moment, I didn't know what he meant. Then I did. "He was here to watch you. The way Uriah Heep could watch Eric, through his own eyes. Because—"

"Because I am David Copperfield," Charley finished. "Yes. The monster in the cellar. The secret at the heart of the new world. That's how she knew where the book was for the Artful to steal."

"That's how she knew you were on your way to her right now too. And, when she knew you were here, she slit his throat."

She hadn't even bothered to read him away—too much effort,

probably, with everything else going on. Like turning off a device that was no longer needed. Only with more blood.

"'David Copperfield as Narrator,'" Charley said.

"What?"

"It's a lecture I give in my third-year course." He took a deep breath. "Um."

As I said, it used to be my job on long car journeys to watch for the signs. I wasn't surprised when he ducked quickly behind the moldy sofa, and I heard the harsh, painful sound of him throwing up again and again. Nor could I blame him. I felt my own stomach churn.

The sounds of gunfire and shouts from outside were growing louder. I bent down by David Copperfield, removed the blindfold, and closed the staring dark eyes that were far too familiar. He was still warm to the touch, but barely.

This was who Charley was. As much as he was the child upstairs—more, perhaps—he was this. Maybe I really couldn't do this after all.

When Charley emerged, he was shaking, and deathly pale. That seemed to be his near-permanent state today.

"I'm sorry," he said.

"It's all right," I replied. I should, of course, have said much more.

He took another breath, and ran his hand through his hair. "Okay. We need to find Beth again, and we need to find her fast. Once she gets into that battle, the damage she'll inflict will be catastrophic."

"She'll kill you," I said. "She'll kill everyone."

"I think—if I can get there, just close enough to see her, I should be able to read Beth back into Moriarty. The textual Moriarty, or at least my reading of Moriarty. Exactly as I did to the Hound, and the Jabberwock. And then I should be able to read her—him—back into the book. If I can do that—"

My heart jumped. "Seriously? You can just get rid of her?"

"I can try. I have to. And then I can take control of the city. It's mine as well. I can make it all go away."

"All of it?"

"Yes." He said it very quietly; then he raised his head and his voice. "Yes, all of it. I promise."

"All right then." I hesitated. My hopes had soared a moment ago.

Now I felt uneasy. Something was going on in his head, but I didn't know what it was. "Charley—about what Beth said—"

"Let's not talk about that," he interrupted. "We don't have to. I understand why you didn't tell me; I shouldn't have been angry. It's fine. All of it."

It wasn't, of course. It was the opposite of fine. But we didn't have the time, and I at least didn't have the words.

Charley opened another garden door, onto the stairwell; this one, we left swinging behind us. The tiny patch of Edwardian children's literature looked oddly beautiful in the shabby Victorian Gothic.

The room from which we had fallen was deserted when we ventured up the stairs—deserted, and devastated. The walls were blackened and scorched; the floor was now half-wooden and half-hard-granite. The ghost of cruel childish laughter danced around its edges, so faint it sounded like a sigh. The place could have been gutted and abandoned for years. The sounds of the battle below—it really was a battle now—drifted in from the wide-open window.

The body curled up in the center of the room was smaller than David Copperfield's had been, and less recognizable as a human being. Nonetheless, this time I saw it at once. The damage all radiated from it. It lay in a clear circle of concrete surrounded by ashes, like a macabre fairy ring.

"Charley..." I said. I was speaking to my brother, not the diary creature, but to my surprise the body in the circle twitched slightly in recognition. He was alive.

"I know," Charley said. He kept his distance. "Beth's done with him. She'd nearly exhausted him anyway. If she wants to use him again, she'll just read another one out."

I bent down by his side, wincing as my bruises protested. He *was* alive, but I saw at once that he wouldn't be so for long. His eyes were closed; that one twitch and the slow rasp of his breathing were the only indications that he was still with us. He was burnt almost beyond recognition. Parts of his face and hands no longer had the texture of flesh but of charred paper. I didn't want to touch him in case he crumbled into ash. I didn't, if I were truly honest, want to touch him anyway. I was afraid to.

If you have difficulty believing your brother isn't real, try seeing him dead or dying in two vastly different forms, as two vastly different people, while he's standing behind you both times as the person you grew up with. And then try to tell yourself it isn't killing you inside.

"Send him back," I heard myself say. "Quickly."

"I don't have his book," Charley said. He still hadn't come forward. "Beth does, somewhere."

"So? It's your book. It's your diary."

"From fourteen years ago! I don't remember what I wrote."

"Of course you do," I said. "You remember words, especially important ones. And I have a feeling those ones are seared into your brain."

He sighed, and didn't deny it. "He wouldn't thank me. He doesn't want to go back. I don't blame him. I would rather die here than go back into that moment—assuming there's even anything to go back to."

"He's twelve. He doesn't get to choose."

"Yes. He does. He's twelve, and he's not real, and he's nothing but anger and fear, but unless he's a danger, he still gets to choose. He's no danger to anyone at the moment."

I bit back my instinctive retort, because I knew it would be the wrong one. "Okay," I allowed. "You may be right, in principle. But he can't choose. He's dying. You can't know what he'd want, or if he'd be right to want it. So save him. Just in case."

"I really don't think I can. I don't understand him. I never understood him."

"Try."

Charley sighed again, but he bent down next to me. The diary Charley stirred again as his older self laid his hand gently on his shoulder, and he made one tiny sound, somewhere between a whimper and a moan.

"It's okay," I said to the child, on reflex. I nearly reached out and touched him then, but restrained myself; I didn't know how that would affect him going back. "You're okay."

His eyes opened slowly, just a little, so I could see the glimmer beneath his eyelashes. He tried to speak, but his voice was gone. I don't know what he wanted to say.

"It's okay," I said again. "It'll be over in a minute."

It was. The broken child gave one shiver, then his eyes closed with a long, tired sigh. Charley blinked, and sat back on his heels.

"I'm sorry," he said. "I tried. I couldn't do it."

I looked at the tiny figure. I couldn't seem to feel anything at all, except that someone had grabbed my chest and was squeezing very hard. "He's dead?"

"I set him on fire, Rob. The fire that killed Miss Havisham. Yes, he's dead."

In that same moment, the city rocked. The floor shuddered as if struck by an earthquake; the sun flickered like a light bulb; the skies above screamed. I put my hand to the ground quickly to stay upright, and felt it quiver beneath my palm.

"What the—?"

"I told you, he's gone," Charley said. Once again, I couldn't read the expression on his face. "Part of the city was being created by him. It's all Beth's now. And mine, if I can take it back. She'll be struggling to hold it without his help."

I reached out and touched the shoulder of the diary Charley. He didn't crumble into paper. He was warm and substantial, and I wished I had touched him earlier, so he wouldn't have spent the last seconds of his life utterly alone. I wished I had caught him that day at the courthouse, when I'd felt his eyes asking for my help. I wished a lot of things. My eyes were hot then, and I blinked and quickly looked away. He deserved better than that, I know. There wasn't time.

"Why has Beth just left us?" I asked. I stood, and limped over to the window. The streets were darker now, and the sound of shots was like thunder in the sky. The courtyard was spilling with people. They had broken down the barred gate, and were running forward to crouch behind the old beer barrels and gravestones spotting the ground. (I have no idea why there were gravestones, or even if they had been there when we crossed the yard. It seemed to make sense at the time, and still does.)

The Witch's motorcycle was at the head of the charge; she stood in the saddle, teeth bared, dark hair streaming like a comet behind her. The Scarlet Pimpernel sat behind her, raising his rapier high. Beth's creations were coming out of the house to meet them: the same blank-eyed criminals we had seen in the streets, weapons of their own in hand. The Witch pointed her wand at a burly, square-jawed man, and he turned to stone as he raised a pistol. It didn't matter. There were more of the same man, piling out behind him.

Somewhere beneath it all, I realized with a stab, were the lights of Courtenay Place, with its partygoers and commuters and diners. And Lydia. Somewhere, beneath all this, was Lydia.

"She thinks that if she sends men to take us, she's likely to lose them," Charley said, answering the question I'd almost forgotten I'd asked. "They'll be read away by me, or altered beyond use. I'll do my best, at least. And if she comes herself, I'll try exactly what I want to try now. She knows that. She was ready for it before Millie came and interrupted. Now she's just hoping we'll wait it out, and let her fight this battle before our war begins."

He joined me by the window. He was limping too, though he scarcely seemed to notice. His face was pale, and utterly remote. I wondered in that moment how I could have ever missed that he wasn't real.

"Is Millie there?" he asked. "Can you see her?"

I squinted through the dark and the rain that was beginning to fall. It only took me a moment.

"There," I said, pointing. "There by the oak tree. Holmes and Dickens are with her."

She was pressed against a tree, her head turned to shout something to Dickens, a pistol in her hand. I wondered where she had found it, and if she knew how to use it. It wasn't the sort of thing one learned in a Millie Radcliffe-Dix Adventure, or in urban New Zealand, but I wouldn't put anything past her. She stood next to a slight, muscled Polynesian man with a weapon made of curved bone in his hand—a man I recognized immediately. Not for the first time that day, I felt I spike of pure, perfect wonder.

It only lasted a moment. Something else caught my eye.

"Charley," I said suddenly. "There's Beth."

"Where?" he said, then followed my finger. "Yes, I see her!"

Beth-Moriarty had just entered the field. Her people fanned out in front of her, crouching behind armored shields and the kind of assault rifles I was surprised to see until I remembered the action thrillers I'd found in her basement. She, sheltered by them, looked as though she were going for a stroll in the Botanic Gardens. Her hair was crisp, and her cardigan was in place. Her hands were empty of weapons. Instead, they held a stack of books.

"Oh God," Charley said, a second before I too realized what was about to happen.

I didn't see the title of the book she opened, but I know what it was. I know because I saw Sherlock Holmes disappear. One moment, he was at front of the line near Millie, a revolver in his hand and every long limb wired for attack. The next, he was gone. There was barely a chance for him to falter, flicker, and look toward the wall of characters behind which hid Professor Moriarty; though I'm sure that he did, and that he recognized the feel of his own nemesis taking possession of him and throwing him away. He was simply gone.

Beth threw his book to the ground, and opened the next.

"He's not dead," Charley said. "She's just sent him away. I can bring him back."

"Holmes, perhaps," I said. "Dickens too; perhaps Millie, in some shape or form. They're yours. Not the others. If she keeps going, you won't be able to save them."

"No." He shook his head. "She did that in *seconds*. It took me ages to reread the Jabberwock to the point where I could send it back— and that was just from a poem."

"She's been reading a very long time. But you read the Jabberwock back in the end. You can read her back too."

I'd hoped to remind him why we were here; it worked. New resolve flushed into his face. "Give me a second."

He had the paperback in his hand, but he didn't open it; just held it, loosely, like a touchstone. His eyes were fixed on something very far away; his voice, when it came, was a whisper almost too quick to be heard over the gunfire.

"'It is with a heavy heart that I take up my pen to write these the last words in which I shall ever record the singular gifts by which my friend Mr. Sherlock Holmes was distinguished...'"

I looked out the window again. Beth had paused in her reading away, and new people were materializing. These were harder, meaner—and less human. I didn't recognize the characters, if they were indeed named characters, but I recognized their type: gargoyles, gremlins, goblins. A horde of flying monkeys rose from what must have been *The Wizard of Oz*. They grabbed Lancelot, lifted him in the air, and dropped him like a stone. He flailed with his sword as he fell.

"Look out!" I called—uselessly, on instinct. The instant before he hit the ground, he stopped; suddenly, with a snap that must have wrenched his back, but he stopped. Matilda was standing a few feet away from him, her eyes wide and her face pale. She lowered him gently to the ground—ignoring, to my horror, the tall, cloaked figure approaching who could only have been Count Dracula.

I didn't have time to call out this time, even instinctually. With a high, fierce war cry that carried over the battle, the man wielding the bone leaped in the air. Between one second and the next, he was an eagle, beak and claws poised to tear. He descended on the vampire like a bolt from the sun. I saw them go down, and lost sight of them in the rush.

"You really need to hurry up," I said to Charley.

He ignored me, and kept his focus on the book. He wasn't reading the story, exactly. His voice leaped from line to line as though skipping stones.

"'—the recent letters in which Colonel James Moriarty defends the memory of his brother, and I have no choice but to lay the facts before the public exactly as they occurred. I alone know the absolute truth of the matter—'"

"I didn't know Moriarty had a brother," I said, startled.

"Rob, please, I'm trying to do a reading. I'd really appreciate it if you didn't—"

"Okay, point taken. Carry on."

The courtyard was filling up with statues as the Witch circled; the Scarlet Pimpernel held the handlebars now, and she stood on the back like a Roman charioteer. Matilda, now with a cut across her cheek, hurled the statues toward Beth; her living shield took the blows. The Darcys moved across the battlefield as one, canes in their hands. The eagle soared, swooped, claws scattering blood. Distorted monsters sprang out of the air near Beth's head, howling and snarling. Beth-Moriarty stood as she had before, before the chaos, another book opened in her hands. She raised a hand to turn a page.

And then, so briefly that I almost missed it, I saw her change. As the Jabberwock had a few hours ago, she flickered, her shape morphing into something taller and thinner before snapping back to her more usual form. My heart gave a leap.

"I think it's working," I said.

"Moriarty's so complicated," Charley muttered, more to himself than to me. "So many cultural connotations beyond his actual function in the text. Doyle really just created him to kill off Holmes so he wouldn't have to write any more stories…"

Suddenly, he gasped; a sharp, painful gasp, as though he'd been surprised by a dagger. He stumbled forward, dropping the book, and caught himself against the window ledge. I looked at him and then out at the courtyard. Beth's head was raised to look directly at our window. It may have been my imagination, or it may have been a metaphor, but I felt the force of her gray eyes strike us.

"What is it?" I said to Charley.

"I don't know," he said tightly. "She's doing something."

"She's looking at you now."

"I know." He winced, and his hands tightened on the window ledge. "Okay. That hurts. Never mind. I just need to—"

"Look, calm down," I said, because I could see him starting to panic. "What's happening? She's not flickering anymore."

"No. I've lost it. It's not working."

"Is it because you're not close enough?"

"I don't—no. No, it was working before. She was changing. I could feel it working."

"So why won't it work now?"

"I don't know!" His voice raised. "I really don't! I don't know how I ever made it work in the first place."

The city was definitely growing darker. Outside, the buildings creaked and grumbled as if a step away from prizing themselves free and walking toward us. Something stirred beneath the ground.

The darkness at the heart of the Dickensian world. It was just an expression. No, it was an idea, set down in words. And here, that was everything.

"If you can't take her," I said, "can you take the world back from her, somehow? Reread it into something a little more safe?"

He didn't answer.

"You love Dickens. You don't read it like this. I've met your Dickens—I know you don't. So what part of your book has Beth ignored? What offsets the darkness?"

"What?" he said distractedly. He shivered, and made an extreme effort to collect himself. "Um...I don't know. I can't..."

"Think!"

"I *can't*! I don't know why, I—it's just not there. The city won't listen to me anymore."

I looked out at Beth-Moriarty, at her eyes fixed on the window. A horrible conviction settled over me.

"I think she's reimagining *you*," I said. "Just a little, maybe, but..."

"I think she is too," he said. "I can feel it. She's trying to make me into David Copperfield, just as I'm trying to make her into Moriarty. David Copperfield didn't write Charles Sutherland's book, and he can't summon. He's not a threat to her."

"Okay. So don't be him. Stop focusing on Moriarty for a moment, or Dickens. You need to focus on who you are."

"I can't," he said. "I have no idea who I am. Not anymore."

I knew what he meant. I had no idea who he was either. I'd seen him in too many different forms, in too many different lights. I was one to criticize him for never living more than half in the real world. It seemed to me in that moment that Charley had always been more than half a dream figure to me.

"You're a reader," I said. It was all I could think to say. "A summoner. Hold on to that."

"I'm trying," he said. "I don't think that's enough. I can't keep that and lose everything else, it doesn't work like—" He broke off with a gasp, and doubled over. Suddenly, horribly, he flickered and distorted as the Jabberwock had done in the Street. It only lasted a second, then he was back, straightening, his face white with pain and effort. But it was obvious what was happening.

"She's reading you right back into your—into *David Copperfield*, isn't she?" I said. "The book, not just the character."

He nodded tightly.

"Okay," I repeated. I tried to sound as calm as I could. "You really need to fight back, or you're going to be reinterpreted out of existence."

"I *am* fighting back," he said, through gritted teeth. "I really am.

I'm trying to hold on to who I am, but it's not like finding an interpretation of a character in a story. I can't—don't!"

He'd flickered again, and I'd lunged forward to grab him instinctively before he stumbled. He wrenched himself backward out of my reach, his image solidifying briefly as he did so.

"Don't touch me. I don't know what would happen to you if I go when you're in contact with me."

"Nothing's going to happen," I said firmly. "I'm not going into a book. I can't. I'm real."

"I pulled you through the crack in the wall to the Street. I pulled you into a cloud to bring you here. I don't know where the boundaries are anymore."

"Nothing's going to happen because you're not going anywhere," I said. "Come on. You said that we're all stories."

"When?"

"In your book. This book. The one we're practically living in. It's in the conclusion."

"You said you hadn't read it."

"I might have been lying about that."

He looked at me in disbelief, then laughed a little. The laugh was strained, but it was genuine. "You're horrible."

"That's right. But you still said it. You must have believed it. So what does it matter if you started out as a story too?"

"I was eighteen, up all night and very highly caffeinated when I wrote that conclusion. It's more emotion than criticism. Besides—my story's a lie. I don't know what's true anymore. It's not that I'm upset about it; it's just a fact. An intellectual problem. I don't *understand*. You have to understand a story to interpret it. I don't know who I am."

"That's rubbish," I said to him firmly. "You're Dr. Charles Sutherland."

"And how am I supposed to believe that, when the reason I *need* so urgently to believe it is that I'm *not*? If I were Dr. Charles Sutherland, I'd be real. No reader in the world could make me otherwise. Beth can only read me into what I actually—" He flickered again. It lasted longer this time, and his sharp intake of breath dissolved into a cry of agony.

"Charley?"

His image phased wildly in and out of focus, then settled. "I'm here, I'm still here," he said, but faintly. His face was streaked with tears. "God, that hurts."

"I know." I didn't, obviously, but I could imagine. As Dad said, Charley is a lot tougher than he looks. If he says something hurts, it really does. "But—look, that's because it's wrong, isn't it? It's because you're not hers to read."

"It's because I don't want to be sent away." Of course, he had to be right and I had to be wrong, even now. Even about this. "Not like this. I know how Uriah felt now; I'm so sorry I did this to him; I didn't realize. I don't care if there's a book to go into or not. I don't want to leave. I want to stay here."

The ripple came again, and took him. This time, he didn't manage to hold it back for more than a few seconds. He screamed.

For just a moment, a fraction of a second, the wavering form that had been Charley shrunk to nothing. Through the fractured light, I glimpsed a tiny, swaddled bundle. I thought I had felt sick before; now, I felt bile rise in my throat.

Because obviously, Beth wasn't trying to read him into the strong, capable Dickens David Copperfield who had materialized in Charley's hospital room. That wasn't what he had been read from. She was trying to read him back to the beginning, to the infant who had been born, as he had been informed and believed, on a Friday, and had cried as the clock struck twelve. He was going to be undone to the very first moment of his birth, and then he was going to disappear back into a book or nothingness or whatever there was for fictional characters outside this world. He was right, it didn't matter. He would be gone.

And then he was back, sunk to the ground, shuddering, his jaw set in determination. He was faint around the edges, and his skin had the translucency of ice, but he was still there.

There had to be something I could do. I'd come to protect him. It couldn't be true that now, at the crisis, all I could do was watch.

Outside, a scream came as someone was hit—by bullets, by fire, by magic. It was one of ours. Moriarty's people wouldn't scream. They would die without a sound, and they would kill without a sound. And they would kill everyone. It didn't matter how brave Millie was, or how clever. When Moriarty was finished with Charley, she would destroy them all with a thought.

I heard a roar.

I turned to the window in time to see the sky shatter with light: the white light that brought a character into the world, or took it away again. This time, it brought a dragon. It filled the sky, furious and terrible. Red, knobbly skin, smoky black wings, fierce orange eyes that blazed fire. It opened its jaws, and the roar came forth again. The entire city quivered.

There were a lot of places a dragon could have come from. They're the oldest stories; possibly they're older than story. *Beowulf* had a dragon, Norse sagas had dragons; they were part of Chinese legend and medieval folktales. But I knew this dragon. It didn't come from legend, and it didn't come from Beth.

"That's *A Lion in the Meadow*," I said slowly. "That's Mum."

I don't think Charley heard me. He was locked in his head, somewhere beyond words. But he had heard the roar. Slowly, with great effort, he turned his head toward it.

"Look," I said to him gently, the way I might have in those few months before he could talk, when he was still mine to teach everything I knew. "Do you see it? It's the dragon from the picture book, the one she used to read us. She's come for us."

Something worked behind his eyes, in the muscles of his jaw. His mouth opened twice before he spoke. "I see it," he said.

Beth must have taken her eyes from Charley for just a second. The Jabberwock had sprung to meet the dragon. It spilled into the world: leathery, sinuous, impossible. This time, it had wings that propelled it into the sky. The two great monsters collided above the Dickensian nightmare city.

Underneath them, in the midst of the battle, I saw my parents. Dad stood close to Mum, Matilda held protectively in his arms as I could still remember being held. Mum stood beneath her dragon. She wouldn't have needed a book to summon it. The book had been the source of her first creation when she was a child. She had read it to us a thousand times.

"Okay," I said. A calm had settled over me, real instead of pretended. I crouched down beside Charley. "You need to know who you are? You're Dr. Charles Sutherland. You're a supremely annoying word genius who went to Oxford at thirteen and wrote the world we're standing in. You can quote Dickens and Conan Doyle verbatim, but can never remember where you left your phone. You're stubborn, you're kind, you're brave, and you're too smart for your own good. You apologize too often, forget to buy milk, and have terrible taste in friends, because seriously, *Moriarty*. You're my brother."

"I'm not your brother." His voice was strained, but it was back. "Beth was right about that. I—David Copperfield's brother died as a baby. They had the same eyes. I've never been your brother. We're not even related."

"For God's sake, Charley, I've known you since you were a day old. I grew up with you. How much more related do you want to be? If you're not my brother, then tough, because I am sure as hell yours."

I saw a shiver go through his body, and he looked up. His eyes caught mine, the way they had when I first saw him, the day after he came into the world. And they were nothing like my eyes, and they were Dickens's eyes and probably David Copperfield's, too, but they were also his.

He believes what you tell him, Eric had said. He saw himself as I saw him.

"I know you," I said. "I remember you. And you are not going anywhere."

Another cry from outside the window. This one was barely audible over the gunfire. The dragon and the Jabberwock fought in the sky.

I stood and offered Charley my hand.

He flickered once more as he took his place by the window, but he barely noticed. His attention was once more directly at his archnemesis. This time he didn't say anything, even to himself. He looked at her.

And she felt it. I saw her teeth bare in a flash of white. It only took moments this time before her image began to twitch, then change.

"You've got it," I said—quietly, this time, so as not to distract him. Hope rose in my chest. It wasn't only Beth. The characters around her were beginning to falter without her explicit orders to guide them. The city itself was darkening, and there were ominous creaks and groans from the house around us. The whole world was straining at the seams.

Beth broke Charley's gaze, motioned to two characters to follow, and turned back to the house.

"What—where is she? Where's she going?" I asked. "Is that it?"

"She's coming upstairs," Charley said. He was no longer fading, but there was a transparency to him. Light seemed to be coming from somewhere behind him, and shining through him. He was tiring. "She's coming to face me properly."

I could hear footsteps coming up the stairs. I remembered being in Charley's flat, only a week or so ago, waiting for the Hound of the Baskervilles to come break down the door.

"Don't give up," I said. There had to be more I could do than this. There had to be. "You never give up. There, that's something else about you. You're a complete pain, but I've never once seen you give up."

"You can stop telling me things about myself now," he said. "I've got that. Besides, I think you're just finding new ways to tell me I'm a pain."

"How about the fact that you used to be terrified of spiders until you read *Charlotte's Web* when you were five?"

"Stop it!" he said, but he'd smiled. The light around him solidified. "I thought we agreed never to talk about that."

The door opened, and Beth-Moriarty came in. Two characters flanked her. I think I recognized a Fagin, all red hair and knobbly eyebrows, and the other may have been Bill Sikes. Beth-Moriarty's perfect gray hair looked a little less perfect that it had been. That wasn't all. I thought, with a start, that she looked taller and thinner, her forehead higher and her eyes a little more deep set. Her head oscillated slowly from side to side as she glared at us.

"Copperfield," she said. Her voice, too, sounded lower, with a gravelly hiss it had not possessed before.

"Moriarty," Charley said.

"You won't beat me," she said. "I am better than you. That is indisputable fact."

"We're not fact," Charley said. "We're fiction."

Beth-Moriarty smiled. For a moment, the two of them looked at each other. There was no reading being done, I don't think. They simply looked, and saw each other.

And then the Fagin standing at Beth-Moriarty's side drew out a knife and stabbed her through the heart.

It was so quick, and so unexpected, I didn't realize at first what had happened. I'm not sure anyone did. Moriarty screamed, a high, shrill sound of more anger than pain. The city convulsed. The floor rocked under my feet; the walls around us bulged and flew apart; the sky was suddenly the color of blood. Outside, I could hear the cries of the combatants as the ground split into jagged lines.

Fagin stepped forward. His features blurred and melted, his red hair sprouted, and once again, I found myself looking at the face of Uriah Heep.

XXIX

"Master Charley," Uriah said. Beth-Moriarty was on the floor, gasping and choking. The knife in Uriah's hands glistened red with blood. "Or is it Master David? Do tell me which you prefer, won't you, sir?"

"Uriah," Charley said, deliberately calm. "What are you doing?"

"What am I doing?" he repeated. His limbs twitched. "What does it look like I'm doing? What am I always doing? Rising above my station. I'm Uriah Heep, Master Charley. A threat to the social order, and the truth at the heart of it. It's what I do."

"I thought you were with Dorian," I said.

"He thought so too," Uriah said. "Dorian Gray. Such a witty, aristocratic person. So beautiful and clever. Do you know what Moriarty did to him, Master Charley? Him, and those who followed him? She welcomed them into her city, and then she melted their bodies into words. All of them. I hid in the form of one of her soldiers. I heard them scream as they were torn from the world."

I felt rather than saw Charley shiver.

"You told them to come to her," I said. "Dorian, and the Artful Dodger, and the rest. All of them."

"Oh, I would never presume so far, Master Robert. They would never have believed me, if I had *told* them that the other summoner would lead them to greatness. They didn't realize I was telling them. I didn't, not in words. I just whispered, and they believed what they wanted to believe."

"Why? What did you want?"

"I wanted them to come here," Uriah said. "It would be too conspicuous for me to come on my own. I wanted her to deal with them. And then I wanted to deal with her. With both of you. I wanted the city for myself."

"You can't control it," Charley said. "You have no power over it. You need to stop this."

"That's what they all say," Uriah said. He smiled: not his horrible, obsequious smile, but the one with fury behind it. "'Stop it, Uriah. Keep to your place. Be umble.' That's what this city is, you know. You should know, you wrote about it. The darkness. The rage and pain of thousands like me, kept in our places until we die there. My place? This *is* my place. It's always been my place. Not hers. Not Dorian Gray's. Not yours, Dr. Sutherland, David Copperfield, Dickens's favorite child. *Mine.* Control it? I don't need to control it. It's part of me. Let it spread until it devours the whole world. It's *mine.*"

Footsteps sounded on the stairs, a flurry of them, brisk and quick. I turned my head for a moment, toward the open door. In that one moment, Uriah grabbed me by the wrist, spun me around, and pressed his blade to the soft part of my throat.

There are a lot of things for which I'm truly ashamed during this whole affair—deeply ashamed, where I doubt I'll ever be able to dig them out. Letting myself be grabbed by Uriah Heep at that moment, by contrast, was nothing. Moriarty, after all, had been caught off guard by him only moments before. He was strong, supernaturally so; I was battered and off balance after my fall through the floor. I was prepared to protect Charley, not myself. But, illogically, what shot through me as the knife-edge bit my skin like a midge was pure humiliation. How *could* I? What an *idiot.*

Then I saw Charley's eyes wide and his face still, and a chill of real fear touched me.

There was a crowd of people in the room now. Millie had entered, accompanied by perhaps twenty fictional characters of assorted shapes and sizes. Her army, I assume. Any of them could have taken Uriah Heep with one hand, yet none of them moved. Because of me. If they moved—if anything happened to twitch Uriah's fingers—I would be dead. It seemed such a stupid thing to be stopping an entire city in its tracks.

"Uriah," Millie said, too calmly. She was breathing heavily, perhaps from the stairs or the fight or some combination thereof. "We've taken this house. I've one more group to come up from the courtyard, and it's all over. We can take you too. Don't do this."

"You know I can do it now, Master Charley," Uriah said softly. He ignored Millie entirely. The red-brown eyes were fixed on my brother. "Not like the first time we met. I've grown since then. If any of you come near me, I'll kill him."

"Let him go," Charley said.

Out of the corner of my eye, I saw Millie turn toward the Scarlet Pimpernel and whisper something. He nodded quickly, and left.

"You can't send me back," Uriah said. "Not in time. If I feel even a tickle that makes me think I'm starting to go, I'll slit his throat and leave his corpse behind me. And if any of you come near me, I'll do the same."

"And what if one of us decides we don't care that much for Dr. Sutherland's brother?" That was one of the Darcys. Jane Austen apparently has depths of heartlessness I didn't suspect.

"Shut up, Two," Millie said.

Uriah smiled. "Oh, I don't think you'll decide that. Not when you think about what Dr. Sutherland might do to someone who makes that decision. I have some of his thoughts in me, you know. They wouldn't be very kind on that point."

"Don't any of you dare move," Charley confirmed, without looking at the Darcys. I was reminded painfully of the time I had seen him present at a conference when he was sixteen. I knew his heart was pounding and his nerves stretched to the breaking point, but his words had been as deliberate and precise as the knife point at my throat. They were so now too. "Let him go, Uriah. I told you already I wouldn't put you back. I promised."

He snorted. "As I think I've said before, Master Charley," he said, "I'm umble, not stupid."

"Charley," Millie said. "Something's happening to the city."

"I know," he said, without looking at her. "It's dangerous, I keep telling everyone. It needs to be read away."

I finally found my voice around the blade at my throat. "Then read it. Quickly."

"If you do," Uriah said, "he dies. I'll do it. I don't want your brother dead. It's you I need gone. But I'll do it."

"I know," Charley said. His voice caught just a little. "And you can have me, of course you can have me. Just let him go."

Eric was right. Charley is so much weaker around me.

Around us, the city raged. It creaked and groaned: the noises our house made settling at night, but so much louder, and it wasn't settling, but rising up. The sky outside was a red so dark it was almost black. The darkness beneath the text. And still nobody moved.

If I just thrust my neck forward quickly, the blade would slice my throat. The thought came to my mind, and I knew at once that it made sense. Uriah wouldn't have me then. He would have nothing on Charley, now or ever again. He could be put back. It could all be put back: Uriah, Moriarty, the city. Lydia could come back. Charley could be safe. It could all be put right again.

I felt the steel against my throat, and I knew I could do it. My heart was racing so fast I would probably bleed out in seconds.

One move. That was all it would take.

I would have done it. I hope I would have, at least, despite how sick the thought still makes me. But at that moment, the Scarlet Pimpernel came back. With him was Charles Dickens. In the house he had written, he glowed twice as alive as he had in the hospital. His clothes were richer and more flamboyant, despite the dirt and a tear or two in the fabric. His dark hair around his flushed face seemed to stir in a breeze that touched nobody else. His eyes were bright as stars.

"The house is ours," he was saying. "Satis House. I must say, if it weren't for the dire nature of these circumstances, I would be unable to forgo the opportunity to explore further. I always thought it among my most vivid creations. Now, Sir Percy said that you wanted me for some—"

He stopped short at the scene before him, and the twinkle faded from his expression. That was nothing compared to the reaction of Uriah Heep. I couldn't see his face, twisted around as I was, but I heard the gasp he gave right in my ear. It was a death rattle.

Uriah Heep, I realized, had not known Charles Dickens was among us. He must have been gone, along with Dorian, by the time he and Holmes had reached the Street. And now, in the middle of a crumbling Dickensian world he was trying to claim as his own, he was face-to-face, for the first time, with the author of the story of his life. The author who knew—who had seen to it—that the story of his life was not really his at all. It was named for David Copperfield.

"Master Dickens," he whispered.

"Hello, Uriah," Dickens said.

I could feel Uriah shaking. His grip tightened on my arm, a convulsive squeeze that hurt. His breath came quick and fast on the back of my neck. He was terrified.

"Uriah, put down the knife," Dickens said. "You must know you can't succeed. Not here. I didn't write you to succeed. I wrote you to fail, so better people may be happy."

"You wrote me as a scapegoat," he said, in the same broken whisper. "You wrote me to be punished, so your precious David Copperfield wouldn't have to be."

"I'm sorry," he said. "But this world was never meant for you."

"No…" With me still tight in his grip, the knife still at my throat, Uriah took a shaky step back, then another.

We had all, I think, forgotten about Beth-Moriarty. Perhaps Charley hadn't—he had a good memory for fictional characters. But she'd been so quiet, there on the floor; I hadn't even noticed the rasp of her breathing since Uriah had grabbed me. I'd thought of her as dead. She had looked dead.

As Uriah took a third step back, almost on top of her, her eyes flashed open.

They had been gray before. Now, they were the same absolute black of the Hound of the Baskervilles, in his monstrous form, and like him they seemed to burn with phosphorous light. I have never seen so much hatred on anyone's face, not even Uriah's, and I never want to again. Her hand had shot out and grabbed Uriah Heep by one bony ankle.

He shrieked, the same wail of outraged despair I had heard the first night I met him, the night in the English department. As then, it chilled me. It was the cry of a specter, or a shadow. It took me a moment to realize the cause. He was starting to flicker. I wrenched myself out of his grip, and seized the knife from his hand; he writhed a little in resistance, but not much. Already, he was warping out of existence.

"No!" he cried. "No, you can't, you *can't*—"

Beth-Moriarty tightened her grip. "If you are clever enough to bring destruction upon me," she said, but it scarcely seemed to be her saying it, "rest assured that I should do as much to you."

There was a flare of light, bright and harsh. Beth-Moriarty drew her breath sharply, shuddered once, and slumped. Her eyes closed.

Uriah was gone. He hadn't even had the chance to scream.

For a moment, none of us moved or spoke. Not even me, suddenly finding myself free of a knife to my throat. Not even Millie, usually the first to react in any situation. Not even Dickens. We all just stood there.

Charley, in the silence, bent down over the body of Beth-Moriarty and laid his hand on her shoulder. She vanished in a tiny flare of light.

"I know she thought there was no book for her to go back to," he said. "But you never know."

The city heaved. The buildings and streets outside were mere shadows in the dark now, but I thought I could see them move. I felt, once again, the ground beneath my feet ripple. It shook us awake.

"Charley..." Millie said, softly but urgently.

"I know." He stood very slowly, as if everything hurt almost too much to move. "It's okay. I have it now." He closed his eyes.

It wasn't dramatic, as so much else that day had been. It was gentle, almost imperceptible, like a plant unfurling to embrace the sun. Like the growth of the tree at the bottom of our childhood garden, which I couldn't think of as less beautiful because I now knew it was also a grave. The sky lightened, and the light fell on the crooked houses lining the crooked streets and healed them. The ugly slashes in the walls closed; the cobbles settled; the shadows in the room smoothed and retreated. They didn't disappear: nothing disappeared, not the dirt or the shabbiness or the disorder. I could still feel the darkness there, quivering. But it was fading. It no longer overwhelmed the city.

This was it, I thought. This is the way the world disappears.

Then Charley's eyes opened.

"Is it safe now?" Millie asked.

"It's stable," he said faintly. He swayed and caught himself. When he spoke again his voice was firmer. "Beth gave me the key to her interpretation. As Rob said earlier, it wasn't a very balanced reading of Dickens. I've made it less dark. It wasn't too difficult, apart from the scale. It's a terrible oversimplification to trace everything about Dickens's world to one childhood trauma. There's more to Dickens than anger."

"But it's still hovering over Wellington?" Millie checked.

He nodded. "I'll read it all away soon. The whole city. Just...give me a minute, won't you?"

"Give us one too," she said. "I have a few of my people still downstairs. A few of Beth's too."

"Where are Mum and Dad?" I asked.

"Downstairs," Charley said, at the same time as Millie. He shook his head at my expression. "I have the whole city in my head at the moment. I know where everyone is."

"They're with the wounded," Millie said. "They're all right—your father took a spear cut from a goblin, but the Duke of Wellington will patch him up. Your mother's trying to gain control of the dragon. She made it beautifully, but it follows its own rules. Since we're inside, though, I could—"

"Don't let them come up," he said. "Please."

I went over to him as Millie motioned Dickens and the bloodthirsty Darcy to follow her out to the landing. Charley turned to me at the same time, so we nearly collided.

"Are you all right?" he asked, before I could ask him the same. "Did Uriah hurt you?"

"No worse than last time," I assured him. I rubbed my neck; my hand came away streaked with blood, but not too much. "Why does he keep holding knives to my throat? Didn't you say Uriah Heep is David Copperfield's shadow self, or something? Is there something we should be talking about?"

He smiled slightly. "Only if you put down that knife first."

I realized then that my desire to protect him, the desire I had chafed at for years, really had very little to do with how frustratingly helpless he could seem. He wasn't helpless now, frustratingly or otherwise. He was holding a whole world, about to save another. And I wanted to protect him more than I ever had in my life. I didn't care what he could handle. He shouldn't have to.

"We're nearly done, aren't we?" I said. "You just need to read the city back, and it's over?"

"Yes." He was very tired. "Yes, it's over then."

"All right," I said. "Only a little bit longer then. Just…hang in there."

It was a stupid reassurance, and he must have known it, but he didn't say so. He didn't even seem to think so.

"Hang in there," he repeated. I saw the resolve strengthen on his face. "I can do that." He paused. "Rob—"

"All clear downstairs!" Millie's voice came. She entered the room. "We need to get out of here."

"Good," Charley said. He turned away from me. "So it's time."

"Yes." Millie hesitated, uncharacteristically, and bit her lip. "Charley…I don't know how it was for you, but we barely got into this city. The place is surrounded. Patrol cars, barricades, all sorts. If you go out there, it might be difficult for you to find the time and space to—"

"I couldn't anyway," Charley said. "I wouldn't be able to see the city out there, much less touch it. I need to be right in the middle. I'm guessing at the middle, of course, but I assume it's about here. It's Satis House. It's where the past haunts the present. It's where hearts are broken. It fits."

Millie nodded. "And—I don't know if you know this, either, but according to your mother, you're—"

"It's all right," Charley said. "I know."

"Well. That might mean that when the city disappears—"

"I know," he repeated. "All of it."

"What do you know?" I demanded. My weary heart had quickened in alarm. "What are you talking about?"

He ignored me for the moment. "You'll have to get them out," he said to Millie. "You and Rob. I'll hold this place still as long as I can, but make it quick. And whatever you do, make sure Mum and Dad get out too. If you have to make up a story about where I am, do it. When it does start to go, I'm not sure how long it will take. It might only be the space between heartbeats."

She nodded. Her face was white. "I understand. I say, I do wish—"

"It's all right," he repeated. "Honestly. It makes sense. The Street will go, too, I'm afraid, if the new world's reached it, but try to stay together if you can. All of you—Beth's people, too, if possible. Things are probably going to be difficult for you all now."

"I'll handle it," she said. "Not to worry." She gave him a quick, fierce hug. When she pulled away, I saw the glint of tears in her eyes, and something in me chilled. I hadn't known Millie Radcliffe-Dix could cry.

And then, all at once, I knew what they were talking about. If there had been a picture of my soul, as there had been of Dorian's, it would have turned to ice in that moment.

All of it. That's what he'd said, all the way back downstairs, beside the body of David Copperfield. He'd make all of it go away.

I'm such an idiot.

"Good luck," she whispered.

"And you," he said. She gathered herself, visibly, before she turned away and raised her voice. I heard a faint quaver in it, but nobody else would.

"Come on, chaps!" she called. "We need to get out of this place before it goes for good!"

He'd more than just said it. He'd *promised* me.

This was what he'd been promising.

I went over to Charley. He was still watching Millie, and I couldn't read the look on his face. But his eyes shifted to Dickens for a moment, who was standing in the doorway. Dickens nodded very slightly, and smiled. Charley nodded back. They had never had a chance to exchange words.

"You're not staying here," I said bluntly.

"Only a little while." He finally turned to me. For a moment, I could see the Dickens in him. "Then the city's going away, and I suppose I'll go with it. Wherever it goes."

I had to swallow hard before I could speak. "You can't—"

He laughed tightly. "Rob, please, stop telling me I can't. I can. I can do anything, remember?"

"You said I didn't believe that."

"That's because it's not true. But I can do this—I have to. This city can't stay here. It doesn't fit. It's going to keep growing, and it's going to swallow up everything and everyone that gets in its way."

"Right. But you're in control of it now, aren't you? You can stop it growing."

"I can. I am, right now. But it's already done too much damage for that to be enough. Half the city's gone. It's already taken Lydia. It needs to go, and I'm the only one who can send it back."

"But if you send it back—"

"Everyone inside it goes too," Charley said. He would have sounded almost preternaturally calm, had he not been trembling. "Everyone fictional, at least. I still don't know where they go—into their books, into nothing—but you were there at the tunnel. They go somewhere. That's why you and Millie need to get everyone out, and let me send this city away."

"And you go with it."

"Yes," he said. "Yes, I go with it."

My chest tightened. "Don't be an idiot," I managed to say, in something like my usual voice. "What am I supposed to do after that? What am I supposed to tell Mum and Dad—that you've just dissolved into the written word?"

He almost smiled. "You can't expect me to think of *everything*..."

"I'm serious."

"You're supposed to do whatever you want to do," he said. "I'm serious too, Rob. You're supposed to get out of this mess, find Lydia, go back to your life, and try to remember that I did my best to fix all those things in it I broke, all right? Oh, and tell Mum and Dad—I don't know. Tell them I'm sorry I didn't go to see them last weekend." The resolve on his face flickered for a moment. "God, this is hard."

"Good. So don't do it."

He shook his head quickly. "No, I shouldn't have said that—it's not important how hard it is. There isn't another way. I told you, it makes sense. Narrative sense. It's how stories work. For order to be restored, there needs to be a sacrifice."

"This isn't a story."

"You aren't. Lydia isn't. But I am, and this world is. This moment is too. It's why I've been here, all this time. I've spent twenty-six years learning to read and to summon and to love your world, so that I can be right here, and do this one thing, for it and for you. I was always this."

"You weren't this. You were my brother."

And I realized, too late, that I had said it in past tense.

Charley must have noticed; it was exactly the sort of thing it was his job to notice. But he didn't point it out.

"I know," he said. "And thank you for that, so much. Now please, Rob, just go. I'm trying to hold an entire city in my head, and it's very difficult."

"This is ridiculous," I heard myself say, but it sounded weak. Because I could see it, exactly as he'd told it. I could see how this was his story and how it always had been. I could see that my role in it had never been to protect him; it had only been to give him strength enough to do what he needed to do, for everyone's sake, because he could tell himself he was doing it for me. I could see all that. But I hated it. It wasn't *fair*.

Millie's hand was on my arm somehow. "Come on, Rob," she said. "Come on, we have to go."

There had to be something more I could do. There had to be something more I could say.

"Thank you," I said. Charley nodded, very slightly, and smiled.

Millie led me out. I couldn't have found my way on my own. We passed streets, and buildings, and sky. A dragon, perched on the cupola of an iron-gray building, sent a roar out over the city. With every step, I wanted to turn back. I didn't.

And then, at once, the mists around me cleared. My city—the real city—stood before me, in a blaze of sirens and helicopters and electric lights. Millie was in front of me, and Dickens and the Darcys and several other walking metaphors. A voice was shouting from a megaphone, in a blur of words that made no sense.

Had it gone already? Was that it?

I whirled around, and looked back. The cloud was still there, as it was when Charley and I had entered it not so long ago. I had stepped beyond its border, that was all. It was lighter now; not only thinner on the ground, but burning with the faint glow you sometimes see in the sky during a very cloudy sunrise.

"Rob?" Dad was there, solid and reassuring, Matilda still nestled against his shoulder. She looked pale, and her eyes were closed; he had a bloodstained cloth wrapped around his forearm, and his face was streaked with dirt. "Oh, thank God. Susan!"

Mum pushed past a Darcy, and her face melted into relief. She wrapped me in a tight hug. "Thank goodness. I thought—how could you go in there without telling us?"

"Where's Charley?" Dad asked. "Did he come out with you?"

I didn't know how to answer.

The shadow was still in front of me. I put out my hand, and it passed straight through. No going back now. The whispered sensation on my skin was like a goodbye.

Charles Sutherland, age twelve
Extract from diary (dark blue)

I don't want to write about what happened today. I'm sick of words. I'm sick of their elusiveness and their sharpness and their beauty and their hurt.

But if I don't write it down, then it will still be there in my head, and that will be worse. So I will set it down in the plainest words possible, and rob it of its power. This is how it happened.

Today I was crossing the edge of the netball courts, behind the bike shed. I should have known better, but I was reading while I walked and I forgot. Some Year Nines saw me—the ones who despise me for being their age and in Year Thirteen. I don't really know why this bothers them so much, and I don't care. I hate them. If they were in a book I wouldn't, because they would be rounded characters who had their own voice and they would be interesting. But my knee still hurts, and I hate them.

I didn't look up until I heard their voices, and then I closed the book quickly and wrapped it in my arms because sometimes they go for what I'm carrying rather than me. I don't care what everyone says, damaging books is worse than damaging people. People heal up. Books never do. The marks always show.

There were five guys, all bigger than me. I backed up against the bike shed until my backpack hit it, and prepared to wait it out. Usually they just push me around a bit until they finally push me out of their circle, and then I can run away while they laugh and feel good about themselves. That's what they were doing when one of them shoved a little too hard and I fell down. There was a puddle right there, and all I could think was that if *The Adventures of Sherlock Holmes* fell in a puddle, the pages would dry warped and crinkled and it would never be the same. So I twisted, and came down hard on my knees and elbow rather than putting my hands out to stop myself. It hurt, but I think I managed not to make a noise. I think. Things had never gone this far before; they all seemed much taller from down on the ground.

That was when I looked up and saw Rob. I could see him through the gaps in the legs of the other guys. He had been crossing the courts, but he had paused, and he was looking right at me. I was so ashamed, because I shouldn't need him to rescue me, but deep down I was relieved. I was cold and hurt, and I was starting to be really frightened. I *wanted* to be rescued. I wanted it all to go away.

He didn't rescue me. He saw me, but he didn't come over to me. He left. He looked at me, and he turned, and he walked away. And it was like—never mind what it was like. It was like Rob turned and left me to get beaten up by a pack of Year Nines. It doesn't need a simile. I didn't have a simile then. I had nothing but the cold feeling right down in my stomach. It was as if my brain stopped working.

Nobody else was there. I could hear voices in the distance, from the fields, but they weren't going to come this way. It was just me and them.

The others didn't see Rob, or I think they would have stopped anyway. They didn't stop. The next thing I knew, a boot connected with my ribs, hard. Perhaps I was meant to get out of the way—I would have, had I not been watching Rob go. But I was watching, so I didn't, and I wasn't even braced for it, so it really hurt.

"Stop it!" I said. I don't know why. I knew they wouldn't.

They laughed.

And I don't really know what I felt then. I can't understand it. I was alone, I was scared, I was suddenly furious, my heart was racing, and even Rob didn't want to protect me. Somehow, all those contradictory feelings surged in one big wave, and what came to my head was *The Adventures of Sherlock Holmes* in my hands. I saw the text, word perfect, and I understood, in a flash, that it was about the power of intelligence and deductive reasoning over brute force. It made so much sense that I forgot where I was for a moment; all I felt was pure exultation. And then, I pushed that feeling, and I directed it at them.

I saw the flash of light, because I was looking for it, but they didn't. The first they knew was when Sherlock Holmes grabbed one of them by the shoulder. Not roughly; the way he'd separate a bunch of urchins brawling in the streets. But they weren't expecting it, so they flinched. Then they saw him, in his tall, hawk-nosed, sharp-eyed Victorian glory. They looked at him, and then they looked at me.

"Get away with you," Holmes said.

And they ran.

I don't care what they did. It doesn't matter. My knee's still sore, and my ribs when I forget and let my schoolbag bump them, but I've done worse to myself falling off my bike. And it was expected. It's how they and I interact. I don't think they even hate me really, despite what I said before. It's just a game, and I forgot the rules for one minute and gave them a free penalty. Then I changed the rules altogether.

I don't care what Rob did either. He was right. It's not his job to look after me, not if he doesn't want to. If I can't deal with five thirteen-year-olds, then how am I supposed to deal with going to Oxford in eight months? He won't be there to protect me then. He'll be on the other side of the world. If he hates me that much, he never has to *see* me again.

I care a little bit what Rob did.

But I care a lot more about what I did. I shouldn't have lost control like that. I shouldn't have used Sherlock Holmes like that. It's not what he's *for*.

And the worst part is, I enjoyed it. I enjoyed that they were frightened of me. I enjoyed being powerful. I enjoyed the feeling of watching them run, like my blood had turned to melted ice. (Melted ice is water, Sutherland. But I know what I mean.) I even enjoyed that they might tell other people. I wanted everyone to know.

Then it died away, and I was kneeling on my own on the cold ground, with the water soaking through the knees of my trousers and stinging where the gravel had got into the scrapes, and it was like the blood rushed back into me.

Holmes said, "Are you quite well, Sutherland?"

I started to say I was fine, but suddenly I was shaking, and then I realized I was starting to cry, and then I couldn't stop. I *hate* crying. It's so inarticulate and helpless. And this was in front of Sherlock Holmes. I basically wanted to die.

Holmes put his hand on my shoulder and waited for me to get back under control. Then he said, "You've learned from this. You're an intelligent person; you will not have to learn the same lesson twice."

"It won't happen again," I said. My voice still wasn't quite mine. "They'll never touch me again. Anyway, I'm only at school a few more months."

"Education never ends, Sutherland," he said. "It is a series of lessons, with the greatest for the last."

And I know that's from "The Adventure of the Red Circle," but it didn't mean it wasn't for me.

Rob just came home from rugby practice. I heard him pull up in the car. I know it's him because he still stops and starts the engine getting it into the driveway. I'm not going out to meet him, but I don't think I'll write any more.

XXX

The police rushed forward to us at once, to take us by the shoulders and usher us away from the wall of cloud. We had come out right where Charley and I had come in, but the alley where I had parked my car was inside the barricade now, and the edges of the new world were lapping a few feet away from the car door. I don't know how much of Courtenay Place was lost: it had been growing ten times faster in that direction, toward Millie's street.

I was being taken to the back of an ambulance; someone was holding me down and pressing a stethoscope to my chest. They must have thought we were people who'd been inside the danger zone when the city came. Just as well, because some of the characters were in need of serious medical attention. Many of them were bleeding from gunshot wounds and sword thrusts. I saw Matilda being wheeled away on a stretcher, two of the Darcys being given oxygen and blankets. Quite what the paramedics would make of them, I had no idea.

These thoughts ran through my head, but I couldn't focus on them. I couldn't focus on anything very much. I saw Millie talking to the police officers; normally, I would at least want to know what she was saying, if not take over myself, but I didn't even listen. I felt a paramedic prodding me, and it seemed to be happening to someone else. I heard the same paramedic asking me questions, quietly and then more insistently, and I heard myself give my name without recognizing it as my own. I must have said something about my brother still being in there, because I distinctly heard the paramedic reply, "A lot of people are still in there, mate. What's your brother's name?"

That seemed such an important question that I'm not sure I answered it at all. If I did, I have no idea what name I said.

The paramedic went away after a while; I stayed sitting, because I didn't feel confident about my ability to stand. My ankle was throbbing from where I'd landed on it earlier. The world about me, ironically, didn't seem real at all. It was just a chaos of lights and voices.

"It's taken Cuba Street now," Millie's voice said beside me. She was standing with her arms folded tight to her, as though she were cold. "So that's the Street swallowed with it. And these people are already starting to be puzzled by us. We're going to be out in the open now. It doesn't matter, as long as Charley can send the world away."

"He will," I said. I knew that better than I knew the answers to all those questions the paramedic had been asking, including the ones about my own name. Charley could do anything.

"I know he will," she agreed. "I just heard on a police radio that what they call the cloud is breaking up. I can see it myself. It'll go at any moment."

Any moment. I'd seen a lot of things read away over the years. I knew it could happen in the space between heartbeats. Any moment, and this nightmare would be over, and my city would be back, and so would Lydia, and so would my life.

"You can't let him do this," Mum said. She and Dad had been detained by the paramedics too; she must have broken free, because all at once they were both there. Her face was streaked with tears. "I'll do it. I must be able to. I'm a summoner as well. And it wouldn't take me with it, would it?"

"You couldn't do this, Mrs. Sutherland," Millie said. "I wish you could, but it's Charley's world now. You'd have to reinterpret it first, then read it away, and that would take you years."

"I read his book," Mum said. "It's not so complicated."

"I've read it too," Millie said. "It jolly well is. Besides, it's not the interpretation. It's the size. That thing is chapters long. And it's covering miles of real ground."

"Just let me try! Take me across the threshold! You know it won't accept us without you."

"Let us both across the threshold," Dad said. "Like Susan said, we won't go away with it. What harm could it do?"

"It could ruin everything! Don't you think I would, if I could? And you don't know you won't go away with it. None of us knows anything anymore."

"He's our son," Dad said, and Mum gave a convulsive shiver. I knew she was thinking what it must have cost Dad to say that and mean it. But it was true. I remembered my certainty when Charley's birth certificate had come back. In a way, I had been right to suspect he was adopted. But I was also right that whatever else he was, he was ours.

"He's my friend," Millie returned. "If there was any other way, then I would take it—I'd read it away myself, if I could, and go with it. But we can't save him at the expense of the world. It would be wrong, and he would hate us for it."

Mum turned to me. "Rob..."

"He made me let him go." I barely recognized my own voice. "He wants to do it. He thinks it's right. It makes sense."

"It may make sense," Dad said. "That doesn't mean it's right."

I barely heard them. All I could think about was Charley on a rainy day behind a bike shed, watching me walk away and leave him to his fate. I was doing it again. The circumstances were very different from his point of view. But from mine the view was the same. I was walking away, and he was watching me go.

"You abandoned him," Eric had said. "And he was more powerful on that day than he had ever been when you were at his side."

It was true. I had abandoned him. I had seen him in trouble, and I left him in it. It was the worst thing I had ever done. And Charley had come into his power on that day because of it. He had been under attack, and he called the world's greatest detective to his aid. Sherlock Holmes hadn't protected him; Charley protected himself. He had been strong, and angry, and alone. Nobody at that school had ever touched him again.

But who needed that kind of strength? I'd seen it now, in physical form; I'd watched it burn itself alive. It was the strength of a scared, hurt twelve-year-old who realized, one cold afternoon in a schoolyard, the person he loved and trusted more than any other had thrown him away. Charley didn't want to be that. He had been telling me so every time the phone rang in the middle of the night.

He had said, in the hospital, that he didn't know why he kept phoning for my help when he had gone so long without it. Eric could have explained that, as well: he would have said that I made him less than he was. Lydia thought something similar, and so had my parents, a long time ago. Perhaps they were right. Yet I think, perhaps, they had underestimated him. Perhaps it had very little to do with his weaknesses, and everything to do with mine. Because he didn't want *me* to be the person I had been in that schoolyard either. He wanted me to be the person who would drop everything—do anything—to protect him, even when he could protect himself. The person who would kill the whole world to keep him safe.

I know that was why I always came. However much I complained about it, I wanted to be that person too.

Charley knows everything about stories. I believed him when he said that this was how his story went. But this wasn't only his story. It was mine.

"I can't do this," I said. I really just said it out loud, but Millie heard me. She paused in her argument with my parents, frowning. The drizzle was clinging to her hair, curling it to wet tendrils around her face.

"What?"

"I have to go back in."

"You can't stop him, Rob. If you could, I wouldn't let you. He was right. This is the only way."

"Then there *is* no way. Because I can't do this."

"You don't have to do anything," she said. "He does. Rob, don't you think I'd *rather* there was no way at all? There is. It's this way. We don't get to choose."

But that was the problem. I did. I *was* choosing. I had already chosen, in the moment when I let Millie lead me out of the written world. Losing Lydia had been Beth's fault; this really was mine. I had deliberately let it happen. And if I let that choice stand, I would never be able to forgive myself. I would always wonder if I had, on some level, *wanted* Charley gone, and know on every level that I did not. Charley and Lydia were both my family, and both their worlds were part of mine. I couldn't let one go to save the other. There had to be another way.

But was it too late to change my mind? Millie wouldn't take me back in, any more than she would Mum and Dad. She had been written to do the right thing. Charley would have read it into her. A sneaky worm of a thought came to me that perhaps this was it then. If there was no way back in, and I could tell myself I had been practically marched out by Millie and the others at gunpoint, then...

No. There had to be a way. It was one of the very few things Charley and I had in common—maybe the only thing, unless you count hating brussels sprouts and preferring vanilla ice cream to chocolate. I never gave up, either.

Could Henry get me there? He was fictional, just like Millie and the others. He could pass through. And he could take me, too, if I kept a hold of him. The trouble was, he was all the way back at Charley's house. By the time I got there and back with him, I would be too late. Even if I got in my car right now—

My car. Suddenly, I knew. Excalibur. The sword that Charley had pulled from *Le Mort Darthur*, all that time ago, to save me from Uriah Heep. It was in my car. I'd put it there just this afternoon—only hours ago, though it felt like longer—when I'd gone to pick him up from the university.

It would pass through. It was from a book, it had to. Whether it was alive or not shouldn't matter; it was whether or not it was real. And if I were holding it...

I didn't know for certain. I never knew any of this stuff for certain. But my car was right there; it would take seconds to test it. And it made sense. Charley is always very big on things making sense.

I didn't stop to think. I got up off the back of the ambulance. I forgot how sore my ankle was and how weak and shaky I'd felt only moments before, forgot that Millie was standing right next to me, forgot everything except where I'd left my car keys (my jacket pocket) and where I'd put Excalibur.

"Rob, what are you—?" Millie asked. I ignored her. I ignored my parents as well.

The sword was still in the trunk of the car. I had laid it diagonally across the old blanket I kept there, and it gleamed in the emergency lights. I picked it up and curled my hand around the pommel. It fit there like it had been created for me. In some ways, of course, it had.

"Rob?" I don't think Millie knew what Excalibur was, but from the tone of her voice, she could work out what I intended to do with it. "Rob, don't you dare—"

I turned toward the wall of otherworldly fog, tightened my grip on the sword and, injuries or no injuries, I ran.

I faltered just a little, the moment before I hit the cloud. If I were wrong about Excalibur, I could just disappear. Just step into the mist and vanish, as Lydia had vanished. Presumably I'd come back if Charley dissolved the city, of course, but that didn't quell my instinctive revulsion at the idea.

And if I were wrong to do this... if I were just *wrong*...

I'm so sorry, Lydia.

I entered the city again.

XXXI

It was like stepping into the end of the world. At once, my eyes were blinded by a white glow, harsh and pitiless as a flare from an atomic bomb. Almost as blinding was the noise. It struck me in an endless roar. It took me a moment to realize that it was made up of words. Hundreds of thousands of intermingled voices, each crying over each other in fragments.

Chapter One. I am Born

You have been in every line I have read.

Whether I shall turn out to be the hero of my own life, or whether that station will be held by anybody else...

And the mists had all solemnly risen now, and the world lay spread before me.

These pages must show.

Usually, when Charley puts something back, it goes with a flash of light. Just one flash, between one heartbeat and the next, and it's gone. But Dickens or Uriah Heep or the Cat in the Hat was a good deal smaller to hold in a thought than an entire world. This was a flash drawn out over minutes. And for once, I wasn't watching it from the outside. I was inside the light.

Think of a story, I remembered belatedly. It was what Charley had told me to do as we passed through the edges of this world. It looked as though it was all edges now.

There was so much light, I could hardly see. I made out the outlines of buildings, and of streets, and of lampposts, and of steeples and domes and roofs. It didn't help, because they weren't in the order they had been in before. They weren't in any sort of order at all. Lydia and I had been to an exhibit of Escher lithographs once—it came to the museum on tour, and it was a rainy weekend. The city now felt like those prints. Paths went nowhere, or doubled back on themselves. Buildings folded over like the pages of a book.

Liminal space. The space between two worlds.

Where the light was strongest, there were no buildings—at least, none of bricks and mortar. They shone through with words. The city at the edges dissolved into block text, and the ground under my feet was shifting with printed sentences. In places the buildings looked like thinly painted watercolor over newsprint. In others there were holes torn through walls or across the sky itself, and words teemed from those holes—or out of them, I couldn't tell. Everything was in motion. And noise. There was so much *noise*.

There was no sign of Charley. There was no sign of anything so concrete. All signs were starting to break down.

A story. I needed a story.

And I had one.

"My name is Robert Sutherland." It was the story I told myself without thinking every day. The world around me paused to listen. *Chapter One. I am Born.* "I was four and half years old when my brother was born. I want him back."

The words twisted before me, and writhed into the shape of Uriah Heep. He stood there bleeding ink around the edges. His mouth when it opened was a rip in the world.

"You don't want him back," Uriah Heep said. "You never wanted him at all. I know you."

"You don't know me," I said.

"I *am* you," he said. "I am the part of you that hates, and resents, and dreams of revenge. I am the part of Charles Sutherland that he won't acknowledge, the part that hates you too. I am the child buried under the tree, the narrative sacrifice, the life lost so that David Copperfield could thrive. I am the darkness at the heart of the world, the darkness that even Dickens couldn't defeat."

"Fine," I said. "You're all of that. But I still want my brother back."

"If he comes back," Uriah said, "he'll bring all this with him. Chaos, and story. It's what he is."

"I know. I still want him back."

"He'll destroy your world."

"I know." I wasn't being defiant. I was too tired for defiance, and Uriah Heep was too elemental to defy. Besides, I agreed with every word. "I know he will, one day or another. I don't care. I want him back."

"Why?"

"Because whatever he is," I said, "I knew the first day I saw him that I would destroy the whole world to keep him safe. I thought it was a feeling. Now I suspect it was also a prophecy. Charley would probably call it narrative foreshadowing. Either way, it was true. It still is."

"That doesn't make any sense."

"It doesn't have to," I said. "It's a story."

And then I saw him.

He was standing there in the midst of the disintegrating world, the book open in his hands. Its pages were glowing, casting light about the streets and on his face. The words that were spilling out of it or into it, that were making up the city, were making him up as well. They flickered behind his eyes and shone through his face.

He was David Copperfield, and Sherlock Holmes, and Charles Dickens. He was Dr. Charles Sutherland, author of the world that was crumbling around us. He was words, and thought, and memory. He was a creature of metaphor and simile, of hopes and autobiography and dead people. And he was my brother.

"Charley!" My voice was lost again in the gusts of words streaming around us, but somehow he heard me. He looked up. I saw his eyes blink, darken, and focus on my face. The world around me faltered as his attention diverted. In front of me, Uriah Heep dissolved into text.

"I've come back for you," I said.

He didn't answer. I think he heard me, but he couldn't afford to listen. His concentration was taken up with trying to hold an entire city in his mind.

"Come on." I took a step closer and held out my hand. "Come back with me."

His face was utterly remote. I'm not even sure he was behind it anymore. I kept moving forward anyway.

"I'm sorry I let you do this," I said. "I'm sorry I let you be scared, and worried, and hurt. I'm sorry I let you think I didn't want you. I'm sorry for reading you the way I wanted to see you, all your life. That's enough to be sorry for, okay? I *refuse* to be sorry I lost you."

It was hard to walk now. I glanced down, quickly, and saw that this was because the cobbles beneath my feet were falling away.

The streets and buildings and lampposts and sky were fading. Already, I thought I could see the neon lights and straight lines of the real city beneath it, Courtenay Place on Friday night. The city was a whisper in the mist, nothing more, and in moments it would pass away and leave nothing at all, not even the mist.

I wasn't fading. I was still real and solid. Wherever the city was going, I wasn't going with it.

My brother was. Before my eyes, I saw him blur about the edges, and then I saw his face translucent and his body all but transparent. For just a moment, his eyes shifted again to meet mine, and his mouth twitched in a tiny smile. It was the smile he had given me before he boarded the plane for England, when he was thirteen and I was seventeen, and we were both leaving home for the first time. My heart had given that treacherous little tug then, because I had known that he was terrified. And then he had gone through that gate, and out of my life.

"Don't you dare," I said.

I don't really know, in that moment, what I was trying to do. I don't know if I thought I could bring him out, or if I thought I could go with him—into a book, or into nothing, wherever it was fictional characters went. I only know what I did and what happened.

I knocked the book out of his grip and grabbed hold of his hand.

The world shattered.

Chapter One. I am Born

I existed, and I didn't exist. I felt the real world and my brother's world, pulling at me and tearing me apart.

Whether I shall turn out to be the hero of my own life...

I saw, as if from above, the long ramshackle line of Courtenay Place wreathed in fog. I saw that fog lift, and the streets of Wellington hard and glittering in the streetlights.

I saw the city, Charley's London, solid and real, made of words and thoughts and ideas and interpretation, sprawling out as far as I could see. It was disappearing: not into nothing, as Moriarty had feared, but into something I couldn't begin to understand. It was passing into pure language. In another moment, perhaps, I would disappear with it.

For this moment, we were here. Liminal space. The space between two worlds. A fictional landscape to be traversed. The place where the impossible happened.

... or whether that station will be held by anybody else...

"No," I said. The words were strange: not so much heard as absorbed into the narrative around me. "Not this time. It's my turn."

I closed my eyes. I didn't know how to close read, or interpret. It had never made much sense to me. But I knew the feel of a case coming together out of a myriad of details; I knew the feel of being in touch with something bigger than myself. It was the feeling of a story being told. I told this one.

"My name is Robert Sutherland," I said. "I am thirty years old. I live in Wellington, New Zealand. I was four and half years old when my brother was born."

I saw myself at two, playing by the creek while my mother held my hand. I saw myself at four, peering into a crib and feeling my heart tugged from me. I saw myself at seventeen, walking away from a schoolyard fight; at twenty-two, a brand-new lawyer in a city that I loved; at twenty-six, asking Lydia if she wanted to go get coffee sometime. I put out all the threads I could to my real world, and I held them tightly.

And then I let this world in. I saw myself playing Pac-Man with Sherlock Holmes, chasing Uriah Heep through the English department in the early morning, standing under the shelter of a tree in the rain watching a crowd of stars. I saw the Street in all its shambolic glory. I saw all the times Charley had tried to show me something beautiful and I hadn't wanted to look. I let it all become part of the story. It wasn't as hard as I thought it would be.

I couldn't see Charley through any of this. I couldn't even feel his hands in mine. But when I heard his voice, I knew that I was still, impossibly, holding on to him.

"What are you doing here?" the voice said.

"I came back for you," I replied.

"Why? Who are you?"

I nearly told him. Something stopped my tongue at the last moment. It was too big a question. I felt, very strongly, that the wrong word here would ruin everything.

"You know who I am," I said instead.

"I don't..." The voice was slow, hesitant. "I think I do. I don't know. I think you shouldn't be here."

I laughed at that. It was strange, in a place of pure language, to hear my own laugh bounce around and come back to us. "Well, you might say that. But neither should you. I came to get you out."

"Oh." He paused. "Who am I?"

And then I understood. I had helped him read himself back before by telling him who he was. That wouldn't work this time. He had already gone too far; if I tried, what I would pull out would not be the Charley I knew but some figment of my own interpretation. That was what Eric had accused me of doing to him his entire life. If Charley was to come back, he would need to bring himself back.

"Who do you think you are?"

"I don't know," he said. "I think I was trying not to know. I think..."

I spoke the first thing that came into my head. The first story.

"Do you know what I thought of this afternoon?" I said. "When we used to play around the tree out back. Do you remember?"

"I think so." His voice grew a little firmer. "Yes. We used it as a pirate ship. You helped me get to the top branches."

"Exactly. Remember that one evening, when the storm clouds rolled in while we were in those branches? You were only about four or five. We started to climb down when the first drops fell, but it came over so fast we had only just reached the bottom when the clouds burst. We just stood close to the tree trunk and stared at it. It was raining so hard and the clouds were so dark that it was like night had come early. We could see the lights of the house in the distance, behind the veil of rain. The fire was going. And you made the stars come out."

"Yes." He said it with wonder. "I remember that. The crowd of stars. They were from Yeats."

"I know. I don't think you meant to make them; the poem came into your head, and you hadn't learned to shut up about poetry yet. They weren't like proper stars—I mean, scientific stars. They swarmed around our heads and glittered in the branches like fireflies. When the rain caught one, it would hiss, and steam would rise from them. But they weren't fireflies. They were real stars. More real than real. And the garden around us opened up, and the air felt thin and crisp, and it was as if we were miles above everyone, us and the tree alone on top of the entire world."

"And then Dad came out to get us with the umbrella," he said. "Mum sent him. I had to put the stars back, and they told me off, but not too badly because we were soaked through. We got dried off, and were given hot chocolate by the fire. You let me read your comic book."

"Did I? I don't remember that part."

"I do," he said.

He was in front of me now. I could see him. I could see all of it. And the city glowing with the light of pure meaning was the most beautiful thing I had ever seen.

... *these pages must show.*

The world came back together.

We were right where we had been before, on the high street of the new city, only the streets had quieted. It might be more correct to say that the streets were utterly quiet. Nothing moved, nothing stirred: not a breath of wind, not a bird, not a whisper. The air felt too hushed to breathe. Even the sky overhead, still and high and the palest blue, seemed to contrive to make as little noise as possible.

My hand was still around Charley's; as the feeling returned to my body, that was the first thing I felt. His hand was barely substantial when I had taken it. Now, even as I stood there, I felt it solidify. He formed around it, as a ghost out of the air.

"Hey," I said. Almost before I'd spoken, warmth and feeling rushed back into his face. He drew a sharp breath, then coughed. His hand slipped from mine as he crumpled to the ground, still coughing. Air rushed into his lungs for the first time in a long while; his heart took its first beats. His body shuddered as life entered it again.

"Steady." I crouched down beside him and put my hand on his shoulder, partly to support him, mostly to reassure myself that he was real and solid. "Just breathe."

"I'm okay," he said breathlessly. "Give me a minute. What—?"

Another fit of coughing grabbed him before he could finish the question, much to my relief. I didn't want to have to explain what happened. The cold certainty that had been mine only moments ago evaporated in the light of day, wherever this day was. I was no longer sure what had happened, or if it was right.

Charley caught his breath, and sat up.

"Take it slow," I said. "I think you just read yourself back to life."

"I didn't mean to." The confusion on his face was beginning to clear. "I was almost gone. Something called me back. I—"

He turned to look at me.

"That was you, wasn't it?" His eyes were suddenly brimming with hurt bewilderment. I didn't care. He was back behind them, and that was what mattered. "What did you *do*?"

"I saved your life, I think," I said. "Beyond that, I was hoping you'd explain."

"I almost had it! You pulled me back. You made me pull myself back."

"I know that much. But where are we? We're not in a book, are we?"

As I spoke, I knew the answer. I had just been as close to the inside of a book as I would probably ever get. It was nothing like this.

"No." The question distracted him briefly. "No, I don't think we're in a book. I don't know where we are. We might have just snapped back to reality. This might all be overlaying Wellington, right where it was before... Why did you *do* that? I told you to get out!"

I snorted. "And since when do I do what you tell me?"

"I meant it, Rob! You could have just ruined everything!"

"I know," I said. "Fine, it was stupid. But I couldn't do it, all right? I wasn't going to let you just fade away like that."

"Did it occur to you that maybe I *wanted* to just fade away like that?"

"Not really. And if it had, I would have only come to get you sooner, because that would be disturbed. Did you?"

He didn't quite answer. "It was my choice."

"Well, tough. It was my choice not to let you go. God knows why. I wish I had, if you're going to be this much of a pain about it."

He made a small, inarticulate noise of frustration, and I knew he was backing down. He wasn't very good at nonacademic arguments.

"If you've ruined it, then Lydia can't come back," he said. "Nobody can, but not her either."

"Do you really think," I said tightly, "that I hadn't considered that?"

The last of the fight drained from him. "Of course you did." He sighed. "I'm sorry. I didn't mean any of that. I just—I'm tired. And I thought it was over."

I felt that sharp, familiar tug in my chest. I'd resisted that feeling for about twenty years: inconsistently, which made it worse, and stupidly. "It's okay," I said. "I'm tired too. I understand."

I did. I understood more than I wanted to, and a lot more than I wanted to talk about.

"Can you stand yet?" I asked.

The idea caught him off guard, as if he'd forgotten that might be a good short-term goal. "I don't know. Yes. I think so."

I got to my feet, and he followed. It took him a couple of attempts, but I held back, and he made it in the end.

"I'm okay," he said, and this time sounded almost convincing. He pushed his hair back from his eyes, and looked around. "I don't actually think we've overtaken Wellington. I don't think you pulled us far enough for that. We might just be partway, like the *Oliver Twist* house, or even less substantial. Then Lydia should be free. The cloud would have lifted enough for the real world to bleed back through. I can let you out, and finish the unreading. We just need to find the edges of this place."

"You're not reading anything else away." Some of the between-world clarity had returned to me. "Not now. Whatever's here, whatever world we've made, we made it together. It's done."

"I don't quite understand what we *have* made, yet."

"I've never understood any of these unreal places," I said. "Let alone this one."

There were no walls at all, that I could see. The streets really did seem to go on forever. They'd grown. I wondered with a thrill of fear if I'd been wrong, and we really were in a book. Lost in a book. It was difficult for fear to strike too deep, though. It was too quiet. Even my feelings seemed muffled.

I don't know how long we stood there before we both saw, at more or less the same time, that someone was walking toward us. We turned to each other.

"Are you seeing that?" I asked quietly.

He nodded.

"Who is it?"

"I don't know." He ran his hand over his eyes. "I can't tell. There's too much fog."

The figure was coming closer. I felt my muscles tense, painfully, and was reminded again of every blow and tear they had suffered already today. Whoever it was made a dark shadow through the haze. They seemed to be hesitating too. Perhaps they were as unsure of us as we were of them. That would be hopeful, if it were true.

"I don't suppose you can tweak the atmospheric conditions at all?"

I didn't mean it, but Charley's brow furrowed slightly in concentration, and a moment later the fog lightened. Sunlight crept into the shadows and a breeze danced down the street, stirring the mist and blowing it away.

The figure came out of the few shreds of fog that remained. A short figure, dressed in jeans and a long coat, with curls that bounced and eyes that, when we drew near enough to see each other, kindled in relief.

"*There* you are, you two!" Millie Radcliffe-Dix exclaimed. "I've been looking for you fellows everywhere!"

I think my mouth may have dropped open. It's never done that before. This was its limit.

"How on earth—?" I tried to say, and stopped there.

"Oh, thank goodness," Charley sighed. I think he was just too tired to be surprised. "If you had been something hostile, there is no way I could have dealt with you. I think I'm about to pass out."

"Don't be modest," Millie said cheerfully. "You are certainly about to pass out. Did you just lift the fog?"

"Rob told me to."

"I didn't mean for you to *do* it," I protested, finally finding my voice. "You don't have to take everything so literally. What are you, six? Millie—how did you *get* here?"

"Through the Street," Millie said. "It was the strangest thing. The shadow lifted, first of all. Central Wellington came back. The Street's still where it was before—it hasn't gone anywhere—but it doesn't stop anymore. It just winds on and on, as far as I can see. I thought—well, that's a Charles Sutherland–type thing to happen. If you two were anywhere I could ever find you again, you'd be here. So I started looking. I can't tell you how glad I am to see you."

"The new world's become part of the Street?" I said slowly.

"It does sound peculiar when you put it that way—I would say the Street's become part of the new world—but yes. They've been reaching for each other all this time. They've finally joined."

"We knew they'd do that," Charley said. He was frowning. "But why—?" His face cleared suddenly. "Unless—"

"Here we go," I sighed. I was resigned to weirdness by this point.

"I was putting it back. I was putting it all back. And then you stopped me, Rob—you grabbed me right when I was somewhere between reality and fiction. That's where the Street always existed: not quite in the world, and not quite out of it. That's where we've stopped. Right on the border between worlds."

"But—you said the cloud's gone?" That had only just caught up to me. "The real city's back?"

"All clear," Millie confirmed. "This is tucked away behind the wall, the way we always were. Everyone who was swallowed up is back—I don't know Lydia personally, but I'm sure she is too. You'll have to introduce us."

I'd never felt relief like that. My knees nearly buckled underneath me. She was back. I hadn't killed central Wellington, and I hadn't killed Lydia. She was safe.

"She doesn't know about what I can do," Charley was telling Millie. "Rob doesn't want her to know."

"Don't *you* start getting at me for that," I complained.

"I'm not. I'm just saying—Millie wanted to meet Lydia, and if she did—"

"She'll have to know now, anyway," Millie said. She sounded regretful—actually, she sounded suddenly sad. "Everyone will. I had to tell the police about this place, or they wouldn't have let me come. So now they've seen a city disappear in front of them, and a woman walk through a wall, and they're about to see two more people come out of one. And some of the characters they're examining don't quite pass as human on close inspection. We're going to have to tell them something, and I really think it's going to have to be the truth."

Charley nodded. He had known this all along, I suspected. Perhaps it was one more reason why he had wanted to disappear.

"I think so too. It's exactly what we were afraid would happen, isn't it? Beth brought us out in the open. We're in the new world after all."

"But not Beth's new world," Millie said. "Beth wanted to erase the real world and populate it with her own creations. She wanted to retreat into a made-up past. This is the future." She paused. "Dorian said—before we lost him—that we couldn't stay secret forever in the modern world, even with the Street. He said the one advantage the Street had given us was that we weren't alone anymore. We had a place where we could find each other, and a place from which to make a stand. They can't get in here, you know—not without us helping them over the threshold."

"Beth wanted to use that advantage to start a war."

"We need to strike peace. And jolly quickly. There's an army out there looking very uneasy, and our people are in their custody. But at least we can negotiate from here. This city is ours—assuming it's no longer dangerous."

"No. Well, no more than anything fictional is a little bit dangerous. There's darkness here, but there's also hope, illustrated by the network of connections between people across the social divides. I covered that in chapter ten. It balances."

"Sounds like life."

"It is." He paused. "How are the others? You said they were in police custody?"

"Except for Maui, and a few that he took with him. He flew away, and when the police looked, some of the others had vanished too. They thought it was magic, but it was a trick, of course. Bound to be. Misdirection, and all that. But the others are still being held. Some of them are in a bad way."

"Well," Charley said. "We'll go get them, to start. The rest we'll just have to write as we go."

"We will." Millie looked at him, then hugged him suddenly. He hugged her back, just as tightly, and for a moment they seemed to fit together, as though made of the same material. I looked away, obviously.

"Come on," Millie said. "Let's go out and meet the new world."

The world was waiting. When we came out through the wall, having walked through the familiar street, the small alley off the Left Bank Arcade was ringed with police and army officers and even a medic or two. New barricades were up, blocking off the entrance at both ends. My most immediate impression, though, was of faces. Pale faces, dark faces, round faces, thin faces: perhaps only about ten altogether, but all looking at us. I was used to being looked at, in a courtroom, but not like that. For one thing, each face was accompanied by the barrel of a gun.

"It's all right," Millie said to them. Somehow, her Jacqueline Blaine voice made the guns seem a little foolish. "I said I'd bring them out. And I have. Now will you let the others go?"

"Which is the one you told us about?" The speaker seemed to be in charge. "The one you say sent the cloud away?"

That was a hopeful emphasis, at least.

"I'm the one you want," Charley said. And at once, all the faces that were on us were only on him. I saw him shrink from them, instinctively, then unfurl and brace himself to meet them.

"We need to talk, I think," he said.

The man nodded.

I wanted to be there with him; actually, if I were honest, I wanted to be in front of him, between him and whatever was about to come. The trouble was, now that I was out here, I also couldn't stop thinking of Lydia. My body was straining against itself to get out and find her. I didn't say anything, but Charley obviously knew.

"It's okay," he said quietly as the policemen conferred among themselves and their radios. He smiled a little, with effort, but he meant it. "Really, this time. Go. We've got this."

I tried to say thanks, but my voice had stopped working, so I just gave him a nod and left. One of the policemen made a half-hearted move to take hold of me; I gave him my best counsel-for-the-defense stare, and he moved off. I suspect he had no more idea of what he should be doing than the rest of us.

I raised my phone to my ear as I started to walk, then run, to Courtenay Place. It was ringing.

The streets were a swarm of people: people who had been trapped inside the cloud when it descended, people who had been trapped outside while their loved ones had gone, reporters and officials and God knows who else. I pushed through, searching desperately, and telling myself she was going to be exactly where she said she would. She had to be.

She was. I saw her standing at the base of the giant statue of a tripod across the road from the theater. Her phone was in her hand, as was mine, and I could see the same strained look on her face as had been on mine as she scanned the crowd. When she saw me, her face relaxed.

She pushed toward me through the crowds, so that we met in the middle. When we did, I caught her in my arms, and she did the same to me, and we held each other tightly.

Dr. Charles Sutherland, age nineteen

Extract from Dickens's Criminal Underworld. *Oxford University Press, 2012*

The opening lines of *David Copperfield* may be the most perfect in the history of literature; certainly they are among the most well-known, and the most well loved. Because they are all our opening lines. They are how our stories all begin.

This is why we love Dickens; why today, when many of the social issues this book discusses have become history, he is still among the most popular authors of all time. We love Dickens because he tells us that things happen for a reason, that chance encounters mean everything, that we are all—rich or poor, good or evil—bound up in the plots of each other's lives. We love Dickens because he tells us that life is funny, and cruel, often both at the same time. We love Dickens because he tells us the truth, when the dominant strand of contemporary postmodern literature so often tells us that there is no truth. And there isn't, perhaps, not that can be put in words. Truth, at least complete truth, isn't held in words. But there would be no truth at all without them. It lies behind them and lurks around them and shines through them, in glimpses of metaphor, and connotation, and story.

We love Dickens because he tells us stories, and because he tells us that we are all stories. We are. We are more than stories, of course. But we have to start somewhere. And there are many worse places to start than, "Chapter One. I am Born. Whether I shall turn out to be the hero of my own life, or whether that station will be held by anybody else, these pages must show."

Charles Sutherland, age two

Hello. My name is Charles Sutherland. I am two years old. This is the first thing I have written down ever. I made the letters but not the words because I wanted to get them right. Now I have written them down and I exist. Things in writing exist. They are not always true. But they exist.

My favorite books are *The Hound of the Baskervilles* and *Green Eggs and Ham*. And the first part of *Great Expectations*. I havent read the rest yet.

XXXII

For the next few days, everything was chaos. I think I had expected the shell-shocked calm that follows a major storm, if I had expected anything. It wasn't; or if it was, the calm lasted less than the time it takes to draw breath to scream.

At first, there was a very real chance that the Street's inhabitants, Charley included, would not be allowed to return to the Street or anywhere else again. They were liminal creatures once more, this time existing in the spaces between laws: they were illegal refugees, yet they had brought their own world with them; they were dangerous monsters, yet they were human beings. There was real talk of taking them into custody, and unofficially, I'm sure there was real talk that if they went in, they would never come out. Had I realized this, I would never have left Millie and Charley alone to negotiate their own release. But I did, and perhaps it was for the best. By midnight, someone made the decision, probably out of fear for their own life, to let the Street's inhabitants back through the wall without a fight; many of Moriarty's freed creations went with them. And so the first painful steps toward a new world began.

The Left Bank Arcade became a border between reality and fiction, guarded by barbed wire and armed forces, lined with reporters and police and sightseers. Academics and scientists insisted on their right to study the creatures formed from words. Various literary estates put in claims, without being quite sure what they were claiming and why. Critics wanted to meet Charles Dickens. Readers wanted to meet Mr. Darcy. There were other, more dangerous calls: cries for them to be cataloged, deported, destroyed.

Lydia and I were outside the furor, though we had storms of our own. She was hurt, scared, and furious. I understood this perfectly, and should have just asked her to forgive me. But I had too much of my own hurt, fear, and fury shut up inside me, and as soon as we reached home, the closing of the front door was an opening of the floodgates. One of us started shouting, the other shouted back, and soon we were in the midst of a blazing argument that was probably heard across the new borders of reality. Arguments are meant to clear the air. This one, when it finally burned out, filled it with smoldering resentment like the acrid aftermath of a chemical fire.

But the air did clear. The floodgates did close. I am, I think all this has proved, neither as articulate nor as intelligent nor as kind as I need to be, but I'm not a complete idiot. The following morning, I went up to Lydia, who was sitting by the window after a night that had probably been as dark and sleepless as my own.

"I'm sorry," I said.

She nodded. "Your father called," she said. "He and your mother want us to come over as soon as we feel like it. They say this affects all of us, and we need to talk it through. Charley, too, of course, but nobody can reach him."

"Yes." My heart sank at the thought of that particular family meeting; not, this time, because Charley was going to be a problem, but because he was going to be hurt. "Of course. Do you still—I mean, do you want to come?"

"Yes." She knew what I was asking. "Do you want me to, this time?"

"Yes. God, absolutely, yes."

A tiny smile crossed her face; just for an instant, but it was there. "I talked to your father; he wanted to talk to me, otherwise I would have come to get you. Your mother kept an even bigger secret from him than you kept from me, and he's forgiven her—or he's trying to. He's far more forgiving than me all around, of course. But let's see how we go."

And we did.

We didn't see or hear from Charley directly in all that time, but we saw a good deal of him. The whole world did, though Millie tended to take center stage. She and Charley were the spokespeople for the new world. They were the two who had, after all, lived and worked between both worlds with the most success for years. There were negotiations to be made, with the New Zealand government and the United Nations and anyone vaguely official. The new world could keep reasonably safe from attack, sandwiched between realities, but it had no resources of its own: if it was to survive at all, its people needed to come and go between the borders to trade for food and supplies. There were many who didn't want it to survive. There was a question of whether any characters would be prosecuted for their perceived roles in Beth's invasion, though no damage had in the end been done, or even simply prosecuted for living illegally in the country for so long. There was a lot of fear, mingled with genuine curiosity and sympathy, and a good deal of real hate.

And at the heart of all, as Uriah Heep had once predicted, was my brother, Dr. Charles Sutherland, David Copperfield. I sat on the couch, Lydia curled up next to me, and we watched him and Millie on the television being shoved past cameras on their way to negotiations. Millie looked terrific, of course—the girl adventuress grown up—but Charley had, once again, become someone I didn't recognize. Or rather, someone I had glimpsed once before: in front of a lecture hall, his face glowing as he told a room full of students about the darkness at the heart of Dickens. He was exhausted, I could tell, but he looked self-possessed, otherworldly, and brilliant.

"There's no law against what we are," he said, in answer to a question, "not just because there's no precedent, but because there is no law against a person being made of ideas, intuitions, interpretations, and language. If there were, nobody could ever step outside their door. Excuse me, please, we're expected somewhere..."

"Is it true that literary interpretations like yourself are highly unstable?" a reporter asked.

He laughed a little. "You'll have to take that up with Derrida."

I had no idea what he meant, but plainly a few of the reporters had suffered through classes in literary theory, because they snorted.

There was no sign of Eric among those taken from the new world, or anywhere else. His ferry had left from the harbor: the last one before all transport to or from the city had ceased. I didn't know if he had truly escaped, or where he had escaped to. I didn't want to know.

My parents had been forced to return home without seeing Charley. I tried to phone him a few times, but it went to voicemail. I had no idea, as usual, if that meant he was in the Street, he was talking to the prime minister, or he had simply never had his phone on him in the first place. He never called me back. He seemed, from what I could see, to be surviving without me. So I forced myself to hold back, keep my distance, and wait until I was needed.

Then, late on Friday night or early Saturday morning, the phone rang.

"Hi, Rob," Charley's voice said.

"Hey!" I said, sitting up straight in surprise. I'd assumed it was one of those endless reporter calls. Lydia and I were lying in bed, talking quietly in the dark, and I'd only picked up the phone to unleash some choice insults. "Hey, where are you? How's it going?"

"Okay," he said. "I think. Things have quieted down on the Street—in the City, I mean. There's still a lot of talking to do, but we've reached a temporary truce with the government. Negotiations are suspended over the weekend while the government talks over the terms. In the meantime, nobody's going to come and take us away in vans, or experiment on us, or try to deport us back to our books, all of which were real possibilities, so that's good. Rob—I'm sorry, but can I come and stay at your place? Just for tonight, maybe the night after? I don't have anywhere to go. There were people at my house when I went there—I don't know who they are, but none of us are really safe outside the Street. I don't even know what's happened to Henry. I've been staying with Millie, but as I said, things have finally quieted. I don't want to stir it all up by being there. Not everyone thinks I should be welcome, given what I can do. I wouldn't ask, except—"

"Of course you can, you idiot," I said, finally managing a word in edgeways. "And Henry's in the back garden. He practically *is* the back garden, actually. Couldn't you have made him a little smaller?"

"Blame Conan Doyle," he said, and sighed. "Thanks. Would it be too strange for Lydia, though? After what happened? Ask her, seriously, I won't mind."

"Is that Charley?" Lydia whispered, sitting up in bed beside me. I suppose there are only a few people I call idiots on a regular basis.

"Yeah," I said, looking up from the phone. "He can come stay, right?" I asked the question as if it were a foregone conclusion, but I was a little worried.

"Of course he can!" she said. "He's family."

I don't deserve Lydia. I really don't.

"Did you hear that?" I said to Charley. "Get here as soon as you like. I chased off the reporters and that one spy from the secret service across the street, so you'll have a clear run to the door. Do you need a ride?"

"No," he said. "Thanks. I'll be right there."

I thought about insisting we pick him up, but restrained myself. He'd battled Moriarty and taken possession of a Dickensian underworld. He could probably handle whatever form of transport he was planning. Probably. Even though it was raining.

Charley seemed to be hesitating. "Um... are Mum and Dad going to be there?"

"Do you want them to be?" I had an idea where this was coming from.

"No," he said. "No, not right now."

"Then no. They're not staying here—they're at home. I've convinced them to stay quiet, so nobody will look too closely at what Mum can do."

"The government doesn't know," Charley said. "I made sure of it."

I was fairly sure Mum meant to tell them herself, once she was sure that it wouldn't put Charley at any further risk. She felt it was cowardly to stay hidden while Charley and Millie took the weight of two worlds on their shoulders. But I didn't mention that. "Come on over. There's leftovers in the fridge and hot water in the shower."

"Thank you," he said. "Honestly, you might have saved my life. Be there in a second."

He hung up.

"How did he say he was coming?" Lydia asked. She was propped up on one elbow, watching.

"He didn't."

"Right." She yawned. "Well, you'd better go turn the porch light on, I suppose. For all we know, he's coming on a dragon."

I made it out into the hallway just in time to see a door appear in the middle of our freshly painted walls. Not the green, weather-beaten *Secret Garden* door this time: this was carved wood, curved, and opened from the center. A wardrobe door. A portal. A door from another world.

Charley stepped out, bringing a blast of snow-speckled air. "Hello," he said. He stared about him in wonder. "It worked. It actually worked. That's incredible."

"Tell me you didn't come from Narnia," I said.

He shook his head. "I wish. Just from the Street. It's snowing there now."

"It's spring."

"Not in Dickensian England. Millie says wait until we get to Christmas."

Lydia came out from the bedroom behind me, obviously drawn by the voices. She blinked once at the wardrobe door, but only once, and she didn't comment. "Oh, hi, Charley," she said. "So glad you could make it."

"Thanks for inviting me," he said. "Um. How are you both?"

"All right," I said. "You look terrible."

This is probably exactly the kind of thing Eric meant, but too bad. I know that I've tried to underestimate him, on purpose, for the sake of my own ego, for a long time. He's not useless. He's not hopeless. He has, in fact, both use and hope. But he'd also been through a heck of a lot this week, and he *did* look terrible. He was wound so tightly I felt that if I touched him he'd shatter like glass.

Lydia gave him a quick hug, took him by the shoulders, and looked at him critically. "Right," she said. "You know where the bathroom is. Go stand under hot water for at least twenty minutes. Rob will find you something to change into, I'll reheat some pasta, and then the couch is all made up for you. Don't try to be polite. That can wait. Go!"

Lydia has *three* younger brothers. Can you imagine?

We never got to the reheated pasta. After he came out of our bathroom, wearing a long-sleeved shirt I'd dug out and a pair of my old tracksuit pants, Lydia sat him down on the couch, handed him a drink, and went to get a plate. I went, too, to help dish up. In the two minutes that took, he had quietly curled up and fallen so deeply asleep that our coming back failed to stir the slightest response. Lydia wanted to wake him, but I thought it was probably best just to find him a blanket and leave him. I ate the pasta instead. It was the compassionate thing to do.

After a while, we went back to bed for the few remaining hours until daybreak. There didn't seem much else we could do. We talked a little more, quietly. Lydia dozed after a while, I think. I just lay there, staring up at the ceiling. I got up once or twice and went into the living room, to keep the fire stoked. It wasn't really cold enough for it, in the middle of spring, but never mind. It was snowing in Dickensian England. Each time I went out, he hadn't stirred since the time before, and the firelight was flickering across his face.

We let him sleep through to lunch the next day, then Lydia insisted on shaking him gently awake for toast and a Cup-a-Soup. I don't think he really woke up all the way at first, but he sat up and ate what she gave him. And I have to admit, he did seem a little better afterward. He spoke to us, at least; the night before, it had seemed as though all his words were gone.

"Thanks," he said. "I'm sorry to be such a nuisance."

Of course he was.

"You're not a nuisance," Lydia said. "You're a guest. And frankly, as guests go, so far you couldn't be lower maintenance."

"She's right," I said. "It's been like having a dead body on our couch, without the awkward police interrogations."

Lydia kicked me without looking in my direction. But Charley smiled a little, so it was worth it.

He finished his soup, and tried to get up and rally and be sociable. I took him out to see Henry, who had to be restrained from leaping all over us in delight. (What is fine for a terrier is dangerous for a creature the size of a lion.) But it was obvious he was still desperately tired. When Lydia passed the dirty mugs off to me and told him to go lie back down, he didn't need much persuading.

We did the dishes quietly in the kitchen, trying not to wake him.

"Is he really okay?" Lydia said. "He was in intensive care not that long ago. Then he was text, or imagination, or something. In between those times, from what you told me, he fell through a floor."

"Well, it's not like he could go back to intensive care, even if he needed to," I pointed out. "The Street's the only thing keeping people like him safe. Outside, he'd likely be hauled off and interrogated—or dissected. But he's fine. Or he will be soon."

"You both will," Lydia said. "I'm sure. But I think you and he do in fact need to talk."

"We don't need to talk," I said. "Brothers don't really do that sort of thing."

Lydia raised an eyebrow. "I don't know if you've noticed, oh pillar of masculinity," she said, "but your particular brother rather likes words."

I flicked the soapy liquid at her, but couldn't exactly argue.

So, when it was time for dinner, I left Lydia to prepare it—she gave me a hard look, but she let me get away with it for once—and went into the living room where my particular brother was still dead to the world. The sounds coming from the kitchen were starting to revive him. He stirred, and I saw his eyelashes flicker.

"Hey," I said.

He opened his eyes, and blinked a couple of times before he focused on me. "Oh," he said, still drowsily. "Hey. What time is it?"

"Probably about time to eat again," I said. "Proper food, this time, not in a mug. Do you want to get up, or are we bringing it in here?"

"No, I'll come." He propped himself up on one elbow, and rubbed his eyes. "Thanks. Just give me a couple of minutes?"

"You have twenty," I said. "Go right back to sleep afterward, if you want to. Though Mum and Dad would appreciate a phone call. They've rung me five times today. I keep telling them you're still alive, but—"

"Maybe tomorrow," he said. His face had suddenly hardened.

"Come on, Charley." I sat down on the arm of the couch. "It's nobody's fault. You ought to know that as much as anyone. How many times have you brought someone out of a book you didn't mean to? Would you rather she had sent you back?"

"She could have told me," he said. "It's not like I wouldn't have believed her! She knew exactly what I was, all those times I . . . Well, you know how it was. I knew I wasn't right, obviously. It was hard to miss. I used to ask her why. She could have told me. And you. She could have told both of us."

"She could have," I had to agree. That still stung me as well. "But she was trying to protect you. Actually, I think she might have been trying to protect all of us."

"I know that. Of course I know. I just . . ." He shook his head. "I want it to be somebody's fault, I suppose. And I can't help thinking that she *made* me this way. Which is ridiculous, and unfair, because if she hadn't made me, I wouldn't exist at all. And I don't know how Dad's going to react to me now that he knows."

"He doesn't care," I said. That was an overstatement, maybe, but true enough in the way that mattered. "He's a little overwhelmed, obviously, but—"

"Obviously. Mum metaphorically cheated on him with Charles Dickens."

I snorted despite myself. Charley's sense of humor can come out of nowhere at times, like a blade in the dark. "It doesn't change how he feels about you. How could it? You haven't changed."

"I have, as far he's concerned," Charley corrected me. "What we see when we look at people is just a bundle of our own interpretations, and—"

I rolled my eyes. "Oh shut up. He loves you, you idiot. You want to feel upset about what you are, then fine, you're entitled. But don't put it on us, okay? We don't care."

"I know," he said again. "I know I'm not being fair. I'm not really upset about what I am—well, not very. It's just not what I thought I was, and I'm trying to get used to it. I'm trying to get used to it in the middle of trying to defend what we are to the world, which is a nightmare. And—this sounds ridiculous, but I hate being noticed. Millie doesn't like it either. She's spent all her life trying to be normal. We both have. And even in the best version of the new world we can build, that's not really going to be possible now."

"True," I conceded. What could I say? It wasn't. I could say that might not be a bad thing, and it would be true, but it would always be a hard thing. And I couldn't help him with it.

We sat there for a bit. I could hear Lydia ostentatiously clattering pans on the benches, trying to tell us she wasn't eavesdropping. She wasn't, but she was probably overhearing. There just isn't any privacy between the living room and the kitchen in our house.

"Look, Charley…" I hesitated so long that he sat up and looked at me properly. "I'm sorry for that day that Uriah Heep kept talking about. When I saw you getting bullied, and let it happen. I shouldn't have walked away."

"I never blamed you for that," Charley said. He looked surprised.

"I was upset by it, maybe, but that was because it confirmed that even you had given up on me."

"Given up on you?" I repeated. "Who did you think had given up on you? You were being pushed all the way to the top."

"And people hated me for it," he said. "Even some of the teachers— they didn't think I deserved it. I was smarter than most of them, by a complete fluke of nature, and they had to watch me achieve higher in their subjects at twelve than some of them had in their lives, without ever seeming to work at it. I understood. I might have felt the same way. It wasn't fair. And it was far worse for the other kids—especially for you. I understood that too. Even Mum and Dad—right about then, they were starting to talk about how I was going to take up my Oxford scholarship, who was going to take care of me, who would be here for you over the holidays if they both relocated to England with me and yet how much it would hurt if we split the family in two. Not to mention how worried they were all the time that someone would find out what I could do and take me away. I was the cause of that. They loved me, but they didn't know what to do with me. I didn't fit into anyone's plans, and I was ruining them." He shrugged and looked away, suddenly self-conscious. "I don't know. Everyone thinks the world is ending at twelve. I just meant—I never thought of what you did as being a reflection of you. I saw it as reflection of me."

"But it wasn't," I said. "You know that now, right?"

He didn't answer.

"I used to hate you bringing those things out of books." I didn't quite know what I was saying until I said it. "I told you it was because they were so much trouble, but really I hated it more when they weren't. Like Holmes. I was jealous of them."

I meant that I was jealous of him for being able to make them, but when I heard my own words, I realized that they were just as true in the other sense. I was jealous of them, because Charley seemed to need them so much. And when he had them, he no longer needed me.

"I started out making them for you," Charley said. He smiled a little. "The very first one, the Cat in the Hat, remember? It was your favorite book. I thought you'd like him. Only Mum made me put it away. And afterward, you never seemed to want them. You just told me off and helped me catch them and put them back. But when I came without them, you just told me to go away. So after a while—a long while, when I was eight or so—I just started making them for me. You'd stopped spending time with me. They always would."

"You substituted Sherlock Holmes for me?"

"Well. You did grow up to go after the truth of crimes for a living."

"I don't go after the truth," I said, and tried not to say it bitterly. "Like Holmes or anybody else. If anyone's Sherlock Holmes, you are. I investigate my clients' claims, and I present them as convincingly as possible. Maybe I tell their stories."

"Well, yes," Charley said, as if unsure where I was going. "That's telling their truth, isn't it?"

That shone a light on something I had been fumbling after for a long time. Just a brief one, but it was a start. I turned it over in my head for a while experimentally, then put it away for later.

"I haven't heard any other summoners announce themselves," I said. "Do you think you and Mum really are the only ones?"

"Possibly," Charley said. "Millie has a theory that there's only one natural-born summoner every century or so. The real Beth was the last one. Mum would be the next. All this was brought about only because the two of us came into being with our gifts intact, and changed everything. But I don't know if I believe it. For one thing, we know the gift isn't unique to the English language, because of Scheherazade, so it's highly likely there are summoners in other countries even if there are no more in the English-speaking world. I think they just haven't dared come out until they see how things unfold. I don't blame them. A couple of times this week we've seemed poised on the brink of the war Beth wanted after all."

"You won't let that happen."

"No, we won't. But I don't know what we'll do if we're not given permission to live and work on New Zealand soil. The Street isn't self-sustaining. We don't have our own resources. As it is, a lot of people behind that wall are deeply frightened, and Millie doesn't know what to tell them. Also, we don't know what to do with the dragon. I know Mum meant well, and it saved our lives, but it's a mess of contradictory readings. I can't do anything with it. It just flaps around the city, nesting on the sturdiest chimneys."

"'The dragon stayed where he was,'" I quoted, "'and nobody minded.' That's how the book ends."

"Well," he said. "Here, that's only where everything starts."

"You know I'll help, don't you? If you ask me to. I know something about legal questions. I'm probably the only lawyer in the business related to a literary character."

"Only if you want to," he said. "I mean, I'd love it, we'd all be very grateful, but—"

"I want to. I really do."

"All right." He smiled. "Then that would be great. And I'll phone Mum and Dad after dinner. I promise."

"Good." I hesitated, wondering whether or not to ask the question on my mind.

"What is it?" Charley asked.

"Well. I probably shouldn't ask this, but...who are you now? You nearly went into a book. And then you read yourself out, with my help. Are you the same person who went in, or did you...change yourself, in some way? Did I change you?"

"Well, of course." It was almost defensive. "That's what people do to each other every day, and to themselves. Are *you* the same person who nearly went into a book?"

"That's different."

"I know," he conceded. "Everything's different now. But I don't know how to answer any other way. I don't feel substantially different. I—do I *seem* different?"

"No," I said. "Of course not."

It wasn't quite true. As he said, everything was different now. Our lives had altered around us, and of course we were all trying to alter to fit, to the best of our abilities. But I still knew him, and that was what he was asking.

"What did it feel like?" I asked. "Where were you going, when I pulled you back? I think I saw some of it. But you went further than I did."

His face turned thoughtful. "I don't know," he said. I don't know why he always says he doesn't know the answer to a question before he answers it. It's just him. I waited. "It felt like I'd slipped through the gaps in the text, and I was falling deeper and deeper into what lay behind it. I've spent my whole life doing that, in some shape or form. Trying to see the glimpses of truth behind words, or in words. I think that's what I was falling into. It was so close, I could almost touch it. Or become it."

"You're making me sorry I pulled you out," I said.

He shook his head. "Don't be."

And I wasn't. I didn't even mind that he had made me miss the rerun of last night's rugby match because he had been asleep in the living room all morning, or that from now on I was going to be known as the lawyer with the fictional brother, or that my world had changed forever into something strange and elusive because I had forced him back into it. I wasn't sorry.

"Did you know there's another ending to *A Lion in the Meadow?*" Charley said. "An earlier version—it's hard to find these days. Mostly it's the same. But in that version, the mother learns her lesson, and never makes up a story again."

"God, that's boring," I said. "No wonder they changed it."

After dinner, and the dishes, and the feeding of the Hound of the Baskervilles, Lydia left us to go pay a last-minute visit to her hotel. It was opening tomorrow, along with most of Courtenay Place. The last of the lingering Dickensian fog had cleared. I left Charley curled up reading a book by the fire, and followed Lydia out to the car. The wind was blowing from the coast, and I could see the city lights in the distance.

"Are you sure you don't mind?" I asked her. "I mean, all of this..."

"Will you stop asking me that?" she said. "The only thing I mind is that I missed Maui, apparently. Not to mention Frankenstein. You'd better introduce me to the ones left on the Street. I mean it: I want to meet Millie Radcliffe-Dix. I loved those books growing up."

"Apparently," I said, "a lot of people did."

As I came back inside out of the cold, there was a flare of light by the fireplace.

"Oh," I heard Charley say. "I'm sorry..."

"It's okay," I said. "He can stay if he wants to."

"Are you sure?"

"Why not? There's an inflatable mattress in the closet somewhere."

I glanced over at the figure now sitting in the armchair by the fire. "Hello, Mr. Holmes."

"Good evening, Mr. Sutherland," replied the great detective, and his eyes when he inclined his head were warmer than I'd seen them before.

I changed into pajamas and poured a mug of coffee, then I went to join them. Charley had moved on to *The Princess Bride*; Mr. Holmes was reading Agatha Christie. I had a lot of reading to do myself, in self-defense, and because I was interested now. I had finished *David Copperfield* two nights ago. I was halfway through *Great Expectations*.

"It's better than *David Copperfield*," Charley said, when he saw me open it.

"Are you allowed to say that?" I asked. "Considering."

"If *I'm* not," he said absently, because he'd already returned his attention to his own book, "then I don't know who is."

It was quiet as I settled in to read alongside Sherlock Holmes and David Copperfield. But for the crackle of the fire and the ever-present whistle of the wind outside, it was as quiet as it had been in the city, after everything changed. And for a moment, the space between heartbeats, I felt I could glimpse the world Charley saw. A world of light and shadows, of fact, truth and story, each blurring into one another as sleep and wakefulness blur in the early morning. The moments of our lives unfolding as pages in a book. And everything connected, everyone joined, by an ever-shifting web of language, by words that caught us as prisms caught light and reflected us back at ourselves.

"We changed again, and yet again," I read, "and it was now too late and too far to go back, and I went on. And the mists had all solemnly risen now, and the world lay spread before me."

Acknowledgments

Special thanks are owed to my agent, Hannah Bowman, for pulling me out of the query trenches, supporting me, and reading far more of my drafts than any human being should ever have to. Also to my editor, Sarah Guan, for asking page after page of impossible questions and teasing out the heart of the story in the process. You both taught me to write.

Thanks so much to the amazing team at Orbit/Redhook for everything they've done to make this story into a book. Lisa Marie Pompilio's art is breathtaking, and I'm honored to have it on my cover.

This book is a love letter to literary analysis, so thanks are owed to the English department of Victoria University of Wellington. You all taught me to read. Please know that although the Prince Albert University bears curiously geographical similarities to Victoria, none of its fictional staff are in any way based on you. (Not even you, Charles, I swear.) Also, Harry, I'm sorry about the insult to Kipling.

Any interpretations I have of *Great Expectations* have grown from David Norton's lectures in ENGL209, which I was fortunate enough to hear first as a student and then as a tutor. Thanks also to the many scholars and biographers whose books and articles have illuminated Dickens for me. (It was obviously just for me.)

Most importantly, thank you to my family: my parents, for their love, support, and belief, and my sister, Sarah, for her insight, enthusiasm, and kindness. This book wouldn't exist without you.

Thank you to my rabbits, O'Connell and Fleischman, who are just rabbits, and that is everything. Also to the guinea pigs, Jonathan Strange, Mr. Norrell, and Thistledown, who weren't actually born when this book was written, but who would have helped if they could.

And lastly, thanks to Charles Dickens, Oscar Wilde, Mary Shelley, Arthur Conan Doyle, Jane Austen, Margaret Mahy, Roald Dahl, C. S. Lewis, Emily Brontë, and the other authors whose creations grace the pages of this book. You're wonderful. Your words are wonderful. I'm sorry for what I did to them.